Precious Pawn

Precious Pawn

Mary Martin Devlin

Cuidono Press

© 2014 Mary Martin Devlin

All rights reserved. No part of this book may be reproduced in any form or by any means, electronic or mechanical, including photocopying, recording, scanning, or by any information storage or retrieval system, without permission from the author and publisher.

ISBN: 978-0-9911215-1-9

Cover Artwork:
© 2014 Julia Proctor

Cuidono Press
Brooklyn NY

www.cuidono.com

This book is for A. and M.

Author's Note

The unpublished memoir of a provincial French aristocrat, the comtesse de L— (1730-177?), inspired this novel. Excerpts from the memoir, translated by the author, are interwoven with the text.

Book One

1

The Comte de Fautrière, my father, after having served and held for a long time a post in the Court, which made him known and loved by the King, had a disagreement with the prime minister, who banished him to his estates in Burgundy. He spent several years there with my mother, one of the most beautiful and respectable women of her time. I had two sisters, who were placed with me in a convent, and a brother, godson of King Louis XV and the Queen. . . . My father, having brought a criminal suit against a priest on one of his estates, asked for and received permission to go to Paris to plead his case. Thus, he departed with my mother and his son, leaving the three of us girls in the convent where he had placed us.

Several years later he came back to the provinces and sent for us.

Diane de Fautrière shoved her chapped, chilled hands under the folds of her voluminous shawl. The room was cold, even though logs blazed high in the broad expanse of the fireplace in Mother Superior's private sitting room, where Diane and her sisters anxiously awaited the arrival of their father. It was early spring, and winter had made an unexpected return to the Burgundian countryside, spreading a thick, white rind of hoar frost over everything. A magical snowy crust sparkled on the trees in the orchard and enclosed the tiny pink and white buds in icy capsules. Through the clouded windows of the sitting room the sun slanted palely, without warmth.

The eldest of the three sisters, Diane had slept fitfully. The night before, after evening prayers Sister Barnabas had come scurrying along in her rodent-like way, through the long, narrow dormitory where the girls slept to tell them that their father would be calling on them in the morning. Her white wimple a bit soiled and slightly askew, she had said only that the comte de Fautrière had returned to his country estate near Beaubéry and was expected to drive over from his chateau at Corcheval sometime during the morning.

Sister Barnabas would never leave the convent because she would never have a dowry. Her father was the village blacksmith in Beaubery, where Diane and her sisters went with their grooms to have their horses shod. For the young novice, Diane and her sisters were glamorous figures of that distant, enchanted world of the aristocracy. Their name was one of the oldest in France's nobility, a name associated with the royal house of the kingdom. It made no difference that their dresses and ribbons were sometimes frayed and out of fashion, especially compared with the showy elegance of the wealthy daughters of trade or finance, such as little Lucie Fargeau, whose silks and velvets were often encrusted with tiny pearls. But Lucie Fargeau would never be Lucie de Fargeau; she would never have the precious *de* that proclaimed nobility.

"Oh, if only he would get here!" Diane said. "If only we knew why he is coming." She dreaded the moment when her father would walk through the double doors of the antechamber and back into their lives, for she associated sudden disaster with her father's sporadic intrusions into their quiet lives in the convent. Several years before, the King himself had banished her father from court, not just the customary ten leagues from Versailles, but complete exile to his country estate. Though still a little girl Diane had felt this humiliation envelop the entire family. Then came the death of their pudgy, light-hearted brother Louis-Etienne, crushed by his horse in a hunting accident. And, of course, the money shortages. There was no end to those.

Diane groaned in exasperation. They had been standing like faintly quaint little dolls in the same spot since Sister Barnabas had left them to return to her duties in the sewing room. They dared not sit down for fear of showing disrespect to their father and to Mother Superior. Soon it would be time for the morning *goûter*, hot milk and sweets from the kitchen.

Catherine yawned and stared sullenly at the arabesque patterns in the carpet beneath her feet. "Do stand up straight, Catherine," said Diane. "You know how Papa hates to see you slumped over and gloomy. He should be here at any minute. I wish we could have some sweets. I'm starved this morning."

"You're always starved in the mornings. You should have eaten your lentils at dinner like the rest of us. Stuffing yourself with sweets, you're going to have brown, rotten teeth like Sister Cécile and smelly breath like a sick old cat."

Diane did not much care what Catherine had to say about her teeth. Catherine was just jealous, if the truth be told. In fact, Diane was vain about her beautifully even white teeth. Every day during their walk through the south gardens, she would quickly break a twig from a sweet laurel bush and would chew on it until it was soft and feathered, then she would surreptitiously clean and polish her teeth, even in chapel, when she should have been praying or giving her responses.

"I think I hear his carriage," said Sophie, turning eagerly toward the large double doors that led to the plain and drafty antechamber of Mother Superior's sitting room. Beyond the antechamber lay the cobblestone courtyard of the convent. Sophie, the youngest and the frailest of the three sisters, though almost ten, looked scarcely more than five or six years old. She had always been a sickly child, with a listless appetite and little strength to join her more robust sisters in their childhood games. She wore a pale blue striped frock, one that her sister Catherine had outgrown and that Clotilde, the girls' only maid, had adjusted to Sophie's diminutive frame. This morning Sophie had awakened with a cold, and her pink, irritated nose made her small, wizened little face look more pinched than usual.

Moments later, Diane heard voices coming nearer, the sound of high heels on flagstone.

"And here they are, Monsieur le comte. Your little girls . . . and what do you think, hein? The country air and quiet have made them even prettier." Mother Superior held the comte's arm coquettishly, leaning against him as he stood quietly studying his three daughters for a moment.

"Well, now, my darlings, aren't you pleased to see your father? Can't I have just a smile and a tiny little kiss? I'm the early bird, come to welcome spring with my lovely ladies of Neuilly-les-Dames."

Diane watched in awe as her father swayed toward them. Indeed he did seem some sort of exotic bird in his magnificent clothing sparkling with precious stones in the morning sunlight. Alençon lace flowed from the velvet sleeves of his pink coat and cascaded from his throat. The heels of his shoes were red and very high; a soft, floppy bow fell across their front. He wore bright blue stockings clasped just beneath the knee by a deep pink garter. His wig, parted in the middle, fell slightly below his shoulders and was powdered a mauve gray. Two purplish-red circles of rouge accentuated the chalk white paint on his face. On his cheekbone beneath the corner of his right eye he had placed a black silk beauty patch cut in the shape of a crescent moon. And the perfume!

Like a country yokel Diane stood gaping at her father. She could not help herself. How grand he looked! And how wealthy! He was a far cry from the local aristocrats whom she glimpsed around town and in the inns on her infrequent excursions into the nearby town on market days to make visits or to buy combs and trinkets at Madame Rufinac's shop. Most of them, like the young marquis de Saint-Amand, handsome though he was galloping about on his fine Arabian mare, dressed exactly like the peasants who worked their fields. Crudely cobbled boots, soiled tobacco brown leather vest, fustian coat and breeches, shirts and stocks gray with age and yellow with soil. And they smelled like the fields and barnyard, too.

Of course, her father had never dressed like a rustic lord, even during his exile from the court when he had had to depend on the local gentry for society. He had hunted with them, had sat at their gaming tables, but he had never forsaken his meticulous concern for his appearance. Diane could not imagine a man in the entire kingdom as handsome as her father, not even the King.

At the convent there was always a steady flow of visitors from Versailles taking up residence in the convent, especially during the spring when the battles started up again. They captivated her, these ornately dressed creatures, parading the latest fashions, purveying the rawest gossip. They made more real her ardent fantasies of someday playing a part in that enchanted world at Versailles, and she vowed to herself for the thousandth time that she would learn the ways of the beautiful women at court. At the bottom of her ribbon box she kept a small miniature of the King, a present to her mother, the comtesse, at the christening of her first child, a son, the King's godson.

Like an Italian dancing master, the comte de Fautrière pirouetted from Diane's embrace to enfold Catherine and Sophie in his arms, all the while murmuring lovingly and glancing toward Mother Superior for approval.

The comte and Mother Superior seated themselves comfortably, like old friends, near the fire, while Diane and her sisters remained standing politely near their father's chair. Through the east window of the sitting room Diane watched as their trunks and modest packing cases were loaded atop the carriage. So . . . they were leaving the convent today, this very morning. Clotilde, dressed in her best frock, but still wearing her broad apron, stood near the fountain chatting with one of the comte's footmen.

"And when will the demoiselles return to take up their studies again, Monsieur le comte?" Mother Superior was saying. "You mustn't let them desert their books too long, you know." She leaned forward confidentially, knowing that the comte would appreciate her little joke. No one, especially Mother Superior, took seriously the educational activities of the convent.

"Ah, who shall say, my dear Madame? They will spend a holiday at Corcheval, amusing their fond old father. Perhaps a few weeks, perhaps until the rains and fogs return in the autumn. The dreary, pestilential fogs of the country! Then, I shall have no choice, then I shall have to return to Versailles to rescue my spirits from the country doldrums," drawled the comte. His voice was low and intimate, and he could not keep his eyes off Diane.

"On the other hand, Madame, I do like what I have found here. Perhaps I shall not return to Paris alone," he said, rising abruptly and bowing low over Mother Superior's slender hand.

The comte's huge carriage lumbered along in the fine midday sun, which had banished the morning's crystal frost. The girls sank back against the dozens of cushions and watched with fascination this elegant stranger who was their father.

"Why, you ninnies, you're staring at me like some kind of specimen in a cage!" the comte teased.

"Tell us about court, papa. Tell us about some of the women," Diane said.

"Some naughty women," Catherine said, glancing defiantly at her sisters.

"Hmmm. Let me see. Naughty. No . . . not that one. Not naughty enough for convent girls." He gave Catherine a stagy leer, and they laughed merrily. "Naughty. Let me see, have I ever known a naughty lady? Ah, me, probably not. But, now here's a very naughty lady. Was. For she's long gone, may she rest in peace. The duchesse de Berry, you know, the Regent's daughter. She had an enormous jam closet fully stocked that she kept right there in her bedchamber. In her bedchamber! Imagine that! Such a pig she was, really. And what was the result of all that stuffing herself with jams and breads? Besides, of course, the buckets of fat and flab that she accumulated. A big tub of lard she became. Her teeth, before she was twenty, her teeth were all rotten. A black hole that stank to high heaven. That's what her mouth was. Towards the end she did not even take the trouble to use a fan the way polite women do. She breathed her stinking breath right in your face."

Catherine leaned forward and glared at Diane. "You see, I told you so, eating all those sweets that your friends in the kitchen slip into your pockets. Your teeth are going to rot and fall out before you're twenty years old!"

Oh, my, sighed the comte, can't that poor child think of anything other than badgering her sister? I thought she might have changed. Outgrown it. Catherine was the plain one, he thought, looking her over with a cold eye. Her pale blue eyes looked faded, old beyond their years, for she was only twelve. But she had lovely blond hair, masses of it, neatly arranged in heavy curls pulled back from her angular face. She had a strong jaw and a firm chin, and from the governess's tales of Catherine's behavior in the third-floor nursery, this plain little girl with the firm jaw could be belligerent and stubborn.

"Oh, well, then," laughed the comte, "I'll have to appoint little Sophie guardian of Diane's beautiful white teeth, for they are beautiful, you know, and we wouldn't want anything to happen to them. So, you'll have to watch over them, Sophie. Make sure that they don't rot and fall out before your sister is twenty!"

Sophie giggled and writhed with pleasure, and Diane was delighted by her father's witty compliment.

"Will we find maman at Corcheval, papa?" asked Sophie, as the carriage approached the entrance court of the chateau.

"Not this summer, *ma petite*. You know your mother has not been too well of late. The winter in Paris left her tired. The grippe twice, and she still has a hacking cough. No, she preferred to remain in Paris to rest, to be near her priests and her charities. Why, do you think you will miss her? I do believe that I am going to be jealous," and he smiled hugely at his own humor.

For answer Sophie grabbed his hand and shyly smiled.

The comte stepped down quickly from the carriage and swept into the chateau, leaving the footmen to attend to his daughters. The day had turned warm, and the old stones of the chateau glistened in the sun. Corcheval was one of the grandest chateaux in Burgundy, and the comte's most valuable and profitable estate.

Before the fortunes of the Fautrières began to dwindle away as bad harvests, greedy speculation, the gaming tables and an extravagant way of life took their toll, the family had possessed fifteen of the grandest chateaux in the lush Burgundian countryside. Their decline started well before Michel de Fautrière inherited the lands and the titles that went with them. As a very young man, gloriously handsome, with titles that resonated down through the illustrious history of France, Michel de Fautrière seemed destined to reverse his father's loss of income and lands. He made an advantageous match with Aurélie d'Ancy, who brought him an old, respected name from the *noblesse d'épée*, though not as old or as renowned as his own, and rich fertile estates in the Charolle. After the family signing of the marriage contract, the old comte had stood, lost in reverie, rubbing his hands with glee.

The old comte, however, had not reckoned on his son Michel's utter extravagance, which far surpassed his own. Though Michel did not share his father's ruinous addiction to gambling, he arrogantly refused to concern himself in the slightest way with the administration or cultivation of his immense properties and thus was gulled, fleeced, and swindled by a succession of crafty stewards before he realized that he was not a rich aristocrat after all. In fact, he was not far from being poor. Instead of retrenching, economizing, and making the most of what little remained, Michel de Fautrière went to Versailles to play the courtier's costly game of dancing attendance on the King and his powerful ministers in the hope of any lucrative crumbs that might fall from the monarch's gold-lined pockets. The comte had multiplied his lavish expenditures with his usual recklessness.

Diane followed her father up the broad expanse of the entrance steps and into the large foyer where a grand stairway led to long corridors of bedrooms on the second floor. She did not entirely trust her father's sunny mood, for she knew that he hated the country. *I do like what I have found here,* he had said, looking directly at her, his eyes bright. What could he have meant? She intended to find out before his jolly humor turned sour.

The comte watched absentmindedly as the servants busied themselves with the girls' trunks. Sophie and Catherine rushed forward up past the great sweep of the staircase toward their little rooms on the nursery floor. As Diane prepared to follow her sisters, her father stepped forward and touched her arm.

"Not you, my darling. You will remain on the second floor."

"Clovis," he said, turning to the old footman, who had been his personal servant since the comte's childhood, "Clovis, take Mademoiselle Diane's things to the yellow rooms, if you please."

Through the open doors of the library Diane could see her father seated at his writing desk, sorting papers impatiently. He did not hear her as she cautiously stepped forward toward him.

"Papa," she said timidly, as he looked up from his papers, smiling broadly.

"Already settled into your rooms, have you, *mon trésor?*" He knew why she had rushed down so quickly from her unpacking. She wanted to know why she had left the small, stuffy but familiar, bedroom of her childhood. To be moved into a suite of rooms that had always been reserved for his fussy, haughty, unbearable mother-in-law the marquise d'Ancy, one of the finest suites on the second floor, deserting her sisters in the homely old nursery rooms under the eaves.

"Do please sit down, my darling. Don't stand there like a stick! Show me how graceful you can be. Come, sit there, and be easy with your father." The comte opened an embossed leather satchel and bunched together a large sheaf of papers before shoving them carelessly into the satchel.

He rose from his chair and seated himself in the green silk fauteuil facing his daughter. Sunlight from the broad French doors opening onto the terrace glowed about her face, lighting her tiny earlobes with pink flames. His daughter's beauty fairly took his breath away. A sudden surge of joy almost made him dizzy.

"And how old do you think you are, *ma jolie?*" he asked, tilting his head to one side, a quizzical, amused look on his face.

"Thirteen . . . almost fourteen. This October." Diane's rich, firm voice betrayed none of her anxiety. "I'll soon be fourteen, but Catherine is already twelve."

"Of course, of course. I may be forgetful, but I do somehow remember how old you children are. And you are almost fourteen. Your mother was married at fifteen, which is to say, my dear, that you are now very much a young lady, and soon to be a young lady of fashion."

Diane grew chill with fear. "You don't mean that I am to be married, papa," she asked in a horrified whisper. Only two months ago, Diane's thoughts flew back in a panic, her only real companion, Sylvie de la Béage, had been dragged, weeping uncontrollably, into the family carriage, and given in marriage to a pimply-faced young man with offensively expensive clothes. Sylvie was fourteen. And her family was as poor as Diane's and, like hers, their name had coursed through the history of France for centuries. Sylvie had resigned herself to passing her life in the convent, knowing full well that she had no distinctive beauty or talent to make a marriage without a dowry. Then one day Sylvie had been called into the parlor to meet her parents and this contemptuous young man—Roger Griffeau, was that his name?—who talked in a loud nasal voice and giggled at his own lame witticisms. The next day Madame de la Bécage had come to announce triumphantly to Sylvie that marriage contracts would be signed, that Sylvie would be the bride of Roger, the eldest son of a rich tax-farmer who fancied a daughter-in-law with noble blood. Diane had passed a sleepless night by the weeping Sylvie, and she had cried sincerely as she helped her friend gather up her pathetic belongings. Long afterwards Diane could still hear the rumble of the carriage wheels on the cobblestones of the courtyard and the echoes of Sylvie's awful bellowing sobs as her father thrust her into his carriage. The comte's return to Corcheval, his luxuriously flamboyant clothes, his increasingly high spirits as he gazed at her: was it now her turn to be bartered away to some repulsive young man?

"I'm not going to be the wife of someone like Roger Griffeau, am I?"

"Who in heaven's name is this Roger Griffeau?" the comte threw back his handsome head, hooting with laughter. "Don't be a frightened ninny, Diane. Eventually, yes, you will be married. Though the way you carry yourself like some rustic dairymaid will not make you any man's prize possession. Look at you! Sitting in that chair, your knees spread apart as if you were settling in to milk a cow! Lift your chin; square your shoulders . . . that's it. Very nice, my darling."

Diane felt a prickling rush of shame along her neck. She did not need her father's ridicule to know that she was clumsy and coarse in her manners.

"Naturally you need to acquire certain social graces. You must learn to dance, and to dance well, to sing a little, and to play the piano. To speak Italian, a sophisticated French instead of this dreadful near patois that you've become accustomed to in the convent. But, come along here, let's have a look." The comte rose and suavely took Diane's hand as if inviting her to a minuet. "Come, let's just do have a look," he said as he guided her toward the long, gilded mirror tilting forward a little from the wall next to the fireplace.

"Now, tell me, do you like what you see? Oh, forget about that drab little frock. It looks as if you might have pinched it from pious old grandmaman. Anyway, it's a bit quaint, isn't it?" The comte gazed raptly at Diane's rather clouded reflection in the old mirror. The sunlight bathed her luxuriant blond hair in a diaphanous silver light. Her eyes were a deep grey, the color of glistening wet pebbles in the shallow bed of a clear stream, and her dark brows swept over her beautiful eyes in a smooth, wide arch. Fashionable ladies at court prided themselves on their small bow lips, painting on the bow if nature had failed to provide one. Diane's mouth, however, was full, richly sensual, expressive. It was her complexion, above all else, that set her apart as a rare beauty: her skin glowed with health, smooth, creamy white, translucent at the temples. At the left corner of her lips, and slightly above them, she had a small, round, raised black mole.

Word of his eldest daughter's wondrous beauty had reached him in Versailles and in Paris, where he would sometimes hear her being discussed with reverential awe by some stranger who had heard a description of Diane from another stranger who had just returned from a hunting party at such and such a chateau in Charolais and had passed by the convent at Neuilly-les-Dames for a game of quadrille and gossip before returning to Paris. At first, the comte had paid little heed to the flattering tributes to his daughter, for there was always someone at one's elbow or one's levée who had a reason to fawn and flatter. Actually, the comte had been rather slow to take his daughter's great beauty into the calculations surrounding his giddy life at court. Very slow indeed. It was only after Monsieur de Tourmelle, who had recently acquired the rich lands adjoining Corcheval, had abruptly appeared in his sitting room one day to ask for Diane's hand in marriage—Diane, whom Monsieur de Tourmelle had never seen. Her reputation as a great beauty had aroused him to make his offer, and a munificent one it was, too. Naturally, the comte had declined. He had no intention of handing over his one remaining jewel into the rough, acquisitive hands of this upstart squire.

Before the week had passed, however, the comte made up his mind to pay his daughters a visit in their remote convent. After all, his arch enemy, the ancient Cardinal de Fleury, had finally died a few months previously at the overripe age of ninety in 1743, the only agreeable thing the old fool ever did, the comte said. In 1735 the comte had played a conspicuous part in a plot against the cardinal, which had failed. In retaliation, the King, utterly devoted to his old tutor, exiled the comte to the lonely boredom of his country estates. It had taken years and countless petitions to return to court. With the cardinal dead, the comte's schemes to advance himself in the King's favor might finally prosper.

Father and daughter remained standing before the mirror in silence. "Do you realize how beautiful you are?" the comte finally asked in a low, solemn voice.

Diane stood perfectly still as her father carefully framed her blond head with his hands. Gazing into the mirror, he murmured, "My dear, can fortune fail to shine on a face like that?"

2

He was so very nice to us, especially showing a little partiality to me, perhaps because, as he never tired of repeating, I much resembled him, and because I then had such a pretty face. We spent the entire summer in the country.

As Diane descended the grand staircase on her way to join her sisters in the garden, servants and footmen borrowed from the marquis d'Ancy's staff swarmed busily about the vast foyer and into the long, narrow salon on the east side of the chateau where the ball would take place. A dozen *frotteurs* with soft brushes clamped to their shoes whirled about the ballroom, buffing the parquet floors to a golden glow.

Since their return to Corcheval, Diane and her father dined together almost every day, and from time to time he would invite a few guests, keeping a watchful eye on her ability to entertain them. She was a willing and eager pupil. Sometimes at night as she listlessly allowed Clotilde's practiced hands to undress her and prepare her for bed, Diane felt exhausted from attuning herself to her father's every wish, his every expectation of her. But the thought of leaving the country behind, of embarking on the great adventure of Paris and the court, where her father enjoyed the company of the King himself thrilled her waking moments, and often at night, she awakened suddenly from a deep sleep, with a rush of images of the glamorous life that her father had promised her.

The days, weeks, months had sped by as the comte turned the massive old chateau of his ancestors into a whirling round of parties of every sort. Musicales, late night card games, large and small dinner parties, and now, later on this evening in late August, a masked ball, *le dernier cri* from Versailles, for even the local gentry knew that the King himself delighted in masked balls. A select group would attend the formal supper, then would be joined by numerous country neighbors for the ball. Though to economize had been one of the comte's reasons for spending such a long time at his country estate, he was furiously squandering enormous sums on entertainments. The estate orchards and gardens no longer sufficed to feed the flocks of people who came from chateaux at a considerable distance to frolic at the comte's expense for a few days.

Catherine and Sophie, their arms linked and their heads bowed, were already walking toward the chateau's park at some distance from the house. At the sound of Diane's steps along the gravel pathway, they turned around and came back to walk with her. Childlike, Sophie broke into a run so that she would be the first to kiss Diane, who stooped and swept her tiny sister into her arms.

"Oof, Sophie. You're getting as heavy as a bucket of lead!" The warm months at home with Clotilde fussing over her, bringing her extra cream cakes from the kitchen and letting her pad along in her footsteps during the day, had brought a healthy glow to Sophie's cheeks. To Diane, accustomed to her little sister's convent pallor, she looked almost robust in her faded old cambric gown, rusty and frayed along the hem.

"It's almost eight in the morning, Diane! Soon you will be like papa, getting out of bed at noon!" laughed Sophie. Wide-eyed, she looked at her older sister in awe. Sleeping late was for Sophie the surest sign that Diane had left the nursery for good and had joined the grown-up world.

"Good morning, Catherine," Diane said.

"Ugh, you look awful this morning. Were you out all night long with papa at Uncle Philippe's *cavagnole* party?" Catherine knew that her sister had not gone to the party, but she also knew that she *could* have gone. Diane's new status in the family set her teeth on edge and sharpened her tongue.

Diane turned her most dazzling smile on her sister. That smile never failed to find its mark. It was like a slap in Catherine's face. The morning was too beautiful and her new life too exciting to spoil with quarrels. For Catherine, given the chance, would pick and bait until she got what she wanted: an unpleasant scene. It wasn't fair, Diane knew, the way papa fussed over her, the way he had always made her his favorite without caring how much Catherine would be hurt. No wonder Catherine grew peevish and lashed out at her. Still, it was too fine a day to spoil with quarrels.

They turned into the broad central pathway lined with dark green topiary shrubs, which their father had modeled after Fouquet's grandiose park at his chateau at Vaux-le-Vicomte. At some distance, at the very end of the central pathway stood a hexagonal little chapel, a charming jewel of a structure that the comte had designed and built for his pious wife, Aurélie. That was where they buried Louis-Etienne, Diane thought, the brother I can hardly remember now, buried under a shiny new bronze plate that looks as slippery as water.

The girls stopped to toss fistfuls of gravel from the footpath into the fountain pool, Sophie chortling as the exotic fish swirled about in frantic confusion.

For the comte, descending the broad steps of the terrace, the girls, with their gleaming blond curls and graceful little figures, formed a lovely composition that brightened his otherwise foul mood. Selfish and self-centered though he was, the comte loved his daughters more than he ever had his only son, whom he even now guiltily dismissed as a dullard. A dullard largely because Louis-Etienne actually seemed to enjoy the military life; he had thrown himself into it with such relish that the King seemed genuinely pleased when the comte purchased a commission for the boy. Michel de Fautrière had looked upon his military service merely as a duty, the only profession, other than the clergy, for a young man of the *noblesse d'epée*. He loathed combat and the bloody chaos of battle, and though he had distinguished himself in the never-ending military campaigns of Louis XIV, the comte had been secretly happy when his wounds on the fields of Villaviciosa obliged him to retire from the King's forces.

"What on earth are you doing to my beautiful pool, you nasty creatures," said the comte in a loud voice that made them start.

"You'll foul the water and kill those gorgeous fish that cost me a fortune!" he continued, feigning anger.

He cut a very striking figure in his riding clothes. He wore no wig, and his thick chestnut brown hair with not the slightest trace of gray was tied neatly behind his head with a narrow, black ribbon. He had not painted his face, only a faint suggestion of rouge on his cheeks, and the deep-set wrinkles about his mouth and eyes were less obvious. But it was a dissipated face, pale and pinched from the excesses of the previous evening. A thin brown stain filled a deep line in his upper lip, the only evidence of the comte's addiction to snuff, for his perfectly shaped teeth remained spotlessly white.

"Are you going out to ride, papa?" Diane asked.

"I'm riding over to Ancy for dinner." He sat down a little wearily on the broad stone curve of the fountain. "I promise to bring back a great basket of plums from your Uncle Philippe's orchards. It's ridiculous, really, that we should have to get plums from someone else's orchards. If my steward weren't so confounded lazy, he could rid our plum trees of disease."

His voice whined in mounting irritation. The burden of his neglected lands, of problems needing his attention made him cross. In Paris, living mainly on credit, milking his estates of their increasingly slender income, he could forget about the diseases in his orchards, the crumbling roofs over his stables, the disastrous rains and the even more disastrous harvests. In Paris the glitter and glamour of the courtier's life, the hours lost in the honeyed luxury of velvets, diamonds, perfumes, and, for the comte, the carnival of the senses, made it easy for him to forget the responsibilities he loathed.

"Will you be coming back before the ball tonight? Or will you drive over with Uncle Philippe?" asked Diane. She was eager to have her father's help in getting ready for the evening. She had appeared at several of her father's large dinner parties this summer, but each time he had very carefully prepared her for the occasion, selecting her dress and jewelry. With fanatical intensity he supervised every detail of her toilette. Tonight would be their last extravagant entertainment before their departure for Paris, and she did not want to displease him.

"Yes, of course, *mon trésor.*" He smiled and lifted his handsome face toward the sun. Bah, what need he worry, after all? A jewel like his daughter was worth a dozen of the best estates in Burgundy. Easily.

"No, no, no . . . " said the comte, rising from his chair in exasperation. "That's far too fussy, Clotilde!" He snatched the comb and brush from Clotilde's boney, worn hands, and gathering a thick mane of Diane's lustrous hair, began slowly, with intense concentration, to work with it.

"You see, the face must not be overwhelmed, even if the hair is as beautiful as Diane's." The comte bent over the dressingtable and searched through a heap of pins. Stark white paint, already cracking at the corners of his mouth, cast a bluish shadow over his face. Diane watched him anxiously. She wanted to soothe him, to reassure him with her beauty that soon, after she had become an accomplished young lady in Paris, he would never have to put on that worried scowl again. He had no idea how hard she would work to refine her tastes, her manners.

Diane kissed her hand and laid it along her father's painted cheek. He smiled absentmindedly into the mirror. He brushed, he combed, he wound narrow ribbons encrusted with rubies and diamonds around each heavy tress. He was nervous and tense; his hands trembled slightly as he slowly coiled her hair into place.

"How lovely I look, papa!" For she did look supremely beautiful, her pale white skin glowing with only the slightest touch of rouge along her cheekbone.

"Of course you do," her father replied rather crossly. "In Paris you will have someone who knows how to dress your hair so that I won't have to waste precious time doing it myself."

Clotilde stood waiting with the pale blue satin slippers that Diane would be wearing. She knew very well that the comte disliked her, had always disliked her, because she was just a country maid who had been raised with the comtesse, who treated her like part of the family. When the comtesse married Michel de Fautrière, Clotilde followed her to Corcheval as her most trusted servant. She watched jealously as he fussed with Diane's hair, swaying on his absurd high heels, sniffing and complaining irritably as he fashioned Diane's hair according to his fancy.

"You are so clever, papa!" said Diane, anxious to rouse her father from his quarrelsome mood. He could be so wonderfully high-spirited, affectionate and gay. Then the next moment he could fall into his dark mood and lash out at someone as kind and gentle as Clotilde, who looked after them in the convent as if she were their real mother. And sometimes his ugly temper would turn against Diane, too, as if she were responsible for all the awful things that were going to happen to them. The awful things had to do with money. Diane knew that much. She knew that the comte was using borrowed money to pay for her fine new clothes, as well as his ostentatious new carriage and hectic entertaining. Money borrowed from Uncle Philippe.

"Will Uncle Philippe and Odile be coming over tonight?"

The comte had invited those of his neighbors whom he considered just that trifle more sophisticated than the others, and naturally Philippe and Odile, who had assembled a house full of guests fleeing the heat of an unusually scorching summer in Paris. The comte had planned a masked ball, with perhaps some prankish blindman's bluff, accompanied by strolling musicians, in the formal gardens of the chateau in the bleached light of the moon. Afterwards, there would be several gaming tables, for the comte's country neighbors were as addicted to the pleasures of gambling as courtiers in Paris.

Uncle Philippe was the marquis d'Ancy, her mother's only living brother whose largest properties lay only three leagues south of Corcheval. Normally, the marquis and his young wife Odile would be spending the summer season in their chateau near Fontainebleau with the *habitués* of the court within easy reach. Odile was passionately involved with the intrigues and politics of the court, where her provocative behavior had tantalized more than one minister. She loathed the hushed fields and rural simplicity at Ancy, where the fourteenth-century chateau, damp and uncomfortable, had received few improvements over the years. This summer, however, she fretted that she was restless, that she needed the soothing air of the country, the blessed quiet of Ancy and its healthy pleasures.

Having to attend to some nagging business on his properties a few villages distant from Ancy, and also, like the comte, needing to escape the ruinous expenditures of life at court, Philippe agreed to his wife's suggestion. The summer days had melted away in the most agreeable fashion: if nothing unforeseen happened, he should be able to return to Paris with very welcome additional funds, and Odile had happily adjusted to life in the countryside far from the frenzied pleasure-seeking of court society. The continuous festivities at Corcheval had very successfully held Odile's monstrous boredom at bay.

The comte laughed. "Odile would never miss such a party! Would Odile ever miss *any* party, even if she had to crawl to it?" Diane saw his saturnine face brighten with pleasure, and she was displeased without really knowing why.

"And I want you to observe her closely. She is one of the most fashionable women in Paris. She will help you get rid of your country stiffness. I've had long talks with her. She knows how she can help you before your debut in Paris society. Mainly, my dear, you need to learn how to make delightful conversation. Witty conversation will carry you further at court than great beauty, believe me. And Odile happens to be one of those rare women gifted with both beauty and wit."

To Diane's mind, Odile was no great beauty. She was a small woman with sharp, pointed features like a little fox or a ferret. Her eager, brown-black eyes darted quickly about. During conversation, her deeply set little eyes would tirelessly sweep about, searching restlessly as if she might cry out her boredom at any moment. She made Diane feel ugly and ill at ease. But Diane was awestruck by her dress and her jewels. Diane had never seen such luxurious silks and velvets, stiffly encrusted with jewels. Her stomachers were so tightly laced that her huge white breasts, astonishing for such a small woman, rose so high that the dark circle of her nipples could be glimpsed whenever she leaned forward.

"I've never heard Odile say anything profound or witty," murmured Diane.

It was almost ten o'clock, and the silvery light of the full moon had turned the formal gardens of the chateau into a place of enchantment, just as her father had predicted. Diane, fully dressed and uncomfortable in her elaborate gown, sat near an open window listening to the crunch of gravel as the carriages of their guests arrived. She ran her fingers slowly over the seed pearls sewn into the bodice of her gown of pale blue silk, sent down from what her father said was the most fashionable establishment in Paris, and it must have been so, because the package was perfectly elegant—purple glazed cotton tied up with yellow satin ribbons. She was thrilled. She had never before worn such grown-up clothes. After weeks of expectation, she was finally being allowed to join her father in entertaining at a late hour. Although some—Odile for one—had been critical of the comte's decision to introduce his daughter to Parisian society before her fifteenth birthday, the comte had made up his mind.

"Your father is ready for you now, mademoiselle," said Laurent, the tall, handsome footman whom the comte had recently added to their retinue of servants. It was rumored that Laurent was the natural son of an aristocrat and that he had been kept in domestic service to protect him from a laborious peasant's life. Sweet-natured and slow-witted, the result of virulent fevers soon after his birth, Laurent would accompany the comte and Diane to Paris and serve as her personal footman. His eyes sparkled with simple pleasure every time he looked at Diane. Already he was devoted to his young mistress.

Diane allowed herself few misgivings as she followed Laurent down to the supper table where the evening's guests were already assembled. Feeling awkward in her heavy new gown, she watched her step carefully as she descended the great staircase and drew near the dining room, glowing warmly from quantities of candles along the walls and on the sparkling table.

As Diane stepped forward into the room, the sudden hush and her father's broad smile set her entirely at ease.

"As you see, Diane is joining us tonight. My lovely daughter. Don't you think she looks *exactly* like me," he said, making a face.

"No, no, Michel. Don't be absurd. Your daughter looks like a vision, an angel. Besides, I don't see any snuff stains around that beautiful mouth," Roger Saint-Valérien's brick red neck bulged in hoarse laughter at his own jesting. The comte despised this coarse country squire, but Roger's reckless, profligate gambling made him ever welcome at the comte's tables.

As Diane took her place at the far end of the table, she felt the tiny, ferret eyes of Odile following her. It was Odile who sat opposite the comte as his hostess. Diane looked quickly around the table for her Uncle Philippe, who was chatting with a heavily painted young woman whom Diane had never seen before. He suddenly turned and smiled broadly toward his niece, giving her a conspiratorial wink.

Thirty or forty guests, Diane could not tell exactly how many, animated the long, narrow dining room, busy with footmen in the comte's burgundy and silver livery. The brilliant display of her family's possessions—the fine porcelain china, the heavy ornate silver and serving dishes, the immaculate white tablecloth and fine crystal—filled her with pride. In the tiny upstairs nursery she and her sisters had always taken their meals with Clotilde on a small table stained and bruised from its many years in the nursery. She and her sisters used plain cups and bowls of pewter, dented and misshapen.

Diane reached forward, lifted her glass, and drank deeply, delighting in the chill, dry wine. Suddenly, she felt like enjoying to the full the pleasures of the life that her father held out for her. Balancing her fragile wine glass in her hand, she turned to the young man seated on her right, Armand de Mézières.

"I understand that you will soon be going to Paris with your father," he said, leaning toward her, his left hand caressing the softly crumpled silk neckcloth knotted at his throat. Armand de Mézières was spending the summer months with Odile, his cousin, who sat like a queen surveying the guests around the comte de Fautrière's table. Armand dressed in the very latest fashion from Paris and the court, for he had left his father's country estates four years ago and had joined the throng of idle, pleasure-loving young courtiers in Versailles. Odile said that he had become something of a favorite with Louis XV and that as a result would receive one of the richest benefices in the kingdom as soon as the old abbot died, which was expected soon. In anticipation of this bountiful future Armand had allowed his debts to accumulate with lazy indifference.

"Yes. My father and I will make the trip to Paris on a river barge all the way to Paris. It's the latest thing, isn't it? I mean, a house barge with all sorts of luxurious appointments. My father designed ours himself." Diane felt lucky to have as her dinner partner Armand, who according to Odile was an amusing and altogether handsome young man. And indeed he was. His soft elegant clothes hugged his robust frame tightly, their very feminine suppleness accentuating his masculinity and strength. An early childhood injury had damaged the eyelid of his left eye, leaving it with a permanent droop. To her great surprise Diane found herself excited by the languorous expression this lowered eyelid gave to Armand's swarthy face.

"I must say that I prefer a large, commodious carriage myself," said Armand. He bent his head closer to hers and lifted the corners of his lips in a slight smile at her girlish enthusiasm.

"Odile says that you hunt wild boar with the King at Rambouillet."

"And at Fontainebleau," Armand replied with a self-satisfied smile. Really, she was quite charming. And terribly beautiful, despite all that Odile had said about her lack of finish. How was it she had put it? Her country convent ways. She certainly looked the epitome of worldly refinement tonight. Even the old-fashioned design of the sapphire and diamond earrings glowing on her dainty pink earlobes enhanced her stylish perfection. Yes, perfection, that was the word. Armand smiled at the prospect of a delicious evening of flirtation, followed by the serious business of gambling until dawn.

"I say, I rather fancy the look of your yellow sapphires by candlelight, don't you?" Armand ran his fingers under the bracelet loosely draping Diane's small-boned and delicate wrist. Amused by his subterfuge, Diane merely smiled and returned his playful gaze, allowing him to take her hand carefully in both of his, to turn the bracelet this way and that, studying it as if he were an experienced jeweler making an appraisal of critical importance.

At the end of the table Odile watched the young pair with a frown, recognizing the familiar games of seduction and conquest. Really it was foolish for a woman in her position, a woman of the world sought after by some of the most powerful men at court, to give a second thought to this adolescent slip of a girl, still backward and shy. But the truth was that Odile did give her more than a second thought. Armand must simply be bored this evening. Michel de Fautrière's boastful pride in his eldest daughter verged on the absurd. What sort of figure would she cut in the exclusive circles of Parisian society? A woman needed more than a beautiful face and an exquisitely shaped body to make her mark there.

The table hummed with conversation and laughter. The comte as usual had enjoyed his own wine too much, and he longed to escape the closeness of the huge dining room. The heat from dozens of candles and dozens of heavily perfumed and perspiring bodies was oppressive. Outside the terrace doors the park glowed in the cool moonlight. But the footmen had only begun to serve ices, and no one at the comte's table seemed disposed to put an end to the cordialities at table. Only Odile, opposite him, looked bored and restless, her sharp little features lax, the corners of her lips drooping in weariness. She paid little attention to the interminable anecdotes of her neighbor, who half-reclining on his elbow, lazily droned on and on about his seduction of the Marquise de Vintimille long before Louis XV took a fancy to her.

Almost beside herself with vexation, Odile fanned herself furiously and stared straight ahead at Michel de Fautrière, willing him to look at her, to recognize her discomfort, and to rise from the table, thus freeing her from the heat and boredom. Armand and Diane continued their colloquy of slow smiles and low murmurs. Indeed, indeed, Michel would have his hands full with that one, to be sure.

Diane took another sip of wine and carefully smoothed her hair in an unconsciously coquettish motion. For the first time she was experiencing an altogether odd kind of pleasure, an intense thrill she could not understand that surely must be part of the grown-up world of her father, the world of the court. Armand murmured something about her hand, and she leaned forward to catch what he was saying.

Suddenly, Armand looked up and caught Odile's cross, ill-tempered stare. Impertinently, imperiously, she did not turn her gaze from the young pair, and Armand chuckled to himself, anticipating his pleasure in calming Odile's jealousy. Jealousy he most assuredly knew it to be, for while Odile had mastered many of the ruses of intrigue and manipulation, she had never learned to disguise her own powerful emotions.

Diane turned to follow Armand's eyes. Odile was staring at him with boldness and familiarity, a look such as Diane had never seen pass between a man and a woman.

"Are you enjoying your stay at Ancy?" Diane asked, feeling clumsy and cold, the warmth and excitement of Armand's attentiveness abruptly vanishing.

"Not really." Armand replied, pulling down the corners of his broad mouth into a pout. "It's isolated, you know . . . Ancy. Your father the comte is the closest society we have. Most of my cousin's guests are getting ready to return to Versailles and then it will be too dreary. And it's damp, the chateau. That foul moat seeps through the walls and into your bones."

"You don't care for a moat?" asked Diane, her lovely gray eyes wide in disbelief. "I adore a moat such as Corcheval had long, long ago. Now we have only that modern reflecting pool that papa dreamed up. Really so ugly and not at all romantic."

Armand threw back his head and laughed. "A moat. You adore a moat! What a wonderful, wonderful little innocent you are, my dear little Diane. Come, your father's getting up from table. You must let me show you the beauties of that reflecting pool you scorn so much."

As Diane rose from her chair, which a footman deftly slipped out of her way, the elaborate dress that had in the beginning of the evening felt so weighty, stiff, and cumbersome now seemed light and easy about her slim, shapely body. Swaying slightly as she turned toward Armand, she steadied herself on his outstretched arm. She thought it odd that she should feel dizzy, giddy, her stomach queasy, never imagining for a moment that her father's fine wines had anything to do with these new sensations.

For a moment Diane stood gathering admiring glances, and the chill that had come over her after she had caught Odile staring at Armand in such a strangely intimate way disappeared as her awareness of her own beauty returned.

"Wouldn't you prefer a game of hide-and-seek in the gardens?" Diane asked with a mischievous smile.

"If you like," replied Armand. He saw her glance briefly toward her father and was amused. Such a little girl really, but such a breathtaking woman. Armand wondered how much she knew or guessed of her father's notorious hide-and-seek games of that summer. Perhaps that mischievous smile meant that she knew a great deal indeed.

With immense relief, before some of his guests had finished their ices, the comte de Fautrière had heaved himself up from the table, his head heavy from far too many glasses of wine. If I am not careful, I shall be as fat and greasy as Roger Saint-Valérien, rooting through his food and swilling his soup like a sow at a trough. The comte despised himself for playing false with his lean, elegant body, which meant everything to him.

The long table, which at the beginning of the meal had been a thing of beauty, now displayed the messy stains and litter of food and drink. A footman opened one of the long doors to the terrace, and the candle flames flickered in the sudden gust of cool, sweet night air.

The comte saw his daughter stagger a little as she stood up and leaned a little too insistently on the arm of young Armand de Mézières. A flash of anger ripped through him. He had complete contempt for women who drank too much. He watched Diane disappear through the terrace doors with young Armand. His daughter's beauty made his heart race, both in joy and fear. He would keep a wary eye on her; he did not intend to let any mishap snatch away this precious pawn.

Diane ran down the stairs, then swirled around in the noisy gravel to face Armand. Behind her in the grove of evergreens bordering the pond, she heard a woman's throaty laughter. The full moon spread its pale glow over the elaborately sculpted shrubbery, which appeared black-green in the moonlight. The fresh night air gently stroked her cheek and lifted the damp ringlets from the nape of her neck. Of a sudden she felt wonderfully invigorated.

"Let's play hide-and-seek," she said. "We don't have to wait for the others." She knew every turn, every quirky recess in this garden where she had played since childhood with her sisters and cousins. The unfamiliar mood and sensations that she had experienced at table with Armand vanished; she felt more like herself, ready to romp and play with her sisters in the great gardens. She ran toward the fountain in the center lane and waited for Armand to catch up with her. In the distance she could hear the disturbing melancholy lament of a nightingale.

She watched as Armand strolled toward her, unhurried, almost indifferent to her. She could hear the rowdy voices of some of the guests at the foot of the garden where large topiary figures of jungle animals cast huge pools of shadow.

"Would you like to play hide-and-seek, Armand?" she asked again, but less enthusiastically. He was a sophisticate from court, after all, hardly the sort to enjoy the childish games she played with her sisters.

"Why not? I'll turn around, close my eyes, count to ten, then come searching. But don't hide yourself down there in the darkness where you might see some things that a very proper demoiselle shouldn't see—or rather, not just yet."

Armand turned around to face the chateau, put his hands over his eyes and started to count.

"You go and hide," said Diane. "I already know all the best hiding places. It wouldn't be fair."

Armand continued to count. "Five . . . six . . . seven . . . "

Diane took to her heels, streaking down the gravel path toward her mother's chapel, whose grey slate roof glistened like silver in the moonlight. As a precaution she left the path and darted silently over the soft green lawn to the rear of the hexagonal chapel. There, as she well knew, a sturdy shaft of ivy had spread its branches all the way up the brick wall. The base of the shaft was more than strong enough to hold her weight. Quickly, she kicked off her slippers. As nimbly as her heavy gown would allow, she climbed the clinging ivy as far as she could and still keep a firm footing.

Struggling to quiet her breathing, she listened for Armand's footsteps on the gravel path. Her fingers dug into the ivy, and she almost lost her footing when a patch of young tendrils tore away from the wall in her hands. Bits of loosened mortar sifted down to the ground, with the sound, it seemed to her, of an avalanche. She waited and listened, the sound of voices at the far end of the garden now muted, her own breath loud in her ears. She turned her head and flattened her face against the wall. Suddenly, she could hear Armand, very near, whispering her name. She pressed herself into the wall, her arms and fingers aching for a firmer grip.

As she shifted her weight to her left foot to find a more restful position, she felt a warm, caressing hand under her heavy skirt, moving slowly up her right leg, up her calf to her thigh. She turned with a startled cry and fell heavily into Armand's arms. He pressed her roughly to his body, twisted her face, and held it firmly between his broad peasant-strong hands as he kissed her. With both hands Diane pulled down on his grip on her face, struggling to free herself from his hot mouth. He panted and trembled, drawing his breath in loud, labored snatches.

Diane pulled back her head with all her strength and hit her head against the brick wall with a thud. For a moment she stood stunned without moving, listening to Armand's harsh, uneven breathing. He said nothing, but he did not move his eyes from her face.

"What have you done?" she asked in a whisper. She could not imagine what had happened to the clever, attractive dinner partner who now stood before her as a shadowy stranger gasping for breath.

"What have I done?" Armand echoed. "What have I done?" he asked again in sharp, cold irritation. "Why, I've done only what you wanted me to do. Only what your father wanted any man to do. Dressing you up like a Versailles courtesan, parading you in front of all the country barnyard animals. Instead of leaving you in your convent where you belong."

Diane sank back against the wall and covered her ears with her hands. "I don't understand why you say such things," she said, looking up as he stood, stiff and impassive. "I don't understand why you say these things about my father."

Armand said nothing, merely stood there, looking down at her with a contemptuous smile. He reached down to take her hand and help her to her feet. Her complicated coiffure had come undone, spilling heavy twisted braids of hair down her back, and her stockings were stained and torn.

"Shall I help you back to your room?" he asked.

"No, please don't," she said weakly.

"As you like. I'm off to the gaming tables," he said, "where I've no doubt I'll find better entertainment. Good night."

In her stocking feet, forgetting her new satin slippers in her haste to get away from the hateful garden, Diane ran away from the chapel, across the rose gardens and into the long, arching row of linden trees that lined each side of the drive leading to Corcheval. When the drive curved out of sight of the chateau, she stopped for breath and turned to listen. No voices, not a sound except for summer insects rasping in the thick foliage of the trees and dance music from the ballroom.

Her steps dragged as she made her way around the pool to the rear of the chateau. Her feet were sore, her chest ached with each deep, ragged breath. She felt dirty and ashamed but could not understand what she had done to feel this way. One minute she had been a little girl, absorbed in a child's game from which she had abruptly plummeted into the brutal, mauling grip of a stranger. She sat down finally on a stone bench where the kitchen maids often gathered in the late morning to chatter, to crack nuts, to peel vegetables and fruits for dinner. From the other side of the chateau came a few stray voices in the garden. She could hear the faraway clatter of a carriage departing down the long drive and wondered if for some reason her father had decided not to set up the gaming tables after all. She rose to her feet, seized with panic that Armand might have recounted to her father what had happened behind the chapel. Dizziness forced her to collapse again on the kitchen maids' bench. For another few minutes she sat quite still, listening for sounds in the chateau.

Slowly she rose to her feet and quietly made her way into the house toward a narrow stairway to the second floor. She had no need of the candle and flint box, for moonlight flooded through the high windows in the entryway. From the back hallway she heard the sound of a bottle crashing to the stone floor and the angry cursing of a footman. She had no idea of the time. It seemed an eternity since she had left the supper party with Armand and skipped so innocently into the garden. A last heavy coil of her hair slipped from its pins and startled her as it collapsed against her cheek.

A door opened and slammed, and she heard a buzz of voices in the distance. At the end of a long series of empty formal rooms she could see a pool of light coming from the two rooms which had been set aside for gambling. With relief Diane turned toward the stairway.

"Will you stop playing the little bitch!"

Her father's angry voice cut across the silence of the back hallway. Diane stifled a cry. There was no mistaking her father's voice, muffled though it was by distance. She had heard him quite plainly. For a moment she thought that he might be in the back garden overlooking the pool. But surely his voice had come from inside the chateau. She ran her fingers through her tangled hair and began walking across the empty rooms toward her father's library, a large, elongated room extending behind the chateau's two formal sitting rooms.

She caught a glimpse of herself—disheveled, the bodice of her tight, heavily embossed dress twisted askew and her stockings torn and dirty—in a dimmed mirror. She thought she heard a woman's voice and the heavy thud of an overturned chair. She waited until her breath came more slowly, then continued her way toward the library.

One panel of the double door stood slightly ajar, but all was tranquil. Gradually she became aware of a woman's low murmuring, hoarse as a cat's purr, and the liquid slapping of flesh on flesh, as in a child's game of pat-a-cake pat-a-cake. Diane moved cautiously to the door and pushed it gently aside.

Utterly bewildered, she stared and stared, the scene before her reverberating like some gigantic, mocking puzzle. In the clear light of the moon she saw Odile sprawled face forward over the arm of the rose satin canapé, her naked breasts hanging down like large, snowy globes, her voluminous skirts twisted up around her waist. Behind her stood the comte, groaning and panting, his chest bare and glistening with sweat, pumping frenziedly against Odile. The comte's sun-browned hands kneaded the firm, full flesh of Odile's white breasts.

An immense crackling roar set up in Diane's ears like the combustion of dozens of bonfires springing into flames. Clumsily, she reached out to steady herself against the door, which swayed back and forth in her hand.

Without pausing a moment in his frantic thrusting, the comte turned his head toward the doorway and hissed: "Go away!"

Until well past the early hours of dawn Diane sat at her window and stared down into the intricate, clipped order and beauty of the garden. She could scarcely remember how she had reached her room. Or how she had dismissed her new maid, Marianne, perched on a chair fast asleep, her jaw slack and mouth agape. Without her help Diane had fought free of her cumbersome gown and dropped it to the floor. For a long time she washed her face and hands before sinking into a chair by the window.

Diane did not see her father again for almost three weeks. The comte left for Cluny the following morning to oversee the last details of the furnishings of the houseboat that would return him in grand style to Paris and the court. Diane spent all of her time with her sisters and dreaded the loneliness of her bedroom and the terror of her dreams where her father, wild-eyed, hissed at her.

In her thoughts the awful scene played itself over and over again, a puzzle wearing down her nerves, electrifying her with fear. At times she thought that it had not happened at all, that the memory of Armand's warm hand on her thigh had fevered her imagination. Then she would hear her father's fierce whisper and would shrink with guilt and shame. Had he recognized her at the door?

When the comte returned to Corcheval in mid-September, the evening air had already taken on an autumnal chill and stray, yellow leaves fluttered along the gravel drive. Suddenly business-like, the comte dismissed with a wave of the hand a last flurry of invitations that had accumulated in the silver platter on the cherry commode in the great foyer. Every day the comte whipped his horse over the fields for dinner with Philippe, who finally relented and made yet another loan to his impecunious brother-in-law, all the while insisting that this would be the last. With his beautiful daughter at his side, the comte determined to spare no expense in returning to Paris in a style befitting a Fautrière.

3

My father, whose affection for me seemed to increase with each passing day, decided to take me with him to Paris. My sisters were sent back to their convent, and we left during the month of October. We traveled by way of the Loire River on a barge that my father had had specially designed to accommodate his entire household. . . . At last we arrived in Paris, very weary and tired of traveling.

It was a fresh October morning in 1743 when Diane de Fautrière caught her first glimpse of the throngs of Paris. As the comte de Fautrière's heavy, slightly listing houseboat made its ponderous way up the busy silvery lanes of the Seine, she felt as if she were entering a foreign land.

"Look at the people, papa! Do you see the woman in the funny dress? Over there . . . the tall one with the white bonnet that dips and swoops with wings. And there's another one, see? Just next to the steps of the quay."

"Those are women from Brittany, from a region west of Paris," the comte laughed, settling a shawl around her shoulders against the morning chill. Her father's laughter warmed her heart. He loved her this morning, he was proud of her, she could tell, his eyes gleamed with pleasure as he looked at her.

"But, oh, look at the bridge. All those buildings leaning against each other. They're tottery. And so many of them!"

"An eyesore that's what they are. The King despises them. He'll have all those filthy stalls torn down and carted off the bridge. Then, the Pont Neuf will be as beautiful as ever."

The King! She could scarcely believe that she was entering a world where one day she would actually meet the handsome king in her miniature, secreted away at the very bottom of her ribbon box and the thrilling subject of her girlish fantasies. To one and all in his kingdom Louis XV was Louis *le bien-aimé*, Louis the beloved, idolized by his people.

"Paris is having a party just for you, *ma petite*," said the comte, waving a gloved hand toward a gaily-decorated Place Dauphine, as they passed under the Pont Neuf.

"Is the King giving a fête for his mistress . . . for the duchesse de Chateauroux?" asked Diane, leaning forward for a better look at the square.

"His mistress? His mistress! What would a pale convent flower like you know about mistresses?" The comte chortled gleefully and squeezed his daughter's hand. "I shall have a talk with Mother Superior, that sly hussy. What on earth is she putting into those innocent little heads, I ask you." The comte dabbed a pinch of snuff on the back of his hand and sniffed loudly. "Where do you get these ideas, hein?" He chucked Diane under the chin. "You are a funny one, you are," he said.

"Everyone talks of the duchesse de Chateauroux, papa. And how foolish the King is about her."

Spellbound, Diane had listened to stories of the willful, imperious duchesse de Chateauroux from visitors to Neuilly-les-Dames. The Queen, old and fat and frumpy, had no power at all. Everyone said so. Nonetheless, the King had loved her with all his heart for a long time, ten years. But after giving the King ten babies, the Queen had turned to her prayers and the King to other women.

Diane knew the list by heart, and they were all sisters: the de Nesle sisters. He began with Madame de Mailly, plain and unvoluptuous, but gay and lively, ever docile and eager to please. Around the King, who suffered from chronic boredom, she created a world of cozy supper parties and entertainments where the shy, insecure Louis could relax with his favorite courtiers. In the antechamber of Madame de Mailly's *petits appartements* in Versailles, these courtiers would gather in the late afternoon and wait patiently for hours, hoping to have an invitation to sup with the King and his mistress. After the meal the King himself would grind the coffee beans and make coffee for his guests. Diane could scarcely imagine it: the King himself handing a cup to his guests!

In time Madame de Mailly shared the affections of the King with her younger sister who, far away in her convent, dreamed of becoming his mistress and connived with Madame de Mailly to make those dreams come true. Louis fell hopelessly in love and arranged a hasty marriage for the young girl with the comte de Vintimille. At Versailles, the strictest etiquette ruled who could or could not become the King's mistress. She must belong to the nobility, and she must be married. It was strictly improper for the King to have a liaison with an unmarried woman.

In the palace at Versailles the comtesse de Vintimille lived in a specially designed suite near her sister Madame de Mailly and soon became pregnant with Louis's child. In giving birth to him, the young woman, who had achieved her heart's desire in capturing the heart of the King, succumbed to childbirth fever. Devastated, his great joy abruptly ended, Louis sought consolation with his ever devoted Madame de Mailly.

The baby was a son, and he lived on at the palace, archly referred to by the courtiers as the *demi-louis,* an allusion to the coin, which

Diane found not at all witty. How could it be witty when the unhappy story of the poor young comtesse causing the King such grief brought tears to her eyes?

And then came the next de Nesle sister, one that none of the aristocratic guests at the convent could stomach. They positively hated her because of her awful power. While the King mourned his young mistress, the marquise de la Tournelle, the prettiest and certainly the most ambitious of the sisters, saw her chance to step into this void in the handsome monarch's life. Madame de la Tournelle was as shrewd as she was charming. From the very beginning, she planned her strategy down to the last detail. She chose as her collaborator and consultant in her conquest of the King, the most notorious seducer in this age of cool, calculated lust: the duc de Richelieu. With his help the marquise toyed with the King, refusing to yield to his ardent desires until he had granted every single one of her demands. For the marquise de la Tournelle and Richelieu, her colleague in seduction, wanted power, power to dip into the golden treasuries of the kingdom, to dole out munificent benefices, to name ministers and governors, to influence policy. In short, to rule France.

Louis lost his heart to Madame de la Tournelle, made her his official mistress and granted all her wishes, including the banishment of her sister Madame de Mailly from Versailles. Louis installed his new amour in charmingly intimate apartments in the palace, and soon gave her the title of duchesse de Chateauroux. Louis' infatuation with his willful mistress knew no bounds. In Diane's imagination the duchesse was a figure from a romance, distant and mysterious, and every new scandal a tribute to her irresistible power over the King. And in her bolder daydreams Diane already saw herself a witty, captivating beauty, taking her place at Versailles among the clever women who, like the duchesse de Chateauroux, with a lift of an eyebrow or a shrug of the shoulder, wielded the kind of power that would bring her father the kind of hommage due a comte de Fautrière.

"We're pulling up to that quay on the Left Bank," the comte said, anxiously aware of the captain's difficulty in handling the massive houseboat.

Diane watched with delight the small, narrow boats, so low slung that it looked as if a boisterous wave might capsize them, which ferried a handful of passengers from one bank to the other. Fishwives stood along the quays and shrilled the day's catch, glistening in row upon pungent row. Coachmen led their horses down muddy banks to drink from the river. Diane was glad that she did not have to share this moment with her sisters, with dour, practical Catherine, who never found anything exciting, or with little Sophie, who found everything exciting.

The houseboat pulled up to the quay with a mighty thump that sent them lurching against the rail. Behind them, Diane heard glasses and dishes crashing to the floor. The comte stiffened and swore beneath his breath. Two emaciated little boys, their bony shoulders sticking through holes in their ragged shirts, struggled to prop a broad plank against the deck. After shouting a few instructions to his captain, the comte took Diane's arm and helped her down the plank to the riverbank.

"Papa," she whispered. "The little boys."

"What? Oh. Hmmm." The comte rummaged hurriedly in his satchel and threw the boys a fistful of coins.

The narrow cobblestone streets twisting alongside and away from the river were slippery and treacherous. The comte handed her into a hackney-cab, a *fiacre*, he called it. A little frightened, Diane stared at the chaotic jumble of people and vehicles crowding around the bridge—smart black carriages glistening with gold and silver, heraldic insignia painted on the sides and soft, buttery leather interiors of the palest pastels; small open hackney cabs with expensively dressed men in powdered wigs; crude wooden carts rumbling along behind pairs of yoked oxen, downward staring, resigned.

With a sigh of satisfaction, the comte settled himself in his seat. He was back in Paris, ready to give battle at court once again, and this time he believed that he returned armed more effectively than ever before. He looked down at his daughter's lovely face touched by the pale morning sun and smiled. Her eager eyes darted here and there, bright with astonishment. She raised her hand and swept back a heavy wave of silvery blond hair that had fallen forward over her forehead. It was a gesture of natural grace. She has no idea of her great beauty, he thought, no idea at all. No capricious, coquettish mannerisms. No artifice. He would change all that. The comte, like the artists of the age, preferred stylized women, women who had no intention of leaving anything to nature or to chance.

With paints and patches and powdered wigs she would stop a man's breath and muddy his judgment. And a man whose judgment was muddied by desire could be very useful. Very useful indeed. Since the interminably long reign of Louis XIV with his Madame de Montespan and still more his Madame de Maintenon, no one who knew Versailles and the way power was manipulated would dispute the role of women in the intrigues that raged around the corridors and antechambers of the palace. It was the age of women, of beautiful, intelligent women who relished power and knew how to wield it. Diane would make a spectacular match, and the comte would be able to warm himself in its glow.

A little abashed, but unable to help herself, Diane held her perfumed handkerchief to her nose as the fiacre rumbled through dirty, narrow streets. Recent heavy rains had done little to wash away the filth that accumulated in jagged heaps along the way. The comte's footmen, dressed in velvet liveries, raised their noses primly above the clamorous squalor of the streets. A bellman in bright gaiters and a three-cornered blue hat cried out for householders and shopkeepers to sluice down the streets.

The tangle of narrow, muddy streets gave way to broad, sweeping avenues as they approached the new mansions in the Faubourg Saint-Germain. They drove past the Palais du Luxembourg, gleaming softly in the morning sun, and circled the gardens, deserted now except for an old man cleaning damp, black leaves from the gravel paths.

They stopped at an imposing black wrought-iron gate, wide enough to accommodate two large carriages side by side, on the rue des Trois-Pavillons. Two porters in dark marine blue uniforms with gold braid leaned forward at precisely the same moment, like mechanical toy figures, before solemnly swinging open the broad gates.

They entered the rather small courtyard of a large, four-story *hôtel particulier*, only recently constructed. Diane, accustomed to ancient feudal chateaux, often with careless bric-a-brac additions, and the humble stone and timber houses of villages and small towns, thought that this fine house must surely belong to the King or to one of the princes of the blood.

"Will we be staying here, papa?" The comte was watching her now with amusement. "Is maman living here?"

The comte scowled as he always did at any reminder of his wife, who had for years been merely a remote, disapproving shadow in his life. He could not recall when he had last seen her. Surely, in the winter, before he had left for Corcheval, but perhaps not even then. He ought to discuss Diane's future with her. On the other hand, it was not really her affair.

"Does this look like your mother's sort of house? The sort of thing that would appeal to a descendant of the Ancys? Your mother lives on the rue Hyacinthe. Not far, you'll see. You must call on her as soon as you're settled."

They reached the wide *perron* with a great curving stairway at each end. A footman in the comte's livery opened the door, and Diane was astonished to see her maid, Marianne, already busy with servants carrying her boxes and cases up the stairs. The gleaming foyer with its polished marble and stately columns bespoke wealth and comfort and luxury. Great wealth. Warily, she watched as her father ran a practiced eye over every detail of the reception rooms.

"I'll leave you now, *ma petite*. I have a frightful number of people to see, and the best place to see them is at the duc de Bourgogne's levée, which I should be able to reach with time to spare, especially if the duc stayed late at the gaming tables, as he is known to do. Are you quite sure you'll be happy here, Mademoiselle de Fautrière?" he asked with a teasing smile.

"You're leaving me here? What am I to do here by myself while you're away?" She was bewildered and not a little frightened. She knew that in the country her father often bragged about his rooms in the palace at Versailles and never mentioned a residence in Paris.

"Don't worry. By the time you get settled and get used to your new home, your home in Paris, I'll call on you with some friends.

So freshen your toilette, make yourself beautiful for papa and his friends. Never fear. I'll be here so often that I'll make a nuisance of myself. You'll be ever so happy to see my back going down the steps after dinner."

"I'll be living here alone? In this huge *hôtel*?" She felt sure that he must be making fun of her. How was it possible that this beautiful mansion was hers alone when her father never stopped complaining about his revenues from his estates in Burgundy? But, then again, the harvests this year might have been exceptional. Perhaps, papa now had all the money he ever wanted. The fall harvests, of course, there were so many fields, so much wheat. Suddenly, she felt like a princess in a fairy tale, magically coming to life in a dazzling new kingdom.

"Naturally. You'll see. Your friends will have their own establishments, too. Perhaps not as grand as the rue des Trois-Pavillons, but then again, they are not de Fautrières, are they? Get settled as quickly as you can. For you have plenty of work to do, my girl."

4

No sooner had we settled in than my father engaged for me tutors in music, dance, drawing, Italian, Latin, and French . . . . My father corrected me continually and criticized me for my ridiculous behavior. As soon as I had observed several ladies, I understood perfectly what he meant, and I began to imitate them. My father associated with the highest society of Paris and socialized with those favored by the Court.

In the outer rooms Diane could hear Laurent and the other footmen preparing the house for the evening, closing shutters, and locking doors, lighting candles and lamps. The silence of the immense house enveloped her. She gazed with satisfaction around the beautiful, luxurious room. Often, awakening in the ivory and gold splendor of her bedroom, she would have to think hard to remember how she came to be surrounded by such beauty. She felt cosseted, snug and protected in a warm cocoon of wealth.

Laurent moved with muffled steps across the room. He lit the candles in the sconces above the massive commode and drew together the heavy velvet draperies at the windows giving onto the small paved courtyard. It was only five o'clock in the afternoon, but the frosty winter skies had already filled the room with dark shadows. She looked up and smiled as Laurent placed a dainty lamp at her elbow. Lately, she had taken up writing poetry, and she had almost finished a sprightly ode to surprise her father on his saint's day.

She longed to show her father that she deserved the wonderful world that he had revealed to her. Her father as the hissing demon of her nightmares had been banished forever. She could not bear to think of returning to the bleak provinces and the dreary humdrum life there, cut off from the brilliance of Paris. She did not care that her lessons meant headaches, scoldings, and hard work. She would do everything she could to turn herself into the most polished young woman in Paris. Except for the dirty little voice teacher, a thin little man whose scruffy, unpowdered wig seemed too small for his large head with its bulging forehead, she liked her masters and was eager to please them by learning as fast as she possibly could.

Diane knew that Odile, and perhaps Uncle Philippe as well, thought that she was trying to do too much, too fast. She frowned and bent her head to her writing. The comte had engaged every conceivable instructor: he had set her to learning Italian, dancing, the viol, the piano, voice, and even French, which she spoke with a provincial accent, though of course she was improving with every passing day. Now and then, she could turn a very pretty phrase, and her father would simply glow with pleasure.

Even the intricate protocols of dress and language and manners of the court at Versailles had to be learned and practiced. In Paris and elsewhere in France the court, with its own complex etiquette and rules of conduct, was known as *ce pays-ci,* "the other country." She learned that in the other country she must scratch at a door, not knock. There, ladies affected a kind of step that looked more like gliding than walking, and so she practiced that glide until she was dizzy and her legs ached.

Painted faces also had to observe the rules of rank. Until Diane was presented formally to the King and Queen at court, she must content herself with a small dab of rosy pink rouge in a circle on each cheek. After her presentation she would be able to wear dark purple. She had to learn intricate family histories, who had been born with what name, who had been ennobled when, to recognize immediately whether a title had been purchased and what members of the sworded nobility had stooped to marrying fortuned commoners. Within a few weeks, she could tell just by looking at the painted faces of women promenading at the Palais Royal whether they were of the *noblesse d'épée* or of the lesser *noblesse de robe*. With the zeal of a voyager setting out on a long and perilous journey, Diane stored away every detail, holding fast to these precious signs and symbols that assured her that the world she was seeking was indeed just as exalted and fabulous as she had dreamed it was.

Diane knew that her father was more than pleased with her progress. Her French had improved impressively, which delighted him. One day, catching him out in a fib, she turned to him with a mock serious pout and said, "I must conclude, papa, that I have a more dependable relationship with the truth than you." Diane had a decided gift for grave, witty remarks, he declared, and he could not wait to pass along her clever remarks to his friends at court.

But he had obviously made up his mind to be patient, to bide his time until she could make her debut in *le grand monde* and capture its capricious attention. She had been in Paris for over two months, and he had not yet introduced her to his circle of friends at court.

More mysteriously for Diane, her father continued to say nothing about her mother. Until one day, when, after taking tea and droning companionably on into the late afternoon, as he stood up and carefully adjusted his lacy cuffs, he said, in the most casual way,

"Your mother has sent round word that she has returned from Brittany. Apparently, Philippe wrote to let her know that I had brought you to Paris. And she would like to see you. Naturally."

Since arriving in Paris, she had wanted to see her mother more than anything in the world. Now that her mother was expecting her to call, Diane grew uneasy. As long as she could remember, her stomach would cramp into tight knots at the thought of her mother and father. They were such distant figures, weaving unpredictably in and out of her life. As a little girl in the convent, she had a bedtime ritual of trying to picture her parents' faces in her mind before going to sleep. But she never could remember what they looked like. Smells, though, she did remember. Her father smelled of sandalwood. And her mother? What was it? Eglantine, yes, wild rose.

She placed a ribbon in her notebook to mark her place and rose to dress for her call on her mother.

Being of a delicate disposition, she preferred to retire from the tumult of the world in which my father reveled.

Diane's carriage—a dainty, very elegant affair purchased especially for her with her own footmen in emerald green livery—drew up before an imposing building that dominated the rue Hyacinthe. The comtesse de Fautrière lived in a rambling apartment that occupied the entire second floor, a residence far less impressive, certainly, than her own daughter's.

"Perfect, mademoiselle," said Marianne. If Madame la comtesse was indeed the pious prude ridiculed by Odile, there would be nothing in Diane's dress or grooming to give offense.

"Are you sure? I don't look too drab, Marianne?"

"Not at all. What an idea! Your mother will be so pleased to see you again that you may even be invited to stay for supper. Unless, of course, the comtesse is supping with friends this evening."

Diane was immediately reassured by the gold and white opulence of the foyer to her mother's apartment, though the stairway was of polished wood, not marble like her own, and the steps quite worn.

A stooped, old footman took her cloak and ushered her to a sitting room, where Diane sat down by the fireside to wait for her mother. Several books lay open on the canapé next to the window, as if someone had abruptly decided to leave the room and would return to the canapé and begin to read again. It had been over three years since she had last seen her mother. That would have been in the spring, at Easter, the comtesse had spent a month with them in the convent after they had buried Louis-Etienne at Corcheval. How long ago that seemed. She recalled her mother playing the piano for the Abbesse and her friends in the parlor.

"Diane, is that really you?" A tall, thin woman dressed in white, moved quickly across the room. Diane sprang to her feet and extended her cheek to her mother, who embraced her and placed her smooth, cool face against Diane's.

"I came as soon as I could, maman. I mean, papa said today, as he was leaving, that you had returned to Paris, and I was glad, because I wanted to see you just as soon as we got here. In October . . . " She was tense, breathless, as if she had just run up a flight of stairs.

"Sit down, Diane. Do sit down. *Mon dieu!* What a young woman you are! But you can't be. You're only a child!" Her voice was filled with joy and tenderness. She spoke slowly and deliberately, her voice low and husky, a voice that Diane found familiar because it was so like her own.

As her mother sat down in the chair opposite, her dark eyes were alive with pleasure, and Diane's spirits lifted. The comtesse's movements had the suppleness of a very young woman, and her presence emanated peace and calm. How silly she had been, after all, to fret about what dress to wear. "I'm already fourteen, maman. I mean, I've just turned fourteen, you know."

She did not want to contradict her mother, who sat smiling at her in the kindest sort of way. The comtesse was very tall, but too thin, and her face was pale, almost bluish like Diane's when she was tired or not feeling well, but Diane thought she was one of the most beautiful women she had ever seen. In the Charolle the women in the Ancy family were known for their beauty, Diane had often heard that. The comtesse wore a simple muslin dress and no jewelry except for heavy gold teardrop pendant earrings. That her mother could turn her back on fashion yet look supremely lovely filled her with admiration. Why, she made women like Odile, who fancied themselves the height of fashion, look tawdry, like those brazen creatures strutting in their garish finery around the Palais Royal.

"And how are your sisters? Catherine and little Sophie? Would I recognize Sophie, I wonder? Just a wee one at Corcheval three years ago."

"Oh, you would, maman, you would. Sophie is a little pet, forever wanting to be petted, that is. She is Clotilde's favorite, her *petit chou*, and Clotilde makes no bones about it. But, then, Sophie is everyone's pet at the convent because she was sick a lot last year. But now she's fine, of course. Catherine is very good in her studies. She is far ahead of me in embroidery. I'm clumsy with my hands, the sisters say, and I don't concentrate the way Catherine does."

The comtesse still leaned forward in her chair, but she no longer smiled. She gazed sadly at the lovely stranger facing her, the lovely stranger who was her daughter and very nervous. Four strangers. Diane, Catherine, and Sophie . . . And her son, Louis-Etienne, a stranger, too, though for many years the only thing that gave meaning to her life was seeing him. Occasionally. When he came begging for money to tide him over until . . . until the next time he came begging. Louis-Etienne, too, a stranger, there was no denying that. She could still remember her elation at his birth, when she was young and in love with the handsomest man in Charolais, Michel de Fautrière. More than anything else she had wanted to give a son and heir to her moody young husband. As she lay sweating and panting in the pain of childbirth, the dingy, coarse skin on her knees reminded her of the hours and hours she had spent kneeling on the stone floors of the family chapel and on the rush matting of her bedchamber, praying, please God, not a girl, not a girl, praying for a fine boy to make Michel happy and proud of her.

God had answered her prayers, but the baby was weak and helpless. She had begged Michel to let her nurse him with her own milk so that the baby would grow strong at her breast, so that she could gaze down into his eyes as he fed on her strength and grew to love her. Obscurely, she knew that she was counting on this red, wrinkled little form to share her painful loneliness.

At first, Michel had thought she was mentally enfeebled from the ordeal of childbirth, perhaps she was running a fever. But when she persisted and even twice fondly put the frail infant to her engorged breasts, Michel grew angry and accused her of making herself look ridiculous. "Do you want to make both of us the laughingstock of Burgundy? The King of France is this child's godfather, and the Queen is his godmother! Are you out of your mind? Do you want fingers pointed at you, and sniggering laughter behind your back? Why not get down on your hands and knees and scrub floors then? No woman of your rank nurses a baby! You know that as well as I do!" he cried, his neck red and swollen with fury. "Peasant women do that!"

Later that day, while Aurélie slept, her father-in-law the old comte and Clotilde—her Clotilde who had been her faithful servant and friend—had taken Louis-Etienne away to a wet nurse on a farm near Flavigny, twenty kilometers over bumpy, rutted roads from Corcheval.

Three months later, when it was proper for her to go abroad, she and Clotilde went to visit Louis-Etienne in the dirty, earthen-floored thatched house of the wet nurse. The rains had been heavy, and the muddy roads sucked stubbornly at the wheels of the carriage. Twice Aurélie leaned out the window and scolded her driver to whip up the horses. She could not remember ever being so overwrought with anticipation. It had been so long since she had felt her child in her arms!

Weary and chilled, Aurélie felt all her joyous expectation disappear when the carriage came to a stop before the lonely cottage at the edge of a scraggly field. What could her helpless little son possibly be doing here? Two large-eyed children, their aprons dirty and torn, sat in the mud playing with a broken bowl and a handful of chestnuts.

The wet nurse, a wide snaggle-toothed smile spread across her face, leaned out of the low door at the sound of the carriage. Inside, the house reeked of smoke and the remnants of the dinner meal, which were still scattered about on the table. Madame Laferre, the wet nurse, motioned cheerily toward the corner where a crudely made cradle was tucked away behind a bench and a broken chair. "It's to keep the little ones away from the babe," said the wet nurse, lifting aside the bench so that the comtesse could come close to the cradle.

Aurélie looked down at the tiny vacant-eyed baby staring up at her. He moved his head from side to side, as if he might be able to see her. His hands were swaddled tightly to his side. He had thick black hair and a bright red sore festered on one side of his tiny mouth. He smelled of stale urine.

The wet nurse waited expectantly as the comtesse turned away from the cradle. "A good baby, he is. The little gentleman is a good baby. A quiet one." She paused a moment, as if suddenly remembering a forgotten errand. "But, madame, a baby means work, doesn't it? And my back giving me the fits every time I stoop to pick him up. When he cries. And it's always at night when I'm trying to get my sleep after all the work that's on my mind during the day. And when the little gentleman finally decides that he'll get some sleep, here goes my little tyke howling his head off for his own sup, too," and she pointed toward a coarsely woven reed basket on one side of the hearth.

"Clotilde, have Albert and the footman bring in the baskets," the comtesse said wearily.

The wet nurse had resumed her broad smile. She pulled a tall-backed chair toward the hearth where a deep bed of ashes glowed under a large black kettle. "Sit down and rest yourself, my lady. You look a bit peaked. And well I know the feeling. It's not easy, bringing the little ones into this hard world, whatever the menfolks may say."

"No, thank you, Madame Laferre, we must be on our way to be back at Beaubery before dark. The roads are muddy and slow." She sounded as if she barely had the strength to utter these few words. "I've brought some ham and venison from Corcheval for you and your family . . . and other things." Her voice trailed off. "Some linens for the baby. For Louis-Etienne, of course."

The footmen and Clotilde brought in several large baskets of meats and preserves and apples and pears from the chateau larders and stood waiting to be told where to put them down.

Madame Laferre looked eagerly from basket to basket. "We'll put them over here on the bed," she said. "And I'm ever so grateful, my lady. And my husband will be, too, when he comes in from the fields."

But when the wet nurse raised her eyes from the daintily packed baskets, Aurélie had already left the house.

In the carriage Aurélie closed her eyes and sank back against the cushions. Clotilde placed a soft pillow behind her head, but she knew her mistress well enough not to try to talk to her. Clotilde gave the footmen directions for returning straightaway to Corcheval. For a long time Aurélie lay back in her corner of the carriage, oblivious to the buffeting and jolting of the journey. Then she sat forward, her back rigid, and gazed blankly into the gathering dusk.

During the dark chill days of that winter Aurélie spent most of her time in bed, speaking little, rarely getting dressed. Her young husband lost patience with her dull mood and rode away to Paris, where he told any of his friends who bothered to ask that his wife was suffering from a *crise de nerfs*. Secretly, he hoped that whatever she had would not spoil her beauty and leave her with a sallow complexion.

Louis-Etienne was almost three when he returned to Corcheval. The old comte had died of a fall from his horse in the spring, and Michel was now the comte de Fautrière and Aurélie the comtesse. When Louis-Etienne arrived at the chateau where he was born, his parents were away at court where Aurélie was being presented to King Louis XV. In late summer when they returned briefly to Corcheval, they brought back a tutor for the little boy, a Monsieur Nicholas, a stocky, squat young man, who, the comte said, knew a little English.

A suite of small rooms in the attic up under the eaves had been freshly painted as the nursery, and Louis-Etienne lived there, taking his meals with his tutor in the nursery. Every day, or almost every day, Louis-Etienne would be bathed and dressed in crisp, clean clothes and made to scrub his nails until they hurt. With his tutor following a few steps behind, Louis-Etienne would call upon his mother during her toilette and pay his respects to her, bowing formally over her extended hand. The comtesse thought that he was perfect. A perfect little stranger.

Diane was born in Paris in 1730 when the comte and comtesse still resided in a drafty Renaissance mansion on the rue Jacob. To Aurélie's great surprise, the comte had been enchanted with the little girl and had chosen all her names himself. This time Aurélie scarcely noticed when the infant was taken from her arms and handed over to a wet nurse. Her friends and her own experience with Louis-Etienne had convinced her that her children, the offspring of her swollen, aching body, would never be a real part of her life. She would carry them in her body for months, bring them red and crying into the world, then strangers would take them away and keep them until the babies themselves came back to her as polite strangers.

For days before Diane's birth she had busied herself with selecting the laces and gowns for her *relevailles*, the period during which, as a well-born woman she would receive her friends while reclining prettily on a chaise-longue in her exquisite laces and flounces.

Diane was taken away, and the comtesse paid no attention. Those were the days when she desperately used every means to attract Michel's attention, when she would flirt outrageously with almost anyone just to make her husband turn his head and look at her for more than a few seconds.

But Michel was amused instead. By now, he made no secret of his liaisons with the marquise de la Gallière and Alexandrine, the Russian princess who had taken Paris by storm. Aurélie watched with numb misery as her handsome young husband drifted from actress to actress and in and out of the arms of some of the most desirable women at Versailles. When she raged and cried, he laughed and called her a bourgeoise with low tastes. "To be faithful to one's wife is something the lower ranks do. I should think that you would have a better sense of style," he would say as he settled his cloak about his broad shoulders and climbed into his carriage and departed for the night.

But that was long ago, and she marveled that she had ever had the energy to care so much. There had been two more children, two more little girls—Catherine and Sophie—for Michel was determined to protect his succession by at least two male heirs. But after the third daughter was born, Michel remarked coldly that he found it now pointless to think further of another son.

Eventually, Aurélie capitulated to the way of life of their aristocratic friends, just as Michel had said she would. Like their circle, they established entirely separate apartments, and when they met, they were beautifully polite to each other. Quietly, without display, she withdrew from court circles, finding deep solace in her religious activities, while Michel continued his frenzied pursuit of the pleasures of Versailles.

One of the large logs burning in the fire broke in the middle; the flames flared up hotly, throwing orange and red shadows about the faces of the two women. Diane had stopped talking, worried that her mother had become bored with her stories of the petty miseries and triumphs of life at Neuilly-les-Dames.

The comtesse smiled as if rousing herself from a dream and reached for the pull rope next to the mantelpiece. "Could you stay for a little supper, Diane? It won't be anything fancy, but we can carry on our visit. Would you like that?" Her voice was gentle and kind.

"Oh, yes. Thank you, maman." Her mother was every bit as nice as Clotilde had said. Diane did not feel afraid of her at all.

Later, as Diane prepared to leave, the comtesse said, "Don't go just yet. Victor will bring up some hot milk and cakes. That will give us a chance to talk a little longer."

The comtesse settled herself and took up her tapestry hoop. She brought a pair of miniature scissors trimmed with ivory from the side pocket of her gown and snipped a thread and tied it neatly in a knot on the underside of the tapestry. "I sent word for you to come to me this evening because I wanted to tell you of my plans."

"Your plans?"

"Yes, my plans. You know, this evening, you have brought me such happiness in coming to see me, in letting me get to know a little better my beautiful young daughter. Such happiness."

"I'm glad, maman," said Diane gently as she watched her mother's worried expression, her sweeping eyebrows crumpling into a scowl.

"Diane, I have decided to retire to the convent. To the sisters of Charity in Villeneuve-la-Petite." Her words echoed forlornly around the huge room. The comtesse gazed calmly at her daughter, as she slipped back into her chair.

"But why? Why, maman?"

"For many reasons. Many good reasons. And I have thought about this decision for several years now. If you like, I have been preparing myself for the religious life for some time."

Diane felt her cheeks go hot with shame at the idea of her mother joining the pitiable wraiths haunting the cloisters, the impoverished widows, the undowered daughters—inevitably plain and as demure as sheep—the displaced wives who had struggled to escape an abusive marriage only to end up in the bleak exile of the convent. Society's rejects. Forgotten by all, by family and friends. And the convent at Villeneuve was not even fashionable. A poor, provincial abbey run by an order that depended on the duc de Toulouse's benevolence. Her mother would be one of those pathetic women who had failed to find an honorable place in society.

"But what will papa say? And Uncle Philippe? Does Uncle Philippe know?"

The comtesse raised her hand slightly as if to calm Diane. "Of course I've talked to my brother. Philippe has always been my best friend; you must know how close we've always been. Philippe does not find my decision strange or unreasonable." She placed her tapestry hoop on the window seat and folded her hands. In the candlelight she looked beautiful and young, her cheeks flushed with health, her blue eyes clear and shining.

"And papa? Surely you have an obligation to papa and to the family, our position, to remain here, the comtesse de Fautrière in your rightful place in society. You ought to go about more, maman, there's no earthly reason why you should hide away here in this huge, drafty place with shabby little curés shuffling in and out in their dusty old *soutanes*. Why do you do it, maman? I don't understand. And now you want to molder away in a convent!"

"On the table near the canapé, Victor." The comtesse's arthritic old footman moved toward the far end of the long room and slowly lowered the heavy tray to the table. He bowed stiffly toward Diane before leaving the room with a deliberate, measured step.

The comtesse lifted a pale green cashmere shawl from the window seat and drew it tightly around her shoulders.

"But what about papa? What does he say?" asked Diane.

"Your father knows of my intentions and approves of them. Quite approves, as a matter of fact."

"Approves?" Diane's voice rose in disbelief. "What will people say? What will they think? That you've crept away to a dingy convent because the family can't afford to keep you in proper style in society?"

"Precisely," said the comtesse, gently, without anger, enunciating every syllable.

"But how can that be?" Though she was far from being hungry, she gulped down her cup of spicy hot milk and, without waiting for her mother, nervously reached for a slice of lemon cake.

"There is no need to go into the muddle of your father's affairs, and they are a muddle, believe me, and always have been. Whatever he is, your father is not a reasonable man where money is concerned." The comtesse spooned coarse lumps of sugar into her cup of hot milk and paused a moment, musing, stirring the milk with unhurried strokes. "For some time now he has been borrowing heavily from Philippe. My dowry, of course, and my family's estates—Châtillon and Audicourt as well—have been scattered to the four winds. Audicourt was sold just before you and your sisters went to Neuilly-les-Dames together." They had quarreled bitterly when she learned that Michel had sold her beloved Audicourt, lovely old Audicourt with its round *pigeonnier*. Her grandfather had the servants shovel it out each time one of his tenants' children married, a precious wedding gift, those wagon loads of pigeon manure; none of the other peasants in the region had a seigneur as generous as the old comte d'Audicourt. She and her sisters would decorate the wagon and the horses with bright ribbons and flowers and would ride alongside on their ponies, all the way to the farmhouse where the treasured manure would be ceremonially unloaded into huge, new baskets and carried to safekeeping in the barn. She had loved Audicourt and the summertime and bright meadows smelling of thyme and rosemary.

"Philippe's funds are not inexhaustible. He can't go on financing your father's recklessness. Philippe is having trouble like everyone else. This living at court, away from the planting and harvests, it's ruinous. Philippe is not the only one being careful with his money these days. But your father simply will not listen to reason." She spoke flatly without emotion, staring peacefully into the fire.

"But how can that be true, maman? Papa has been so generous with me. I mean . . . my gowns, the latest fashion and all done by

Madame Clarisse herself, never her assistants. My gowns are richer and more luxurious than anyone else's. Madame Clarisse says so. And the shops have papa's word: I can buy whatever I like, he told me."

"Of course. Of course he would. He has to outshine them all. One way or another," said the comtesse grimly. "And besides, it's all part of his scheme, isn't it?"

"His scheme?" asked Diane, although she already knew what she was about to hear from her mother. "Do you mean his scheme to become minister of the royal establishments? I know that's what he expects from the King. If only papa has enough supporters."

"Oh, yes, a ministry, by all means. Another rung up the ladder. Your father is trying to work his way back into the inner circle, back to his favored place before the Cardinal de Fleury fiasco."

Diane had never heard her mother speak about the other country and its politics. She had always seemed distant from the heavily perfumed crowds swarming through the vast mirrored corridors of Versailles. But, of course, during those long, lonely years with her sisters in the convent at Neuilly-les-Dames, her mother had been one of the most admired women at court. And she remembered her father, slouching in a chair before the fire at Corcheval, discussing with her mother ways to end his exile.

"Which he may well do with a great deal of luck and better judgment than he has demonstrated in the past. Yes, certainly, the opulent show which my brother has been financing is intended to get attention. The right kind of attention. But I gather the minister's position is the second step in your father's scheme."

The comtesse paused a moment and raised her clear gaze to Diane. "You, of course, as you may be well aware, are to complete the first objective of his scheme. That first objective is to find a brilliant *parti* for your hand, a suitor who will be happy to bestow a huge portion of his earthly goods on the father of his dowerless bride."

"There's nothing really melodramatic about his scheme," the comtesse added, studying the panic in her daughter's face. "And it is not at all original. This kind of marriage contract is becoming commonplace: a young lady with a title from one of France's noblest houses . . . and a young lady, like you, beautiful beyond words. It's a bargain many a suitor would be happy to strike."

Diane twisted her napkin into a tight ball. Sylvie, her eyes swollen shut after a night of tears in her narrow dormitory bed. Sylvie, dragged away by her father and angrily shoved into his gleaming new carriage; everyone watching, silently, some with satisfaction, some with pity. Some, like Diane, with fear.

"But, maman . . . a *mésalliance* . . . Papa would never make a contract with a bourgeois, would he? Papa is so proud. I've heard him myself, making fun of aristocrats who marry a big purse. He hates that. He despises a *mésalliance.* Do you remember, the comte de Villemorin's son who married a shipbuilder's daughter, a shipbuilder from Bordeaux? Papa said to Uncle Philippe that Villemorin was stupid, no one could be that poor, and that no bourgeois would ever have enough money to put his feet under the Fautrière dinner table." Her father, so arrogant and fastidious. No, he would never give her away like Sylvie's father to a puny rich oaf with a coarse accent and bright, vulgar clothes. Maman has spent too much time alone, away from society and the court. Besides, when did she ever see papa? How could she know what papa would do?

"You may be right, of course. Still, don't expect too much. Don't build your hopes too high."

"Oh, papa can be silly, I know that. But papa wants the very best for me, I know he does." But even as she said it, Diane knew that it was not so.

"There are three of you, remember? And what with the money borrowed to buy Louis-Etienne's commission"—the comtesse crossed herself—"at a ruinous rate. Philippe has already told your father that he will have to go to the Jews for more money."

"Even so, maman, if you shut yourself away, everyone will know how bad things are with papa, everyone will think worse of us, and nothing will ever go papa's way again."

"Oh, come, come . . . what an imagination you have!" The comtesse smiled and shook her head. "And what if I told you that I want to go to Villeneuve and help the sisters in their work with the poor? What would you think of that, Diane? Would you think that your mother has grown old and foolish?"

"I don't know what I would think, maman. I hope that I won't have to think of it at all. Ever."

5

When the comte entered his brother-in-law's dressing room, Philippe was still being shaved by his valet. The air was close and stuffy, smelling of leather and tobacco. The comte cast a furtive, envious eye at the handsome toilet articles of heavy, chased silver scattered carelessly about the marble-topped table next to Philippe's chair. Philippe seemed hardly the sort to surround himself with items of such luxury. He gave the impression of being indifferent to refinements that the comte found utterly indispensable. Philippe's secretary, a pimply young man from the country, sat at a desk sorting a heap of papers into separate packets which he then tied neatly with string, his tongue protruding in concentration.

"I didn't see you last night at Saint-Amand's," said Michel, trying to sound off-handedly jovial. He was bristling with anger. Since his return to Paris, for well over two months, Philippe had been playing some sort of game with him, avoiding him in public with a short dismissive nod when their paths crossed and sending down word that he was *invisible* whenever the comte came to call. Odile apparently was under orders to play the same game. He had seen nothing of her since she left Ancy.

"Saint-Amand's crowd is addicted to faro, which bores me stiff. There's no conversation. Everyone's too busy panting over cards and quarreling." Philippe had been enjoying his nice warm shave until his sister's husband had spoiled it. What Odile saw in this mincing dandy he would never know. Of course, Odile would spread her legs for anything with a cod, from lackey—and God knows there had been plenty of those—to princes. Thank God, he did not have to depend on her for children. Elisabeth had not exactly been the light of his life, but at least she had given him six healthy children before she went to her early grave. With Odile, who could say whether it was his child or the head footman's? Fortunately, he had never had to decide. Rumor had it that Odile kept her Parisian abortionist in silks and laces.

"What brings you out so early, Michel? It is early, isn't it for you and your crowd?

"Not really," replied the comte, stifling his anger at Philippe's insolence.

Philippe's stout frame filled the chair in which he lounged. He closed his eyes with a sigh of annoyance. Michel's heavy perfume—was it some sort of rose?—made him slightly queasy. With short, deft motions, Roger trimmed the marquis' thick black eyebrows, then stepped back to survey his work.

Philippe could sense Michel's anger, as he paced about the room, swaying on his high heels. Michel was wearing a mint green velvet coat and rose breeches with light green stockings. What a ridiculous peacock, thought Philippe. He knew exactly why the comte had been calling so assiduously, and he enjoyed watching him stew.

Roger buffed his master's face to a pink glow with a soft towel. From a row of wigs, he selected one rather low in front with two shoulder-length braids tied with black ribbons. After adjusting the wig, he powdered it lavishly. "Enough! Enough! Let me breathe!" said Philippe impatiently, shaking away towels and rising to his feet.

"Are you going to the King's *levée* this morning, Michel? If so, we can go along together before the roads to Versailles get clogged with carts." Philippe dismissed his annoyance with Michel. There was no reason to let him get under his skin.

"Yes, certainly, one always tries to attend His Majesty's *levées*. I missed one day last week, and he noticed. He noticed, can you imagine that! He said to the Cardinal de Bernis, 'I haven't seen Fautrière. Is he ill?' The Cardinal told me himself. And others heard His Majesty say it, too."

He was carried away now, Philippe could see, on his little tidal wave of vanity. What an utter fool, always intriguing, spying, betraying, forever hoping that a golden apple will fall from the King's pocket into his hands. With the way he spends money, he is going to have to hang on to the royal coattails till the day he dies.

"Emile, I'll need my papers on the Briare estate as well. And make sure that every document is signed."

"Very well, Monsieur le marquis." The secretary, knowing that he was being dismissed, hurried to collect his papers and bundles.

"So, Michel, shall we go along to court? You have your carriage, I suppose, though how you manage to get around in Paris with that enormous rig, I can't imagine."

"I've another carriage for town, though I'm quite happy with the six horse. Very convenient. And the duc de Richelieu's coach is far larger. Makes mine look more like a hackney." He knew that Philippe was taking a swipe at what he considered Michel's extravagance. The coach had in truth been rather a disaster, although it had made the trip down to Corcheval pleasanter by far. Since the duc de Richelieu had had his immense traveling carriage fitted out with a bed, a fashion had been started, and every courtier, whether he could afford it or not, spent reckless sums of money to outfit absurdly large vehicles with every conceivable luxury.

"Another carriage!" exclaimed Philippe, feigning surprise, for he had already heard of his brother-in-law's new carriage with its large coat of arms heavily gilded on each door. He steered Michel through the small dark library that adjoined his bedchamber to the door to the corridor.

"If we could take just a moment, Philippe," said the comte, and there was an ominous whine in his voice. Philippe stopped and waited, his ill humor growing.

"I know you'll find this surprising, but I'm afraid that I must call upon you for another temporary loan. Oh, not enormous, you understand, but just enough to tide me over until some of the estate revenues begin to trickle in." Though with everything going to rack and ruin, he wondered how many revenues would show up in his pockets at the end of the year.

Philippe waited a moment before replying calmly. "Actually, dear brother-in-law, I am not at all surprised. Your ability to throw money to the four winds never ceases to amaze me." His tone turned icy and caustic. "But, tell me, what has happened to the considerable sum of money I lent you before I left Ancy? That loan, as I recall, was meant to tide you over as well."

"I've made some very important investments with it."

"Investments? Investments? What on earth are you talking about? There isn't another South Sea bogus stock company started up again, is there? I thought all that lot had been run out of town."

"No, of course not. By investment, I mean that I finished paying off the construction and equipment of the houseboat with . . . with your very generous loan."

"Do you mean to tell me that you sank 75,000 *livres* into that river whale?" Philippe spluttered.

"No, that's not all, naturally. You forget about Diane. I've had to set up an establishment for Diane. Provide her with clothes, maids, a staff, a carriage. Tutors. And they cost a great deal of money. But the poor girl can't go about in society fresh from a pokey convent in the country without any finishing. Why, she barely learned a correct French in the convent."

They had reached the bottom of the great central staircase, and Philippe turned to his brother-in-law. So, this whining fop was cleverer than he had supposed. Michel had not been slow in figuring out that Aurélie's children could loosen Philippe's purse strings quickly enough. Especially Diane. Poor beautiful little Diane. She had always been his favorite niece. Even as a small child she had resembled Aurélie with her pale blond hair, her thin, nervous face. And like Aurélie, Diane would be used as a pawn by this scheming, vain little dandy to get on in his scheming, vain little world.

"So. You plan to make a lucrative marriage with Diane, and then what? Have you figured out exactly how much she will fetch on the open market? Of course, you have!" Philippe could feel the blood pounding heavily at the back of his head. With anyone else it seemed, he could always keep his temper under control, but let him so much as look as this mincing fool, and Philippe would get apoplectic.

"Do you have anyone in particular in mind? Or do you intend to parade her about Paris and Versailles hoping that someone with a grand title and more money than he knows what to do with will pick up the scent?"

Michel sucked in his thin nostrils and shot out his chin. "You are in a fine mood this morning, aren't you, my dear brother-in-law? I know that you can be crude, but I would never have expected you to speak of your sister's child in this way." Ordinarily, Philippe could be counted on to maintain his mask of familial bonhomie, the good spirits of a robust man in fine health. Lately, however, Michel had noticed that Philippe, every time they met, appeared to struggle with his notorious temper. Perhaps his liaison with Odile was beginning to nettle Philippe after all.

"But, to answer one of your questions. No, I do not have any particular *parti* in mind, though with her name and her beauty, I have no doubt that Diane will have plenty of suitors. I must simply select carefully, that's all."

"That's all very well, but I should think that another year in the convent would do her no harm. She's only fourteen, Michel. Surely she could be left to her innocent pleasures a little longer before being fed to the barracudas at court."

"The barracudas at court! What nonsense! Diane is ecstatically happy to be in Paris. Ecstatically happy! And why shouldn't she be, after being holed up in a musty, dull convent for years? And what is all this stupid dismay over her tender age? Aurélie was only fourteen when we married, and no one rolled his eyes to the heavens, least of all your parents. How old was your wife—your first wife— when you were married? Not more than fifteen, I'll wager."

The comte's voice had become shrill and insistent. Why must he always be surrounded by interfering fools who wanted to tell him how to run his life?

"Steady . . . steady. There's no need to shout, *bon dieu!*" As much as he disliked the comte, Philippe hated a family squabble, especially in his own house. "It's beside the point that women of Aurélie and Elisabeth's generation and the generations before them married at such an early age. Times have changed. And customs have changed. We know more now than we knew in the old days. Women today, for very sound reasons, are marrying much later, and you know that as well as I do."

"Oh, so I'm to keep my daughters at home so that they can become better breeders? So that their husbands can be sure of having more and more heirs? That's not *my* problem. What do I care whether Diane has one or one dozen brats?" the comte spat out his words.

"Be that as it may, I'm afraid that you're catching me at a very bad time. I'm making some major repairs at Ancy and building a flour mill, a large up-to-date one, at Saint-Julien." The footman stood waiting with the door open. The icy cold air had turned his nose red. Philippe had no desire to discuss these matters in front of the servants. "I thought perhaps of going to call on Diane to wish her well. Where is she staying, or did you say?"

"I found a very nice place on the rue des Trois-Pavillons. 8 rue des Trois-Pavillons."

"Ah, *très chic*, *très chic,* indeed. You didn't think at all of placing her with her mother and cutting back on expenses in that way? Or here with us? Odile certainly wouldn't mind, and it would be perfectly proper. And perfectly adequate, too, I might add."

"Your sister, I am told, leads a very reclusive life. I hardly think that she would enjoy having an active young lady under her roof, disturbing her peace," replied the comte coldly. "I take it then that even a small loan of a few thousand *livres* is out of the question?"

"Look here, Michel. I won't go over again what I think you should or should not do. You know how I feel about Corcheval and its timber and lands. You've already got a gold mine there that you're turning your back on. At this point I suggest that you try to negotiate some short term loans with someone like Samuel Molé. Or even Abel Bertrand."

"With Jews? I'm to run to the Jews now?" The comte's high-pitched voice rose hysterically. "What kind of family feeling do you have, what kind of kinsman are you? I'm not asking you to risk anything. I'm asking only for the simple courtesy of a small loan to pay off some of my current expenses."

"Michel, I believe we've gone beyond the point of 'simple courtesies,' don't you? I repeat, my best advice to you is to secure a loan from Molé. With the campaign in Flanders you may be able to get something to your advantage. Provided you're prepared to bargain your terms." Philippe made no effort to hide his disdain. "I'm late for the king's *levée*, and so are you." He held his soft-brimmed hat in his hand, but instead of putting it on, he hastily shoved it under his arm and, bareheaded, hurried down the front steps. "*Bon sang*, I do believe it's going to snow!"

Michel stood watching him depart through the courtyard gates. The iron wheels of Philippe's carriage screeched unpleasantly against the frosty cobblestones as it turned out onto the street. Michel shivered, humiliation settling about his shoulders like a heavy, wet cloak.

6

He had sent word to [the marquise] of his return to Paris with me, describing me as having fine qualities of intellect and character but not of physical beauty. He had told many of my wretched looks . . . . I can truthfully say that my father greatly enjoyed the astonishment of those who saw me after having heard his description. Listening to the excited praise of me was like a delicious balm to him, and he never failed to add: "Don't you think she looks like me?" In truth, my father was a very handsome man.

Diane and Marianne bent their heads into the sharp wind that made them cling to each other for support as they rounded the corner onto the rue du Faubourg Saint-Honoré. They were hurrying to get a glimpse of *La grande Pandore*, the doll that would display every detail of the latest fashions for the woman of the world. Each year the couturiers of the rue du Faubourg-Saint-Honoré created the doll as a model of elegance for fashion-conscious women who wanted to copy the Parisienne from hat and coiffure to stockings and shoes. And after the stylish folk of Paris had adopted the latest trends, it would be shipped out to the four corners of the world where devotees of *la mode* eagerly awaited its arrival.

Foul smelling mud and filth filled the streets, and the two girls lifted their heavy skirts and shrank back against shop walls to avoid getting splashed by the carriages and carts in the congested narrow street.

"We'll never get close enough to see," said Diane, catching her first glimpse of the crowd of men and women, some in their carriages, others stepping gingerly around in the muddy streets, craning to get a look at *La grande Pandore*.

In truth, Diane did not really care. Since her visit with her mother, she had lost all taste for shops. After their talk, she had felt chronically guilty: guilty of frivolity, guilty of knowing—and enjoying knowing—the latest gossip. Guilty of being resplendently dressed in heavy brocade and some of her best pieces of jewelry while her mother sat beside her in a simple gown of plain muslin. Since coming to Paris, when she was not working hard on her lessons, Diane spent delicious hours in the fitting rooms of her dressmaker, her glove maker, her shoemaker, her jeweler. Even her shifts and stockings were of the finest silks and exquisitely made. She was fond of opening the drawers of the enormous armoire in her dressing room and running her hands over the pile of soft, supple undergarments.

Like her father, Diane loved fine clothes and each day spent hours with Marianne poring over finery near the Louvre and the Faubourg Saint-Honoré. Madame Clarisse's little shop was number 43, next door to the premier glove maker of Paris. The opulent tastes of Louis XV and his court had created a demand for ingenious craftsmanship in luxury items of every sort, where price was no object. A sought-after dressmaker like Madame Clarisse knew her value as a fashion arbiter to a young woman like Mademoiselle de Fautrière, who was already proving to be an excellent, receptive customer.

"Let's go home," Diane said wearily, tugging on Marianne's sleeve.

"What's wrong with you? You're not ill, are you?" Marianne sounded prim and authoritative. They were close in age, Diane almost fifteen, and Marianne approaching twenty, and they had become good friends, for Marianne knew how to maintain a discreet line of formality between servant and mistress. Marianne was a lady's maid, more of a lady-in-waiting to Diane than a servant. In Paris and at the court at Versailles all the women of high fashion sought out the prettiest and liveliest young girls to be their maids in order to create around themselves an ambiance of feminine mystery and allure that a homely maid would damage or destroy. Marianne was certainly as pretty as any lady's maid in the city. Not as tall as Diane, she was less statuesque but more curvaceous. From her dark abundant hair to her small, slim feet Marianne was a young woman of considerable sensual appeal.

"Well, we're not going home empty-handed. You still have to try on your new gowns. Come along. Here, let me show you what elbows are for," Marianne said, taking her mistress's hand and tugging her along through a group of heavily perfumed courtiers, bright as exotic butterflies in their colorful taffeta cloaks.

"It's superb! Exquisite! You're a young lady of taste, just like your father, of course," said the comte, stroking the beautiful lace on Diane's bustier. "Shall I tell you a funny story? The English! Those sorry English! Do you know what the lacemakers in Flanders have taken to doing? They force-feed—like geese, you know— fine lace like this to cats, or lapdogs, send the animals along their way across the Channel, and once there, they slit open their guts, and, *voilà*, expensive Flemish lace imported without paying a shilling."

"Oh, papa, you made that up! You're disgusting!" Diane cried, as her father guffawed.

"It's all too true, *mon trésor*. Dreadful race, the English. Keep an eye on that spaniel of yours when they're about," he said solemnly, glancing roguishly toward Marianne, who was arranging dozens of pairs of soft leather slippers in neat rows along a shelf. She paused a moment and returned his gaze, straightening her shoulders and arching her back. The small square room off Diane's bedchamber had been turned into a dressing room, mainly for storage of the quantities of feathers, ribbons, gowns, boots, shawls, hoops, and shifts that Diane's numerous fittings had produced. Madame Clarisse had chosen soft colors, many of them pastel variations of yellow and gold, to flatter Diane's splendid complexion and her blond hair.

"Now that Madame Clarisse has worked her fingers to the bone providing you with these beauties, it's time to get you out and around the salons. It's time to dazzle, my darling." Clearly, he thought, he had to start putting his plans for Diane in motion. Waiting around for more loans from dear Philippe, who, God knows, had more than enough money to spare, was a disgusting waste of time. He was finished groveling to Philippe, of all people. One or two friends at court, after getting a look at Diane, would surely come up with enough money to get him into marriage negotiations for her hand. That settled, he could relax and busy himself with improving his position at court. Damn. If only he weren't so clumsy and inept at hunting. There, Philippe really had him bested with the King. Philippe was one of the King's favorite hunting companions. But the comte always ended up making a fool of himself and spoiling the game for everyone else, including the King. He had not been invited on one of Louis' hunting parties in over two years.

Instead, the King was more inclined to ask him along on excursions with his mistress to one of his chateaux outside Paris, such as the chateau de Marly. It was an intimate setting, and the comte made the most of these trips. The comte had hoped that once Louis had cut loose from Marie Leczinska and had started to indulge his carnal appetites, he would lose his obsession with hunting. It hadn't happened. And, although he was already showing signs of a keen, very keen, sexual appetite, he still had to have his women served up to him on a platter. And Bachelier, that sleek, rich valet of his—or pimp as some courtiers called him, Bachelier knew how to keep the King happy with women. And Richelieu! He could read Louis like a book! Richelieu had the King in his pocket these days, Louis so besotted with the duchesse de Chateauroux that she was allowed to pick all the latest ambassadors. The comte's spirits sank. He had never been clever enough to amuse the King with women or with hunting or entertainments that would display his wit. But with Diane and a brilliant match . . . ah, the King would sit up and take notice. The King would see him in a different light.

"The marquise de Sabran has been asking for you; so let's begin there," the comte said, gay again. "We'll go round in a week or two, perhaps sooner, if I think you're ready. She'll have some of her usual crowd and two or three young people on whom you can try your charms. It's time to dazzle, *mon trésor*."

The comte put his hand on Diane's arm, pausing a moment after the footmen had taken their wraps.

"Let me have just one last look," he muttered. He lifted his hand and tugged very gently at one of the small ringlets just over her ear, smoothing it into place.

"You are magnificent," said the comte, looking genuinely moved. Diane thought that his voice trembled. "Just remember, as you walk up to the marquise to be introduced to her party, remember that you are the most beautiful woman in the room. Don't forget that. It will keep you from having a stiff, scared look on your face."

They turned to the great staircase and began to climb slowly, Diane lifting her skirts carefully so as not to catch her foot on her petticoat. He glanced at her quickly. "And part your lips. Don't smile. Just let your lips fall open a little. Otherwise you'll look too severe." Her father sounded nervous again.

The footman had scarcely announced their arrival when their hostess, the marquise de Sabran, her expression a curious mixture of recognition and surprise, came rushing toward them.

"Michel, you've kept us waiting. As usual, you great nuisance!" she said, rushing through perfunctory kisses. "And this is . . . ?" she asked, staring round-eyed at Diane.

"My daughter Diane, of course," said the comte, looking smug as he tried to hold back a grin. "I believe I wrote that Diane has joined me in Paris."

"Yes. But, you fool, you wrote that she was plain. Now, what was it you said? That she was plain but pleasant, was that it?" The marquise stepped back, looking in amazement at Diane from head to toe. "Why, she is absolutely beautiful," she muttered, as if talking quietly to herself. "As beautiful as a flower!"

"What did you expect, *mon amie*?" asked the comte, with his odd, high-pitch whinnying snicker. "Don't you think she looks exactly like me?" But the marquise had taken Diane by the arm and was leading her away triumphantly to a group of her guests.

"Do have a look at what the comte has brought us from Charolais!" Suddenly quiet, the group turned to look at the marquise and the young girl who trembled on her arm, a half-smile so rigidly fixed on her face that her lips twitched.

Cocky and relaxed, beaming condescendingly, the comte stood slightly behind Diane and the marquise. He had been a fool to worry about her "presentation." But then he was a perfectionist in everything he did. And perfectionists worry.

"*Mes amis,* the comte de Fautrière you already know. Probably only too well," the marquise said with a slightly affected giggle, "And this is the 'homely little thing' he has been hiding from us since he came back from the country. His daughter, Diane de Fautrière."

Diane tried not to think of the hush that was beginning to settle over the room, conversations stopping here and there, and she could feel the eyes of others in the crowded room turning toward her as she curtsied gracefully, slowly fixing her eloquent grey eyes on each in turn.

"Just when I thought the winter season was becoming insufferably dull," said Emile Pontavieux, his small black eyes gleaming with pleasure. Emile Pontavieux was one of the richest tax-farmers in the country, and his oldest son, despite his bourgeois family and his obsequious manners, had just married the marquise de Sabran's daughter. Diane smiled warmly toward his tall, extravagantly bewigged wife, who made no effort to disguise her careful scrutiny of Diane's jewelry.

"Now, let's just move along this way, my dear. I want everyone to get a good look at you."

Diane let herself be steered gently around the enormous room crowded with perfumed courtiers in satin and lace and women in towering white wigs and panniers so wide that only one or two women in the entire assembly dared to sit down. All eyes, or so it seemed to Diane, followed her as the marquise led her about from group to group. She willed herself not to yield to panic, knowing that her father's eyes, too, were observing her performance. Some of the names of the guests were familiar to her, well-known personages at court who were the staple of her father's gossip. She encountered a few smiles, guardedly friendly, but most of the guests scrutinized her with undisguised calculation, especially the women.

"Now I shall leave you in the very best of company," said the Madame de Sabran, leading Diane toward some young people seated at a card table near the concert room. "I want you to meet Madeleine de Chastelmarne, my niece who has come up from the Poitou to live with me. And this great lout is her cousin, Jean-Christophe, the chevalier de Rosnières." The young man laughed jovially and raised his hand in greeting.

"Now, I must find that rogue who claims to be your father. He shall get a few unkind words from me for pulling this latest trick. Believe me, I was quite unprepared to have such a beauty set my salon on its ear this evening. Just listen to them buzz!"

The spacious and dazzlingly bright room had indeed grown noisier since Diane and her father made their entrance. As she sat down, Diane realized that her knees were shaking and that she was panting slightly.

Madeleine turned toward Diane with a bright smile, and a tall young man whose back had been turned as she approached, rose quickly from his chair and helped her to her seat.

"Now, you can ignore your father and the marquise and have some fun with us. We're playing quadrille, and I already know that you play only too well. Be forewarned, Armand," she said, slapping the wrist of the tall young man who had stood up to hold Diane's chair.

Diane swiftly turned her head toward the young man. Armand. Armand in the garden and the game of hide-and-seek. She felt a hot flush sweep up her neck to her face. Armand sat calmly gazing at her with a sly smile on his face, his left eye half-closed by its drooping eyelid. With his thumb he flicked a playing card against the felt of the round table.

"Well, well, you've left the country behind you, Mademoiselle de Fautrière? And all those funny country games? Hide-and-go-seek, isn't that a favorite in Charolais?" Diane stared at his hand, thumping the card again and again against the table.

"I should stand and bow properly, Diane," said the chevalier de Rosnières from across the table. "I should stand and bow properly to a beautiful young lady named Diane. But, lord, I'm too drunk," and he belched loudly as if to illustrate his point.

Madeleine laughed and pushed his elbow off the table. "Not as drunk as all that, Jean-Cristophe. So, as usual, we can count on Armand to know every pretty woman in and *around* Paris." She emphasized *around* and gave Armand a long, intimate look. She had noticed Diane's deep blush. I shall have to find out about that blush, she said to herself.

Armand lowered his eyes. "Let's play cards," he said. "Mademoiselle de Fautrière loves games. And, as you say, is quite good at them."

Stung by his rebuke Diane bristled, remembering his harsh words to her as he had stormed angrily away from her behind the chapel. They began to play, and she forced herself to pay attention to every card, and as the interminable game dragged on into the late hours of the evening, she forgot the knots of panic and shame in her stomach. Soon she was laughing gaily at Jean-Cristophe's silly blunders and his hangdog adoration of her. She did not mind when Armand leaned on his elbow and gazed at her with his oddly provocative hooded eye. And when Madeleine suggested that they interrupt their game, give it up as hopeless, and take a refreshing turn through the empty concert room, both Diane and Armand noisily objected, banging their cards on the table, and, laughing merrily, bumping shoulders together in rough camaraderie. Later still, after the crowded room gradually began to empty, and she felt Armand's stockinged foot caressing her instep, she abandoned herself to the dark pull of pleasure. The sounds in the large formal rooms became distant and muffled.

"Look at that!" said Armand. "Tsch! Tsch! Such a blunder! You must surrender your cards. You're out of the game!"

They had been among the last guests to straggle into their carriage and depart into the windy night. The comte was jubilant. And, as always, slightly drunk.

"It could not have gone better! A triumph! I knew it, I knew it!" He slapped his hands gleefully against his thighs, lost his balance, and lurched against Diane. With one hand, Diane pushed him gently away. The comte appeared not to notice. "You were adorable. Adorably regal! Like a queen, you sailed into the room, as pleasantly as if you were settling down at your dressing table. Like a little queen, *mon trésor.*" He had taken Diane's hand in both of his and drunkenly squeezed it. His hands were hot and unpleasant. On the pretext of adjusting her hood, she pulled her hand away, then tucked it underneath her cloak.

"Do you know, that young fop who fancies himself so much . . . uh, you know, the marquis de la Chétardie. He was all over me, showing me a miniature of the Czarina Elisabeth. A miniature that she had given him when he left Russia last January. He fluttered about—did you see him?—showing the miniature to everyone saying that you are the living image of the Czarina."

Diane had seen the miniature, which the marquis carried on a gold chain in his pocket. A small porcelain face with pointy features. How boring papa is when he drinks! He will jabber on and on, slurring his words.

"The living image of the Czarina. How silly. Everyone there could see that you look exactly like me . . . exactly like me. Of course, you know, they say the Czarina is still madly in love with Chétardie. She showered him with gifts —money, jewelry, and gold, plenty of gold—before he came back. He's the only ambassador from France to get rich in Russia. He's rich! Great god, the man is rich! And all because of the Czarina and her infatuation. 'Never will they tear France from my heart!' That's what she told him. Whispered in his ear at some ceremony, that's what he told Odile."

The wide carriage scraped the gateposts noisily as it pulled into the courtyard of Diane's mansion. The comte fumbled free of his cloak and lurched forward to kiss her goodnight. Diane could not wait to get away from him. She wanted to be alone, alone in her soft, enveloping bed, alone to remember and to dream, not of her triumph in one of the great salons of Paris, but alone to summon back that delicious sensation of Armand's insinuating foot stroking her ankle.

7

My father was a violent man.

"Is it yours? Is it yours? Of course it is, you fool!" Odile tore at her skirt with her hands, fighting to pull down her heavy skirt over her broad hoops, which bobbed from side to side. "You disgust me!" she snarled in a hoarse whisper. "You disgust me! You and your dirty tricks!" A thread of saliva dribbled from the corner of her mouth, creating a shiny path over a large black velvet patch.

The comte leaned against the cool marble column and adjusted his clothes. From the broad graveled paths of the gardens he could hear a woman giggling and muttering drunkenly. The comte and Odile had found each other for the first time since Corcheval at the Friday night masked ball at the Opéra. The comte could not stay away from these masked balls. He craved their lewdness. The excitement of flirting with lowborn strangers and later coupling in the dark arcades surrounding the Opéra. And sometimes, like tonight, with a blue-blood from one of the oldest families of the nobility. The evening had followed its familiar pattern, and finding Odile behind a black-feathered mask had been just the stroke of luck he had been searching for.

"Why all the fuss? You're behaving like a shopkeeper's wife! Why not see your Madame what's-her-name and have done with it? As before? Many times before." He felt a little dizzy. He inhaled deeply from his scented handkerchief.

"That's just the problem." Odile's narrow face suddenly looked old and wizened. "She won't do any more. She says there is not enough money in the world to pay her to do another one. For me. I thought I'd never stop bleeding the last time. She says I'd surely die. It would ruin her reputation. And it's your fault!" she choked out the words, her anger returning like a heavy, stubborn weight. "I should have let you do it the way you do with the duc de Brabantes and the nasty little boys in his crowd. You like it that way, don't you? Then I wouldn't be pregnant by one of the biggest fools at court!" She turned aside and spat.

"Odile. Odile, behave yourself, my darling. You know as well as I do that it could be any number of people. Except your own husband, of course." How dare she rant at him, the little slut! Making herself available to every man at court. And then blaming him for ruining her figure for a few months. "I seem to recall that Armand, your young friend—and is it, relative?—was most attentive at Ancy this summer."

"Leave Armand out of this. You are not fit to pronounce his name! Scum like you!" She lifted her skirt and used her petticoat to wipe her brow and neck. They listened for a moment to the sounds of a quadrille from the ballroom.

Then Odile jerked her head forward and pushed her face close to his. "Listen to me, my dear Michel!" she hissed, her lips curling with contempt. "You just may be in for the surprise of your life! Armand, my relative and my friend, is going to have the pleasure of deflowering that innocent little convent prude of yours. It seems that pure and proper Diane is panting after my cousin and can't wait to . . . "

The comte seized Odile's neck with both hands and spun her around against the column. "What's that you are saying? What! What!" With his right hand he struck Odile alongside the head. The sound of the blow crackled along the arcade. He turned his back and strode quickly toward the river and his waiting carriage.

❦

The comtesse's carriage pulled away from the rue Hyacinthe one morning in April, and Diane, having slept quite late after a party at Madame de Sabran's, was not there to see her off to her new life in the convent.

The evening before, shortly after ten o'clock, Diane had rushed up the stairs to her mother's sittingroom to say farewell. She was shown to the comtesse's small, drafty bedchamber, plain and modestly furnished in contrast to the cashmere-draped luxury of Diane's own bedchamber. Her mother was preparing for bed. They embraced tenderly, and the comtesse seemed unwilling to let her go. Her eyes were moist with tears.

Since that first visit after Diane's arrival in Paris, mother and daughter had fallen into a comfortable pattern of visits. In the late afternoon when the house was at its quietest, the comtesse would often hear Diane's carriage pulling into the courtyard, and she would hurry to the top of the stairs to welcome her to a corner in her huge dim sittingroom. Much to her surprise, she had grown very fond of her oldest daughter. Diane was quick and alert and vulnerable. She had taken to the idea of refining herself into a highly polished and desirable object with a seriousness and enthusiasm that made the comtesse smile in spite of herself. And such wistful longing for the court. She was so intent, dear child. Her beautiful gray eyes probed everywhere, observing, judging, puzzling. Though lately Diane had been restless, distracted, never quite settling into her chair.

"I really must go, maman. My friends are waiting in the carriage. I shall miss you horribly, but I'll write every week and come to the convent to visit when I can." Her voice sounded tinny and insincere, even to her own ears.

"Of course, you will, my darling." The comtesse released Diane's hands and turned toward her prie-dieu at the foot of the bed. It was the same old prie-dieu that had sat at the foot of her bed in the chateau of Ancy where she had grown up and that had followed her from the convent to Corcheval and then to Paris. Her stern-faced mother's needlepoint tapestry, now worn and discolored, covered the small knee-rest.

As Diane closed the door behind her, she saw her mother kneeling in prayer, her head slumped down over her clasped hands. Diane hurried down to the waiting carriage. From the doorway she could hear Armand's hearty laughter.

Dust motes and puffs of scented powder danced in the thick shafts of sunlight flooding Diane's dressing room. It was almost noon. The Abbé de Montfort had just hurried away, hoping to find the marquise de Sabran still at her toilette.

Like any other popular young woman of high society, Diane now awakened every day sometime before eleven o'clock, her convent habit of rising early and walking in the morning dew in the gardens a thing of the past. Sometimes after a party she did not return home and crawl wearily into bed until dawn. Already she had her own circle of favorites who joined together in going to the Opéra, to the theater, to balls, and to supper parties. Already she had her own devoted admirers who arrived sometime before noon in her boudoir while her maids and Marianne assisted her through the coquettish stages of her toilette. They sent her bouquets of hothouse flowers, wrote poems about her little spaniel, and got into fierce arguments over which lace should trim which gown.

After her mother left Paris for the convent, she had at first felt abandoned and afraid of facing alone the demands of her father. Gradually, her guilt over the luxuries of her life had faded as she persuaded herself that the family destiny was now up to her: she alone, armed with sumptuous gowns and jewels would through her marriage rescue her family from debts and the threat of impoverishment. Her father would be proud of her, and her mother would leave her shabby convent life behind forever.

"Now, this necklace, mademoiselle, would make you the envy of all Paris. You see, beautifully matched, immaculately white with just the faintest rosy glow." Dagueneau, the King's jeweler, held out to

Diane a black velvet square over which he had draped a magnificent string of pearls. Uncle Philippe had said that she could choose anything she liked for her saint's day.

"Pearls! No! Pearls are so boring, dear Diane," groaned Jean-Christophe. "Unless they are worked into the bodice of a gown that will set them off. Dull, dull, dull. You mustn't think of it. Show her something more exciting, monsieur." He waved his huge pink handkerchief impatiently in great swoops. Armand sat to one side of Diane, shaking his foot restlessly, a mocking smile on his broad, handsome face. Marianne smiled brightly at Jean-Christophe. Poor thing, he did try so hard. And Mademoiselle Diane scarcely realized that he was there. But Monsieur Armand— well, that was a different story altogether, wasn't it?

Without a word Armand rose from his chair, gathered up the pearls, and draped them around Diane's slim neck and across her bosom. Their eyes met in the mirror of Diane's dressing table, Armand's drooping eyelid almost closed over his left eye. He stepped back, and as he withdrew his hands, his long fingers caressed her warm breasts before sweeping languorously up her throat.

Diane's throat and cheeks flushed red, and she placed moist palms against her throat. She thought she would faint with desire. "I should like the pearls, monsieur," she said, her voice little more than a hoarse whisper.

Monsieur Dagueneau rubbed his hands together with satisfaction. "The marquis will be exceedingly pleased that you have made such a happy choice," he said, darting a malicious glance toward Jean-Christophe, who slouched in his chair, staring, annoyed, at the fevered glow of Diane's cheeks.

In the hallway below came the sound of doors opening and closing in hurried succession. They all turned expectantly toward the pink and gilt lounge just off Diane's dressing room.

"Still at your toilette, *ma petite*," said the comte, briskly stepping aside for the departing jeweler. "Well, well."

Diane could tell by the haughty, piercing tone of her father's voice that he was in a terrible humor. She judged correctly. The comte could barely contain his fury. He had not slept at all. He had been driven straight home and had spent the early morning hours cursing Odile and debating what to do about his reckless daughter, so stupid and spoiled that she risked ruining all his plans.

"You, of course, know the chevalier and Armand de Mézières," said Diane softly, by way of entreating her father to acknowledge the presence of her guests. "The Abbé de Montfort has just left," she added lamely, wondering what could be vexing her father now.

"So. I've missed the lard bucket, have I? Such a pity!" he said.

Armand sensed that something was amiss as soon as the comte strode into the room, and he wanted no part of the prissy man's foul mood. "Jean-Christophe and I must be on our way as well, monsieur." Armand glanced over his shoulder at the chevalier, who picked up his heavily plumed hat, bowed over Diane's outstretched hand, and sheepishly hurried from the room.

Diane lifted the heavy string of pearls from her neck and held them toward her father, who stood motionless with his back to her, watching the departure of the two young men.

Suddenly he moved his hand to the thin rapier at his waist, and with a practiced movement, whipped it out of its sheath, and brought it crashing down on Diane's dressing table, scattering rouge pots, powder and patch boxes and jewelry in broken confusion on the floor. Her little dog, fast asleep at her mistress's feet, yelped and fled under the bed. A vial of perfume smashed into ragged shards that flew out into every direction. Marianne drew back against the door to Diane's bedchamber.

With a disdainful kick the comte righted an overturned chair and sat down.

Abruptly he sprang to his feet and deftly ran his rapier into its sheath with a cold, metallic whir.

"I think the time has come to tell you why you are here in Paris, my dear child, and not back in your grubby little convent with your sisters." His face white, the comte was breathing heavily. He did not bother to wipe the perspiration from his wrinkled brow. Diane watched him struggle for breath.

"Or . . . more to the point . . . why you are NOT here in Paris. You are not here in Paris to moon around for the likes of a cretin such as Armand de Mézières. Do you understand what I am saying? Or is your head so stuffed with convent claptrap that you have mistaken him for the rising star of the King's firmament? Armand de Mézières is everyone's poor relation, a puffed up sycophant without a *sou* who will be exceedingly lucky if he ends up with a benefice that he can milk dry." The comte shook snuff onto the back of his hand and inhaled in short, barking snorts.

"You are not to see him again. Not here. Not at your uncle's house. Not at the marquise de Sabran's. Not at the Opéra. Not anywhere."

Even at the far end of the drawing room Diane could hear the noise of the servants cleaning up the debris of her father's rage. She had sent Marianne with a note pleading a headache to the marquise de Sabran and excusing herself from dinner and the theater. She sat alone near the window holding an unopened book of poems in her hand and watching the puffy spring clouds beyond the trees of the little square.

Her father's white face, his lips curled in scorn. Diane felt sick with shame. She was guilty. She knew that very well. She deserved his wrath. If only he knew, he would have slashed at her with his rapier. He would have whipped her cheeks to a bloody pulp. For weeks now she had been intoxicated, day and night, awake and sleeping, with Armand. With Armand and his teasing lips and hands that gave her so much pleasure that she craved but did not fully understand, his mocking smile that made her wild to please him.

After Madame de Sabran's supper party when Armand had caressed her foot with his, she had found him everywhere she went. Everywhere. Always smiling his half smile. Mocking her with his sleepy eyes. Daring her. To what? He ridiculed her ignorance and said that he would teach her everything she needed to know to be the most desirable woman in Paris. Teach her what?

And now her father's violent rage had once again awakened the demons of guilt and shame. Mostly shame. How far she had fallen from her duty to rescue the family from all its impending ills. She wished her mother were here, still leading her strange secluded life on the rue Hyacinthe with shabby priests shuffling about, noisily eating their dinners and droning their stale homilies over the roasts and desserts. But the comtesse was gone, shut away in a convent, doing good works and praying for souls. Praying for me, thought Diane. Oh, *ma mère,* pray for me! she whispered, remembering her father's wrath.

Book Two

8

A country squire from Burgundy, an infantry captain, came to Paris on business and saw my father, with whom he dined frequently. He fell madly in love with me. The gentleman was rich . . .

$\mathcal{A}$ flurry of polite applause burst out as Diane finished singing a frothy melody by Lully, the old Sun King's beloved composer. A trifle sentimental and girlish in her delivery, mused the comte, beaming with satisfaction as Diane gave a sprightly curtsy and was led to her seat by Jean-Christophe. Yes, a trifle sentimental, but the new voice teacher can take care of that detail. Details, merely details. The girl has made remarkable progress, no question of that. Money well spent. A little over a year, and look at her! The center of attention in every fashionable salon in Paris! Well done, my girl! Well done! The comte watched the prince de Soissons rise from his chair and make his way to Diane. Well done, my girl!

The comte felt someone tug at his elbow and started from his reverie. It was Jean de Tourmelle. He moved his chair closer to the comte's, so close that Tourmelle's vinegary breath was overpowering. The comte ostentatiously brought his large perfumed handkerchief to his nose.

A huge, hulking man, Jean de Tourmelle looked more like the peasants on his enormous estates in Burgundy than an aristocrat at the world's most brilliant and glamorous court. Not that long ago his family were indeed prosperous peasants whose vineyards supplied the King's table with some of the best wine in France. They had accumulated great riches, enough to purchase a title and to buy their sons regiments to serve in Louis XIV's many wars. They were ferocious fighters, these robust sons of Burgundy, and the old sovereign had smiled upon them and increased their honors and lands. Tourmelle was almost forty years old, and he had spent most of those years either at court or on the battlefields, most recently in Prussia, where his horse had twice been shot from under him and where he had earned the highest honor of the King's service, the Cross of Saint-Louis. Battlefields were more to his taste than the teeming corridors and antechambers of Versailles.

"Like a bird. She sings as lovely as a bird, that daughter of yours, comte." Jean de Tourmelle's plump, glistening lips stretched wide with pleasure. He cocked his head. "Remember, comte, you've promised to introduce me to your charming daughter, and tonight will be the night, hein?" His large mouth hung open expectantly. Two of his front teeth had been broken off at a slant and had started to decay. "Hein? Tonight? After supper, of course, when I can have a chat with the girl."

"Actually, I intend to send her home after supper to get to bed early. She's been a little fragile lately. Though she's certainly looking superb tonight." It would do no harm to keep the man at arm's length a little while longer. And it was true, Diane was still fragile. The girl was so emotional. He had not meant her any harm, though, God knows, he was beside himself when Odile—damn that slut!— had told him about Armand hanging about Diane and Diane acting like a bitch in heat. Or so Odile said. That bastard Mézières! Fit to be tied I was, what father wouldn't be with a daughter like Diane. And I only wanted to frighten her, put some sense into her head. And frighten her I did. Thank God, Marianne had enough sense to fetch me. Diane's a sensitive child. Too sensitive if she can make herself sick like that.

The comte twisted away from Jean de Tourmelle and got to his feet. For two months now this country neighbor had hounded him, that was the only word for it, hounded him at every turn for an introduction to Diane. He had not yet made another marriage proposal, though. Which struck the comte as somewhat curious.

He had received four serious proposals, enough to confirm his notion that Diane's lack of a dowry would not prove a handicap in making a brilliant match for her. But the proposals had not been quite brilliant enough. The comte de Somaize, for example, an illustrious name but his estates were as moribund as the comte's. Or, almost. No one seemed to have as much bad luck with harvests and flocks as the comte. A few months after Diane's debut in the marquise de Sabran's salon word of her wonderful beauty had spread rapidly at court and in Paris. And more than her beauty. There was something about her. Even the comte could sense that. He could sense that intriguing appeal of childish innocence and naiveté lingering behind the facade of her exquisite manners and poise. She could look so pure with those deep gray eyes under those swooping brows. And then suddenly so sultry . . . suddenly so *impure* . . . that was it. The comte fancied himself a connoisseur of women, but he was not sure that he had ever met a woman with his own daughter's ambiguous attraction.

"Are you going in to supper?" asked the comte. Most of the audience in the marquise's concert room had risen and had begun to drift toward the dining room. The comte wanted to stall Tourmelle a little longer. There were nasty rumors about Tourmelle, and he needed to know more about him and his fortune, reputedly enormous, before he showed him any signs of encouragement. He had tried to pin down something more specific about Tourmelle's bad reputation, but he had run up against a blank wall. Some talked of his having abducted a woman from Prussia during the fighting there, but was that enough to account for the funny looks and evasiveness when Tourmelle's name was mentioned? Odile would know. Odile was the first to sniff out any dirty mess at Versailles and the last to let it be swept under the carpet. Be that as it may, he could not go to Odile now. He wanted to stay as far from her waspish temper as he could get. God knows what scandal she might be spreading right now about him.

The comte pulled at his lace cuffs. "Shall we have a pinch of snuff and a turn about the terrace before going in?" He would question Tourmelle, discreetly, of course. He mustn't dare let any whiff of scandal become associated with Diane, not even remotely.

The comte liked the way the big brute of a man followed him meekly out onto the terrace into the clear autumn air. A likable fellow, this Tourmelle. And rich, by God.

Diane ran down the steps after Madeleine and Jean-Christophe and fell into step between the two cousins. They walked down into the Jardin du Luxembourg, their arms intertwined. The three young people had become inseparable. After dinner each day they would play quadrille or lansquenet, gossip, part for a few hours, then they would meet for the promenade hour on the smooth graveled paths of the Tuileries. Jean-Christophe escorted the two young women to lectures at the Collège de France and helped them choose their patches and ribbons and fans. After theatre and supper, which they almost always took together at the marquise's townhouse, a stately beige sandstone giving onto the Jardin du Luxembourg, the three friends would stroll together along the neatly groomed parterres of the garden before escorting Diane to her gate in the rue des Trois-Pavillons.

In the spring, before Diane's illness, Armand de Mézières had joined them every afternoon for cards, and sometimes he would sing in a sweet baritone voice if Diane could be persuaded to accompany him at the piano. It was now November, and Armand had not yet returned from the country.

Diane breathed the crisp night air. Her heart swelled with contentment. The old pains were fading, like rheumatism yielding to the healing warmth of the sun. With infinite tenderness her father had enticed her back to health and gaiety, to indolent pleasures, to affectionate friends, full of laughter and high spirits. Gone were the nightmares of the early morning hours. She stretched her arms to sunlight and sprang from bed even before Marianne brought her chocolate. She had erased from her mind the image of her father's rage. And the memory of Armand's bewitching voice whispering in her ear. Gone, forgotten. She closed her mind to the future and the inevitable: marriage to that faceless stranger.

Every morning she woke with joyous anticipation of the quiet familiar church on the rue Jacob, with its handful of faithful old women dressed in black and a few monks and *curés*. For months she had not missed a single morning, not even when she had such a bad cough and fever that Marianne begged her to stay in bed and drink her medicinal teas. She would sit and pray, and during the sermon she would let her mind drift to pleasant daydreams of gowns, balls, parties in the chateaux outside the city. Diane was much admired, and she knew it. Though she had not yet been presented at court, she was steeped in the gossip of its licentious behavior. She knew that her father had received numerous proposals for her hand, and she approved of his slow, calculating negotiations. In losing her girlish innocence, she had a clearer idea of her own worth, and she reveled in the certainty of always being the most beautiful woman, no matter where she went.

She dreamed the sermons away and left the church in her elegant carriage feeling at peace, contented. She had never looked more radiant. Since her illness after her father's outburst in her dressing room, the comte had denied her nothing. With Marianne and Madeleine at her side, she went everywhere, her curiosity about life at Versailles and Paris insatiable. She sang, she danced, she wrote playful occasional verses for her friends, she played cards, she worked hard at her lessons, especially Italian, and she allowed herself to be adored by young men by the dozen. Of all these, Jean-Christophe was her favorite. His worshipful gaze followed her everywhere, and to prove the seriousness of his ardor, he more than once appeared, bleary-eyed with sleep, across the dark, dusty pews at Saint-Jacques.

She was no longer tormented by the disturbing desires awakened by Armand. Whenever she saw him, rarely these days and always from a distance, she felt only a brief stab of longing that she found she could comfortably ignore. Only a few months ago she would never have believed that her life could be so vivid with pleasure. And as each day passed, brimming with peace and satisfaction, she prayed that her body's intense cravings would never again betray her.

They passed through the gates to the garden and under a lantern at the corner. *If only I could go on like this for the rest of my* life, Diane said to herself, with my two friends always at my side, the laughter, the gaiety. Diane could not imagine anyone more sophisticated than Madeleine. Tall, with thick dark hair clustered in stylish ringlets around her heart-shaped face, Madeleine dressed in the height of fashion. Before anyone else in their circle Madeleine appeared in skirts so wide that she had to turn sideways to enter a door. Even her aunt, the marquise, had hesitated before adopting the new *pannier*, which Bourdaloue had denounced as wicked in more than one sermon in the King's chapel at Versailles. However, the marquise made up for her miscalculation by being the first to have fauteuils built with diagonally extended arms, elegant carved arms swooping outward, to accommodate ladies in broad skirts. The chairs were a marvel and soon started a vogue.

There were few strollers in the garden, and their voices echoed in the inky shadows of the giant yews. The three friends turned back at the end of the path and headed toward Diane's gate.

"Ah, what a beautiful evening!" Diane said. "I do love my life now. My lessons, Madeleine the cynic and Jean-Christophe the poet, the shops, the parties. Parties every night of the week, and soon there will be more. Papa says that when the King gets back to Paris, all the fountains will stream with wine, and there will be balls and parties everywhere to celebrate the King's recovery."

"And to celebrate the King's dismissal of la Chateauroux. They say she narrowly missed being stoned to death, sneaking back from Metz," said Jean-Christophe.

Madeleine laughed. "Just you wait. The celebrations won't have finished before the ladies start queuing up to take la Chateauroux's place in the King's bed."

"But, what are we thinking? How can we celebrate the King's miraculous recovery until Armand returns to Paris," said Jean-Christophe. "We need Armand to have a proper party. Isn't that right, cousin?"

"Don't joke! Don't you dare joke about that!" said Madeleine in a low, angry voice.

"About what?" asked Diane, and Jean-Christophe felt her hand tighten on his arm. "Joke about what?"

Neither of the two answered. They walked along in silence. At the end of the deserted street, near the corner, they could already see the porter at the gate of Diane's house.

"Nothing. There's nothing to joke about. It's just that Armand has had some urgent business in the country, that's all," Madeleine said reluctantly.

Jean-Christophe cleared his throat and began to whistle softly. A little too ostentatiously, Diane thought, pleased that the mention of Armand's name had brought only a brief jolt to her heart, and then, nothing. Calm. Peace. She took a deep breath.

"*Voilà*, mademoiselle." Jean-Christophe said, bowing low over her hand, as they stopped at Diane's gate. The old porter stood waiting to close the gate behind her. "Until tomorrow, beautiful lady. I shall rise with rosy-fingered dawn and swiftly fly to your side!"

"Where? What nonsense is this?" asked Diane.

"No nonsense at all, fair lady. We shall rendezvous at seven o'clock precisely at the Church of Saint-Jacques. I've caught a great dose of piety just by being around you night and day!"

"Oh, la! We shall see how pious you are when your feet hit the cold rushes on your floor in the morning!" laughed Diane, her heart overflowing with affection for her tall, gangly friend.

A haze of steam hung over the bathtub, and tendrils of dark hair clung to her temples and the nape of her neck.

"More hot water! I'll catch my death of cold. The two of you standing about while my bath water turns to ice," Odile scolded. Her head cradled against a satin cushion, Odile closed her eyes as Ninon, her maid, massaged her plump round arms with perfumed oils. A small woman, Odile's feet barely touched the end of the bathtub, installed with a stately canopy and green velvet side curtains edged in gold braid near the fireplace of her bedchamber. Odile lifted a glass of brandy from a small round table and drank.

"My God!" she moaned.

A footman struggled toward the tub with a large bucket of hot water.

"Almost boiling, madame," he said, averting his eyes from Odile's nakedness. He slowly began to empty the bucket into the tub.

"That's enough!" cried Odile, suddenly sitting upright, splashing water from the narrow tub onto the carpet. Her huge breasts, ordinarily snowy white, were beet red. Ninon bent over Odile's back and began to knead her shoulders and neck.

It was late afternoon on a dark November day, and the large bedchamber in the fashionable mansion on the rue de Varenne was as hot and humid as a lush tropical forest. The high windows were shuttered and the curtains drawn. It had been snowing since early morning, and the streets below were silent except for the slipping and scraping sounds of a stray carriage. Wizened old peasants predicted a terrible winter of snow, ice, and deprivation. Already, in Auvergne, cattle were starving, their frozen bodies abandoned in the fields.

"Another brandy," Odile said weakly, slipping back down into the water. "Ah! my God!"

A draft of bitter cold air wafted through the huge room and stirred the ruffles on Ninon's sleeves.

"What on earth? Odile! Have you filled your room with boiling kettles?" Armand strode across the room, making a great show of cutting through the thick steamy mist with his handkerchief.

"Armand! Armand!" Odile shrilled gleefully. "Is it really you? I don't believe my eyes!" Water rippling from her body, she spread her wet arms as he bent to kiss her on the lips. Odile leaned back against the pillow and brought her wet hand to the back of his head and held his mouth against hers.

He withdrew from the kiss, his hand lingering over her slippery breast. "Damn! That water's boiling hot. And my lace is wet! Damn!" He sounded genuinely annoyed, but Odile lay back and laughed and clapped her hands.

"When did you get back? And is everything all right? Are you all right?" she cried, her eyes brimming with delight.

"Of course." He scowled and pulled a deeply cushioned chair close to the hearth and sat down, pushing his heels up to the fire.

"Well? What else? Tell me. Are you on good terms with the King again?"

"How should I know? I've been buried in the country, remember?" He spoke with weary surliness. Abruptly, he rose and stepped quickly to the side of the steaming tub. He knelt and brusquely pushed Odile's head back and kissed her roughly on the lips, then lifting her body slightly, he covered her large, pendulous breasts with swift, voracious kisses.

Odile gave a sensual laugh and pushed his head away. "You big fool, you're getting sopping wet!" She held his tousled head between her hands and gazed at him with adoration. "Did you miss me?"

"No, not really," he yawned. "I missed my flaming little convent girl. Diane." Odile shoved him away in a show of anger.

"More of Mademoiselle de Fautrière anon. Now, be serious. What about your . . . your trouble with the Prussian officer."

Armand took off his waistcoat and rolled back the cuff and sleeve of his left arm. He sat studying Odile's naked body under the water. His drooping eyelid gave him a grave expression. He reached into the water and carefully ran his hand over the protruding mound of her stomach.

"You didn't have that when I left for the country," he said, raising his eyes to hers.

"You just don't remember," she said impatiently, pushing his hand away. "It's nothing. And you are not answering my questions."

"I told you. All is settled." He rose, pushed down his sleeve and returned to the fire. "It would have to be, wouldn't it, if I'm back in Paris."

"I mean, my friends at court tell me that the duc de Gesvres believes you were vicious in the duel, the duc says you seemed so intent on killing the Prussian."

"Ah . . . " groaned Armand. "That prissy old duc de Gesvres! What would he know about dueling? The only thing he cares about is his needlepoint and his gaming tables, greedy bastard!" Armand kicked angrily at the fender with his boot heel. "Are they still talking about me at court?"

"Alas, my lucky darling, no. The brouhaha over the King's recovery, and his recovery of his appetite for his mistress, and then her sudden death from some sort of fever, that's what tongues are wagging about up under the eaves at Versailles. The scandal of Monsieur Armand de Mézières and his duel is not nearly as juicy as the Queen's constant mewling, complaining that the King promised to come back to her bed when he sent his wicked little duchesse packing. But, heigh ho! the King was a dying man when he made that promise, and we all know that our good Louis will promise anything to save his soul. They say the Queen has bathed every evening after supper since the King returned from Metz and la Chateauroux went to her grave! Poor dear old Queen! She must have high hopes indeed if she has started to bathe again!" Odile lifted the glass of brandy and emptied it.

Armand stood and turned his back to the warm fire. "Do you intend to soak in that tub the rest of the day? You're already as red as a beet. What are you trying to do? Get out of there! You're going to parboil yourself."

"Don't bully me. All in good time, darling, all in good time." He noticed that her speech was slurred and that her jaw sagged. She looked older, coarser. Deep lines bracketed her mouth, and her small, dark eyes, sunken in shadows, looked more animal-like than ever.

Suddenly, she stood up in the narrow tub, water streaming down her body and splashing out onto the floor.

"Where the hell is Ninon? Where the hell is a towel?" she said thickly, reaching down to steady herself against the tub.

Armand realized that she was drunk, quite drunk, and felt a hard surge of excitement.

"Shhh! Shhh! Ninon is busy, darling. Here are your towels, and I shall do Ninon's job quite well. Quite well . . . " He enveloped her in soft, warm flannel and began to work his broad, strong hands up her fleshy thighs.

9

The Dauphin married that winter. He went to greet his fiancée, Marie-Thérèse at Sceaux, ten miles from Paris. The Marquise de Sabran, who was rather fond of me and whose beautiful and charming niece was one of my dearest friends, asked my father permission to take me to see this meeting to which all of Paris was rushing.

It was early morning on a blustery February day in 1745, and Diane had been up since five o'clock in a frenzy of preparation for her trip to the chateau de Sceaux, where the Dauphin was to meet his bride-to-be for the first time. The marquise de Sabran had begged the comte to allow Diane to join her party. The entire royal family and all the court would be there to welcome Maria-Theresa, the Spanish Infanta, for a marriage that would strengthen the ties between France and unpredictable, possibly treacherous, Spain. For the first time, Diane would be present at a *grand couvert*, a grandiose ceremonial meal, during which she could watch the royal family display their elegant manners throughout the long, elaborate meal of beautifully concocted dishes.

She smiled, remembering how pleased her father had been at the idea of having her arrive at Sceaux chaperoned by the marquise de Sabran, after all, one of the great notables at court, a lady-in-waiting to the Queen, the grand-daughter of old Villeroy, the King's first tutor, and hostess at the most intellectual *salon* in Paris where guests rubbed shoulders with writers like Voltaire and Diderot.

"We shall be late!" snapped Diane, hunting through the disorder of her armoire for her saffron leather gloves. It was a frosty day, and her hands were so delicate that she did not dare go outside without gloves. At the convent she often had chilblains, and she would cry herself to sleep at night from the itching and pain of the split, oozing skin of her hands. Only little Sophie's hands were more sensitive to the damp cold.

"You *are* in a fuss!" laughed Marianne, looking stunning in a low-cut green taffeta gown that showed off to perfection her small but shapely figure. "You put your gloves with your shawl when you came back from mass. Here, let me have a look at your hem, then we'll go down." Diane had chosen a gown of cloth of gold that fell into graceful folds as she walked.

Inside the marquise's handsome coach the ladies rested their feet on two large coffers of hot ashes. They shed their woolen shawls in the cozy warmth of the carriage as it made its way slowly through the clogged streets of the city. Behind them followed a coach every bit as large with five servants, including Marianne, and provisions of food —and cosmetics—for any eventual emergency.

"Thank heaven, you've been sensible about your *panniers*, my dears. Otherwise, I don't know how we could all squeeze into my coach, big as it is!" laughed the marquise, arranging her skirts and settling back against the cushions. She loved young people and rarely inflicted her sharp tongue on them. "We shall have nothing but misery if the highway to Sceaux is like these streets. We should have left earlier, though my driver told me this morning that Versailles emptied out at crack of dawn, and the roads have been thick with carriages ever since."

Despite the deep creases fanning out around her bright hazel eyes, the freshness of youth still clung to the marquise's ruddy cheeks. Beneath thick white paint her cheeks were sprinkled with deep pockmarks. She was a lively, vivacious woman whose smile could be either wickedly satirical or meltingly tender. The apathetic Queen, forever surrounded by a tight circle of sycophants, depended on her for tedious games of *lansquenet* and occasional advice on her toilettes. Very occasional, however, for the Queen preferred to bundle herself in dozens of layers of ruffles and flounces and shawls and ribbons and bows, crowned with a somber black lace mantilla. She was an absurd sideshow at the most elegant and glamorous court in the whole of Europe, this Marie Leczinska, daughter of a dethroned Polish monarch, not really a blue blood at all in the eyes of Madame de Sabran and many at court.

Nevertheless, the marquise served her as best she could and tolerated, though often with difficulty, for the marquise had a brilliant mind and a sound education, the grim, dull favorites who gathered around the Queen in the evenings to read from religious tracts and pamphlets, to discuss Bourdaloue's latest sermon, and to yawn and sigh in the Queen's stuffy sitting room crammed to the ceiling with religious gimcrackery, holy medals and relics, and mediocre paintings of saints in maudlin postures of various and sundry agonies.

In all fairness, however, the marquise found the Queen a changed woman since the King's "deathbed" reconciliation with her at Metz. After her return to Versailles, she had bathed every afternoon and had put aside her gloomy mantilla except for morning mass. Even when she knew for a certainty that the King planned to bring the duchesse de Chateauroux back to her apartments at Versailles, the Queen clung to her fantasy of recapturing the King's affection, especially after the duchesse's sudden, mysterious death. Only last week the Queen had shyly asked Madame de Sabran to add another pillow to her bed.

As the two coaches slowly made their way down the Champs-Elysées toward the country, Diane had to stifle the impulse to cry out, "Oh, look! Do look!" In the midst of one of the harshest winters in memory, Paris had been transformed into a wonderland of spring. The entire city had been touched by the wand of a fantastical magician. The twelve largest squares of the city had been decorated with masses of freshly cut evergreen boughs. Triumphal arches of spruce, pine, yew towered above the ice slick cobblestone streets, and every house was hung with a profusion of lanterns.

Diane gaped at the dramatic change in the dreary streets that she knew so well. "Papa says that the celebrations will go on for at least two weeks. Every night, he says. Dancing and fireworks."

"Oh, indeed, yes," the marquise said. "Over there, do you see? They're building platforms for the musicians. And over there, the fireworks display. Italian fireworks. The very best. The King is sparing no expense. The King loves a good spectacle. And the court is tired of seeing him mope around over the death of the duchesse de Chateauroux. The Dauphin's marriage will be feted, and the King will dance and play again."

"Oh, do look, my dears," said the marquise. "Every one of these squares has a fountain, and the fountains will spout red and white wine. Those plank tables will be covered in sausages and breads, and heaven knows what all for the people. Poor dogs! They need a full belly and a good time. If this war in Flanders drags on much longer, the King's taxmen will not be able to squeeze out another *sou*. Not another *sou*!"

As soon as they had traveled beyond the city tollgates, the jumble of vehicles crowding onto the main road to Sceaux slowed the horses to an ambling walk. The marquise nodded grandly and waved to friends and acquaintances.

"The King will want to play again, that's a certainty," said Madeleine, with a malicious grin. "The royal hunt, the *chasse au roi*, is about to begin! The King's mistress is dead . . . "

"Poisoned by Maurepas, so they say, but is it true, madame?" interjected Diane.

"No, child, I don't believe it for one minute. The duchesse de Chateauroux has been dead for two months—or almost two months—and every woman in France has her eye on the King and is hoping that the King will have his eye on her! The shopkeepers have made a fortune in paints and patches and gowns and fans! Just wait until the grand balls at Versailles, that's when the really gorgeous finery shows up. The King will not want for a mistress by his side for long. The fair ladies will see to that. One of them has been up to some fancy tricks for months. Dressing in pink and driving around the forest paths in a little blue *berline*. Oh, that mad bourgeoise. She's obsessed. She's wasting her time. The King would not dare take a woman of that class as his official mistress. The court won't allow it. Never," huffed the marquise.

"That may well be," said Madeleine, "But, I know for a fact that the King has sent her gifts of venison from the day's hunt. Compliments of

His Majesty, the King. The King's eye will be roving, mark my words, and someone is bound to be the lucky one. I wouldn't mind being the lucky one myself!"

"Madeleine!" cried Diane, and the marquise laughed.

"Just hold your tongue, young lady, until you see the King for yourself!" said the marquise, enormously amused by Diane's naiveté. "You may be singing a different tune when you see what a handsome man our sovereign is. The handsomest man in the kingdom, I'll vouch for that."

"Handsomer than my father?" Diane asked, awestruck despite herself, unable to comprehend how one man could be both a royal sovereign and the handsomest man in the kingdom as well. In her cherished miniature the King was certainly not as attractive as her father. She had seen the Queen one day, from a distance to be sure, but she had looked like an elderly lady from the country, dumpy and round-faced. The Queen was older than the King, she knew that. The King was thirty-five and the Queen had already celebrated her forty-second birthday. No wonder she looked like such an old woman!

"Oh, yes, my dear, I'm afraid so. If you are lucky enough to see the King up close, he will take your breath away. But, mind you, he's not a lady's man, like your father . . . "

The marquise could have bitten her tongue for making such a faux-pas. She glanced quickly at Diane, but Diane either did not hear or the idea of her father's being a lady's man did not bother her. Catching Diane's eye, the marquise felt a tremendous rush of tenderness for the girl, a desire to protect her, to make her smile and laugh.

Diane became more and more nervous as they approached Sceaux. She hoped that she would not perspire and ruin her new gown. Since coming to Paris, she had heard so much talk of the King and the Queen and the princesses and the Dauphin that they had in a way become as familiar as the weather. Nonetheless, her heart raced with excitement at the thought that in a few hours she would be standing before the grand table, watching the King and his family dine. Everyone said that the King had exquisite manners and that no other mortal could eat a soft-boiled egg with as much refinement as Louis XV.

"Will the King eat an egg today, Madame?" she asked.

"Of course, he will, my darling. Of course, he will. The King considers it an absolute *obligation* to eat an egg at every *grand couvert*!" She has certainly captured my heart, this delicious young beauty, thought the Marquise. "When the King is served his egg, those seated next to him will draw back so that you can watch as he cleverly taps his spoon around the shell. It's quite a lovely sight, to be sure."

The late morning sun had settled over the gray slate roof of the chateau de Sceaux by the time Diane and her party alighted in the large, square courtyard. Lackeys in the duc de Maine's livery hurried about cleaning up cakes of steaming manure from the cobblestones, as coaches and carriages deposited their brilliantly clad passengers before hurrying off to the stables. The flags of France and Spain were draped on all sides of the courtyard and from the windows on the second floor. The marquise soon hurried away to make herself available to the Queen.

Diane and Madeleine joined dozens of groups of courtiers strolling about the paths of the formal garden and the park behind the chateau. The sky was a clear blue, but a strong east wind lashed Diane's face and made her eyes water as she and Madeleine walked about. Inside one of the two square pavilions flanking the chateau, they found a huge, ornate chapel.

"Why, it's circular!" Diane whispered in amazement. "I've never seen a round chapel before."

"Especially one that's stuck inside a square box! What foolishness!" Madeleine said.

But Diane thought the chateau the very epitome of modernity. Not like Corcheval with its ancient, feudal dungeon, a rugged, unflinching tower standing strong and tall since the twelfth century. The park at Sceaux extended as far as the eye could see with evergreen mazes and lakes and waterfalls, whereas Corcheval had only an insignificant little reflecting pool and a pastureland lake. Poor papa, he did try so hard to be fashionable, she thought. But, then, Sceaux was little more than a century old when one of the Sun King's ministers had turned it into this modern marvel. Papa could do the same to Corcheval if ever he became a minister.

"Madeleine, your nose is red! Let's go back inside."

As they wandered in and out of the vast, formal reception rooms in the chateau, they came to the concert room where a crowd of people had gathered around an ornate porcelain clock, which someone said had been specially made in Dresden. Suddenly Diane heard the sharp staccato sound of hundreds and hundreds of heels striking marble floors, a great rushing, beating roar. In a flash, it seemed, the room emptied, the crowd of people running and pushing toward the doorway.

"It's the King, for sure it's the King," cried Madeleine.

The two girls took to their heels and ran first to the wide doorway of the concert room giving onto the ballroom which was already jammed with finely dressed men and women fighting their way to the grand entrance hallway.

"It's impossible, Diane. We'll tear our frocks to pieces in there."

"We should be able to see something from the windows," said Diane.

From the tall double windows they could make nothing of the jumble of people and carriages and horses crowded into the courtyard. Neither of them had ever seen the King's coach. Madeleine thought that she recognized the Dauphin, but Diane insisted that the young man was surely too young.

"Who else could he be?" asked Madeleine crossly. "Besides, the Dauphin is fifteen. And he's tall and slim."

Gradually members of the court drifted back into the ballroom and the concert room. Most of them had had only a glimpse of the King and Queen as they entered the chateau. The Queen, it was said, was annoyed that the Infanta and her party had not yet arrived. The King, however, was in a jovial mood, jesting with his retinue and scolding the Queen for being impatient.

As the afternoon wore on, Diane and Madeleine, like everyone else, bored and restless for the spectacle to begin, drifted back and forth from the garden and ponds to the chateau. Diane's excitement over the exquisite décor—the white marble busts of the twelve Caesars in the library, the rose medallions of Homer and Plato framed in gilded wood—gave way to weariness and lethargy. Jean-Christophe joined them, and they tried to reach the landing of the entrance hall but had to content themselves with strolling around the almost empty concert room once again.

Close to four in the afternoon, as the cold of evening began to set in, there was a great clamor in the courtyard, and word spread rapidly that Maria-Theresa and her retinue had arrived. In the huge ballroom the loud chatter of voices subsided.

"What's happening? Why have they gone silent, all of a sudden," Diane asked in a whisper.

"They're trying to hear the formal greetings down below, I suppose." Madeleine replied.

"We might as well give up trying to get any closer," said Jean-Christophe. "In a few minutes we should move to the dining room and get a place with a good view of the King at table."

Before starting toward the dining room, they stopped to look down at the courtyard once again. Off to the right they could see torches and crowds of courtiers near the landing overlooking the courtyard. There was a flourish of trumpets and the sound of footsteps moving up the grand staircase.

A sudden strong gust of air tugged at her skirts, and Diane heard the double doors of the concert room rapidly close.

"It's the Dauphin and the duc d'Orléans," whispered Jean-Christophe, as the Dauphin walked hastily toward the windows on the opposite side of the room. The duc d'Orléans followed him after making sure that the doors were securely closed. The Dauphin was shaking his head and arguing heatedly with the duc.

Diane knew all about the young duc, and she admired his intense religious yearning. A tall, somber man, unlike his notorious father, Philippe d'Orléans, whose licentious parties behind locked doors at the Palais Royal had led to one scandalous rumor after another during the Regency, the duc d'Orléans wandered in and out of monasteries, unable to find spiritual rest.

Across the room the duc watched nervously as the Dauphin paced back and forth, clearly angry. He rubbed his hand moodily against the pommel of his narrow sword. The duc spoke to him in a soothing voice, but the Dauphin shook his head angrily and raised his voice.

"Of course, I'm disappointed. I have every right to be," they heard the Dauphin say. He looked very young, though he was almost as tall as the duc. His lips and cheeks were painted a deep mauve. Beneath the tight sausage curls of his snowy white wig the hair at the nape of his neck showed chestnut brown hair.

A footman slowly opened the double paneled door, and the chevalier de Montigny entered the room and walked toward the Dauphin. Not one of the three men showed the slightest awareness of Diane and her friends who stood watching, awestruck.

In his arms the beaming chevalier carried an armful of exquisite flowers—pale pink orchids, white carnations, purple anemones, red roses, pure white lilies. From the huge bouquet flowed ribbons of the color of the flags of France and Spain. Montigny bowed to the Dauphin and presented the bouquet to him.

"No, no, and no!" the Dauphin cried, refusing the flowers. He turned his back to Montigny and gazed gloomily out the window. The duc d'Orléans, looking distressed, turned his back as well.

"But, sire," the chevalier said, "You must give the flowers to your fiancée. You must offer them to the Infanta. She is passionate about flowers. Every day, since we left Spain, I have never failed to present her each morning with a fresh beautiful bouquet, no matter how far my men have had to search for them." The Dauphin, his back turned, seemed not to have heard. "Sire? Will you not take the flowers?" Utterly mystified, Montigny looked from the duc to the Dauphin, both of whom remained standing with their backs to the room.

"What is causing this delay? Dinner is waiting." A loud voice rang out. A distinctive, deep voice, a voice that once heard, Diane would never forget: the voice of Louis XV. The King looked quickly about the room and strode briskly toward his son.

Instinctively, Madeleine grabbed Diane's arm. They remained transfixed, the King and the Dauphin merely a few steps across the room. Diane could not take her eyes off the King. Dressed in deep russet velvet with a blush of pink silk flowing from his sleeves, Louis XV was simply . . . beautiful. Majesty, she kept thinking. His Majesty the King.

"Is there a problem, Orléans?" the King asked in a gentler tone. "Is something the matter?"

"The Dauphin, I understand, is quite disappointed with his bride-to-be," the duc replied sadly. "He finds her complexion not to his taste."

"That hideous red hair!" the Dauphin burst out. "It's dishonoring in France. I shan't have it!"

"Don't be childish, monsieur!" the King retorted. "I shan't have that!" The King was trying his best to be stern with his son. Everyone knew that Louis was foolishly tender with his children and that he especially doted on the Dauphin, whom Louis had many a night sat by his bedside and nursed devotedly through his illnesses. "Come now! Take the bouquet and present it graciously to your fiancée. I'm hungry. We've been kept waiting long enough! First by the Infanta, and now by your pettishness, sir."

Without a word the Dauphin turned his face once again to the window. The King stood for a moment watching him.

"Here! Give them to me, Montigny," said the King with an impatient sigh, gathering the enormous bouquet into his arms. He turned away from the men and walked across the room to the three young people who stood watching them.

The King stopped in front of Diane and held out the bouquet for her to take. He said nothing. He did not smile. He simply waited there with the glorious flowers extended to her. Diane looked up into his face and thought she would surely faint. She nudged Madeleine as if to tell her to take the flowers.

"No, Madame, the flowers are for you," said Louis XV, and he smiled broadly, showing even white teeth. With trembling hands Diane reached for the flowers. Louis's ice blue stare did not leave her face for a moment. Abruptly he turned on his heels, the other three men following him. As the Dauphin left the room, he glanced back over his shoulder to Diane, a puzzled look full of curiosity and speculation.

"Oh, I say! What do you think of that?" Jean-Christophe chortled gleefully and kicked up his high heels and pranced about the room. "Diane!" he said, falling to his knees in front of her. "My goddess!"

"Jean, hush! Someone will hear you!" Diane began to pull lilies and orchids from the bouquet to share the flowers with Madeleine, who for a moment was struck dumb.

"Oh, Diane! I can't believe it! From the King's own hands. And they're beautiful. From the King! He was so close that I could smell his perfume! Imagine!"

Diane carefully pulled the bouquet together with the wide glossy ribbons and touched her hand coquettishly to her pearls. The petrifying fear she had felt in front of the King had disappeared as soon as he walked away. In its stead she felt a rush of almost suffocating joy, an intoxicating sense of her own beauty.

"Oh!" she said. "We're too late. We'll never be able to see anything at the *grand couvert!*"

As they entered the immense room, Diane's heart sank. She could barely see the King, only the top of his head, and she could not see the table at all. Jean-Christophe placed himself between them and carefully worked his way to the front of the spectators. They found themselves space a little to the King's right. The Dauphine, who did indeed have a sallow, sickly complexion, sat on the King's right, and on his left sat the Queen. The Dauphin had placed himself next to his mother and, instead of eating, surveyed with weary arrogance the room and the more than two hundred spectators, who stood packed closely together, elbowing each other for an ever better vantage point, and nodding, and whispering. All of the King's daughters, except Princess Elisabeth, who had married the duc of Parma, were present.

The royal family was seated on one side of an enormously long table and had already begun to eat the first course, quail eggs with caviar, served in small, sparkling crystal bowls. The long, narrow table had been placed to one side of the room so that the crowd of onlookers could stand in front of the table and get a better view of the King and his family. Old Louis XIV had believed it his duty to eat all of his meals in public, but his great-grandson sat down to a *grand couvert* only once a week, and, on special occasions, such as this, the formal engagement of his son to the Infanta of Spain. On Sundays shopkeepers and servants could hire places in rickety old hackney cabs to travel from Paris to Versailles, where they could stand only a few feet away from the King and his family as they dined.

Diane could hear the King chatting amiably with the Dauphine, but she could not make out what he was saying over the general hubbub in the room. She longed to have him look at her again, to hold her with his ice blue gaze.

As if commanded to do so, at that very moment, the King lifted his wine glass to his lips and caught sight of Diane, gracefully at ease, the magnificent bouquet of flowers in her hands. Without taking his eyes off her, Louis slowly lowered his glass to the table. Unsmiling, he continued to gaze at her as if lost in contemplation of the utmost seriousness.

Diane held her breath, as the King, without interrupting his study of her, his eyes sweeping over her from head to foot, picked up his spoon and began to eat. At his side the Dauphine chattered along, gesturing with her spoon and smiling, as Louis nodded distractedly now and again without taking his eyes off Diane.

Behind the chairs at the table the personal retinue of the royal family moved back and forth, supervising the service and attending to their needs. The marquise de Sabran brought a small satin cushion for the Queen, who suffered from rheumatism in the back during the harsh winter months. Chill and damp clung to the marble floors and stone walls of the chateau, which for months had stood vacant with no logs burning in the immense fireplaces. The duc de Gesvres took up his post behind the Queen's chair as soon as the marquise had settled the cushion behind the Queen's back.

Madeleine squeezed Diane's arm, for already heads were craning to get a glimpse of the young woman who had riveted the King's attention.

Footmen hurried away with the consommé bowls and brought in huge, steaming silver platters of crayfish and mussels. As the plates were being changed, the King leaned back in his chair, placed an elbow on the table, and waved his hand briefly from side to side.

The Queen noticed spectators near the front of the crowd bending forward and turning to follow the King's stare. An unpleasant scowl spread over her soft, round features as she picked out Diane standing at only a little distance to the right of the King. "Sire," she said, touching his sleeve, but the King appeared to be listening to Maria-Theresa. The Queen gave a disgruntled sigh. She looked like a plump, beruffled turnip in light violet taffeta with lace flounces washing around her fleshy arms and layering the fatty folds of her chin and neck. Over the heavily powdered wig towering over her face, she wore a new black lace mantilla.

Diane was startled to see the duc de Richelieu suddenly appear at the King's side. Louis leaned back in his chair and spoke to him briefly in a low voice, which made the Queen hold herself quite still, trying to make out what was being said. Richelieu strolled nonchalantly away and at the end of the long table walked toward the crowd. Louis bent his head to laugh with Maria-Theresa but followed Richelieu with his eyes.

The Queen, too, observed Richelieu as, with mincing, short steps, he sauntered in front of the spectators. Until he came to a stop in front of Diane. Choking back her fury, the Queen could feel her temples pounding and a hot, itching tightness at the nape of her neck. The lace of her mantilla shook. The huge room which moments before had seemed so cold and drafty was now suffocatingly hot. She hated the *grand couvert*, creeping along ceremonially at a snail's pace, thick, rich sauces oozing from every dish, her corset getting tighter and tighter, her gaseous stomach ballooning hard and tight, her feet and ankles aching, and always the yearning for sleep, for a long, long nap before cards and evening prayers. She looked at the prettified spectators with loathing. Bloodsucking pimps, she said to herself and made the sign of the cross. May God forgive me, she muttered to herself.

The duc de Richelieu stood smiling and swaying at Diane's side. He joked with Jean-Christophe, and, out of the corner of his eye, flirted with Madeleine. With Diane he was less jovial, more formal, though he had jestingly whispered that she must be a mere child, a toddler, and she had replied that she was indeed fifteen years old already.

"Then why have I not seen you at court before?" he asked. "I make it a point to know all the beautiful women at court. They are my abiding interest," he said, opening his snuffbox.

"Because my father has only just brought me to town."

"And who is your father, dear child?"

"Why, the comte de Fautrière, Michel de Fautrière," she answered proudly.

Richelieu knew Diane's father the comte very well. He despised the man. A third-rate schemer who did not have enough sense to stay out of the old Cardinal's way, and a failure, despite his illustrious coat-of-arms. He looked Diane over with a cold eye of appraisal. A golden vision, he thought to himself. Tender grey eyes. A waist the width of a man's hand. Cream and primrose complexion. Delectable! Ah, Louis *is* becoming a connoisseur after all.

Since the death of the duchesse de Chateauroux, the King had become ever more dependent on Richelieu. In the dead of winter the battlefields in Flanders lay deserted until the return of spring and fair weather. Richelieu was free to devote himself to the grieving King.

When the King learned of the duchesse de Chateauroux' death, his grief was devastating. He immediately drew up a list of the duchesse's enemies at court and banished all of them. Every one of them banished to their country estates, not merely to twelve leagues' distance from Versailles. Then, he called for his carriage and departed with Richelieu for La Muette, where the two men stayed up until five in the morning reading and re-reading the duchesse's letters to her royal lover. Louis had sobbed, great honking sobs that crumpled his broad shoulders and bowed his head. The King named Richelieu First Gentleman of the Bedchamber, surely the most coveted position at court, for Richelieu not only enjoyed the privilege of handing his sovereign his nightshirt on retiring but also placed the last candle at his bedside each evening. Richelieu swaggered through the corridors and antechambers of Versailles as never before.

With something approaching awe, Richelieu studied Diane's enchanting face, glowing in the candlelight. She was handling herself splendidly. She did not simper or giggle timidly. She returned his gaze—and the King's—boldly, without fear, her full, sensual lips slightly parted, her lovely chin lifted as if to brave the challenge of a monarch's admiration.

Richelieu caught Louis's eye and smiled in complicity.

"What takes your fancy, young lady, of all the succulent dishes on the royal table?" Richelieu asked Diane, and winked at Madeleine.

Diane observed the wink and was annoyed. "Oh, I don't know," she said slowly, trailing her glance along the table, stopping at the immense platter, an elaborate arrangement of coral orange crayfish and black and gray mussels, placed directly in front of the King. "I think I should like best the lovely crayfish," she said.

Hearing her answer, the King lifted a crayfish from the platter, held it for a moment, then popped it into his mouth. "Bah! They are no good," Louis said, making a sour face.

Diane laughed, a full-throated laugh of deep pleasure, and the crowd abruptly grew quiet for a moment. An intense hum of whispering and murmuring centered around the spectators near the King. The Dauphin looked about suspiciously. There standing in the front row was the girl to whom his father had presented the Dauphine's flowers.

Richelieu saw the Queen motion to the duc de Gesvres, who had moved from his post and was displaying his new gold watch to Madame de Sabran. The duc de Gesvres bent his head low as the Queen whispered in his ear. Startled, the duc straightened. He looked about the crowd, searching right and left, until his gaze rested on Diane. He bent down and appeared to remonstrate with the Queen. The King, unconcerned, his head half-turned away from his wife, consumed quantities of mussels, savoring them with moist, smacking noises as he smiled at Diane. The duc waited for some sort of response from the Queen, who had dipped her bread in red wine and sat sucking angrily on the crust. She muttered something to the duc and banged her wine glass on the table. Without a word, a grim look on his face, the duc de Gesvres left the Queen.

By the time Gesvres reached Diane and Jean-Christophe, Richelieu had departed with Madeleine, for a "turn in the concert room" to see the Tiepolo ceilings, he said. Diane and Jean-Christophe were in high spirits. Madeleine would surely compromise herself, they giggled, going off with the duc de Richelieu, into another room without a chaperone, not even a lady's maid. What on earth would the marquise de Sabran say if she found out, which she surely would? Still, the marquise did not have a reputation for purity either, did she? Diane's face clouded. She had laughed heartily with Jean-Christophe. It was funny to think of Madeleine being naughty with an old roué like Richelieu with such a scandalous reputation. But it wasn't funny to be talked about. To have people stare and snicker and gossip, as they did about the marquise. And her father.

The duc de Gesvres gently touched Diane's arm. She gave a start. She had often seen the duc at a distance. She had never met him, though her father often went to the duc's gaming tables, mostly to see who was losing his patrimony that night, so he said. The duc, a short, little man with a vivid pink and white complexion, wore outrageous colors, extremely high heels, and a profusion of diamond and emerald rings on his stubby, white fingers. He spent most of his time at court with the Queen and her ladies, though he had become a great favorite with the King after teaching him and Madame de Mailly to do needlepoint. The King, like the duc, had become obsessed with it and was quite proud of his handiwork. The King allowed the duc to have gaming tables in his Paris hotel, which had become notorious for swallowing up some of the greatest fortunes in France.

"May I speak with you, Madame?" The duc took Diane's arm and nodded toward the reception rooms. Though the duc had spoken just above a whisper, heads strained toward the pair, the beautiful young girl with the gorgeous bouquet of flowers and the duc de Gesvres.

Diane turned cold with fear. What on earth could this little man have to say to her? First had come Richelieu, who had bandied a few jokes and then gone off with Madeleine. But Diane was not fooled. Richelieu really wanted to know who her father was. After that, he had paid her no more mind, had even seemed to forget why he had sought her out, though she knew that the King had sent him to her side.

"I beg your pardon, Monsieur?"

"If we could only step into the next room. For privacy," he said.

For privacy? Her mind was racing. Why was de duc de Gesvres pulling her away toward the other rooms? Was this another messenger from the King?

"But I shall lose my place." Diane protested. "And I shall not be able to see the King's meal."

The duc de Gesvres glanced nervously toward the Queen, who sat glowering at him. She had stopped eating and sat with her arms folded.

"I'm afraid, Madame, that I must ask you to come with me into the reception rooms." He waited, expecting Diane to make a move. Diane, however, simply stared at him.

"It is the Queen's wish, Madame," he said finally.

The Queen's wish! Diane's head reeled. The Queen's wish? What had she to do with the Queen? To be sent away like a misbehaving child! It is the Queen's wish!

Jean-Christophe took Diane's arm, and she leaned heavily against him as if she were going to faint. The duc de Gesvres stood anxiously watching her, fearful that she would refuse or would make a scene. And then what would he say to that old wet hen? What in Heaven's name possesses her? After all, this is the daughter of one of the oldest houses in France. No one can dispute that. Her father will never forgive this humiliation, never. And he should not. What has got into the old biddy? At her age and after all the King's indiscretions, very public if you please, to begin to behave like a jealous actress throwing tantrums.

"I shall tell anyone who asks that you've been taken ill, Madame. That you've had to leave the room because you have had an attack of the vapors. In this crowd, with all this perfume and . . . other scents. Not unlikely," he said, fussing over her sympathetically, as Jean-Christophe led her away.

Diane could not remember the awful moment of leaving the room under the eyes of all those people. Everyone craning his neck for a look at her. Sent out of the room. Out of the King's presence. By order of the Queen! She remembered clutching the huge bouquet with both hands as Jean-Christophe whispered excuses, working their way through the crowd.

He led her to a fauteuil at the far end of the room. Diane leaned back against the chair and closed her eyes. She felt giddy and sick to her stomach. Jean-Christophe hovered over her. They could hear the low hum of the crowd and the footsteps of servants busy with the ceremonial meal.

A footman appeared with a small crystal glass on a silver tray. "A *digestif*, Madame," he said, lowering the tray. The footman was extremely young, younger by several years than Jean-Christophe, and he watched Diane with bright black eyes, like an alert bird. "The King sends you an herbal *digestif*. He heard that you were taken ill," he added.

"My thanks to His Majesty," she said meekly, taking the small glass and drinking the clear amber liqueur. The footman nodded an acknowledgement and moved toward the door.

Diane caught her breath with a ragged sigh. "I've made a fool of myself, Jean." She looked at him with wide supplicating eyes, dark as night in the blazing light of the immense wall lustres. "We were having such fun. I don't know what happened. All of a sudden everything changed. What *did* happen, Jean?"

Jean took her hand in his and squeezed it reassuringly. "Let's go below, and I'll call for my carriage. I think it best that we leave before the *grand couvert* comes to an end. I'll send word to the marquise."

Jean-Christophe's shining black *berline* with his family's gold and red crest came round in a matter of minutes. The courtyard, bright as midday with the light of hundreds of flambeaux, looked cheerful and gaudy with bright colored flags and bunting.

Marianne, unusually subdued by her mistress's sudden departure from the grand fête, helped Diane into her wraps. Jean-Christophe stood outside in the clear, cold evening waiting for foot braziers to be brought to the carriage. Diane, in the day's excitement, had eaten little. She felt weak and tired and thoroughly humiliated. What would her father say when he heard that she had been sent away from the *grand couvert*? By the Queen! Because the King had given her flowers. Because the King had not taken his eyes off her.

With a loud noise of slamming doors, the marquise de Sabran came running down the broad stairs, her full wide skirts held snugly in one hand, exposing her hoops. She was perspiring, and her broad, handsome cheeks were flushed.

"You aren't leaving!" she said to Diane. "I won't have it! You aren't leaving like a thief in the middle of the night!" She was panting for breath. "That cow! She has no right, and she will apologize, she will apologize! You are not Mistress Nobody from Nowhere. She can't do this, and she knows it. Majesty or not. I've sent for Richelieu," she said, angrily shaking her head.

Richelieu had not been present when the duc de Gesvres asked Diane to leave the *grand couvert*, but the whole court was abuzz with rumor and speculation over the Queen's action. Without a moment's hesitation Richelieu carried Madame de Sabran's indignant protests to the King. Madame de Sabran would make an excellent ally, he judged, if he decided to sponsor the little Fautrière. The marquise sat right squarely in the middle of the pious, niggling circle of prigs in the Queen's retinue, and had such broad and ancient connections at court that the King would not willingly displease her.

"Don't worry, my dear. The King won't put up with this, you'll see. He's a good-natured man and doesn't like trouble, but he won't let an innocent young girl like you be humiliated." The marquise was beside herself. She felt personally affronted by the Queen's fit of ill temper. Diane, poor child, looked like a woebegone waif, abandoned on the streets. The comte would be outraged. What ever got into that insufferable cow! She ought to have developed a thick skin by now. Elephant hide. As far back as Madame de Mailly the King had *always* insisted on giving his mistress official status in the Queen's retinue. Right under the Queen's nose. And she had to swallow it, like it or not. But, today, the King was just having his bit of fun with a pretty young thing who meant no harm. Well, no one had ever accused Marie Leczinska of being smart!

"Don't you think we ought to go, Madame? I really don't feel well." As each moment passed, Diane's apprehension increased. The situation was growing worse, more complicated and more humiliating. Now the King! What would he say when he saw her again? Perhaps he would agree with the Queen. Perhaps he would wonder why he ever gave her the flowers.

She heard the clatter of heels and looked up to see Louis XV descending the stairs with Richelieu. The entrance way blazed with light. Diane had never seen anyone walk like the King, with such an easy, dignified gait. She had heard her uncle Philippe say that even as a child, even at seven or eight years, Louis's step had been majestic.

The marquise rushed to meet the two men and began to remonstrate with the King. Louis listened attentively. When the marquise finished, he walked over to Diane and took her hands.

"Come with me, Madame. I shall ask the Queen to apologize to you immediately. Have no fear." He spoke like a kindly relative to Diane. He smiled, the corners of his eyes crinkling into fine lines. Diane's hands trembled in his. How magnificent he was! The marquise was right, she thought, he takes my breath away. She could smell his perfume. Cinnabar. His teeth were so white that she was sure that he did not use snuff. She wanted to speak, but could not.

"Oh, please no, your Majesty," she finally murmured.

"I think the child needs to go home now, Majesty. This disgraceful matter has been a shock, as you can see." The marquise was in no mood to let the King off the hook by parading Diane before the Queen for a second good look. The Queen would babble anything to make Louis happy. Afterwards she would find a way to be spiteful again.

"As you think best, *chère madame*," the King said. He still held Diane's hands.

"But," the marquise continued sternly, "I want your personal assurance, Majesty, that this sort of thing will not happen again and that Mademoiselle de Fautrière will be welcome at all the court celebration . . . the balls, the concerts, the entertainments . . . everything. Without risking humiliation from the Queen."

"Welcome! More than welcome! Expected, anticipated with the keenest pleasure! I shall not dance, Madame, unless you are there to dance with me." The King lifted Diane's right hand as if beginning a minuet. "And as I love to dance, you must not disappoint me!"

The King bent forward to kiss Diane farewell, a lingering pressing of cheek against cheek. He turned to the marquise and bowed over her hand as she dropped a quick curtsey. The marquise was shocked. Whatever possessed the King to behave so familiarly with a young girl? First, the Dauphin, like a stubborn mule, behaving rudely to his bride-to-be. Then, the Queen acting like an enraged hornet, and now the King kissing and cooing over a child he has never seen before! They were all going mad!

As the marquise put her arm around Diane's shoulder and swept her toward Jean-Christophe's carriage, Diane glanced quickly over her shoulder. The King had already started up the stairs. Richelieu stood watching her departure with rapt attention.

10

The next morning the marquise de Sabran sent a lackey with a gift in an envelope of silk. It was a beautiful mask made of the finest, softest black feathers. *For the wedding celebrations, my beautiful child, may it bring you luck*, her note said. Diane folded the note and stared at the mask as if it were enchanted, as if it contained the secret of her future dreams. Reluctantly, she put the mask away, and hurried down the stairs. She was late for dinner. She had overslept, and so had Marianne. Returning from Sceaux in a trance, her nerves raw with the excitement of the King's embrace and the words he had whispered in her ear, she had plunged into sleep as soon as her head touched the pillow.

Dashing for her carriage, Diane quickly sorted through the visiting cards on the tray in the entrance hallway. The usual, she thought, with a stab of disappointment. Then, on the very bottom of the pile, an early caller, the stiff, gilt-lettered card of Louis-François-Armand, maréchal duc de Richelieu. Her hands shaking, she wrapped the card in a handkerchief and slipped it into the pocket of her cloak, the duc's card another talisman that the King's embrace had not been a wondrous dream.

The marquise de Sabran's guests had already seated themselves in the dining room when Diane, breathless and full of apologies, rushed in. Dead silence fell over the room, as Diane took her seat next to Jean-Christophe.

"She's the one!" croaked the old comte de Verneuil. "She's the one the Queen sent away from the *grand couvert* yesterday!" He pointed his soupspoon toward Diane in triumph, and the entire table broke into prolonged applause. The chevalier de Montigny forgot that he was in the middle of a very good story about the Infanta's stubborn refusal to wear rouge and rose to his feet to propose a toast to Mademoiselle de Fautrière. Diane shrank back as the entire table stared at her.

Under the table, Jean-Christophe patted her hand. There was more applause and laughter and smiles. When Jean-Christophe began to talk to her, Diane turned to him and fixed her eyes on his face, hoping that the other guests would stop staring at her so boldly.

Diane could feel that she was being watched. She looked away from Jean-Christophe and dozens of guests along the table caught her eye, nodded amiably and lifted their glass to her. She smiled feebly and turned back to Jean-Christophe.

"Richelieu will know how to persuade the Infanta, we can be sure of that," the marquise de Sabran said, turning to Montigny, and they all laughed.

Richelieu's name reverberated in Diane's ears. The stiff card with the inscrutable handwriting. She had held it close to her face during the drive to the marquise's dinner, distraught almost to the point of tears that she could not make out the message in the half dozen scribbled words. Or were they merely his signature? Jean-Christophe, too, was talking of Richelieu. And of Madeleine. He was saying something about Armand being in trouble, that he could not prove his sixteen quarters of noble blood for a clerical benefice from the King. Four generations on his mother's side, but only three on his father's.

"And what of the duc? The duc de Richelieu," Diane said, yearning to touch the card again, to hold it close to her eyes. "What does he have to do with Armand's benefice?"

"Nothing. Only that Madeleine is delighted by the whole turn of events, for now she is determined that Richelieu will help find something else for Armand. Something that will make it possible for Madeleine . . ."

Diane thought that he said something about Madeleine marrying Armand, but she could not be sure, for there was a sudden outcry as her father walked into the room, splendidly dressed, his handsome face glowing.

The comte bowed in his daughter's direction before strolling over to the marquise de Sabran's chair. He declined her invitation to sit down and dine. Instead, the center of all eyes, he stood swaying against her chair, joking playfully with her and darting a glance now and again around the table like a restless monarch.

The change in the mood around the table was astonishing. Diane could feel the urgency of the other guests to finish their ices, impatient to get out of their chairs, and to get near her father. Her father! She could see it in their faces. Faces wreathed in deferential, fawning smiles. In one way or another, they were all trying to get her father's attention.

As soon as courtesy allowed, guests flung down their napkins and pressed about the comte de Fautrière, their voices rising and falling in flattery so outrageous that Diane thought her father would surely object. He did not. He beamed, bobbing his head to one and to the other, flush with high spirits, basking in their attention. Diane was ashamed for Jean-Christophe to see her father in this way.

Murmuring goodbye to Jean-Christophe, Diane made her way through the circle to her father's side. She would plead a headache and ask him to leave with her. After a moment, she pulled at her father's sleeve impatiently. He turned his head and gave her a mean look.

"I've just heard the most delicious story," the comte said, with a smug grin, and the crowd about him made high, simpering noises of encouragement. "I've just come from court and heard the most delicious story about our Dauphine, or, rather, our Dauphine-to-be." His friends found this hilarious and laughed and shook their heads as if they could not believe such wit.

"Last night at Sceaux, the Infanta was being prepared for bed by her ladies. Her gown, dressing gown, and slippers were brought in, and the Infanta was asked to divest herself of all that she was wearing, such is the custom, as *we* all know. The Infanta charmingly complied. Then, to the horror of her ladies-in-waiting, it was perceived that the Infanta retained on her little finger an exquisite diamond ring of a rare and exotic color: pale salmon."

The circle growled their disapproval.

The comte raised his hand in a calming gesture. "No, no. You see the Dauphine was ignorant of this rule of etiquette! She did not know!"

The comte waited as a ripple of noises of astonishment passed around the group.

"The comtesse de Guemont, after a moment's hesitation, pointed out the ring. 'You must relinquish it, your Highness,' she said. ''Tis the etiquette of the French court that you must come to us with naught from a foreign court.'"

"'Oh, is this true, Madame?' she asks innocently. And seeing the ladies in her suite nodding in assent, the Dauphine . . . ," the comte paused for effect, "well, the Dauphine simply removed the offending ring from her finger, turned to Madame de Guemont, and said, '*Voilà*, Madame, I make you a gift of the ring that has been worn by the eldest daughters of the kings of Spain from generation to generation for six hundred years!'"

There was a burst of applause and much murmuring of enthusiasm for the comte's story.

Diane twisted with irritation at her father's side. In the past, whenever she had heard snide comments about her father's vain, egotistical posturing, she had angrily shrugged them off. In her eyes he was the very soul of wit, of worldly polish, of elegance and sophistication. He could quote Italian poetry, could sing arias in a sweet, reedy tenor, and could dance the most complicated minuet with careless precision. Who wouldn't be jealous enough to want to make fun of such an accomplished nobleman? But now, on his arm, watching him feed upon such flattery, Diane felt betrayed by her blind admiration of her father. What had come over their friends? Had they no one better to fawn upon?

She looked around in search of Jean-Christophe, but he had already left the room, and she and her father were still surrounded by a clutch of the marquise's dinner guests.

"We have much to discuss, *ma petite*," her father finally said, moving her toward the marquise.

Back in Diane's house, the comte cancelled her plans to visit the King's new aviary at Versailles with Jean-Christophe and Marianne. Instead, he called for tea and cakes—he had not yet dined—and settled into a comfortable *bergère* next to the fireplace in Diane's small sitting room.

The royal family had not yet returned to Versailles before the comte began to hear stories that the Queen had ordered the duc de Gesvres to send his daughter away from the *grand couvert*. In view of almost three hundred people! Of the highest placed courtiers! He had caught the story just by chance, at a gaming table. He was bored, for there was no theatre, no opera, no balls, since everyone of any consequence had gone to the chateau at Sceaux. That morning he had awakened with a pounding hangover and dreadful red eyes. He did not bother to go to the ceremonial meeting of the Dauphin with his future Dauphine. There would be plenty of occasions to shine at the wedding festivities, plenty of exhausting occasions to display his new fashions, his bejeweled finery. So he had had a wretched morning and afternoon, and a boring evening.

Until the evening was suddenly enlivened by the excited talk about his beautiful daughter who had captured the eye of the King! Waves of exhilaration washed over him as he contemplated the future that lay ahead of him as one of the King's *favorites!* The father of the beautiful Diane of Fautrière! He could scarcely contain his excitement.

"Tell me about your excursion to Sceaux," the comte began, after he had finished his tea.

Still irritated by her father's preening performance at Madame de Sabran's, Diane had sat silently watching her father fuss over his tea and cakes and testily hector her servants.

"What is there to tell?" Diane asked crossly. "I went to Sceaux with Madeleine as the guest of the marquise de Sabran . . . "

"Yes! Yes! I know that very well!" the comte interrupted. The girl was maddening! "I heard reports that you were involved in an incident during the *grand couvert,*" he said. "I heard you caused quite a stir."

Diane could tell that her father was brimming with impatience. And she did not care one whit. He simply wanted to hear all the details so that he could run around among the salons this evening, strutting and boasting. Instead, she wanted to tell him how ridiculous he looked this afternoon, crowing over being able to tell a story fresh from court, gorging himself on the most despicable flattery.

Looking past him, toward the gold and white panels of the music room that reminded her of Sceaux, she began to tell him of finding herself with her friends in the concert room when the Dauphin burst in followed by the duc d'Orléans, who obviously was reasoning with the young man, begging him not to behave rudely toward his bride-to-be. She told her father that the Dauphin was obstinate, that he refused to take the bouquet of flowers prepared for the Infanta, that the King himself came to the doorway to find out what was delaying the meal. On mentioning the King, Diane forgot her anger with her father. The excitement of her adventure took hold of her, and she rushed breathlessly through the King's presenting her the magnificent flowers, his smiles as the stately meal progressed from course to course, his comic face of distaste after eating the crayfish that had tempted her. Then, suddenly, from out of nowhere, the duc de Gesvres asking her to leave the room. By order of the Queen.

"She made me miss the rest of the meal!" she concluded petulantly. "I could not watch the King eat his ice, which he consumes in the most delicate manner imaginable, they say."

"What else?" the comte asked, coldly. Every woman in Paris spending a fortune getting tricked out in every conceivable finery and going down on her knees for weeks and months, praying, moving heaven and earth so that the King will glance her way. And here is my daughter, he thought bitterly, being ogled by the King in front of the entire court. After all that, she ends up mewling about not seeing the King eat his ice! *Jésu!* It was clear that he would have to manage her very carefully. Now that everything he had ever wanted in life lay within his grasp. If only Diane did not fumble! Damn the child! She would have to be coached, every move of the King anticipated.

"There is nothing else. I went into the next room with the chevalier de Rosnières. And, oh, yes, the King sent a footman to me with a *digestif* because he was told that I had been taken ill."

"What about the duc de Richelieu? I heard that he sought to learn your name for the King. And that after the meal the marquise de Sabran sent him to bring the King to her. For a discussion of what had happened," the comte said acidly.

"Yes, I suppose so." Diane replied listlessly. Why was he bullying her? Why was he so irritable? She had done nothing wrong, Madame de Sabran had said so. And so had Jean-Christophe.

"You *suppose* so! Don't you remember? Are you so besotted with daydreams about . . . about . . . about," the comte sputtered. For the life of him, he could not remember the name of that preposterous oaf, Odile's cousin. "Mézières. Armand de Mézières," he said finally.

Diane's skin crawled. She said nothing. But she met her father's angry glare without flinching. The sun was setting, its orange yellow glow fixed on the comte's face, illuminating the fine lines, the hairs in his nostrils and ears, the snuff stains about his thin lips. Diane turned her eyes away.

"I don't know how much you know about the duc de Richelieu," he began again, in a more gentle tone.

He waited.

"I know what the court gossip says. That's all," she shrugged.

The comte thought a moment before continuing. He had to be careful. Richelieu was powerful at court now, the King's favorite more than ever before. The comte had to make exactly the right moves. He knew very well that Richelieu detested him, just as he detested Richelieu. They had been enemies for years. Since the comte's fiasco with the Cardinal de Fleury. Even earlier. But Richelieu would like nothing better than to sponsor the King's next mistress. Just as he had maneuvered the duchesse de Chateauroux into the King's bed and many another passing fancy. A woman can twist Louis around her finger. That's the sum total of Richelieu's political wisdom. And look at how many honors have rained down on Richelieu lately! God, it makes me choke, thought the comte. It makes me choke! But he is not going to spirit my daughter away from me and line his pockets with the King's gold! He is not going to stand in my way either! The high and mighty duc must reckon with me, if the King has taken a fancy to my daughter.

The comte smoothed his fine silk hose and stood up. For a few moments he paced before the fire. He sat down again and took a large pinch of snuff, which set him sneezing.

"Damn! I've soiled my handkerchief," he said. "Now, then," he went on. Diane sat silently observing him. "You are going to find that the duc de Richelieu will be very attentive to you during the next few days as the wedding celebrations begin. Be alert to what he says, indeed, do as he says. But keep me informed at all times of his messages and instructions."

Diane wondered whether she should show him the duc's card. But then, why should she? It was only a calling card.

The comte rose, picked up his cane and gloves, and headed toward the door. He had forgotten, or had not bothered, to bid her farewell. She did not particularly care. Sitting perfectly still, watching her father, hips swaying, walk through the open doorway, she felt her heart harden. For the first time, she had a sense of her own power. Perhaps even of power over her father. Was that possible? A smile of deep satisfaction spread over her face.

The whole city surged from one peak of excitement to the other. France had a new Dauphine, a tall, angular Spanish woman with thick, curly red hair and a toothy grin. Already the people said the capricious young Dauphin doted on his bride. She was generous and kind. She had learned to use paints and rouge and patches and to cover her unsightly red hair with becoming white wigs.

Just as the marquise de Sabran had said, every night there was rejoicing in the streets, dancing in the squares, wine flowing from the fountains, and food by the wagonload spread out on plank tables all around the squares. On Wednesday last in the Place de Grèves the fireworks scaffolding had collapsed and crushed three people and injured dozens more. Still the jubilation continued. Every night the great plank tables burdened with food were overturned in a frenzy of pushing and jabbing and screaming, bread and sausages and fruits ground underfoot by the mob. At noonday the cheerless winter sun warmed the cobblestones, releasing the stench of vomit and crushed fruit into the air.

The smug merchants in the elegant little shops in the Faubourg Saint-Honoré closed their shutters and counted their stupendous treasure troves. Heaps and heaps of golden louis. They had exhausted all their ingenuity in trying to satisfy the frenzy of courtiers to outshine each other. "Spare no expense, monsieur!" That had been the constant refrain echoing through the shops. The comte de Vaugirard ordered a suit of cloth of gold with a vest thickly embroidered with diamonds, an outfit so heavy that the comte had to rush panting to a chair after each dance. In order to settle his account with his tailor Monsieur Fandelieu, he was obliged to sell his chateau in Normandy. However, at court the day after the ball everyone said that the King had particularly admired the comte de Vaugirard's suit.

The King himself had never looked handsomer. He had thrown himself wholeheartedly into the gaiety of the wedding celebrations. The crowds of Paris forgave him his lapse in recalling the duchesse de Chateauroux to Versailles after the disgraceful episode at Metz. Louis was once again Louis Le Bien-Aimé, for, after all, the duchesse was dead and moldering in her grave for over two months. Louis had never looked more regal. He was the very picture of health and high spirits. Gone the mournful boredom in his heavenly blue eyes. Every evening ended with a ball and Louis danced every dance, returning to Versailles at six in the morning and rising at ten for mass before starting the stately revelries again.

> *I went to all the festivities in celebration of the wedding both at Versailles and in Paris. I met the King everywhere, and we recognized each other in all our disguises, through the help of the Duc de Richelieu.*

Great bursts of red and blue rockets spread their feathery plumes in the distance over the Place Vendôme. From the open windows at the Opéra Diane and Madeleine watched the ricochet of fireworks across the sooty skies. A sparkling letter "L" coursed high into the night, followed by an "M" and a "T" before arching downward.

As awestruck as a child, Diane watched the thunderous display. She wanted to squeal with delight. But Madeleine, standing quietly by her side, would think her a great fool—as she no doubt was. Her whole world had been transformed into a whirl of intense sensation. The past two weeks had gone by in a blur of excitement. She tightened the taffeta ribbons at her waist. She had lost so much weight that she was more reed-like then ever. Nerves and lack of sleep, a few hours snatched between parties and balls, skipping the large dinner meals because they made her sluggish. But mostly it was nerves, eating away at her appetite. The King had noticed. Last night in the great ballroom at Versailles he had squeezed her waist. "Why, I can span your little waist with one hand now," he had said, gazing at her breasts, which swelled above the lace of her gown.

"We should have gone, Madeleine."

"No, we're much better here. Our gowns would get crushed and soiled at the hems in all that pushing and shoving."

Farther down the broad corridors they could see the ballroom filling with masked dancers, milling about until the musicians took up their places. The long French windows had been thrown open. Before long, the gigantic rectangular room would be overflowing. Anyone in proper dress with enough money to buy a ticket was admitted.

Diane wore a trailing gown of black lace. A broad black velvet ribbon adorned with a single half-opened red rose circled her throat. Richelieu had instructed her to dress *à l'espagnole* to capture the mood of the marriage of the Dauphin with a Spanish princess. The King, he said, would also be wearing a Spanish costume. Diane's gown was utterly simple, and her glowing mass of hair was wound in a tight chignon at the crown of her head. At her ears sparkled her grandmother's sapphire and diamond earrings.

"Are you sure I don't look too plain?" Diane asked.

Madeleine laughed. "Don't talk foolishness. As you must know by now, the King is at your feet, and every woman in Paris and Versailles would like to be at your throat."

There were fewer and fewer bursts of color from the square. Liveried footmen glided along the corridors behind them replenishing candles in the enormous sconces, setting aglow the white and gold panels along the walls.

They could see dozens of carriages moving slowly toward the Opéra. The streets below their window were loud with the noise of vendors hawking their wares, their oranges and roasted chestnuts.

"What is your father telling you? And Richelieu?"

"My father? Why, nothing really, except that he is very careful about what I should wear and what I should talk about with the King. The King says he likes my chatter, it amuses him. So I don't pay any attention to papa. The King laughs at my stories. I tell him stories about the nuns at Neuilly-les-Dames, and he laughs and laughs, all the time telling me that he will have to visit his confessor more often and stay longer on his knees. And Richelieu, well, he flits in and out, mostly to tell me how I shall recognize the King, and to tell me which dances the King will want. That sort of thing."

Diane stopped talking. Madeleine was leaning against the wall, breathing rapidly. Sweat dampened her forehead and beaded her upper lip.

"Are you unwell?" Diane fumbled in her beaded bag for her salts. She removed the stopper from the tiny green bottle and held the salts to Madeleine's nose. Madeleine inhaled deeply and patted her moist brow. Diane took her arm and led her along the brightly illumined corridor to the staircase leading to the next floor.

Madeleine sat down heavily, stifling a groan.

"It's nothing. Only a stitch of indigestion in my sides. I've been eating like a horse lately," she said. Diane looked down at her friend, noticing with surprise that Madeleine did indeed look heavier, thicker about the waist. "We'll rest just a moment, then we'll go back to the window."

"Why on earth, Madeleine? We can wait here until the King and the Dauphin arrive. We may have missed the grand finale of the fireworks anyway. Let's just stay here. You can rest a moment. You look pale."

Madeleine pulled herself to her feet. "I want to watch the carriages coming in. After the fireworks finish, the ballroom will be so crowded that I won't know who's there. I promised Armand that I would look for him," she said reluctantly, moving quickly toward the open window.

"Armand? Why would you be making promises to Armand?" Diane asked, suddenly remembering Jean-Christophe at the marquise de Sabran's table, talking of Richelieu and Madeleine . . . and Armand.

"Why not?" asked Madeleine, turning on her menacingly.

Startled, Diane drew back. Madeleine's plain face was twisted with anger and pain. Could she be really ill? "I only meant that promises are always something serious."

"Which I understand only too well," Madeleine said, her face grim.

"Are you saying that you . . . your hand is promised to Armand de Mézières?"

"I am saying that I have promised to marry for love. To marry only a man I love!"

"And you love Armand?"

"Lord help me, I believe I do. I know I do!" Madeleine whispered.

"But he has no money! You have no money! And he has ambitions for the church—a benefice, a rich abbey."

"I know. His plans for an appointment are botched now, or very nearly so. Besides, he doesn't want to take vows, and he could never get a large benefice without taking vows." They had reached the windows. Madeleine breathed deeply. "The air is so fresh tonight. It clears my head," she said in a gentler voice.

"Does your aunt know? Does she approve?"

"She doesn't know yet. No one knows except Armand and Odile. And now you," she said, turning her sad face to Diane.

It seemed to Diane that her friend had piled upon her an awful burden; the weight of it made her spirits droop. She stared at Madeleine. How many times Madeleine had joked about marriage and the number of lovers she intended to amuse herself with, once she got her rich husband and her lavish household in Paris. Diane had marveled at her cynicism, and had secretly envied it. Madeleine said that loving one's own husband was bourgeois, very bad taste. Only shopkeepers marry for love, she had said.

"You used to say that you couldn't wait to get married so that you could have satin slippers and new gowns and a box at the Opéra where you could receive your lovers."

"I was being silly. I said many stupid things before I met Armand. Oh, he is so tender with me, Diane!"

Diane, remembering Armand's caressing hands, felt her stomach tighten.

Madeleine laughed and wiped her brow. "You'll be the first to go to the altar. Perhaps even before he beds you, the King will find a compliant husband for you. Quickly. It is unthinkable that the King's mistress should be unmarried! You must have a proper husband before you move into your *petits appartements* at Versailles."

Diane wanted to cover her ears with her hands, to shut out Madeleine's talk. She did not want to think of what would come next, what would follow the excitement of the parties, the dances. She did not want to think about the plotting and scheming of her father and Richelieu. She hated her father's badgering, pressing her, wheedling, cajoling, wanting to hear every word the King had said to her, his every gesture, every pressure of his hand, every . . . And her father's spirits rising day by day, his wild hilarity, the duc de Richelieu's serious demeanor, as if he were engaged in plotting his way across a beleaguered battlefield.

A group of courtiers strolling past in black and white domino dress turned to look at the two young women, their masks dangling in their hands.

There was a sudden, muffled rush of feet on the stairs. As Diane turned, she saw a Spanish grandee striding easily toward her, scores of masked courtiers pressing around and behind him. He had a prominent, well-shaped chin, and he smiled broadly, revealing white, even teeth. He was dressed in black velvet with white lace at his throat and wrists, and he wore a wide black velvet mask. Quickly, with shaking hands, Diane tied on her mask, and, like a puppet bobbing along on a string, hastened to meet him.

A thin, silvery blade of light was streaking the horizon as a young woman's carriage pulled into the circular courtyard of the most sumptuous hôtel on the Place des Vosges, far from Versailles in the most expensive *quartier* of Paris. She wearily climbed the stairs and sat, lost in contemplation, before the mirror of her dressing table. It was almost dawn.

The young woman moved a tall candle nearer the mirror and rested her chin on her hand. Across the room Madame Poisson, her mother, sat watching her with anxious eyes. These late night talks, when her daughter returned from the night's grand entertainments, usually gave her great pleasure. Tonight, however, there was something wrong.

"You ought to get your rest, Reinette. You mustn't dawdle before your mirror like that! What's the point? You need your spirits for tomorrow. I should say for tonight. For the ball tonight." Madame Poisson wore no wig, but she was expensively dressed, and her fingers, gnarled and twisted by arthritis, were thick with rings. She sat by the dying fire, a shawl across her lap. Candlelight softened the folds around her face and made her deep set brown eyes sparkle. She was a woman of great beauty, the kind of beauty that could shrug off the damaging licks and swipes of time. At least for a while.

"I'll go in a moment. Every now and then I like just to sit quietly and think before going to bed," the young woman said in a soft, clear, caressing voice. She had dismissed her maid. She preferred to clean her face and brush her hair and prepare for bed alone. She opened a large pot of cream and began to work it into her face.

"I should be careful of the rouges they're selling these days, Reinette. Madame Chantville had a boil on her face that wouldn't heal for months. And now she's left with a terrible scar. Quite disfiguring, though Madame Chantville was never much to look at." Her voice was sweet and melodious, but her common accent betrayed her low birth. "What's the matter, Reinette? Is there something bothering you?"

The young woman nervously rubbed at her face with a piece of soft flannel. She did not know how to begin. But she must begin somehow, she must confide in her mother who would surely know what was best to do.

"I'm worried, maman. Things are not going as well as I had hoped," she said reluctantly.

"In what way, *mon amour*? Aren't you seeing the King? Aren't you dancing with the King every night?" The woman's voice rose, sharp and querulous.

"Yes. Of course. But something has happened. He's not the same for the past two weeks. We dance, we flirt, we whisper and laugh with each other. But he's distracted. He's not really with me, if you understand what I mean."

"Distracted by what? I don't understand."

"Distracted by someone else. There's a young girl. Quite young. I don't believe she could be more than sixteen. The King seems always to be looking over my shoulder when we dance, looking for her. Last night, at the ball at the Hôtel de Ville, they wore matching costumes—the King and the girl." Her voice trailed off wearily.

Madame Poisson's throat tightened. What nasty twist of fate was this? Since the King's mistress died, Madame Poisson had never had a shadow of a doubt that her daughter would one day, and one day soon, bask in her rightful place as the handsome monarch's favorite with her own opulent suite of apartments at Versailles, her own chateaux, her own title. Everyone had said so. Since she was born, since she was a little girl of such exquisite beauty that she melted the hardest hearts, no one had ever called her Jeanne Antoinette. Reinette, "little queen," that was her nickname. And her destiny.

Didn't the old fortune-teller at the Marché des Invalides predict it? Madame Lebon described Louis XV perfectly, in every detail, there could be no question, and Reinette was there by his side, his beloved mistress, his affectionate friend and confidante. Madame Lebon had looked first at the little girl's hand and then into her eyes and had told her that she would be adored by the King of France.

"Who is this girl? What clique at court is behind her?"

"She is Diane de Fautrière. The oldest daughter of the comte de Fautrière. I know only what cousin Binet was able to tell me. But it's an old family, one of the oldest of the nobility. From Charolais, in Burgundy."

Madame Poisson threw a small log on the fire. There was a draft from the window, and her feet were getting cold.

"But she's being pushed forward by one of the cliques at court. She must be."

"I'm not sure." She wanted to bury herself in her warm feather bed and stay there forever, sleeping and dreaming. She stared at her face, a perfect oval, in the mirror. Her eyes with their ambiguous, changing hue looked strained. She bit her lip. I'm not strong enough, she thought. My looks are too delicate. My beauty will give way under all this worry.

"What about the duc de Richelieu? Does Binet know whether the duc has any hand in this?"

"He thinks that, yes, there's a possibility. Richelieu is forever at the King's side, especially now that he's been named First Gentleman of the Bedchamber. The King relies on him and trusts his judgment about . . . women." She lifted a brush to her hair, which gleamed a golden auburn in the candlelight. She bent her head to one side and brushed her long hair.

"This heavy head of hair is a bother tonight, maman."

The older woman was frightened by the tone of defeat in her daughter's voice. For there was reason to be discouraged, reason to give it all up after years and years of preparing, step by step, omitting nothing, overlooking no detail. Richelieu. That was the name she dreaded hearing tonight. Binet wasn't sure; yet there was the possibility. And a young woman of the great nobility, too, with a grand family name. The kind of woman kings took for their official mistress. Not women of common birth like Reinette, a bourgeoise. That's what the world would say, that the King would never take a bourgeoise as his mistress. They are going to be wrong, she thought fiercely. The fortune-teller looked into my little girl's eyes and told her that the King of France would love her. Little queen. That's what we've worked and schemed for all these years. My own lovers believed in her, every single one of them. Le Normant de Tronheim, bless him, "uncle" Tronheim now, spared no expense in giving her the best education. And the lessons, the private lessons with the greatest artists and teachers. Monsieur de Voltaire says that our little Reinette is the most accomplished actress in Paris. And he should know!

"How old did you say this Mademoiselle de Fautrière is?"

"Very young. Not yet sixteen, I'd wager." She placed the brush on the table and turned to her mother. "She is extraordinarily beautiful, maman," she said softly.

"And so are you! So are you! What's more, you're twenty-four years old, a married woman whose salon is frequented by the most talented—and prosperous—personalities in Paris. You sing like an angel, play the harpsichord, paint, engrave—think of that!—act like a professional. No one does Molière better, says Monsieur de Voltaire. You're not only a beautiful woman but an accomplished woman. You know how to entertain a King who is easily bored, who dreads being bored above all else. You know how to use your talents. Now you show me a sixteen-year-old fresh out of the convent who can do as much!"

"I'm glad you waited up for me, maman. Especially tonight," she said, a smile lighting her face.

"Hmmph! Don't make such a fuss, and don't be discouraged. After all, the King was itching for you, even before the duchesse de Chateauroux died."

Reinette stiffened at her mother's vulgarity. "The King showed me many kindnesses," she said, brushing her hair thoughtfully.

"Of course he did. Even after the duchesse learned of your tricks in the forest." Madame Poisson laughed. "That's the kind of spirit you're going to need. You can't just sit back and moon."

"I won't sit back, maman. There's no time for that." She clasped her hands and resumed looking at herself in the mirror. She was thinking that the sun would be full over the horizon soon, and she had not yet gone to bed. She bit her lip anxiously. She needed plenty of sleep so that she would be full of energy at tonight's masked ball. The King hated listless women. He was so strong and energetic, holding her lightly but firmly as they danced. She closed her eyes tightly. Someday he would dance only with her. Only with her.

"You must just push your advantage home, that's all," her mother was saying. "You must make the most of it. The King knows you, or almost knows you. At least, he knows your face and something about you. Remember what the gossips say, the King loves young faces but he's afraid of fresh faces. For the King you are already a familiar face. That is bound to matter."

Madame Poisson rose stiffly to her feet. "Every morning I wake up with a new ache. If it's not my knees, it's my ankles and shoulders," she said, embracing her daughter. "Courage, *mon amour,*" she said.

Reinette looked up and met her mother's eyes in the mirror.

"I think I shall need courage, maman. I'm afraid."

"Afraid of what? Of losing him to that mere chit of a girl?"

"No, maman," she said, lowering her eyes. "I'm afraid that I love him. Afraid that I love him with all my heart."

11

Madame de Sabran panted noisily as she made her way up the twisting stone staircase leading to the maze of apartments under the eaves of the chateau. A powerful stench of urine rose from the cold stone steps. She lifted her skirts away from the filth on the landing at the top of the stairs. Before continuing up the stairs, she paused for breath. In the dark corners underneath the stairs she could see orange peels, rotting apples, and the contents of slop pails hastily emptied there by servants too lazy to walk to the privies in the courtyard.

She pushed her perfumed handkerchief to her nose. Oh, good Lord in Heaven above, preserve me from ever living in this rat hole, she thought. During the weeks when she was attending the Queen, she slept in her own small bedchamber in the Queen's suite of apartments. When she did not have duty at Versailles, she preferred to return to her luxurious mansion at the Jardin du Luxembourg. Why in God's name would Richelieu, who loved comfort and luxury more than any man on earth, keep a residence in this foul hovel? But she knew why. She knew why courtiers schemed and connived, flattered and bribed, for the privilege of having a few square meters in the ramshackle partitioned labyrinth up under the eaves. For what? For the privilege of saying, condescendingly, with a swagger, that one lived at Versailles, near the King. It was one more way of establishing rank, precedence, status.

Madame de Sabran stopped to mop her forehead. The landing was dark. Through an open doorway she could see narrow corridors onto which opened a bewildering number of doors. Down the corridors she could hear the buzz of conversation, laughter, and clinking glasses. A door slammed with a thud, as if someone had fallen against it. The air was close and fetid.

"Is that you, *mon amie*?" To her left she heard the low, rich voice of Richelieu. Squinting through the darkness she saw him standing with a candle at a nearby doorway.

"Just tell me how you manage not to get lost up here and wander around for days searching for your way out? Every time I climb those dreadful stairs, I wonder how old Louis XIV found courtiers foolish enough to want to live here." She was in a jocular mood. Richelieu did that to her. Just seeing his long, pointed nose lifted her spirits. They were easy with each other. They had never been lovers, and she found it hard to believe that women found Richelieu irresistible. Such a reputation the man had made for himself!

"Just wait until you see my new chest of drawers! Come along! Oyster veneer! It's truly magnificent!" He hastily pressed her cheeks with his and led her to his suite of rooms. As usual, his perfume was overpowering. He was wearing full court dress of pink and red cut velvet. The reflection of the colors against his face made his nose look red, the nose of a tippler. Which Richelieu was not. He was a cautious drinker. Poor dear, thought Madame de Sabran, looking at his elegant court dress, that's just about as handsome as he will ever be. Bah! Richelieu did not need to be handsome. He was far too clever.

Richelieu held the taper aloft and guided her through the darkness. In their heels, they were almost the same height, and Richelieu at forty-nine was as slim as a boy of twenty. Richelieu opened a heavy rosewood door with floral carvings. As she stepped into the room, Madame de Sabran was dazzled by the light of dozens of candles placed about the richly furnished room.

"Why, it's magnificent! Truly magnificent, *mon ami*," she said, lost in admiration of the opulent furnishings, the celery green and white wood panels, and gilt work everywhere.

"I knew you would like it. You mustn't think that all of us live like beggars up here. Come, have a look at the chest of drawers Antoine Gaudreau delivered just today." He stood beside an ornate sycamore chest, its sides swelling into glistening curves. "Have a look at the oyster veneer. It's perfect, isn't it?"

"Has the King seen this? It must be Gaudreau's masterpiece. Who would believe that disagreeable little man could produce anything so beautiful!" She ran her hands over the gilt handles of the drawers. Bending over, she could see her plump round face and her pearl necklace reflected in the polished surface of the chest. "Mark my words, the King will want a chest of drawers exactly like this for his private rooms. No wonder he trusts your taste. It's excellent. In every way," she said, looking at him meaningfully.

"That's precisely why I asked you to climb those odious stairs tonight. I knew that most of my neighbors," he said motioning toward the door, "would be going on to tonight's entertainments. We can have some rare privacy here. I don't have to worry about whispering in a corner for a change. Please, take a seat."

Madame de Sabran moved to the far side of the narrow room. Through the large round window placed low in the wall, she could just make out the lanterns in the gardens below. Richelieu's windows faced south. On the opposite side of the chateau the gardens had become a vast, smelly swamp as construction dragged on the new wing cobbled onto the main building.

"So, how do you think our little friend is progressing?" she asked.

"I was about to ask you that question. The Queen has been so capricious since her victory at Metz. Has she said any more about young Fautrière? Does she mention any one else to her ladies? Or to the bogus old fools who sit around and pray with her in the evening?"

"She still occasionally goes off into a rant about Diane at the *grand couvert*. Mostly to justify herself, to defend herself, because I understand that the King came down on her very hard. He was furious, as he might well be. She had no right to vent her spleen on the young girl, and she knows it."

"She has mentioned no one else? What I want to know is whether our girl is beginning to focus the King's attention."

"Doesn't he dance with her every night? That's exactly what I heard. That he has made quite a spectacle of himself in his attention to her."

"He's captivated by her all right. I'm sure of that. All the same, I'm worried that she won't be able to pull it off. She amuses him. He laughs, he sparkles when he's around her. She's lively, she's entertaining with her innocent ways. And you and I know how easily bored he is. If she continues to divert him, she is well on her way to . . . And I've got to work my way around that wretched father of hers. Michel de Fautrière. Stupid fool!" Richelieu frowned and rubbed his hands together.

"Stupid, yes. But not entirely a fool, my friend. Be careful. You must manage him gingerly if you are to be successful with Diane. She's devoted to him. Don't ask me why. But she is. She has tremendous affection for him. Though now and again I notice a rebellious streak. She's developing quite a critical eye, especially regarding her father. Still, don't overlook his power over Diane. It's very real."

"I know. I know. You're right. And it troubles me to have to tread delicately with such an ass. I don't trust him. He hangs on me every chance he can get, but I know he wants to elbow me out of the way. I'm sure of it. That's his style."

"He can't elbow you out of the way. He would be foolish to try. The King hasn't forgotten Michel's scheming against the old Cardinal. The King has an elephant's memory. He may drop a few emoluments into Michel's sweaty fist, but that will be the sum of it. Unless little Diane turns out to be another duchesse de Chateauroux," she said, watching the guarded expression on Richelieu's face.

"The little Fautrière is no Chateauroux," he said finally. "Nor will she ever be. And that's what worries me. She is very young. A child in many ways. Innocent. Too innocent, as the duchesse never was. The real difference is that the duchesse always knew what she wanted, though she did not know how to go about getting it. That's why she joined forces with me. The little Fautrière is so *inexperienced*. A virgin. The King ought to be excited by the novelty of that, if nothing else. But the King is not like most men. He's used to being taught. I don't think he wants to be a teacher." Wearily, he sat down beside her on the sofa.

They sat silently for a moment. The marquise could hear cautious footsteps in the room adjoining Richelieu's sitting room. A clink of silverware. The footmen were setting up for supper in the dining room. It must be close to midnight, she thought.

"I'm afraid you may be right," she said. "I'll have a talk with her. Very soon. She is probably unaware of what is really going on, despite the anxious hovering and coaching of her father. You're right. She is simply enjoying being a beautiful young thing, the envy of every woman in Paris. She may be afraid to let her thinking go much beyond that."

"Indeed. You can well understand why I'm worried."

Worried? Richelieu never ceased to astonish her. Why should he wear himself out conniving to make sure that the next royal mistress would be selected and tutored by himself? What more had he to gain? He had set his cap on being named maréchal de France, and, like a ripe plum, the glorious title had fallen into his hands. Ever grateful Louis. How boring these games are! Richelieu is certainly the wittiest, most—well, almost—learned courtier at Versailles.

Yet he fritters away his intellect and energy on trifles, on protocol, fussing with Byzantine rules of etiquette until the King himself very nearly goes mad. She sighed.

"On the other hand, Diane is a great beauty. The King must surely be ready for that after the de Nesle sisters." She tapped his knee playfully. "No offense intended."

Richelieu did not notice. He was gazing pensively into the flames of the candelabra next to her.

"I might add that I'm worried by evidence of Madame Le Normant d'Etioles' devilishly clever maneuvering."

"Diane told me that the King finds her—Diane, that is—much more attractive and much more interesting than Madame d'Etioles. She told me that several days ago when I called on her. I asked her specifically whether the King had mentioned the beautiful lady in the pink and blue carriages."

"What else *would* the King say?" Richelieu got to his feet impatiently.

The marquise rose and reached for her shawl. "I'll speak with Diane tomorrow, before dinner. We've left too much to her. We've let this matter drift."

If the truth be told, she did not give a fig whether Diane won the King's heart. But she would do what she could to help her old friend's scheme succeed. Besides, Diane de Fautrière would do France and its people far less harm than an ambitious intriguer like the duchesse de Chateauroux. Or that miserable bourgeoise Madame d'Etioles! Outrageous! The woman would stop at nothing! Well, let her carry on like a desperate madwoman. The King would never sully his royal person and position by taking a commoner into the *petits appartements* at Versailles. Diane, after all, was perfect. A beautiful born and bred aristocrat. And she was sweet and innocent. Not a schemer. How on earth would she survive at the King's side?

"And find out whatever you can about what Madame d'Etioles is up to. The rest of the court is laughing at her pretensions," he said, assisting Madame de Sabran to the door. "But I'm not laughing at her. Not yet. Not until Diane de Fautrière is securely installed in the *petits appartements* as the King's mistress.

The road between Versailles and Paris was frozen into gnarled mounds and ruts that cracked carriage frames and broke wheels and bruised passengers bent on shuttling between the theater and fireworks and balls of Paris and the pageantry of the wedding festivities at Versailles.

That night, the twenty-fifth of February, 1745, the grand ball would take place. Court rumor said that the King and eight of his courtiers would attend disguised as yew trees! It was the King's ingenious idea. He would hide his majestic identity behind the familiar shape and boughs of the yew trees outside in the sweeping gardens on the south side of the chateau. Women had been frantically sending their footmen in search of any clue, no matter how small, that would reveal which yew tree would, when the whirl of music and dance had stopped, turn out to be royal.

Madame de Sabran clucked impatiently to her women as they waited their turn to escape the crush of carriages spilling into the *cours de marbre* of the chateau. I have never seen such folly, she thought, yearning for her hot supper and her warm bed and a good book.

Her cumbersome coach and four cleared the main gates, the driver hallooing and whistling imperiously to declare his right of way. The February night was dark and cold, and Madame de Sabran had no regrets about turning her back on the night's glamorous festivities. Her ancient lady's maid had grumbled discontentedly. Old busybody! What did she want poking her nose around corners watching all the swells of court prance by in their absurd finery! The marquise pulled her fur rug about her, and rubbed her hands. The severe cold made the bones of her feet and hands ache. She would soak in a hot tub before going to bed. Let Alphonse complain to his heart's content about heating bath water! She sighed and closed her eyes.

Wheels screeched, the driver cursed and slashed with his whip, as the huge coach scrambled to the side of the road and stopped. The marquise woke with a small, pained cry of surprise, and pulled back the curtains at the window. She shut her eyes against the bright light as lanterns and flambeaux flashed by. The King, she thought sleepily. The King is returning for his supper before the ball. The caravan of horses and carriages thundered by. Her driver waited respectfully as the noise of the carriages and hallooing drivers faded down the road.

Perhaps I won't have a hot bath, after all, thought the marquise, yawning and snuggling down under the rug.

> [A] woman of great wealth and position . . . was seeking his affection through the most indecent and obvious maneuvers. She finally succeeded, although the King had told me that she did not interest him and that he found me much more attractive.

The King impatiently dismissed his attendants in order to eat alone a simple supper of soup and cold beef and bread. He had made a glutton of himself at dinner, wolfing down two roast hens and drinking far too much red wine. He was excited. In a short time his valet would help him get into the yew tree disguise for tonight's ball. The whole court found his idea extremely clever. The ladies would have much ado to identify him tonight. Louis smiled. Diane's face had glowed with pure delight when he told her the secret of how to recognize the royal yew tree.

Louis hummed to himself as he ground beans for his coffee. He wore a deep blue velvet dressing gown and velvet slippers lined in wool. The small dark paneled room smelled of coffee and cinnabar. Louis loosened his robe and sank contentedly into a chair by the blazing grate. Madame de Mailly used to tease him about brewing his own coffee and puttering about like a woman in his rooms as soon as attendants and courtiers had turned their backs. He still missed her. Despite her homely horse-face and skinny rump, she amused him. Simple pleasures. Good food, wit, laughter with familiar faces around the table. He must remember to send a purse round to her convent.

He shifted uncomfortably in his chair, thinking of Madame de Mailly chased out into a rainy night as her sister—and he—stood at a window and watched her lonely carriage depart through the gates toward the highway to Paris.

There was a scratching at the door. Binet, his second valet, entered the room with a furtive look on his face. He was a small man with one shoulder twisted higher than the other. He was devoted to Louis. Binet crossed the room rapidly and bent down to Louis's ear and began to whisper excitedly.

"Why are you whispering, my good man? As you can see, we are quite alone." His words seemed to reverberate around the small, cozy room.

"Sire, my cousin, Madame d'Etioles . . . you may remember crossing her path in the forest . . . while hunting last fall, sire, in the forest at Sénart . . . she earnestly begs your Majesty . . . she earnestly begs . . . " It was all a terrible mistake, and Binet was sorry that he had allowed Reinette and her mother to get the better of his judgment. He knew the King relished his few minutes of solitude, free from ceremony—he had precious few—of sitting about the fire and drinking his coffee and toasting his toes before dressing for the night's festivities. The King was known to be easy with his servants, but he also had a nasty temper that could sting and sting again.

"What is it, Binet? What are you going on about?" Louis said.

Binet scowled and plucked at his ears. His hunched shoulder cast a grotesque shadow against the wall.

"Sire," he paused, losing his courage again. "My cousin is here to petition you on behalf of her husband . . . " His voice faltered, as Louis frowned irritably, putting his cup noisily on the table. "Madame d'Etioles, you recall that you several times made gifts of venison and wild fowl to her table. You recall, she was the lady in pink driving about in the pastel blue carriage and . . . "

"Oh, yes . . . yes," Louis said pleasantly, remembering the lovely young woman with luminous eyes under a pile of sun-filled auburn locks and intriguing green eyes. Or were they blue? Wonderful dancer, too. Until Diane came along, his most amusing partner. "And she is here?" He sounded genuinely puzzled. "You say, she is here?"

"Waiting, sire. Hoping to see you before tonight's ball . . . briefly . . . on behalf of her husband, a tax farmer."

A brilliant flash of emerald washed silk appeared abruptly in the doorway and swept forward into a profound obeisance at Louis's feet. With a magician's sleight of hand Binet disappeared, supplanted by a luscious vision in green. Magic. As if by magic. Startled, excited, Louis stared at the suppliant figure at his feet. Kneeling before him, her firm, round breasts seemed to swing free of her bright green bodice. Her thick auburn hair glowed like sand-polished copper in the firelight.

Slowly she lifted her head. She did not speak. Louis reached out his hand to raise her to her feet. Without taking her eyes from his, she edged toward him on her knees, in a fluid, sensuous movement. Still holding him with her eyes she gently placed her hands on his thighs. With a languorous caress she pushed aside his velvet robe, and began to fondle his naked thighs with long, sweeping strokes. Louis gripped the arms of his chair and threw back his head. He lifted his hips, straining for the pleasure of her mouth.

"Oh, my dear," he moaned plaintively.

Diane glanced out the carriage window. "Look at that crowd! How on earth will we ever get through the gates?"

She was full of impatience, ready for another evening of dancing and laughter and excitement in the King's arms. In the legendary Hall of Mirrors the last spectacular ball of the wedding celebrations was about to begin. At eleven o'clock on this especially inhospitable night of the twenty-fifth of February 1745 a chaotic jumble of carriages and people clogged the Avenue de Paris. Braces of thousands and thousands of candles illuminated the majestic façade of Versailles and the upturned faces of the mob, awestruck, mouths agape.

Richelieu, lounging indolently against the deep maroon cushions of his carriage drawled, "Oh, don't worry, my dear. My men have a way with crowds, you know." He sat upright and tucked back the window curtain to have a look. "Savage brutes," he chuckled, "They'll just have their bit of fun."

Diane drew her ermine cape closer, merely for the pleasure of feeling its silky caress, for Richelieu's carriage was as cozy and warm as a hearthside nook. The cape was hers to keep, a gift from the duc, and her father had said not a word, though he had been furious when Richelieu arrived and swept aside Madame Clarisse's spruce green Lyon silk gown he had chosen especially for the ball. Richelieu had shoved aside the costly gown with a dismissive, "Banal, my good man. This is a *bal paré,* after all." Diane saw her father clench his fist and his neck grow red as fire. She knew that he could not bear Richelieu's *my good man.* But the duc was right. It was indeed a costume ball, the climax of two weeks of feverish celebration. "She shall go to the ball as Diana the Huntress. A knowing nod, I might add, to the King's love of the hunt. And his love of beautiful women," Richelieu gazed into her eyes and slowly smiled. Diane thought her father looked abashed as he swiftly turned his back to them. Richelieu pretended not to notice. "She will stand by the statue of Diana in the Hall of Mirrors, inviting one and all to draw their own conclusions as to which is the fairest."

"But the King will be disguised as a yew tree!" her father had remonstrated. "I chose the spruce green, don't you see, because it makes a pair. The spruce and the yew together. It makes a nice conceit."

Unperturbed, Richelieu plucked the sinuous white gown from its linen case. "And your girdle," he added, holding aloft a magnificent coil of gold. "Now, where is my man to do your hair?"

"No one touches my daughter's hair except me," her father said in that familiar, quiet, strained voice, the one that preceded his violent outbursts. She watched both men carefully, pleased by her own detachment. For two weeks now, she had been enclosed in the magic circle of the King's power, she had seen the change in the way others addressed her, the caution, the deference, and she realized full well that one day Richelieu and her own father as well would curry her favor, would approach her with a tiny corner of fear in the heart. Had the duchesse de Chateauroux not demanded that the King dismiss her sister from Versailles before she herself would grant all his wishes in the *petits appartements?* And had Louis not obeyed her command, standing by the window on a rainy night, watching the departure of Madame de Mailly's carriage, and weeping? Diane knew that she could never bring herself to be so cruel. It was coarse and vulgar to be mean to one's own family. But just to imagine for a moment, to picture herself wielding that kind of power was both exhilarating and soothing.

Before the duc's carriage reached the Ambassadors' Stairs, there was a great deal of shouting, cursing, and shoving so that again and again the massive carriage tilted first to one side, then to the other. Once inside the chateau, Diane lost Richelieu as a crowd of admirers rushed forward to encircle her and to sweep her along to the red damask Salon d'Hercules, where the orchestra was about to take up its instruments to play. The bleacher seats that had been set up in the seventeen towering windows of the vast, elongated space were already crammed with masked spectators.

Bantering, squinting a little, Diane searched the masked Pierrots, scaramouches, harlequins, pirates, and dairymaids surrounding her for her trusted friends, Madeleine and Jean-Christophe.

"Ah, search no further, Diana, for those two madcap cousins," an exceedingly tall and upright lion murmured as he took her hand and led her off to the first cotillion, "I have eaten them both." Diane laughed and stood on tiptoe to look into the dark, infatuated eyes of the duc de Soissons.

What luck, Diane thought, to be led out by a superb dancer and one of the most sought-after men at court. The King would surely be jealous when he saw them together. She scanned the immense space as the cotillion began. Hundreds of people milled about, some dancing, some seated on the bare floor eating delicacies from the two buffet tables set up at each end of the hall. But there was no sign of the King.

As time flew by in dance after dance, and Soissons the lion was swiftly replaced in turn by a bishop, a magistrate, a Persian, and a clown, Diane could not remember ever having so much fun. The wit, the delicious compliments, the laughter, the sumptuous costumes and jewelry, surely there could be no more brilliant society in the entire world.

Suddenly, the music stopped, a blare of trumpets sounded, a heavy thump, then guards called out, *"Place, gare!"* A hush fell over the crowd, women dropped to a deep curtsey, and men bowed to the waist, their swords swishing and banging against the floor, for even lions and clowns could not present themselves before royalty without the sword of nobility. Through a mirrored door the Queen with her retinue entered the hall. She was dressed magnificently in a white silk gown decorated with quantities of seed pearl, and in her hair she wore the fabled Regent and Sancy diamonds. The Dauphin, costumed as a humble gardener, and his bride of two days as a flower girl followed the Queen's party.

"What time is it?" asked Diane anxiously, turning to the fearsome-looking dragon at her side.

"Almost one o'clock. As soon as the Queen is settled in her niche, we'll have a set of minuets." The dragon smiled winningly as he held out his hand. "Shall we?"

One o'clock? But where was the King? He loved to dance; it was one of his greatest pleasures, and he was a wonderful dancer. So relaxed and easy, never impatient, his step always attuned to the rhythm. Where could he be? Usually, the Queen made her entrance hours after the King.

She brushed aside the touch of anxiety clouding her smile as she held out her hand to the dragon. "Why not?" she said.

Minuet followed minuet, interminably, Diane thought, no longer paying much attention to the music or to the sweet flattery of her admirers. What was delaying the King? An uproar started up at the entrance by the Ambassadors' Stairs. Thunderous applause, laughter, pushing, and shouting swept through the crowd. Ah, the King, at last!

"The Turks! The Turks!" someone yelled, and the immense hall roared with laughter. A troop of courtiers disguised as Turks with flowing amber robes and enormous, towering turbans studded with precious stones, pushed their way through the throng.

Diane no longer tried to conceal her panic. Something was going wrong. Where was the King? She turned, and, at a distance she noticed a tall, lithe footman in dark green livery making his way swiftly in her direction. A message from the King, most certainly, though the livery was very odd. But, of course, everything must be kept secret. For a while yet . . . The footman hurriedly made his way toward her, elbowing through the crowd, twisting and turning, with astonishing speed. As she turned to face him, he reached out and placed his index finger on her brow.

"Take that frown off this noble brow, my lady!"

"Jean-Christophe!" Diane cried. "Where have you been? And what are you doing in your footman's uniform, you silly!"

"Cost me not a *sou*, that's why. Tell me about that frown."

"Oh, I don't know," she said evasively. "All things Turkish are such a vogue these days. It's tiresome, really."

At that moment, trumpets blared, and all fell silent. Her spirits soaring, Diane curtseyed gracefully, straining for a glimpse of the King. *"Place, gare!"* shouted the guards, as the King and seven of his courtiers made their way carefully into the assembled crowd. They were dressed identically in dark green stockings, green pantaloons and tightly fitted green jackets. Resting on their shoulders and covering the entire head with horizontal openings for the eyes, nose, and mouth, the disguise was made entirely of yew trees branches fashioned in the shape of the topiary yew trees in the Versailles gardens. Once again, gasps of admiration, applause, and laughter at the ingenious disguise whipped through the crowd.

"The yew trees, that was the King's idea!" Diane whispered proudly to Jean-Christophe.

"But which one *is* the King?" he asked, genuinely mystified. "They all look exactly alike."

"Oh, I can tell. I shall know him immediately." Richelieu had taken great pains to make sure that she would know how to recognize the King. All of the yew trees would be wearing pink garters just below the knee. Only the King, however, would be wearing on his garter a red ruby pin shaped like a rose with a diamond at its center. Richelieu needn't have fussed so much. The King himself had over the past week told her exactly how to recognize him at the next ball. The King adored sharing secrets. She found this wonderfully endearing. What she loved more than anything else, though, were his pet names, his habit of whispering *mon coeur, mon joli coeur— my darling, my pretty darling*—while they danced, his voice like a gentle caress. And when he took leave of her each night, in giving her accolades, he would slowly press his lips, just slightly, only slightly, to the left and to the right of her lips, then draw back his handsome head and look into her eyes and smile, as if he had done something quite wicked and were pleased with himself. His lips, his voice, his perfume—just thinking of him made her knees weak.

Already, the crowd was falling back, making room for the yew trees. Two or three women rushed forward, curtsied, and held out a hand in invitation to dance, for the orchestra had begun to play.

"How bold!" Diane said, as the women led their willing partners to the Salon d'Hercules. "Did you see that? And there's another one." While she and Jean-Christophe were making their way toward the remaining yew trees, Diane was aware that others were watching her.

"*La chasse au roi.* They think they're about to seduce the King," Jean-Christophe said. "Some have seen the Young Pretender here, too, Prince Charles Edward of England. So the ladies have a choice in their royalty."

But Diane was no longer listening. She was staring intently at the garters of the only two yew trees remaining as they came striding purposefully down the long hall. At rather a fast pace, she noticed, and this seemed odd. She leaned to the right, and there, yes! The ruby pin, just as the King had described it! She dropped Jean-Christophe's arm and sprang joyfully into the path of the advancing pair. At last! It was past two o'clock. What had kept the King so long?

Just two steps away from the King, she stopped, waiting for him to bow and take her hand. Instead, as if she were completely invisible, the King strode quickly past her, never once slowing his step or turning his head toward her. Her heart racing, Diane felt dizzy, as if she had completely lost her bearings. Around her, the crowd had suddenly gone very still and quiet, except for some low, furtive whispering. Slowly, she turned and watched the King as he made his way swiftly down the hall.

The other yew tree dropped away and disappeared into the crowd while the King continued alone. He was clearly heading toward the statue of Diana the Huntress! She was both relieved and exasperated. What a simpleton she had been! Richelieu had told her to stand next to the statue. But hadn't that been just a pretty compliment? Smiling now, she hurried down the hall after the King, anxious not to displease him by not being in the appointed meeting place.

As the crowd parted along the passage of the King, she could make out the statue very clearly. But standing beside the statue was a tall, beautiful shepherdess, her shiny dark curls tumbling from her wide straw hat and down around her shoulders. The King came to a halt just in front of her, and the woman's smile was a vision of pure joy. When Diane saw the King take the woman's hand and kiss it, then encircle her waist with a familiarity that she knew only too well, she stopped, overwhelmed by a devastating feeling of loss. She wanted to move, but could not. She remained standing in the King's wake, staring hopelessly after the pair as they started to dance, the lovely face of the shepherdess aglow with happiness.

12

A footman rolled the slipper bath into the Queen's dressing room. After the bathers had brought linens and soaps and perfumed oils, Madame de Sabran scratched at the door. "Your bath is ready, your Majesty," she said, opening the door a little. She heard short steps about the room, as the Queen's tire woman helped her into a robe.

The marquise sighed impatiently and took up her post next to the tub, ready to assist the Queen into her bath. Her Majesty's bathers whispered together as they busied themselves around the dressing table and the tub. The whole chateau is on its ear today, the marquise thought irritably. As soon as she could escape from the Queen's service, she would find Richelieu and would learn exactly what had happened last night at the ball. Failing that, she would look for Michel de Fautrière, though, if the rumors were in any way true, he would be lying drunk somewhere. With his mistress. She fidgeted nervously with her sleeve. What could be keeping the old cow?

The Queen lumbered ponderously into the room and nodded to the marquise, who stepped forward to take her dressing gown. She was dressed in an ample gown of English flannel, a dark, dull ecru, buttoned down to the hem. Madame de Sabran dipped a finger into the water and helped her onto a low step stool. The Queen slipped into the water and one of the bathers placed a cover over one end of the tub.

"Shall I read to you, Majesty?" the marquise asked.

"No, thank you," the Queen said coolly. Her oily, graying hair was plastered to her head, and both her cheeks were blistered by rouge. The old cow is in a foul mood today, thought the marquise. I wager she'll keep me reading and praying with her until the dinner hour. And then some.

The Queen sat soaking in the tub. From time to time she shifted her legs and after a few minutes, she called for more hot water. She sat quietly as the water was being poured into the tub, then with a wave of the hand, she dismissed her bathers and turned to the marquise.

"You did not attend the ball last night, marquise," she said, and without waiting for a reply, continued. "Really a charming novelty, the King's idea of disguising himself and his favorites in yew tree branches." Having lost two lower teeth, the Queen spoke with wet, sibilant sounds. She waited for the marquise to say something.

"Yes. I understand that it was a great success. Really quite charming," Madame de Sabran said finally.

The Queen soaped the sleeves of her gown and dipped them into the water.

"Do you know this Madame d'Etioles?" she asked, abruptly turning her clear gray eyes toward the marquise.

"No, Majesty. I know the gossip about her. As I'm sure you must."

"The King danced only with her last night." Her voice was flat and harsh. Her heavy, round face sagged with disapproval.

"So I've heard."

"What else are they saying?"

They are saying that you needn't bother with your perfumed baths anymore, the marquise thought, then regretted her cruelty. She looked at the folds of fat under the Queen's chin, her sparse, graying eyebrows, her unhealthy blotched complexion, the complexion of a voracious eater. The marquise despised herself for her heartless thoughts.

"I believe they are laughing more than anything else, Majesty. Laughing at this foolish woman for throwing herself at the King." She hoped that her voice was kind and reassuring.

"It's unimaginable! The nerve of this woman, her persistence, why, she never stops, she never gives up!" The Queen said, her fat chins wobbling in dismay.

The marquise laughed. "It is truly unbelievable, as you say. Dressing up in pink and driving out into the forest in a blue carriage one day and the next, dressing in a blue gown and driving out in a pink carriage. How could any decent woman dream up such things?"

"She sounds like a woman possessed," the Queen said. "Possessed of the devil of ambition."

"They say a fortune teller read her palm when she was only nine years old and predicted that she would one day be the mistress of the King of France."

The Queen stared at her, nonplussed. "Yes. I've heard that rumor. The woman is possessed. She will stop at nothing. These are the devil's doings," she said despondently. "The King danced only with her last night."

"Are you sure it was the King? I'm told that there were several ladies who ended up behind stairways last night . . . " the marquise hesitated. Was she speaking too boldly to the Queen? "What I mean is that several ladies thought for certain they were dancing with the King, so wonderfully made were the disguises of the courtiers."

"I'm sure. I'm sure it was the King. He made a fool of himself dancing with her. Just as he made a fool of himself flirting with that little Fautrière creature," she added spitefully.

The marquise thought of Richelieu. What were his plans now that his protégée had stumbled? And perhaps fallen?

"The King, however, if you'll allow me to say, is not such a fool, Majesty, as to treat a bourgeoise seriously. Madame d'Etioles is, they say, extremely accomplished, very well educated. Nonetheless, the fact remains that she is of low birth. And that she is married to a tax farmer. The fortune teller has made mischief in the wretched woman's life, egging her on to aspire to a position that her birth prohibits."

The Queen ran her tongue thoughtfully over the blank spaces of the two missing teeth. "You're right, of course," she said. "The King would never lower the dignity of his rank, he would never bring this shame to his family. To France. For it would be a terrible shame inflicted on the country." She began to soap her neck thoughtfully.

"The little Fautrière, now. She belongs to one of the oldest houses in France." She looked at the marquise, a malicious glint in her eye, for she had heard her friends—her pietistic cabal as her enemies called them—hint that Madame de Sabran and the duc de Richelieu were intriguing to put the little Fautrière in the *petits appartements.* "That's about all she has to cling to right now, isn't it?"

Diane heard the clock in her sitting room strike twelve, and still she did not move. She did not summon Marianne. She ran her fingers over her bell and dropped it into her lap, but she did not ring for Marianne. Her hair fell in tangled locks down her back and over her shoulders, for last night, in returning from the ball, she had simply snatched the pins from her hair. What time had she crept home last night? After dawn probably. The weak morning light was already falling across her bed, and Marianne had pulled together the bed curtains so that she could sleep. But she had not slept.

The door of the sitting room opened, and she could hear the short tap-tap-tap of high heels on the parquetry.

"Papa!" she said aloud to the empty room. Her stomach heaved. She swallowed hard against the taste of sour, burning bile. A sudden rush of tears stung her eyes and blurred her vision, as the comte strode into the room.

He bent his cheeks to hers. "Not dressed yet? Aren't you expected at Madame de Sabran's dinner party this afternoon? As usual? Who knows? You might have an amorous tête-à-tête with your fine friend. Armand." He moved to the window and stood looking at her.

"Oh, papa," she said in a hushed voice. "Armand had nothing to do with what happened. You know that. I sent my regrets to the marquise. Laurent took my card over an hour ago."

She watched her father warily. With his back to the window, his face was in the shadows. His face was puffy, and he wore no wig. As he leaned down to kiss her cheeks, the sharp smell of brandy and snuff had stung her nostrils. Was he drunk? Usually this meant that he would be boring, he would start to drone on and on, repeating old stories, boasting, clowning. But now, this morning, after what happened last night, would he go into a rage again?

"Well, what did you say? That you were otherwise engaged, being the most sought-after belle of the ball?" he snarled sarcastically, his lips curled contemptuously. Diane sat mutely, her hands clasped, her eyes brimming with tears. "For pity's sake, at least have enough spirit to get bathed and dressed!"

He suddenly felt overcome with weariness and slumped into a chair. Like a frightened animal, peering with watery eyes from its lair, Diane followed his every movement. She said nothing. He shook his head in dismay. He had been confident—as had Richelieu, damn him—everything was sailing along. He had never seen the King so giddy, so captivated with anyone. Perhaps with the Vintimille when she first came to court. Yes. And she was young, too. Though Diane is much younger. Damn! He could feel the blood pounding in this throat. To have counted on a silly, prankish girl for so much! How could a child know what it meant to be one of the King's inner circle, to be summoned from the antechamber in the evenings where scores of courtiers would be milling about, waiting to be called, to hear the footman read his name, and then to mount the narrow, private staircase to the King's cabinets for small, intimate supper parties with—what? twelve, fourteen at the most—favorites. *Favorites!* Afterwards, drinking coffee prepared and served by the King himself! The wit, the laughter. The favors! Already he had prepared his petition for minister of the royal establishments. A certain thing! The King would not have stopped there! How could a witless girl, too pretty for her own good, know anything about the world? And the ways of the world?

"Papa," she said. "I did try. I did try, but it was no use. I knew which one was the King. He saw me, I know he did, but he danced every dance with the shepherdess. I waited and waited; we were to dance all the minuets together. It was agreed." She leaned forward in her chair. The comte did not appear to be listening. He lay slumped against the back of his chair, his eyes closed. "Don't you believe me?"

It was true. She had done her best at the ball. It had all been a dream, hadn't it? The King's smiling blue eyes. Cornflower blue in the candlelight. Ice blue in the sunshine. Pressing her hand, her waist, kissing her ear, her eyes, calling her loving pet names in a sweet husky voice. It had all been a dream. A dream that she wanted to go on forever and ever. The King had made her feel like the most beautiful woman in the world. How could she doubt it? And that had given her strength. And joy. She had believed in her new strength.

"Papa . . . papa . . . who was the shepherdess?" she asked meekly.

The comte opened his eyes and stared at the ceiling, where the three Graces in varying hues of blues and greens cavorted with Cupid.

"Madame Jeanne-Antoinette d'Etioles, daughter of Madame Poisson, one of the more compliant courtesans of Paris, daughter of a scoundrel convicted of fraud and in exile, wife of a midget tax-farmer, who, as it happens, is the nephew of Madame Poisson's lover," he said, reciting in a flat voice as if by rote.

He straightened his head and gave Diane a malevolent look. "Precisely the sort of woman to share the life of the King of France, wouldn't you say?"

Diane's hands grew ice cold. Madame d'Etioles! Last night she had been sure of it. But she had kept repeating to herself, it cannot be! it cannot be! The King finds me much more beautiful, he said so . . . he said so, she thought despondently.

The comte closed his eyes again and leaned his head against his chair. Peacefully, as if he had merely roused himself from a catnap.

"Have you spoken with the duc de Richelieu?" he asked, without looking at her.

"No," she said, her voice scarcely more than a whisper. "He called his morning, but I could not see him. I felt unwell. He sent up this for me. A gift from the King." She reached toward the table next to her chair.

The comte's head snapped forward. "What gift? Let me see."

Diane held out to him a small portrait of Louis XV framed in shagreen, the latest craze at court. On the back, the signature of Jean-Claude Galluchat. Louis was painted with his head half turned to the side, his gaze fixed on a distant object. His cheeks were very rosy pink and his eyes very blue.

The comte stood and held the portrait at arm's length, studying it in silence.

"Hmmph!" he said finally, carelessly placing it flat on the table. "Have Marianne pack your things. Tomorrow you leave for Corcheval." He turned on his heels and left the room.

Book Three

13

From her chair on the terrace Diane could see the mowers, lifting their scythes in unison, swinging, bending, in hypnotic, fluid motion. The sweet smell of freshly mown grass and field flowers drifted in the air. Diane, her back to the sun, listened to the peaceful country sounds and wondered why they stabbed her heart with longing for the muddy, filthy, chaotic streets of Paris.

On the path just beyond the lake Sophie was coming from the fields with an armful of Queen Anne's lace, huge sprays of it spilling over her thin, graceful arms. Diane smiled as she watched the diminutive figure making her way toward the terrace. Her little sister adored wild flowers, which she offered to Clotilde or Diane as if they were rare treasures from an exotic land.

"Has Sophie been wandering in the fields again?" Catherine emerged from the house, a Moroccan embossed portfolio in her hands. She had untied the satin ribbons. On this fine spring morning she had elected to stay at home instead of riding about the fields and villages with Pierre, one of the comte's stable boys, an eight-year old with a clubfoot and a chronically runny nose. The two made an odd pair, the handsomely dressed young lady and the ragged boy astride one of the comte's finest Arabic mares. This morning, however, soon after breakfast Catherine had disappeared into the library to prowl amongst her father's musty books and papers.

Diane looked up from her tapestry frame. Her feet, clad only in dimity slippers, were toasting on the sun-warmed flagstones of the terrace. Sophie had slipped behind the sculptured evergreens marking the foot of the garden from which the banks sloped down to a small lake stocked with speckled bass.

"Sophie gets a good dose of sunshine with her walks. She looks stronger and healthier every day," Diane said, determined to ignore Catherine's nasty tone.

"Do the stylish ladies at court go about gathering weeds for their Saint Louis crystal vases?" Catherine asked sarcastically.

"Oh, sometimes. At Chantilly or Sceaux . . . ." Diane's heart skipped a beat. "If there are fields, that is, ladies do collect Queen Anne's lace." Quickly, with an awkward stab of her needle, she bent her head to her tapestry, memories of her journey through a wintry night returning with a fresh, raw sting. When she and Marianne left Paris in the comte's coach, they had drawn the curtains closed, blotting out the now familiar sights—the gardens of the Palais du Luxembourg, the Invalides, the Palais Royal, the Louvre and the Tuileries gardens, the Hôtel de Ville, and the Ecole Militaire, its domes still unfinished. The scenes of her triumphs now mocked her in her humiliation. She did not need her father's sarcasm to feel it in all its galling weight. The searing pain of the night of the yew tree ball when she had stood watching the magnificent shepherdess hold the King spellbound in dance after dance. The same King who had made her feel like the most desirable woman in the world now gazed past her unseeing. That night she averted her eyes from the pitying looks of her friends and acquaintances, for after almost two years in Paris society she was well known, surrounded by admiring looks and elaborate flattery. She saw their astonishment at what was taking place on the night that was to be another triumph for Diane. And, on the faces of some, their satisfaction, yes, at seeing her spurned. After the ball, after the sleepless night, she had welcomed the idea of leaving the court and Paris. Like a coward, creeping away so that she would not have to face the contempt, the ridicule—who knows, perhaps even the humiliation of her name on broadsheets circulating in the streets. She wanted to escape, to get away from the fickle admiration that had swelled her vanity and made being admired her sole occupation, the obsessive center of her existence.

"Of course, I wouldn't know about all that, would I? Never having been to Paris. Or to court. Like papa's little pet," said Catherine, tossing her head angrily.

Calmly, Diane twisted her thread into a tidy knot and smoothed it with her finger. She sensed her sister's barely suppressed rage but said nothing, for she knew from long experience that silence would infuriate Catherine more than any sort of retort.

Catherine was determined not to let go. She had wanted a fight since her father came to fetch her and Sophie from the convent. From a few of the comte's remarks, but mainly from the fact that Diane had returned to the country, Catherine guessed that Diane had misbehaved in some way, had done something perhaps shameful enough to be sent back to the country again. Perhaps not in disgrace, but certainly something was amiss. Catherine intended to pick and goad until she found out. And then she would make the most of it.

"What happened? Did papa's little pet get bored with the excitement of Paris? And papa couldn't stand to see his precious girl unhappy?"

Diane dropped her tapestry hoop, threw back her head, and laughed merrily. "Of course! How did you know? I was bored, certainly, but mostly I missed you, my dearest sister. I missed your delightful conversation. Remember our noisy discussions in the convent about d'Alembert? You were brilliant."

Catherine stared at her in consternation. Her sister sounded quite sincere. Diane smiled sweetly before bending again to her needlepoint. "Anyway . . . ," Catherine said finally with a nervous shrug, clearly nonplussed by the compliment. "He could have sent you back to the convent. Instead of here with your fancy ladies' maid."

Sophie, out of breath after the long climb from the garden, collapsed into a chair after spreading her bouquet on the table.

"Very pretty, Sophie," Diane said brightly, relieved to have foiled Catherine's bad mood so easily. Catherine could pry all she liked, if that pleased her. She would never confide in her what had happened at court. "You must have Laurent put them into a vase right away. They wilt easily, you know, because they prefer to live in the fields."

Catherine loathed Diane's affectionate nature. She looked at her sister's pale creamy skin, her deep gray eyes. On the table Diane had dropped the mask that she always used when she went into the sun. Catherine and Sophie ran about at midday without so much as a bonnet sometimes. Never Diane, though.

Sophie yawned. "I'm ready for dinner. Though I did eat some berries in the grove," she held out her stained hands with a mischievous glance, and Diane beamed, as Sophie knew she would. She had not grown more than an inch or two since they had parted, but her figure had begun to develop. Her small breasts strained against the bodice of her cambric dress. She had Diane's dark eyes and finely shaped features.

"I'm going to dress for dinner," Catherine said glumly. "Will our illustrious father be joining us? If so, there are some matters here that I would like to discuss with him," she said tapping the leather portfolio.

"Catherine! You haven't been going through papa's papers, have you?" Diane asked.

"Why not? Of course, I have. Someone ought to. No one could manage as badly as papa. My ideas can't possibly be as rotten as his. If he has any," she said, her voice heavy with contempt.

The cavernous dining room dwarfed the three sisters as they sat quietly finishing dinner. Laurent and two older footmen hurried in and out of the room, punctiliously serving the three girls as if they were royalty. For a time Diane and Sophie tried to keep a conversation going, but they finally lapsed into silence. How far from the witty, animated dinner conversations in Paris, the card games, the musical evenings, the beautiful crystal and china, the silver service! Diane sighed. It was a magical world, and she had lost her place in it.

She drained her glass of water and called for more. The late afternoon was turning unseasonably hot. Afterwards, she would doze on the canapé in her sitting room while Marianne read to her.

She found it impossible to imagine how she could have endured the bleak loneliness of the country without Marianne, who had poured all her energy into keeping her mistress's spirit from sliding into depression. Corcheval, damp and clammy in the fogs and mists of late winter, seemed withdrawn into a cheerless sleep. The furniture in all the great rooms had been shrouded in coarse linen, serenely gathering dust as the months passed and nothing stirred within the old stone walls, except the cook's brindle cat, stalking field mice and chipmunks. She and Marianne had wandered about muffled in thick woolen shawls, huddling for warmth around the great hearth in the kitchen, like the local gentry.

They played cards—Marianne had learned *comète* just before leaving Paris—they spent hours dressing their hair in fantastic ways, they read to each other from the romances Marianne had thrown into her trunk before their departure, and, as the sun warmed the fields and ancient flagstones of the terrace, they put on their sturdiest boots and walked to Beaubéry, the nearest village where they giggled at the ogling stares of the peasants.

Then, Marianne's gaiety faltered. She lost her appetite and stared gloomily at the empty landscape. Diane wrote to her father that she was sending Marianne back to Paris, to work for the marquise de Sabran, who would surely take her in, but Marianne refused. As did Laurent, who was to accompany Marianne to the city. He would not hear of leaving his young mistress.

Diane noisily cleared her throat and glared at Catherine. Across the table her sister sat playing with her food, her head drooping and the corners of her mouth twisted into a sullen grimace. She was overdressed for an uncomfortably hot afternoon in the country. At almost fifteen Catherine was already taller than Diane, and rounder, more voluptuous. Her thick blond hair, always a little untidy, did little to enhance her plain, sharp features. A long nose gave her face a look of drooping melancholy. Since returning home, Catherine watched Diane carefully, copying every detail of her dress, her manners at table, her walk, and even her makeup, which filled Catherine with disgust. Nonetheless, she studiously painted her face a ghoulish white and smeared large rounds of rouge on her thin, angular cheeks. Diane mistook her sister's dedicated imitation for admiration—or perhaps envy—of all that she had learned in Paris.

"I miss papa," Sophie said in a distressed, little voice. "He makes me laugh."

"He's inspecting his estates across the river. Don't worry, he should be back this evening," Diane said.

Much to her relief, the comte, after his return to the country, treated her with his former affectionate concern as if the hateful, angry scenes in Paris had never occurred. As March turned to April and the old orchards burst into clouds of pink and white bloom, her father arrived, and after a good night's sleep, hurried off to Neuilly-les-Dames to fetch her sisters from the convent. When Catherine and Sophie in their plain muslin convent frocks piled out of the carriage with their crumpled, battered boxes, Diane had to shake herself to believe that days, weeks, months had passed. The familiar world of lessons and matins and vespers and the bells of the convent engulfed her— the smell of candle wax and incense, the cold stone floors of the dormitory.

Their life resumed much as it had been before she and her father boarded the houseboat for the river journey to Paris. Catherine and Sophie, without a murmur, took up their familiar place in the rooms in the nursery at the top of the house, while Diane remained in grandmaman's rooms in the yellow suite. The comte came and went, grumbling about the management of his lands, the indolence of the peasantry, their greed, their backwardness. Uncle Philippe and the marquise would be coming down for the summer season, he said.

He no longer expressed anxiety about his financial affairs, except to remark, casually, that the savings on the girls' convent pension would prove useful. Catherine seemed all but invisible to her father, but, often, Diane noticed that he would stare thoughtfully at Sophie.

Expressionless, the three footmen stood at the double doors of the dining room.

"You must finish, Catherine," Diane said. "Sophie and I are waiting for the next course."

Catherine made no reply. She sat utterly still, studying the messy disorder of food on her plate.

"It's very impolite, you know. Making others wait while you dally with your food."

Sophie dropped her fork to her plate, and Catherine jumped at the sudden noise. She raised her head and looked around with a confused, bewildered air, like a stunned animal.

"What was that noise?" she asked meekly, as if frightened by her own voice.

"Only my fork, Catherine. I dropped my fork. I'm sorry."

Catherine swung her gaze back to her plate and sat looking at it as if she did not know why it was there or what she was doing. She propped her head in her hands and stared stolidly at her plate. Suddenly, she let her arms fall onto the table and pushed herself up, standing swaying against the table. Diane looked up with alarm at her sister's face. It was swollen, and very red around the throat and ears.

"Catherine! What is it?" Sophie cried.

As Catherine turned toward the noise of her sister's voice, she fell crashing back against her chair and onto the floor. With a low moan she turned her face to the cool marble floor.

"Laurent! Laurent! Quickly! Help!" Diane cried out as she ran to Catherine's side.

The comte de Fautrière had lingered over brandy and a long pipe at Roger Saint-Valérien's manor, and as he galloped over the darkened roads to Corcheval, he realized than he was more than a little drunk. And he didn't care. A man with his financial worries had to drink to get by.

His horse clipclopped noisily through Beaubéry, where the villagers were fast asleep behind shuttered windows and doors. A lone goat bleated in a nearby barnyard. As he skirted a huge, damp manure heap near the blacksmith's stable, the comte wrinkled his nose in disgust. God, to get back to Paris again! But patience, patience yet a while. It was best to get out of Paris when he did, after the King had so clearly lost his wits over Madame d'Etioles at the yew tree ball. The court had been in total disarray, as was fitting. The King would never settle a commoner in the private apartments of Versailles. Let him have his fun with her. This, too, would pass. And then, Diane, older and wiser, would return to the scene, more bewitching than ever. In the meantime, the country air—and the prospect of being buried in the country forever—is doing her an immense amount of good. I haven't dropped out of the game yet, he thought fiercely.

The night wind was freshening, and he drew his hood over his felt hat as he turned into the long, steep driveway to the chateau. For a moment he thought that he saw lights, a lantern perhaps. A mare foaling in the stables, most likely. He headed his horse toward the stables.

Unsteadily, the comte crossed the kitchen garden to the back hall and started up the stairway to his room. To his astonishment every lustre along the corridor was alight, and he could hear steps in Diane's room.

The comte hurried toward the open door of his daughter's room just as Laurent emerged with an armful of soiled linens.

"What is it, Laurent?" he asked, his voice thick. He was intensely thirsty. "What is it?

"Mademoiselle Catherine has been taken ill, Monsieur . . . " Laurent's vacant blue eyes blinked in bewilderment.

The comte turned from him and rushed to the room. Its windows and shutters fastened against the night air, it smelled musty and stale. The comte craved a cooling drink of water. The faintly sickening smell of fresh blood, that was the peculiar smell in the room. It made his stomach turn over.

Catherine lay unconscious on Diane's bed, where Laurent had hastily carried her after she had fallen to the dining room floor. Sophie, looking lost and forlorn, stood next to the bed staring down at her sister, pale as death, motionless as stone. Sophie lifted her eyes and stared, open-mouthed, as her father came into the bedroom. At the foot of the bed Diane, her blond head bowed, knelt in prayer on her grandmother's worn old *prie-dieu*.

Dr. Peltier, his old-fashioned wig pushed far back on his bald head emerged from the shadows on the other side of the bed and came toward the comte, his hands deferentially outstretched. He had precious few occasions to visit the imposing chateau de Corcheval. In the neighborhood the elderly doctor was known for his skill in birthing babies—and calves—and for his fondness for scullery maids, the dirtier the better. The comte shook the doctor's dingy hand and looked with wide, uncomprehending eyes at the scene.

"She's been cupped, Monsieur," Dr. Peltier said, lowering his voice and leading the comte away from the bed toward the hallway. "And she has lost consciousness again, I'm afraid."

"But . . . what is it, in the name of God? The girl was as right as rain when I left this morning." The comte's voice was little more than a croak. He searched the hallway for Laurent to fetch him fresh water.

"It's a tertiary fever . . . I would say . . . Though I would not want to rule out . . . " He drew a grimy handkerchief from the pocket of his coat and blew his nose, then wiped his brow. "*Mon dieu*, it's stifling in that room. One cannot breathe," he said, fanning his soiled handkerchief back and forth.

"Rule out what, man!"

The old doctor glanced over his shoulder toward the sickroom. "We shall have to wait and see . . . it could very well be something far worse . . . it might be the smallpox," he said, lowering his voice to a sinister whisper.

The comte turned pale. He stood for a moment, his hand working nervously with the fine lace jabot at his throat, chewing his underlip.

"Diane!" he said finally in a hoarse shout. "Diane!"

Old Dr. Peltier stared after him as he ran, like a man deranged, through the sitting room to the bedchamber. Presently, the comte broke from the room, clutching at Diane's arm, jostling her quickly into the hallway. They were arguing, the comte's voice urgent, breaking in his excitement.

"The nursery! Get back to the nursery and stay there!" he said, pushing her toward the stairs at the end of the corridor. "Stay there! Do you understand me?" His face was twisted in anger.

"Yes, papa," she said, hearing the fear in his voice. Something dreadful was happening to them, and her father could not stop it. She started towards the stairs. "But, papa, what about Sophie?"

The comte stared blankly, as if he confronted with a puzzle. "Sophie? Of course!" He whirled toward the door. "Peltier, man, you will stay the night, won't you?" he asked over his shoulder.

❦

It was late afternoon, and Diane sat at an open window listlessly brushing Sophie's hair. For days they had remained cut off from the rest of the household as Catherine weakened and slipped into delirious fevers. With the calamity of serious illness hovering over the old chateau, it comforted Diane to fall asleep each night in the low, narrow bed of her childhood. The skimpily furnished rooms of the nursery had changed little over the years. The girls' childish drawings—stick figures with exuberantly happy faces, huge yellow suns, and treetops like green balloons—were still pinned to a faded taffeta screen in a rickety bamboo frame. Faraway, in the fields beyond the lake, they could hear dogs herding the sheep to lower pastures.

"I'm bored, Diane," Sophie said.

"I know. Come, let's draw each other's silhouette. Help me find some charcoal."

They picked out bits and pieces of charcoal in an old wooden box, and Diane was clearing the desktops when they heard footsteps on the old stone stairway.

Marianne's face was pale with fear as she stepped into the room. "Smallpox," she said in a whisper. "The swelling broke, they say, and she came out in red spots all over her body." At Ancy, when she was a little girl, the miller's children, all six of them, had been taken away before a week was out. The village church bell tolled over and over, and she had watched as the black-covered wagons carried the small wooden boxes past her mother's door, the wagon creaking, the wooden boxes knocking together with a hollow sound.

Diane shivered. She felt ashamed of herself for her anger with Catherine at table. And before dinner. And all the other times, too numerous to recall. Why was there so little affection between them? She remembered with what joy she had worked on a very special saint's day present for Catherine—a missal ribbon embroidered with expensive, rare spider silk thread, deep gold, shimmering like a jewel in the sunshine. Even Mother Superior had never handled spider silk thread before. Diane had spent all of her own saint's day gift from

Uncle Philippe on the thread because she knew Catherine's fondness for embroidery work. The very next day, walking along the stone path on their way to the refectory from mass, when Catherine saw that Diane was looking her way, she drew the ribbon from her missal and tossed it into the muddy slush of a late November snowstorm. Stung to the quick, Diane watched in disbelief as her sister pursed her mouth in a self-satisfied smirk and hurried away.

But all that was in the past now. Diane promised herself that she would never quarrel with her sister again.

After a few days the comte climbed the narrow stone stairs and sat down heavily in a straightback wooden chair. His long stockinged legs stretched out awkwardly from the low chair. His face was gray and drawn. The lace cuffs of his white shirt were soiled, and his neckband yellow with sweat. The sides of his mouth were stained with snuff, and Diane noticed that he wore no perfume.

"The curé has come . . . we . . . I had to call him." He rubbed his forehead and frowned anxiously. "The curé has given your sister . . . the last rites . . . " He looked at the two girls dumbly, as if appealing for their help. Huge tears rolled down Sophie's face and splashed onto her clasped hands.

"Will we be able to see her again, papa?" Diane asked, unwilling to believe that Catherine could slip out of their lives without a word.

"No, oh, no." He shook his head slowly and studied his hands. "No. It would not be wise. Not until everything . . . is cleaned. And burned." He looked at Diane. "Where did she get it? At the convent? There was no smallpox there. Neither among the sisters nor the boarders. And here in the village . . . nothing. Not a death from the smallpox this year. Only on the other side of Cluny, near Joigny. Old Peltier says that one of my tenants lost his oldest boy lately. Peltier says there's more in the village now."

Diane looked quickly away. She knew that Catherine in her daily roaming about the countryside with the stable boy had been several times to the estate in Joigny, had even boasted of having dinner with one of the comte's tenants. Diane said nothing. Her father looked beaten down by cares.

The comte rose slowly to his feet. "Your mother will be here by sundown. I must attend to her arrival." He shuffled from the room, stooping under the low ceilings.

"Oh, Diane!" Sophie cried, throwing herself into her sister's arms. Diane sat weeping quietly, stroking the little girl's hair until her small body stopped shaking with sobs, until she lay dozing in her arms. She rocked back and forth, cradling Sophie, crooning to her the old nursery songs that Clotilde had sung to them all, to quiet their fears, to comfort their loneliness, to put them to sleep, there, in the homely old rooms of their childhood. At the convent, whenever someone broke out into a fever, the nuns whispered of smallpox and closed doors and fumigated rooms. Not even prayers or candles could save you from smallpox. Foul running sores. Then death. Catherine dead and in a vault under the chapel floor. Like Louis-Etienne. Walking over her sister's burial slab to hear mass, to take communion at the tasseled gold rail, swallowing the wafer and wine, pushing it back on the tongue . . . Catherine-Hélène-Charlotte-Thérèse de Fautrière, dead, underneath the flagstones of the chapel. My sister died of smallpox, she thought, stroking Sophie's hair, my sister died of smallpox.

※

But Catherine did not die. Even as her sisters mourned her in the nursery with its small round windows looking out over the tranquil lake glistening in the spring sunshine, Clotilde, ever faithful Clotilde, was gently raising Catherine's head from the damp pillow and putting a cup of warm broth to her lips, urging her to drink, bathing her poor, infected face and body in soothing herbal potions.

That evening, by the time the comtesse arrived, Catherine had lapsed into a fever that raged through the night and early morning hours. Clotilde wept and protested, the comte swore and called it outrageous folly; nonetheless, the comtesse tied on an apron and took up her place at her daughter's bedside. As Clotilde nodded in a chair, it was the comtesse who lifted her daughter's head for a cooling drink of water and chamomile tea, and as the fever waned at dawn, it was the comtesse who bathed her daughter's thin body and changed her night linens.

As spring rioted in the warm green fields and meadows outside the thick cold stone walls of Corcheval, candles burned far into the night and heavy draperies shut out the sun as Catherine struggled free of the disease. Gradually the terrible fever left her. She smiled at Clotilde, pressed her mother's hand feebly. But she was still too weak to talk, too weak to raise her head alone.

The quiet calm of the sickroom remained undisturbed. The comtesse and Clotilde spoke in whispers, in nods, and smiles, and gestures. In the evening and in the morning, before the pale light of dawn lightened the ceilings over Catherine's bed, the comtesse would fall to her knees on the old *prie-dieu* at the foot of the bed. One morning, as she opened her eyes and began to rise, she saw Catherine smiling at her, a tender, happy smile that lit up her pale blue eyes.

That day Catherine was able to move from the bed to a chair and to eat a slice of roast chicken that Clotilde fetched from the kitchen. For over an hour Catherine, bundled in shawls and blankets, sat in a chair by the side of the bed, holding her head shakily erect, her eyes bright and alert as she followed her mother's movements about the large room.

With each passing day Catherine gathered strength, and the comtesse rejoiced that her prayers were being answered. She kept the room in semi-darkness for fear of injuring Catherine's eyes, the comtesse said to Clotilde. But Clotilde was not fooled. She knew that the comtesse wanted to keep the poor child's face in the shadows as long as possible until the scabs fell away and there was no way to conceal the disfigurement the smallpox had left behind.

Far down the hallway toward the library Diane could hear the tap, tap, tap of her father's high heels hurrying toward the dining room. With a mock serious scowl she motioned to Sophie to sit up straight, and both burst out into giddy peals of laughter. A fresh summer breeze stirred the large bouquet of calla lilies on the dining room table, its immaculate damask cloth and sparkling crystal and china echoing the festive mood in the chateau. Crisp lawn draperies, billowing gracefully at the tall windows, had supplanted the heavy velvet brocades of winter.

"Your sister is coming down for dinner!" the comte said gaily, taking his place at the head of the table. "She feels as strong as a horse, she says. And almost as hungry."

"Oh, papa, you must have just come from a party!" Diane said. "You do look handsome!"

"Is maman coming for dinner, too?" asked Sophie. Even though the comtesse had returned to the chateau for well over a month, Diane and Sophie had not seen her or talked to her. She had remained shut off in their sister's sick room, taking her meals there, sleeping on the canapé bed. She was content to have news of Sophie and Diane and the comte from Clotilde.

"Yes, maman, too, and your Uncle Philippe, as you may have guessed, Sophie, if you can count that high," he said, teasing her, pointing to the empty chairs placed at the table. "Where the deuce are they anyway? The men are waiting to serve."

At the sound of footsteps, the comte and the two girls rose and turned expectantly toward the comtesse. Diane stared at her mother, startled by her gaunt face and emaciated figure. Her long hands looked skeletal as she reached for her water glass and drank. She looked ill; all signs of health had left her face. Her pale cheeks were sunken and slack.

"Catherine will be along in just a moment. Clotilde is helping her with her hair. And Catherine is not at all happy with the cap Clotilde is trying to get her to wear. Clotilde says that Catherine's disposition has not improved one bit." The comtesse smiled and shook her head. "I'm afraid that your sister has a bit of a temper," she said to Diane and Sophie. "Like your father," and she nodded pleasantly toward the comte, who pulled a face.

"Shall we begin?" the comtesse asked. "You've been waiting, and Philippe is just calling in on his way to Cluny. I'm sure that Catherine is on her way."

However, the comtesse was not at all sure that Catherine would appear at the dinner table. She had acted so strangely this morning, after her bath. Like two silly schoolgirls, Clotilde and the comtesse had arranged everything to pamper her—oils, perfumes, powders, the gentlest, most expensive soaps. And Catherine humored them in their little joke. She soaked and bathed in the hipbath decorated with enameled flowers, and before Clotilde could interfere, she pulled on her robe and slippers and sat down at Diane's dressing table.

The curtains at the far end of the bedchamber and in the sitting room had been partially opened. Near the dressing table, however, the curtains were tightly drawn. Catherine adjusted the mirror and peered at her face in the dusty, darkened surface. "Open the curtains, Clotilde. Please," she said, running her fingertips over her face, over the dark, reddish pink scars and the shriveled brown scabs scattered over her neck and face.

The sound of the draperies scraping heavily over the rods at the window tore at the comtesse's heart as she watched her daughter, whom she had nursed so carefully back to life. What kind of death awaited her now? The comtesse stepped toward her, then stopped short. Bright, harsh, blinding sunlight pushed into the room. Catherine blinked, her pale eyelashes fluttering helplessly. The comtesse averted her eyes. She could not bear to watch as Catherine saw herself now, for the first time, as she would always be, as she would be for the rest of her life. Deep, pink scars, smooth and glistening, riddled her face, pulling down the corner of one eye, curling a side of her upper lip. The hair of her left eyebrow was practically gone, replaced by a ragged patch of raw pink skin.

At the dressing table Catherine did not move. She sat studying every detail of her new face as if it were a text that she was learning by heart. She lifted her hands and touched her ears and pushed stray locks of hair from her face. She pulled her hair back tightly, and said with an indifference that sent a chill down the comtesse's spine, "Clotilde. Come here. My hair's a fright. I can't possibly go to table looking like this." Poor Clotilde had not known what to do, how to begin. Much as she loved fussing over the girls' hair, too. But it was hopeless. Her hands were clumsy, and Catherine grew tart and impatient, calling her rude names, despite her mother's gentle pleading. As the comtesse left the room to go down to dinner, Catherine spilled out a box of Diane's ribbons, tossing them carelessly in the air, searching, she said, for "just the right shade of pink."

Catherine entered the dining room so quickly and quietly that no one was aware of her presence. The comte was reminiscing pleasantly with his wife, the two girls listening to their father's tales with delight. He had been drinking since his toilette and was in a jovial, expansive mood. He liked having women around, even when one of them happened to be his wife. These days, unfortunately, Aurélie looked thin, too thin to be truly attractive, and her once creamy complexion was positively gray, but there was no denying that she was a refined woman. A noblewoman in every way, he thought benignly. He stopped in mid-sentence, arrested by Sophie's sharp, startled cry. He turned his head heavily.

"Hello, papa," Catherine said cheerfully, bending to kiss his cheeks. "I've kept you waiting. I'm sorry." With exquisite grace Catherine greeted her sisters in turn and took her seat, while her father, his jaw slack and his mouth round with grief and astonishment, stared after her.

Catherine was dressed as if for a ball in one of Diane's silk and cut velvet gowns made by Madame Clarisse. The skirt was saffron with silver stripes in the petticoat. The bodice set off Catherine's milky white shoulders and breasts swelling over the top of the tightly laced corset. Bright yellow ribbons had been twisted through the thick blonde coils of her hair, fastened into place by Diane's gem encrusted pins.

Catherine settled the folds of her gown around her chair and touched her hair coquettishly. "I made up my face, just as Diane taught me," she said, grinning toward her father. Diane dropped her eyes and tried with all her might to hold back her tears, while Sophie, anxiously twisting her napkin, looked as if she were going to faint.

"Ah . . . ," the comte began, but his tongue felt too thick, he could not speak. He simply stared at his daughter. She looked grotesque. Unspeakably grotesque. She had painted her face with thick white makeup and powder that accentuated the deep pockmarks that twisted her features. One eyebrow seemed to have been chewed away by malevolent insects. Catherine had daubed dark red rouge over her cratered cheeks, and black taffeta patches around her mouth and eyes. Great Mother of God, he thought, his mind reeling, what did I expect, why didn't I remember the scars, what in God's name could I have been expecting? He reached for his wine glass, sick to his stomach.

"I suspect that's Philippe," the comtesse said, determined to dispel the silence weighing upon them, as footsteps echoed hollowly across the enormous room.

14

There was a noisy splash, and Diane looked up from her book just in time to catch a shimmering flash of silver over the glassy surface of the lake. She had fled to the stone bench at the side of the lake in the shade of an ancient linden tree that Clotilde swore had spirits in it on All Saint's Eve. Every day after dinner she escaped to her solitude, to her bench under the haunted tree, while Sophie and Catherine played cards or napped or embroidered and her father drifted about from chateau to chateau, from party to party, and her mother dozed in the sunshine of the terrace until a fit of coughing banished all thought of a nap and sent her indoors in search of a warm, woolen shawl in spite of the hot, cloudless days, one after the other, in monotonous succession.

In the distance, across the garden, Diane watched as Clotilde guided the comtesse to her usual deep chair on the terrace, then turned back into the chateau. Diane quickly gathered up her things and rose to go to her mother. Without really understanding why, she cherished these long afternoons alone with her mother, sitting mainly in companionable silence in a sunny corner of the terrace. Sometimes, though more and more rarely, they would talk, mainly about life at court. Diane found it scarcely imaginable that her frail, austere mother could ever have been a part of the chaotic, licentious sensuality of the other country.

The comtesse's eyes brightened with delight as Diane bent low to kiss her wasted cheeks.

"Shall we read a few *Pensées* together, maman? I never tire of Pascal, do you?"

"Never. Let's read 'The Wager'? But I've forgotten my shawl. The summer sun doesn't warm me now the way it should."

When Diane returned with a shawl, her mother's eyes were closed, her head twisted awkwardly against the pillow. She could not look at her mother in her changed state without deep distress. No matter what Dr. Peltier said, she knew that her mother was gravely ill. The comtesse talked of returning to the convent, and sometimes she would shade her eyes and look yearningly toward the west, toward the purple blue horizon wavering in the heat of midday, but later in the sultry afternoon she would huddle under her shawls in the sunshine of the terrace, reading and dozing until the sun set. Then she would cross the garden stiffly and spend an hour on her knees in the tiny hexagonal chapel. Some days, though rarely now, she went to the chapel in the mornings as well. Diane, who had gone back to her habit of rising early, at dawn when the faintest hint of pink and coral colored the sky, noticed that her mother slept just a little longer each day. Often when Diane came into the kitchen at ten o'clock for her morning chocolate, Clotilde would still be waiting for the comtesse's summons to her room. Her mother said that she would leave any day now for the convent, but she did not. She sat on the terrace and coughed into her handkerchief. Sometimes she would spread open the handkerchief and look at it before furtively stuffing it into the pocket of her skirt. Sometimes she would call a footman who would send Clotilde for fresh linen. At table the comtesse pushed her food around her plate, though Clotilde pestered the cook to make tempting dishes.

The comtesse opened her eyes and gazed confusedly around the terrace as if to get her bearings. "Have I slept long? I thought I saw Catherine racing down the drive with that stable boy."

"I'm sure you did. She probably lost patience with Sophie, tagging along after her from morning until night, like a bothersome kitten," Diane said. "Here, maman, I've brought you some tea."

"Poor little Sophie. She has so much love in her heart. And where is she?"

Diane laughed. "She's with Clotilde. In the back kitchen. Clotilde is trying to teach her how to make starch."

The comtesse smiled and carefully sipped her tea. Diane reached out and touched her mother's gold pendant earrings that she recalled so vividly from the time she had spent with her mother in Paris, before she went away to the convent at Villeneuve-la-Petite.

"I always remember you with these earrings, maman."

"They never leave me. A gift from Philippe . . . He's very fond of you, you know."

Her mother was obviously tiring. Diane picked up Pascal's essays and searched for her place.

The comtesse shivered and turned her face away toward the sweeping lawns parching in the August sun. When the Mother Superior told her that one of her daughters was gravely ill with the smallpox and had been given extreme unction, the comtesse had not once thought that it might be Catherine. Her fears fixed immediately on Diane, perhaps because Diane and the rumors about her and the King had been seething around her for days at the convent. Whenever the comtesse appeared in the stillroom or the infirmary or the garden, the whispering would stop abruptly and all eyes would follow her. Giggling and fluttering her lashes nervously, a young bride whose husband had remained with his regiment in Flanders recounted the story of the Queen's anger at Sceaux, punctuating her narrative with gasps and sighs of astonishment. The King is smitten with your daughter, she exclaimed, clasping her hands melodramatically. How old are you, child? the comtesse had asked. Fourteen, Madame, the girl replied, grinning foolishly.

The comtesse coughed into her handkerchief and leaned forward in her chair. "Maman used to tell the story of being reprimanded by old King Louis's niece for not curtseying to the King's empty bed. Maman was passing through the King's bedchamber with other ladies of the court, and maman had just arrived in the other country and did not know that she was supposed to curtsey to the empty bed. I wonder, is that still the court etiquette? I used to think about that story as I was growing up. What did it mean, paying respects to the King's bed? I still don't know."

Diane felt herself flushing hotly and bowed her head. How much did her mother know of her disgrace? She wanted to tell her mother about the King, his caressing words, his touch. Why had he suddenly abandoned her as if she had not mattered at all? But she could not bring herself to talk of her brief triumph or her crushing humiliation the night of the yew tree ball.

A long-tailed cuckoo, perched high on the back of a topiary giraffe near the chapel, called out its cheery two notes.

"I miss mass," the comtesse said, gazing at the chapel. "Any word about Father Durand?"

"I'm afraid there'll be no mass in the chapel, maman. Not for a long time. Father Durand bent down to look at something on his horse's leg, and the horse kicked him for his trouble. Smashed Father's thigh."

"I'm not surprised. The man never learned the first thing about horses." She paused, then asked, "Do you pray, Diane?"

"I pray . . . yes, maman, I pray. I do. For Catherine, when she was sick, for papa with all his troubles . . . the estates, the need for money, and for you. I pray for you." Diane could feel the hot sun prickling her neck. "But sometimes . . . some days . . . I'm afraid to pray."

"Afraid? Why?"

"Afraid I might pray for the wrong things," she said. Afraid that she might pray that the King would fall under her spell once again, would dance with her, whisper softly in her ear, hold her close, that he would make her the royal mistress . . . with power and privileges that would surpass her imagination, that she would reign supreme in the daily pageantry of the court . . . or that she would make a magnificent marriage, perhaps with a prince of the blood, that she would have one of the most sought-after salons in Paris, filled with wits, poets, playwrights . . . that she would never be stranded in the country, far from the beauty and excitement of Paris.

The comtesse watched her in silence for a moment, then smiled. "You are a curious child. You can say such strange things in a serious way, as if you meant them." She sighed deeply and closed her eyes.

Diane picked up her book and tried to read. She had missed her chance. If only she had the courage to talk to her mother of the desires that assailed her waking or sleeping hours, desires that electrified her with excitement then left her awash in shame and guilt.

A sweltering hush had settled over the chateau. The comtesse stirred under her shawl. "And when does your friend Madeleine arrive?"

"She arrived this morning, maman. You were asleep, and I didn't want to wake you." Diane had welcomed the excuse of attending to her mother. She dreaded Madeleine's sharp tongue, her cutting stories brought back from court about the King and his infatuation with the shepherdess. There had been something angry and bitter in Madeleine's letter, which had followed on the heels of a cold, rather formal note from the marquise de Sabran, requesting the comte's hospitality for her niece. Still, Madeleine had looked so ill when Diane last saw her at the Opera, so alone and desperate.

"She'll bring you some cheer. It's a dreary life for you, my dear, keeping company with an invalid like me."

"Nonsense, maman," Diane said, and she meant it. "You know, maman," she began hesitantly, "The King himself gave me a beautiful bouquet of exotic flowers. At Sceaux . . . "

But the comtesse had already closed her eyes and returned to her own thoughts. At this hour, in the convent, she would be helping the novices with their penmanship, coaxing them to be neater, to trim their quills to a sharp, narrow point, to keep their hands clean. That was the hardest part. After a few moments she began to nod drowsily. Diane smoothed the blankets across her mother's lap and gently removed the unfinished cup of tea from her frail hands. The comtesse smiled weakly but did not open her eyes. Diane turned away, her heart heavy, and started toward the kitchen.

At the end of the garden near the fountain, stood Madeleine, who beckoned. Impatient to be alone with her thoughts, Diane nonetheless hurried down the steps toward her friend.

Madeleine yawned and stretched theatrically. "Dull! Dull! Dull! I shall die of boredom!" She yawned again. "It's worse than I could possibly have imagined. What on earth do you do for amusement?"

Diane sat down on the edge of the fountain and dipped her hand into the bronze green water and watched the wall-eyed, open-mouthed fear of the fish. "Not much. Maman is ill, you know." She observed Madeleine apprehensively. "You'll get used to the quiet."

"No, I won't."

She sat down abruptly beside Diane and swept her eyes over the deserted garden and its elaborate topiary figures. "I'll go stark, raving mad." She waited for Diane to contradict her. "Still, it's better than facing my aunt's fury every day. There's that to be said for being dumped in the country. Besides, as it happens, it suits Armand very well. My being here at Corcheval." She gave Diane a meaningful look.

"Armand?"

"Well, yes. Armand was my lover for . . . let's see, how long was it? . . . well, no matter. Suffice it to say that he was my lover long enough to get me with child, the big oaf!" She watched with pleasure as Diane stared at her, round-eyed, disbelieving. "Not that I blame him. I shall never be one of those women who do that! I love him, I adore him, and that's a fact."

"What happened? What did you do with the child? You are not carrying a child now."

"No. As you see," she said, pressing her hands against her flat stomach. She clasped her hands tightly across her voluminous skirts. "Well, at first, I thought that Mother Nature had taken pity on me. For a time it looked as if the babe would pass away with my monthly flux. At any rate, that's what cut my legs from under me the night at the Opéra when you floated away from me on the arms of the King and abandoned me in my drafty alcove. I began to bleed, and if you want to know the truth, I was in a bad way and foolishly didn't know what to do with myself. Luckily, your Uncle Philippe spotted me, probably figured out exactly what was happening, and escorted me home like the true gentleman that he is. I was out of my mind. And so was my aunt after my maid told her the fix I was in. She raved like a madwoman at my treachery, at my sluttish nature—which I sweetly attributed to my kinship with her—and threatened all manner of evil before she packed me off to her abortionist. Who happened to be in prison for stealing candles from the parish church."

"What did you do? What could you do then?"

"I called in on your uncle's wife and got the name of her woman." Madeleine said flippantly, though she could still recall the bitter coppery taste of fear in her mouth as she hoisted her skirts for the filthy old hag to begin her work. "As a matter of fact, Odile very nicely took me there in her carriage and brought me home to her house for a few days. As a favor to Armand."

Diane shivered, crossed her arms across her chest, and rubbed her arms.

"It is getting a little chilly now that the sun has dropped," said Madeleine, rising to go.

The terrace at the top of the garden was empty. The comtesse had retired for the evening. Dark flocks of magpies swooped low over the box hedges and, turning skyward, showed sparkling white breasts.

"By the bye," Madeleine said, as Diane sat mutely watching the birds swirl against the pink clouds of sunset, "Armand will be coming soon, to Ancy for a few weeks with his cousin Odile. My aunt doesn't know, and isn't to know, if you understand my meaning. I shall count on you, Diane, if I may."

"Certainly, you may," Diane said, quickly if not enthusiastically. She sounded bemused, and she was. "I won't say anything to anyone."

"Especially, say nothing to Catherine. She has a very sharp eye, and I don't think she's awfully fond of me, or of having me here." At her convent school and at court with her aunt Madeleine had seen many, both men and women, who had survived the smallpox, but none whose scars repelled her as much as Catherine's. Today, at dinner, when Catherine, painted and rouged and elaborately dressed with quantities of gaudy ribbons and laces, had sailed into the room, Madeleine had felt her blood run cold. She shrank from the girl and went out of her way to avoid her. At table, Catherine dominated the conversation, wittily, charmingly even, except that there was a menacing undertone to her wit, a gloved claw waiting to slap and maul.

"What's that pretty little building over there? I've never noticed it before. But it's charming. The bricks, such a lovely color."

"It's the chapel," Diane replied laconically. "It's not very old. Papa had it built for maman before I was born."

"Very unusual, isn't it, a hexagonal chapel?" She paused and narrowed her eyes appraisingly. "Is that where your mother will be buried?"

Philippe d'Ancy stood on the steep banks opposite the mill and watched the rain-swollen millrace pound under and over the enormous wooden wheel. Spring rains had turned the narrow, insignificant river Nauxe into a rushing, pushing avalanche of water. The wheel groaned and churned in watery ecstasy.

Contentedly, Philippe, hands clasped behind his back, watched the rhythmic turning of the wheel as if mesmerized. The noise was deafening. The comte touched his brother-in-law's sleeve and motioned impatiently for them to move along across the milldam to their horses tied up at the mill. Both men wore high leather riding boots that covered their knees and the plain beige riding habits favored by their neighbors. The comte, however, had tied his thick brown braid of hair with a large black velvet bow, which fanned out on each side of his tanned face.

The miller's son, a strapping boy, covered from head to foot in flour, poked his head out a window and watched the two men cross the footbridge to their horses.

"Well, Michel, what do you think?" Philippe asked, noting with satisfaction the three wagons tied up in the muddy half moon of grass in front of the mill. Two laborers in leather leggings hefted large baskets of corn from one wagon onto a wheelbarrow. "Was it worth it or not? Look at those wagons, and my man says it's been like this every day, and August not yet over and many a field still to be harvested."

"If you say so, Philippe, if you say so." The comte was bored. And out of boredom, he had agreed to come along to see Philippe's new mill, which for whatever reason, Philippe thought would be passionately interesting to him. It was just another mill, stuck out along a stream on the other side of Ancy.

"Think of the money! That's what I mean. Think of what this

new mill represents in my revenues from Ancy! It's turned the whole place around. Or almost."

The comte did not know what to say next. He stared blankly at the roughly constructed mill house of crude stone and wattle with a thatched roof. "To be sure, Philippe. I don't have much of a head for figures . . . and commerce," he drawled, "Being a military man, you know."

"And that's precisely what's wrong with the nobility of this country!" Philippe snapped. "This isn't commerce. Putting up a well-run flour mill is . . . "

Two youngsters on horseback burst from the woods on the hilltop and raced toward Philippe and the comte. The two men paused and watched them reach the beaten surface of the road and pound toward the mill. One of the riders, a young woman, leaned forward in the saddle, her straw hat almost touching the horse's neck and whipped her horse methodically as if intent upon outracing her companion.

"Why, Michel, that's your Catherine! Bless me! She is riding like a man!"

Before the comte could answer, Catherine reined her horse in front of her father and turned to wait for her companion to catch up with her. Pierre, in ragged britches and a torn shirt, rode barefoot, his twisted, deformed foot pushed all the way through the stirrups of his saddle. He slowed his horse and pulled abreast of Catherine, a snaggle-tooth grin spreading from ear to ear.

"That's my Sultana! My Sultana!" the comte cried, spluttering in disbelief, staring at Pierre's horse.

Catherine threw back her head and laughed, peals of mellow laughter. She looked down at her father, her ragged eyebrow giving her face a perpetually quizzical expression. "Of course, it's Sultana! And your best English saddle, too!"

Philippe could not wrench his eyes from Catherine's ravaged face. What was the matter with him anyway?

"I've come to see Uncle Philippe's new mill once again," Catherine said, pulling him out of his trance-like stare. Her voice was bold, full of authority and purpose. Behind her awful mask she appeared transformed. Philippe could feel her energy, a heartiness, a zest for life. But there was something mean about it, there was a vicious challenge that peered sullenly from those sunken blue eyes.

"What on earth for?" mumbled her father, keeping his eyes on Sultana's rippling, sweaty sides and Pierre's dirty, callused foot.

"For the very reasons you should be looking at it, papa." She said curtly, her lip curled derisively. Or was it the deep scar that pulled it back? "Where will our tenants at Joigny mill their corn and wheat this harvest season?"

Sitting her powerful horse cockily, her blond hair shining in the hot August sun, fresh pink scars twisting her face with scorn, Catherine was taunting her father. Philippe was stunned by her boldness.

"That's for my bailiff to say," the comte muttered. "What I mean is, my people will bring their harvest to the usual place." And for the life of him he could not remember where his tenants milled their grain. Lately he had been trying to pay more attention to these matters, too. He was annoyed, having his daughter scold him about his affairs like a wayward schoolboy. "At any rate, it's no concern of yours," he said curtly. "Thank heavens for that, eh, my girl?" He added, hastily, afraid that he might have wounded her with his tart reply.

Catherine appeared to notice nothing. In her handsome frock, too elegant for riding about the countryside, she sat looking down at her father as if impatient to have her say. "The point is that it should be *someone's* concern!" she snapped. She touched her hand to her straw hat, smiled at her father and her uncle, then spurred her horse into motion. Like a faithful hound, Pierre, his grimy face still stretched with a grin, loped along after her on his superb mount.

The huge, musty library stretching along the west side of the chateau was just beginning to catch a slant of the hot August sun, when Catherine knocked at the door and entered the room. The comte looked up briefly and mumbled a greeting. He was completely out of sorts and did not need the awful disfigurement of his daughter to remind him of how badly his affairs in general were going. He had spent the entire morning searching through every portfolio, every drawer and file in the room for the survey maps and deeds of his lands in Joigny. Papers and untied portfolios littered the floor around the large rosewood desk whose fussy, intricate inlays of briarwood contrasted with the overall sobriety of the room. The desk belonged to that period before his disgrace and banishment from court when, like every courtier currying favor, the comte had ordered a copy of one of the King's desks from Jacques Dubois. It had cost a small fortune and, with its shallow drawers and huge surface, was more decorative than useful.

It was turning into another scorching day, and the comte, wigless and still in his dressing gown and slippers, was perspiring. Ignoring Catherine, he pushed open his snuffbox with his thumb and rapidly sniffed four pinches. Mustard brown snuff dribbled onto his breeches and spotted his shirt. He did not bother to dust off his clothes.

Catherine was already handsomely dressed for dinner in one of Diane's gowns, though her two sisters, like the comtesse, wore simple cambric frocks without hoops, merely a stiffly starched petticoat, to the dining room. She seemed to tower over her father as he hunched over his papers, scrabbling feverishly through them, discarding one heap and turning toward another without sorting or arranging.

"What on earth are you doing, papa?"

"Have a seat, *ma petite*," he grumbled, without looking up. "Ah, you do smell like a wild summer rose this morning. Delightful fragrance. Where did you get it?" He faced her and smiled, his pale blue eyes distracted, worried, sad.

"From Diane's dressing table, where else? Diane appears to be the only one of us worthy of luxuries. Even such a simple thing as fragrances."

"Because she's older. One day you will, too. Once you leave the convent."

"If I ever do," Catherine said grimly.

"Catherine, *ma petite!*" the comte said, immediately cajoling, unctuous. "When did you become so impatient? Here you are, only fourteen, and you can't wait to get out into the big wide world!"

Poor, poor child, he thought. She's too clever. She knows what lies ahead for her. She has only to look in the mirror in the morning. No wonder she is behaving so queerly these days, swaggering about with that gimpy stableboy, acting bossy, dressing up like the queen of the May. God, just look at that lip!

"I shall be fifteen come June," she said acidly, her sunken eyes fixed on him like a coiled reptile ready to strike. "Diane was younger, by months, when you took her away to Paris." She paused. "Does that mean that you're ready to take me to Paris and to court, now that I shall shortly be fifteen." Still standing stiffly erect in her fine gown, she looked down at him mockingly.

"Sit down, sit down . . . you've come to talk. Take those papers off the chair. I can't get up, as you can see. I'm drowning in papers," and a note of annoyance crept into his voice. Where could he search next? He reached for his snuffbox.

"So . . . papa, as I shall soon be fifteen . . . " Catherine lifted the untidy sheaf of papers from the chair. "Papa, what are you doing with all these papers lying about?"

"Searching for a very important deed . . . or rather survey map. It's nothing you would understand. But I need it to get my affairs in order a bit. Get certain matters sorted out . . . " he gazed distractedly over the disorderly yellowing heaps of papers, some tied with faded red ribbon.

"Which estate?" she asked, looking over her shoulder toward the armoire at the other end of the room. "Grandpapa's secretary arranged the maps of all thirteen estates in the old armoire there, on the north wall."

"Who told you?" Stupefied, the comte stared at her. He was stunned that the child would know what an estate map was, let alone where they were stored. "Where did you learn that?" he asked again, as Catherine, her face half in shadow calmly observed him.

She shrugged.

"What else do you know? Perhaps you can tell me what I'm searching for?" He laughed, but his voice had an edge of exasperation. He must get on with it. Locate those foolish papers and get on with it.

"Perhaps."

"What do you mean *perhaps*?" The girl was making him uneasy. Ever since her illness, she had been queer. As if she had somehow got to a place of superiority and were looking down on everyone else. At table she took over the conversation and bullied them all with what she had been reading! Only Sophie listened and asked questions, only little Sophie, so eager to please, to be liked.

"Perhaps I can find it for you if you tell me which estate you're talking about." She nudged a pile of papers with her foot. "It looks as if you have mixed up the accounts and loans with other papers."

"Joigny . . . I'm trying to locate the documents on Joigny." He opened his snuffbox, then snapped it shut.

"Joigny? Oh, well, why didn't you say so? I have the papers. Or most of them." Catherine laughed. "Papa, if you could only see yourself!" She rocked back and forth in her chair, chortling and pointing her finger at him. "Sitting there in your dressing gown with snuff powder dribbled over your shirt and breeches, about to fall off your chair! You are a sight to behold!"

"What, may I ask, are you doing with the Joigny documents? Or with any of my documents, missy!" He was choking with anger. His head trembled, and he nervously pulled at his neckband. "What has possessed you to rummage around in *my* papers! In my private papers that are none of your concern!" He wanted to rise from his chair and throttle her, shake that grotesque mocking head until she cried mercy.

"But you're wrong, those papers are very much my concern," she said, unperturbed. "I think it should be obvious why I should be interested in all the papers in this library." She swept the room with a glance. "You, my dear papa, are so intent on wasting this family's property that every one of us—maman, Sophie, and your precious Diane—should be mounting guard in front of that old armoire by day and by night to keep you from snatching up another parcel of our patrimony and throwing it out the window."

Her voice was growing harsher and harsher, as she rasped out her accusations. The comte sank back against his chair.

"Don't you want to know why I was looking at the Joigny papers?" she asked, regaining her composure.

Her father did not answer. He sat scratching the back of one hand, watching her.

"I took them to study them before consulting Uncle Philippe. Actually, I've examined most of the major documents—and enough of the accounts to know what has been taking place for the last few years."

"Philippe? Showing *my* papers to Philippe!"

"We badly need a mill on that estate, and Uncle Philippe seemed the logical person to consult about the problem."

"Splendid! Splendid! Oh, yes! I spend a fortune building a mill on Joigny when I don't have enough total income from the land to pay my hatter on the Faubourg Saint-Honoré!" He stopped short and blushed scarlet under Catherine's accusing stare. "Where does the money come from? Hein? It costs money to set up a mill. Have you ever thought of that?"

"Of course, I have. You're being absurd, papa." She dismissed him wearily. "A mill takes money, but it makes money. Plenty of money. Especially when you've got tenants and laborers who otherwise have to spend days struggling with their wagons over muddy, impossible roads because the bridges have not been repaired and have fallen in and they have to travel two and three times as far as they normally would just to get to a decent mill. Owned by someone else who pockets the benefit and takes it from your pocket. Look at what's happening, papa! The income from all your estates—rich, profitable lands—dwindles each year. You know that very well. And what is your answer? Spend, spend, spend. Take Diane up to Paris, squander a fortune on setting her up . . . "

"Enough! That's enough! I won't have my decisions, my actions, my . . . judged by a girl . . . a mere slip of a girl . . . a . . . a girl . . . fifteen years old . . . if that . . . " the comte stammered. He was suffocating in the hot, dusty room. He could not breathe. With shaking hands he loosened his neckband and unbuttoned his shirt.

Catherine waited calmly as her father mopped his forehead and rubbed his hands dry. He looked more weary than angry as he took another pinch of snuff.

"Therefore . . . a mill on the estate," she began again, as if her father had merely suffered a minor indisposition, ". . . would produce enough revenues to begin some of the maintenance and repairs that have been neglected over the years."

"*Mon cher enfant,*" the comte said sweetly. He always became more formal and polite when he felt most vicious. "*Mon cher enfant,*" he began again, unable to remember what he had wanted to say. Suddenly his pounding, choking anger fell away, and he felt weary and defeated, as if this pockmarked child of his were a fat, sluggish leech, fastened to his back, stubbornly sucking away his blood, draining his spirit.

"I need those maps right away," he said lamely, distractedly rubbing his hands with his soiled handkerchief. He half turned away from Catherine and began to shuffle through the pile of papers before him on the desk. Around one of the portfolios, a ribbon, yellowed and bleached by the years, broke and, with a dry, crackling sound, papers spilled over the comte's knees and onto the floor.

With a sharp cluck of irritation Catherine rose from her chair and stooped to collect the papers. Dried red sealing wax crumbled in chunks from the yellowed documents.

"Why? What do you intend to do with the papers?" she asked harshly.

The comte did not answer. He picked up a document and held it at arm's length, as if to read it.

"Papa, did you hear me? You might as well answer something, you know." She laughed spitefully, and took the document from his hand and placed it on the desk. "You aren't reading those letters at all, are you? Of course not, you know you need glasses to read."

Like a child, the comte folded his hands and said nothing.

"Besides, I needn't bother to ask what you want to do with the documents to Joigny. I know the answer already. You intend to sell off the river bottom parcels to Roger Saint-Valérien. But what am I saying? Sell? Why no! You are virtually *giving* the land to that beastly pig. Little more than a peasant! Selling land that has been in *our* family for over three centuries to Roger Saint-Valérien, whose grandfather was a stable boy at Corcheval! And for what? Sell it for what? So that you can treat yourself to new diamond bows for your court shoes?

Or . . . so that you can tart your precious daughter up and offer her to the King. Oh, I know what happened in Paris, all . . . "

The comte smashed his fist feebly against the desk, knocking over a stack of portfolios that slid across the desk.

"Shut up! Shut up! Will you not stop!" he croaked, slowly swinging his head from left to right.

Catherine returned to her chair, carefully arranging the folds of her skirt, as if she were sitting for her portrait, or preparing herself for a leisurely tête-à-tête. Her father had slumped back against his chair and stared straight ahead out the window. It had not rained for two weeks and the lush green lawns of the garden were yellow in spots.

Catherine cleared her throat. "Last week I called a meeting of the tenants and heard their complaints. Would you like to hear some of them? No? To sum it all up, then, since you don't appear to be particularly interested, your tenants, papa, are not a bad lot. They need to know that you are going to give them leadership and decent repairs so that they can bring in better and better harvests for you and so that their life is easier."

She stood up abruptly. "I must go. As you say, I'm only a girl. But, I warn you, papa," her voice hardened, "I shall not sit idly by while you bring this family and these lands to rack and ruin. With a little care we can be as rich as a pig like Roger Saint-Valérien. Richer, because we have more land."

Her hand on the door, Catherine turned and fixed her father with her fierce sunken eyes. "In five years, when I expect to be married, I intend to have a dowry so immense that I can pick and choose whomever I want. And I shall want the very best, you can be sure of that."

The double paneled door clacked sharply behind her. From the entrance way the comte could hear Philippe's voice as he gave the reins of his horse to the stable boy. Pushing the heaped papers aside, clearing a space, the comte bent over the desk and cradled his head in his arms. Blood throbbed in his ears, and his throat ached. He cursed himself for drinking too much the night before, for always drinking too much, getting giddy, staying up all hours, and waking the next morning, throat dry, hands shaking, weak and tired. Too weak and tired to stand up to his daughter! To be cowed by a child! Hectored and scolded in the vilest way. All the same, she is right, he thought, I ought to pay more attention to what my steward is doing. Though I'm no more negligent than Father. Why he woke up one morning after a high stakes game at the duc de Gesvres' and discovered that he had lost two estates entire. Not one but two. No one can accuse me of gambling away my lands, not even Catherine. I don't gamble and never will. But a man has debts, and a man of honor pays them off. He clenched his fists. He remembered how nasty his tailor had been about the suits he had ordered for the nuptial celebrations. Madame Clarisse had been much more reasonable . . . nonetheless, Diane's bills were staggering. His hands began to sweat. It would all be well . . . it would . . . it had to be. All was not lost with the King, not yet anyway. He would never presume to bring a bourgeoise to rub shoulders with the court. The princes of the blood would never countenance it. The King would soon tire of Madame d'Etioles' tricks. And then . . . then Diane's fresh innocence would sparkle in contrast. Poor Catherine, so much that she does not understand. The unfortunate child is consumed with jealousy of her beautiful sister and always has been.

He cackled brokenly and raised his head. Propping his head in his hands, he began to laugh hysterically. A dowry! Oh, my God, he thought, the creature has gone mad! The greatest fortune in France—and the noblest name—cannot purchase a husband for a face like that! Tears streamed down his cheek, and still he laughed, the huge room reverberating with his high-pitched, whinnying laughter.

A figure, a young woman in a straw hat with wide blue ribbons was crossing the garden. She carried a shallow basket of cut flowers—blue phlox and huge sprays of white tuberoses—from the parterres on the far side of the chapel. As she approached, the comte recognized Marianne and smiled to himself. Ah! He groaned aloud. I am too tired, he thought angrily, I am exhausted. I feel as if Catherine had been pummeling me about the head for hours. He stood up and tied the sash of his dressing gown. On second thought, Marianne will refresh me . . . like a drink of chilled champagne, he said to himself, walking over the papers scattered at his feet.

15

*B*lack, murky skies rumbled angrily and crashed, thunder clapped and jagged slivers of lightning, thin flashes of blue edged with yellow lit up the garden like the noonday sun, spreading shadows of the giant topiary animals standing patient watch over the battered flowers in the neat parterres. Through the night thick sheets of rain swirled round the ancient gray towers at Corcheval, coursed down the moss-covered walls and cascaded onto the flagstone terrace overlooking the garden. The searing hot drought of August was ending; the cracked, umber fields would soon grow green and springy underfoot.

Behind the glistening, rain-slicked stone walls the chateau was cloaked in darkness, save the tall windows on the far side overlooking the garden and lake. Through the narrow cracks of the partially closed shutters flickered the candlelight of the comtesse's room. For the past few weeks the comtesse spent most of her time seated near the window reading, or dozing over a book or her rosary, for, after a short while in bed, she would begin to gasp for breath and the pains in her chest would become unbearable. Even when Clotilde propped so many large, plump pillows behind her back that the comtesse virtually sat upright in bed, she had to fight for breath. So she sat by the window, watching the night fade into dawn, as Clotilde, open-mouthed, snored tranquilly in a chair near the door.

Soon the chateau came to life in the rain-washed dawn with the bustle of servants throwing open creaking wooden shutters, starting fires in the kitchen, gathering for breakfast around the oak table in the long, low kitchen paved with bricks streaked with paths worn dusty red by generations of kitchen servants in wooden sabots. The upper floors of the chateau remained hushed until the summer sun had dried the flagstones and gravel paths.

There was talk in the servants' quarters that the family would be dispersing before the harvest was done, the comte returning to court, the girls to Neuilly-les-Dames and the comtesse to the Sisters of Charity. But cook shook her head, and Agathe, who did the family washing, rolled her eyes toward the ceiling, as if to make sure that no one was listening, and said that the comtesse would not be going anywhere unless it be to the family chapel across the garden. Agathe had washed the comtesse's bloody handkerchiefs, and she knew what they meant. Some of the younger servants had never seen the comtesse except at a distance, huddled under her shawls on the terrace. But tales of the slim, pious comtesse who had withdrawn to a convent from the wicked world of Paris, who had nursed her stricken daughter back to life, inspired them to look upon her as a saint, self-denying, compassionate, and now an uncomplaining martyr quietly sliding into the arms of death.

The comtesse's illness, however, hung lightly over the summertime activities of the household. Tucked away in the corner of the terrace or garden, and later, secluded in her rooms at the end of the chateau, the comtesse and her sharp, moist cough and all that it presaged became merely another familiar element of the routine of their sun-filled days. Occasionally, Sophie brought her mother wildflowers from the fields—wild columbine and cornflowers and red-orange poppies—and sat for a few moments cautiously eyeing this curious woman who sat in a chair all day long. She helped Clotilde put the wildflowers in vases, arranging the drooping flowers with dainty little hands, diminutive hands with long tapering fingers, and before she left the room the poppies would spill out their gold and black dust onto the table lace.

Even after the arrival of Madeleine, however, Diane refused to give up her daily visits with her mother. After dinner every day she gathered her books and sewing and took up her place at her mother's side. She seemed to know instinctively what her mother wanted or needed: a fresh glass of water, a soothing witch hazel compress for her forehead, reading aloud poetry or Pascal. Diane had given up any idea of telling her mother what had happened with the King in Paris. Why add yet another burden to her sorrowful daily struggle with her lungs? Madeleine, as it turned out, was far too absorbed by her drama with Armand to be interested in taunting Diane about what the court might or might not be saying about the King and Madame d'Etioles. "She's a bourgeois tart. The King may be foolish, but not *that* foolish," Madeleine had said with her usual finality.

As for Catherine, she behaved as if she had not a care in the world. She appeared to have shrugged off any concern for her ruined face. In the scorching hot summer sun she had no pity for her horse, running him over hedgerow and ditch, up hill and across streams, as if she would know every tree, every stone on the vast, extended lands that belonged to her family. Most of the time Catherine missed dinnertime at Corcheval, preferring to accept the more humble hospitality of her father's tenants rather than halt her rambling tours with Pierre. On the rare occasions when she stayed at home, she sailed into the dining room and took over the conversation. She seemed unable to stop talking. She flaunted impious statements by Voltaire and other skeptics and watched with satisfaction as little Sophie stared at her in bewilderment.

When Catherine learned of Madeleine's proposed visit, she expected that any friend of her sister would serve as a delicious target. But Madeleine was not easily shocked by Catherine's irreverence. Indeed, Madeleine was not shocked at all. On the contrary, Catherine's overbearing talk seemed to bore her.

Madeleine was appalled that Diane and Sophie could endure the dullness of the country. Look at these empty salons, she would say, and that desolate garden! So boring! Diane reluctantly joined her friend at supper parties and receptions at the home of neighbors she would have preferred to ignore rather than to stir from the comfortable routines at Corcheval. Madeleine was like a tonic breeze fanning through the dusty chateau. She organized outings on the river, picnics, concerts, and when Armand arrived at Ancy, Madeleine and Odile agreed to produce a play in Roger Saint-Valérien's exquisite little theatre, which had been completed over a month before and which stood empty, unused, still smelling of fresh paints and plaster, its banners waving merrily on the flagpole outside, yet another symbol of Saint-Valérien's social ambitions and swelling income.

Odile and Madeleine argued endlessly over the choice of a play, Odile holding out for a tragedy by Racine in which she would quite naturally play the major role, until Armand decided that it would be a comedy and a comedy by Molière. Odile found it difficult to refuse him anything since he came down from Paris. So Molière it was, and Madeleine chose *Tartuffe*, joking that Armand would make a most convincing hypocrite. "And I shall play Elmire," said Odile, "And mind how you fondle my breasts in Act II, you sly and wily Tartuffe," giving Armand a long look, while he stared back at her innocently, as if impervious to her innuendo. Madeleine cast Diane in the role of Orgon's beautiful, hapless daughter whose tyrannical father tries to force her into marriage with Tartuffe. The choice role of Diane's pert, impertinent maid Madeleine reserved for herself.

"And where shall we place the table, *chère madame*?" asked Roger Saint-Valérien, lumbering bear-like across the stage. "I count on you for every thing, every little detail," he said squeezing Odile's elbow. He and Odile stood near the middle of the small stage surrounded by a rather large rectangular table, several chairs, six candlesticks, and an ornate candelabrum. A bulky, florid man, Roger Saint-Valérien towered over her. A heavy drinker who never felt that he had dined properly unless he fell asleep over his wine and brandy after dinner, Saint-Valérien's round face glowed a fiery red next to Odile's pallid bare shoulders and painted face.

"There are too many chairs. We shall be falling all over them," she said, gesturing to a footman to take the offending chairs away.

In front of the stage, his eyes closed, Armand lay back against a canapé and pretended to sleep. He could hear Odile's high-pitched voice, as artificial as a schoolgirl reciting her lessons, as she began practicing her role, declaiming to Orgon, her gullible fool of a husband about Tartuffe's lechery. The comte, playing Orgon, replied unctuously that she maligned their good, good friend. Ah, it takes a fool to play a fool, thought Armand. The comte is playing Orgon to perfection, to absolute perfection. The sly, treacherous dandy! Though why he should despise the comte so much he did not know. Surely not for tumbling Odile between the sheets. He had never been jealous of Odile and her admirers. What would be the point of that? No, the comte was welcome to take his pleasure there if it suited him, but these days he showed little interest in doing so. Two summers ago the comte had worn the roads smooth between Corcheval and Ancy. Now he stayed over only when he was too drunk to sit his horse, content to fall asleep in his chair with his boots still on. A pity that, thought Armand, with Odile panting after me, creeping into my bed with those clammy, cold feet.

Armand yawned and opened his eyes. The huge rafters and beams were coated gray with thick layers of dust. He closed his eyes drowsily and listened to the scuffle of chairs being moved across the stage.

Suddenly, a cold hand slid down his loosened shirtfront. Clamping his fist around the hand, he jolted himself upright.

"Ah! Madeleine! What the devil are you doing?" he growled. He glanced swiftly about at the rows of chairs in the darkened hall to see whether anyone had seen Madeleine's impudently familiar gesture. Diane had left the little theatre and had gone for a walk with Saint-Valérien's son Jules, who had promised to show her the new fountains in the garden. Two footmen and a carpenter hung about in the shadows along the wall, gazing raptly at the stage where the comte and Odile moved about reading their lines from hand-copied sheets.

Madeleine giggled and sat down beside Armand, nudging him with her hips to make room on the narrow seat.

"Don't worry! No one saw me, if that's what you're afraid of."

Armand slumped down in the uncomfortable canapé and once more pretended to doze. God! He could get no peace! A clever girl, Madeleine, and he liked her spirit. She was like a bold, rambunctious boy, running over with energy, spoiling for fun. But it wasn't fun anymore. Couldn't she see that? They were all like that, these naive girls coming up to Paris from the convent, suddenly swimming in the thick of the intrigues at court and in Paris. Dying of curiosity. Wanting to taste the forbidden pleasures. Madeleine, so eager and willing to find out what the grownups did behind locked doors after the balls and receptions were over.

"I said, no one saw me," Madeleine raised her voice angrily and poked him with her elbow.

"Please. I heard you," he said softly, without turning to look at her.

Madeleine gazed lovingly at his strong, cleanly sculpted profile. His dark brown eyes, the left lid drooping almost shut, stared coldly into the distance.

"What is it, Armand?" Madeleine asked plaintively. "What has happened to change you?" She waited. He sighed noisily. "Have I done something wrong?" Her voice sounded small and childlike.

"Why must you always be pestering me with these questions? Just leave me be! Leave me be!" he spat out. Madeleine put her hand on his arm as he sat up as if to leave.

"Don't go, Armand! We never see each other any more. Only a minute or two. And we never talk. In Paris you said . . . "

"Paris! This is not Paris. Obviously." Armand buttoned his shirt and tightened the silk stock at his neck.

"In Paris you said," Madeleine continued, jutting her chin forward angrily, "we would be able to see each other freely, whenever we wished. And now that I've persuaded my aunt, no easy job, to let me come down to the country, you have better things to do, it would appear, than to have anything to do with . . . "

"What do you mean? We are together! Right here! Right now! We see each other every day. We lunch together, dine together, walk together . . . and now we have this foolish play. Another of your bright ideas." He was choking with impatience.

"Yes, this foolish play that gives you a chance to drool every time you look at Diane! To make eyes at her! Don't think I don't see what's going on! Ever since you came down, you're like . . . you're like . . . oh, I don't know, you're like Jean-Christophe mooning around over her."

"Shut up! Shut up!" Armand stood in front of her, his back to the stage where Catherine as Orgon's mother was extolling

Tartuffe's piety to her maid Sophie. The comte sat to one side of the proscenium arch with Roger Saint-Valérien and whinnied with exaggerated mirth at Catherine's spirited performance.

Madeleine stared defiantly at Armand, hovering angrily above her. "Well?" she asked.

"Well what?"

"You don't deny it, do you? You can't deny it, because you know that it's true! You can't get enough of looking at her and following her around just hoping that you can say something witty and make her laugh. Or quote some scrap of sentimental trash to make her give you a tender look. She's a cold fish. The King has turned her head, and now her father is out to marry her to the biggest fortune in France, and you're nothing. Nothing at all. Worse than nothing." Madeleine's voice rasped harshly in his ears. She was panting, and her eyes bulged angrily.

"And you, my dear," he drawled, slowly, menacingly. "I suppose that you are going to marry for love. Is that what you're saying? And Diane, ah, me! Wretched Diane will marry for money. Fie! Fie! For shame," he said, mocking her.

"I would! I would! I would marry . . . for love!" She sounded suddenly broken, her shoulders collapsed, she bent her head and stared at her clasped hands. "But . . . you're nothing, worse than nothing!" she said angrily, starting up again. "Unless Odile spreads her legs for the right minister you'll have . . . nothing . . . ." Her voice trailed off weakly as Armand strode away from her toward the bright sunshine of the open doors. His footsteps thudded angrily against the crude wooden floors. Catherine looked up from her text and watched as he walked away.

Emerging from the darkness of the renovated barn, Armand shut his eyes reflexively against the brilliant sunshine. Up the sloping graveled walkway, he saw Diane seated on a stone bench while Jules Saint-Valérien held a flimsy parasol over her, shading her from the sun. Smiling, Diane sat looking up at Jules, who was talking animatedly, one foot, sleekly booted in soft brown leather, jauntily perched on the bench.

Armand felt jealousy whip through him. Neither Diane nor Jules took any notice of him as he drew near. Jules Saint-Valérien had the soft, pretty looks of an adolescent girl and was awkward and shy. He was the eldest of seven children and so timid and delicately comely that his robust father seemed ashamed of him. Armand had never heard Jules Saint-Valérien speak in the presence of his father. At dinner parties he would sit silently, slowly chewing his food, not daring to raise his eyes from his plate. Diane must have worked some sort of magic, thought Armand, watching Jules, his chin cupped indolently in his hand, his elbow on his thigh, swaying before her.

"Well, young lovers, aren't you afraid that you'll miss your big scene by dawdling out here in the garden?" Armand asked gruffly.

Diane turned to him with a startled look. It had been Odile's idea to give the part of Diane's lover to Jules, a sop to Roger Saint-Valérien's pride because he had been chucked aside as Orgon when the comte was chosen to play the part. If Roger Saint-Valérien noticed that, with Armand playing the leading role of Tartuffe, there was no other suitable young man to play opposite Diane, he had the good grace not to mention it. "Really? What time can it be? Are you sure that they are ready for our scene, Armand?"

Armand had not the faintest idea and almost said so, but did not for fear that Diane would be angry. She looked lovely sitting in the shade of the parasol, her fine, creamy complexion bathed in a soft pink glow. Armand watched a thin blue vein throbbing in her throat, just below the jaw line, and longed to run his fingertips along it, up her chin, to her softly swelling lips. She looked so lovely. And clean, he thought ruefully. As Odile did not. Nor Madeleine.

"It will only take a moment to find out. I shall just run down and check," Jules said, suddenly unsure of himself in front of Armand. "I shall just have a look." And he trotted off down the hill. "Oh, dear," he said, running back with the parasol, which he thrust clumsily into Armand's hand. "Oh, dear," Jules said again.

Armand watched Jules disappear into the darkness of the theatre. Now that he was alone with Diane, he could think of nothing to say. His angry exchange with Madeleine still rankled him, irritated him like a sore tooth in the middle of a delicious meal.

He realized that Diane sat quietly observing him. "So? Are you amused by the young Jules? Not too countrified for you?"

"Oh, no, not at all," she said sweetly. "He reads a lot, you know."

"No, I didn't know," he said shortly and regretted the petulant tone in his voice. "Young Saint-Valérien is not the sort of person one knows much about. Or that one notices, really."

"I know," she said agreeably, in the same kind, smiling manner, which disconcerted him entirely. As if she knew that it disconcerted him. Madeleine's accusations rang in his ear. Was he as obvious as she made out? Was he indeed twisting and turning in the throes of an absurd infatuation?

He stepped closer to the bench and held the parasol over her.

"Really, Armand, you mustn't tire yourself. I shall simply turn away from the sun and shade my face. You mustn't bother." She treated him with the polite manners of a kind relative—an older sister perhaps? What had come over them both? Try as he might, he could not puzzle it out. When she had first come to Paris, in those fussy, fancy gowns of hers and her country speech and gawky manners, he had been able to twist her around his little finger. She had been intoxicated with him. And then, her father had frightened her away. And Armand had not been sufficiently interested to pursue her. What was she after all but an innocent little creature from the convent? He and Odile had laughed about her, laughed at her, as they made love on the rustling mattress of Odile's canopied bed, the taut ropes of the bedstead sawing and moaning beneath them. Then, what had come over him? Why should he stand before her and hunger to stroke her silver-gold hair, warmed by the sunshine?

Diane touched her hair, pushing a wispy strand back from her forehead. "What's the matter, Armand? Am I losing a pin?"

"Losing what? A pin?"

"Yes. You've been staring at my hair for the longest time. Do I have a pin sticking out somewhere?" She ran her hand over her chignon, fingering each pin.

"No, no, of course not," he said gently. "Your hair is beautiful, not a lock out of place. I was just thinking, that's all. I was wondering when you plan to leave for Paris. Will you be leaving with Madeleine? And your father?"

"I don't know. Papa hasn't said yet." Frowning, she looked away toward the rambling manor house, the brickwork of fresh additions looking raw in the sunlight.

"What do you mean?" Armand had a hollow feeling in his stomach. "Do you mean that he hasn't set a date for your departure yet?"

"He's said nothing. Nothing about my returning to Paris." She looked at him anxiously, as if he could reassure her. "I think that I may be going back to the convent with my sisters."

"Back to the convent? But why?"

"Papa was not pleased with me . . . not pleased at all." She looked as if she were struggling to say the words. "He was angry with me because . . . the King did not choose me after all. He had counted on that. He thought it was a sure thing. The duc de Richelieu did, too. And then the King did not choose me." Her voice had dropped almost to a whisper, but she held his gaze steadily with her clear gray eyes.

"The King was a fool," Armand said.

16

A naked leg, lean ankle, plump and smooth calf and thigh, lay atop a tangle of covers in the large, square bed standing boldly near the center of the room. Marianne slept soundly, breathing heavily, her face turned slightly to one side in the soft down pillows. Late summer flies, fat and lazy, crawled desultorily up the sides of the half-filled wine glasses on the table next to the bed.

Carefully turning his back to the naked woman sprawling across the comte's bed, old Clovis knelt before his master with three pairs of brightly colored shoes.

"The blue pair," said the comte. "I'll take the buckles along . . . no, I'll put the buckles on now." Clovis adjusted the buckles and tightened the slippers over the comte's high instep. "Not too tight, *mon vieux,* you'll have me hobbling across the stage tonight."

The old man smiled and bowed and left the room, carrying the remaining pairs of gaudy satin shoes before him like precious objects.

The comte crossed the room to his casket of jewels and began to place rings on each of his fingers. In the garden below his windows he could hear the noise of steps on the gravel paths and the voices of Sophie and Madeleine walking toward the boxwood maze. The comte paused for a moment to listen, but could make out nothing. Madeleine laughed, a short, flat, mocking sound. I don't trust that one, the comte thought. She's already too hard, too cynical. Two seasons in Paris and the court, even with Madame de Sabran at her elbow shouldn't turn her that sour. The girl's got vinegar running through her veins. Small wonder that Odile's protégé runs from her as fast as he can. Right toward Diane. He's too sly, that one. Armand is like Odile. He wants what he can't get. And he wants Diane about as badly as I've ever seen a man want any woman. That drooping eyelid of his, it makes him look as if he's got his eye out to grab something when you aren't looking. But I don't have to worry about Armand. Not any more. I know my girl, and she has gone far beyond a nobody like Mézières. She has changed since the King gave her those flowers at Sceaux. She is as calm and beautiful as the lake on a hot afternoon. And she has gained weight, gotten a little rounder like Madeleine. Madeleine may not be a beauty, but she can be proud of that figure of hers. I like a woman with long legs. And good, round breasts. He turned toward the bed.

"Marianne! Do you hear me? I won't have the servants finding you in my bed when they make up the room tonight! *Merde!* Get up, girl!"

It's not as if she worked herself to death with Diane. Down here in the country there is precious little for her to do, he grumbled to himself. Even in Paris Diane is not the sort to make demands on a servant. I shall have to think of cutting back on Marianne's wages in a month or two, he thought. I've got to start somewhere. Of course, Marianne won't like that, will she? And if she makes a fuss, I'll send her packing. A lady's maid should never sleep with the men in her household. She ought to know that. Diane will protest. Naturally. She has grown quite fond of the little minx. Diane will weep and plead with me, and I shall have to put up with it. Until I get my way.

There was a short knock at the door. The comte tightened the black velvet bow on the braid of his wig and opened the door slightly. It was Diane.

"Papa. It's maman. She's not at all well this evening. I must stay. I can't leave her like this."

"Nonsense, you're too important in the play. The play's too important," the comte said impatiently. The child always exaggerated. The comtesse was no doubt having a restless day. The summer storms had been fierce the past few nights, and she must have lost sleep. Diane looked distraught. "Oh, all right. I shall come directly."

Reclining against a half dozen pillows, the comtesse sat upright in her canopied bed, so close to one side that she looked as if she might topple out of it onto the rush matting of the floor. Her eyes were closed, and she might have been dozing peacefully in the middle of a hot afternoon in the country. Her lids were bluish gray, her eyes, deep-hollowed, sunken into mauve and blue shadows. Her long, fine silver-blond hair, like Diane's, spread out about her shoulders.

As the comte approached the bed, he saw on the pillow, next to her shoulder, a large, jagged spot of fresh blood—bright, orange red, next to the soft blond of the comtesse's hair. Her hair, it looks clean, freshly washed, as if spread out over the pillows to dry, thought the comte, abashed by the sudden rush of tears to his eyes.

"Madame . . . " he said softly, holding his breath. Diane had left the door partially open for him, and she now stood next to the prie-dieu at the foot of the bed. The windows had not been opened for weeks, and the room smelled stuffy, the air still and lifeless, laden with the odors of camphor and herbs, of mucous and blood, odors of the sickroom. Odors of death.

"Madame . . . " the comte said again, his voice shaky, breaking over the two syllables.

The comtesse weakly raised a hand to cover her throat and opened her eyes. She gazed for a moment at Diane standing at the foot of the bed, then slowly turned to follow the direction of Diane's stare.

"Ah, Monsieur!" the comtesse said in a long sigh.

The comte raised her thin, blue-veined hand and pressed it to his lips.

The comtesse tried to raise her head and fell back against the pillow. With great effort she turned her head so that she could look more directly into her husband's eyes.

The comte stroked her pitifully wasted hand.

"Maman is very upset," Diane whispered, rubbing her skirt nervously. "Since this morning she's called for you, and I didn't . . . "

"Shhh . . . shhhh . . . " With trembling hand the comte reached out and stroked his wife's hair. He could not remember ever being so afraid. Not even at Villaviciosa when his horse pitched him in a ditch and his whole regiment charged forward over him. Then he had known why he was afraid. When his hand trembled, and his throat tightened, he knew why. Looking into his wife's sunken eyes, listening to her rasping breathing, he could feel his knees tremble. Her face was wasted and gray. But still beautiful. On that mild spring day in April, kneeling on the cold stones of the chapel at Ancy, everyone had envied him. He was about to marry one of the most breathtaking beauties in France, trailing behind her wedding train three of the finest chateaux in Burgundy and hectare upon hectare of timbered land. Golden louis coins reaching up to the skies. Aurélie de Fougerolles d'Ancy. He had been so proud of her, of the way men stared unblinking as she strolled, unheeding, unaware, through the halls of Versailles, the mirrored halls reverberating with her silver-blond beauty. He had been so proud of her.

"The chapel . . . ," the comtesse said.

"Ahhh, yes, of course, Madame. "*Your* chapel. The one I built for you many years ago." He smiled feebly. He could feel himself sweating, and his scalp underneath his wig itched unbearably.

The comtesse closed her eyes and brought both her hands to her throat.

"I don't want to be buried in that chapel," she said.

The comte opened the door halfway and peered briefly into the room. "Gone. Good," he muttered, slamming the door shut before hurrying down the hallway. He thought he heard footsteps behind him and turned to see whether Diane was following him. The long, straight corridor was empty. He hurried down the curving staircase, his heels clattering noisily in the empty foyer. Outside, standing in the shade of his immense carriage, Catherine and Madeleine and Sophie were laughing and talking. Madeleine swung a wicker basket of fruit back and forth.

"In we go. We shall be late. Where's Diane?" The comte placed his hand under Sophie's elbow and briskly helped her up the steps of the carriage. "Where the deuce is Diane?" he asked again, just as she ran down the steps, both hands holding high her swaying skirts.

"We shall be late," the comte said irritably, stepping back to let her pass.

"We've plenty of time," Catherine said. She never missed a chance to contradict her father. "The roads are in splendid shape."

Catherine carefully arranged her skirts and lifted her feet as Laurent placed a small round velvet stool beneath them.

"I stopped in to see maman again," Diane said quietly.

"And?"

"She was sleeping."

"You see? You exaggerate. As always."

"But Clotilde is afraid that maman will not last through the night." Sophie crossed herself and stared at her with alarm. Diane looked up at her mother's window as the footman closed the carriage door. "I've sent for Uncle Philippe. He will be a comfort to maman."

"Nonsense! Clotilde is being melodramatic. I saw your mother myself, only a few minutes ago, and she was merely tired. A little depressed, perhaps. Imagining morbid things."

The carriage rocked briefly as Laurent climbed to his seat next to the driver, and they started off with a lurch down the tree-lined drive to the main road.

The comte sighed happily and stretched his legs. "I can't wait to see what our country neighbors will make of us tonight! Splendid idea of yours, Madeleine! Such a tonic, these theatricals!"

"You're behaving like a fool! A stupid, lovesick fool!" Odile snarled, her eyes black and furious. His back turned to her, Armand stood peering round the curtain of the small, improvised cubicle Odile was using as her dressing room. She was wearing thick, white paint and dark red rouge. "She is still the foolish little simpleton that you made such fun of before the King took a fancy to her. That's it, isn't it? You are itching after her because of the King. Don't you see? But she's the same! She hasn't changed a whit!"

"And why should she change?" Armand asked wearily. "The King was charmed by her just the way she is. Her innocence, for one thing. Her purity . . ."

"Her innocence! Ha! But aren't you forgetting, my dear, that the King was not so charmed after all? Else why would he cut her cold the night of the yew tree ball? Your precious Diane might as well not have existed for all the King cared."

"That was all politics. The usual intrigue. And you know it. The King couldn't stomach Fautrière when it came down to that. The King didn't turn away from Diane."

"Then why is he so besotted with Madame d'Etioles that he is having her tutored in the ways of the other country while he is with his army in Compiègne? The scheming little hussy is in the country with the abbé de Bernis learning court etiquette from A to Zed! I have it on the best authority," she said, nodding her head sharply.

"You have everything on the best authority," Armand muttered to himself. "They shall be ready for us soon. You'd better set your mind on the play unless you mean to stumble all over yourself again once you get on stage."

Odile bridled. She had come close to spoiling her big scene with Armand, jumbling her lines and becoming shrill in her confusion. At one point, as Tartuffe moved to caress her knee, she had completely forgotten her lines, and the audience tittered as the silvery, childish voice of Sophie, who also served as prompter, whispered them to her. Odile had expected to dazzle her country neighbors, who had begged and jostled for invitations, had crowded into the small theatre, with her sophisticated performance. Instead, she had panicked and bumbled along like a mechanical doll while the audience howled with glee at Armand's roguish posturing. She no longer felt at ease with Armand. The more he eluded her, the more obsessed she became.

"Damn the play! What should I care? These yokels wouldn't know Molière from Mother Goose!"

"So . . . ," Armand said, dropping the curtain and turning to her, "you think that the King is quite serious about Madame d'Etioles?"

"What?"

"Do you think the King intends to make her his official mistress?"

"How should I know?" Odile asked, exasperated by his hangdog expression. "Why should you care? What difference does it make to you if he does or if he does not?"

Armand turned away and lifted the curtain once again. The

comte might not bring Diane back to Paris if he thought that Madame d'Etioles were more than a passing fancy.

"The King may very well surprise us all," she said, but Armand seemed to be following the play and did not reply. "Maupeou says that the King wants no more to do with mistresses from the aristocracy. They meddle too much in state affairs. They demand too much, and their relatives expect to get lucrative positions. The King may very well stuff a commoner down our throats. Are you listening, Armand?"

Armand heard Diane say, in a low, plaintiff voice, "Do not employ a father's power, I pray you,/ To crush my heart and force it to obey you." The comte scolded her roundly in a pompous manner, and the audience hissed its disapproval.

"You hear that?" Odile asked. "They love it! Even the comte is not too corny for them. Here, help me lace these ribbons."

Armand did not move away from the curtain. "You've changed your gown. Why?" Odile had put on a low cut, dark mauve taffeta gown that displayed her breasts in all their glory.

"My husband is a rich man, remember? I can't go around in the same old frock day after day. Besides, Tartuffe—that's you, my darling—and Roger Saint-Valérien want to see me in a gown that shows off my lovely bosom." Armand pulled tightly at the ribbons as Odile quickly laced them into place. "Hmm? Don't you prefer a low-cut corsage? Or was that before you made up your mind to behave like a simpleton over Diane de Fautrière?" Odile grabbed his arm and pushed her narrow, ferret-like face toward him. She raised her eyebrows, and her forehead wrinkled into deep furrows under the thick paint.

Armand bent his head and kissed her gently on the forehead. "Why must you go on and on about Diane? You're growing tiresome, do you know that? Jealousy doesn't become you. It never did."

"Jealousy! Jealousy! You're delirious! I have no desire to see you make a fool of yourself over that girl. Nothing more! Jealous! You're mistaking me for Madeleine, is that it?" Armand's fling with Madeleine had amused Odile more than anything else. She had known from the beginning how it would begin. And how it would end. Madeleine blustered and boasted and got what she deserved.

"Madeleine can be tiresome as well. And for the same reason."

"Poor girl, she has every right to be wounded by your neglect of her. Her aunt virtually had her under lock and key because of you and your shenanigans. Madeleine had to use all her wits to get down to the country. And all because of you. To see you and to be with you. The poor girl is sick for love of you, never mind her crowing about being a woman of the world! And you flee her like the plague! Hardly what a girl would expect after the fix you left her in."

"Fix? What fix? Madeleine knew from the beginning that it would be . . . that we would have . . . an agreeable little flirtation. That was understood. And we were terribly discreet."

"Discreet, were you? Well, my dear, these agreeable little flirtations sometimes have consequences that aren't very discreet. Not very discreet at all." Odile sat down in a soft bergère that Saint-Valérien had put there especially for her use during the performance. Armand's puzzled expression amused her. She sucked in her cheeks in a complacent gesture and waited for him to speak.

"Do you mean that I made her pregnant? Is that what you are saying?" Armand asked slowly.

"Of course, that's what I mean. What else could I mean?"

"Madeleine has said nothing to me about it. Nothing at all. Why wouldn't she say something to me?"

"Why should she? She is not a bourgeoise, after all. What could you have done that I couldn't do better? She came to me—don't you remember the night of the Opéra ball when you were gambling at the duc de Gesvres' and she was gone by the time you got to the ball.

"And what did you do? For Madeleine when she came to you?"

"I sent her to my woman, what else? As a matter of fact, I took her there myself, even though the foul hag refuses to handle my own business anymore, and the poor girl stayed a few days with me until she was back on her feet. It's not a pleasant affair, you know." She looked at him accusingly.

Not a pleasant affair at all. He leaned against the wall, feeling sick to his stomach. He could feel again Odile's hot, steamy room that November afternoon; he smelled again the sweet, cloying smell of blood. He remembered with revulsion the thick, pulpy mess spreading out bright blood red over the white linen sheets, the feel of it on his hands, sticky, wet, the smell nauseating, turning his stomach over, and Odile laughing, laughing, her narrow white shoulders shaking with laughter. And Odile, her tongue thick with brandy, saying over and over. I got rid of the little bastard, all by myself, I got rid of the comte's little bastard. All by myself. She had laughed, and he had crept away from the dirty bed, the smelly bed where she lay, contentedly sleeping as the foul blood oozed onto the linen sheets.

"Do you have any brandy?" he asked, feeling weak, feeling the foulness of that winter afternoon all over again.

"Jésu!" she cried. "You're as pale as a ghost! Don't faint! Just don't faint! There's some brandy here somewhere. I had a glass with the comte this evening. Oh, for God's sake, where is it?"

She found the brandy and poured him a glass.

"My dear, I had no idea you were so sensitive. You do make such a fuss! Sit down. You mustn't be upset. It's all right now. It's over. Dear, dear!"

Armand sat quietly staring into space, waiting for the giddiness to pass. He did not care what Odile thought. He could not bear the idea of ever touching her again. Madeleine, too. Foul and dirty, the stench of hot, sticky blood. Odile stood at a distance watching him finish his drink.

A hand pushed the curtain aside. Diane leaned forward into the cubicle, her face flushed and moist. "They're ready for you. A part of the set fell over, but Jules and the carpenter have put it back up." She looked at Armand and smiled, "Do hurry, Armand! Now's your chance to seduce Odile!"

"He's done that already," Odile said, her starkly painted face grim and sullen.

From the carriage window Diane watched the faint pink blush of dawn creep over the dewy fields. Everyone slept. Sophie had pulled a lace cap over her curls before falling asleep with her head in Diane's lap. Catherine held herself stiffly in the corner opposite, her head slipping down, down, down to her chest, then with a jerk upward, it would begin again its nodding journey downward. Madeleine slept, the hood of her cloak covering her face. The comte lay sprawled against the seat, breathing stertorously through his open mouth, his legs spread, his wig askew. Poor papa, he likes his wine too much, thought Diane.

She was too worried to sleep. All evening long the pale, emaciated image of her mother had dogged her every moment. She had played her part as best she knew how, which must have been satisfactory for the audience had clapped and clapped and had thrown flowers into a heap at her feet as she and Jules smiled and bowed again and again. Nonetheless, she had felt locked out of the gaiety and exhilaration of the evening.

Afterwards, Madame Saint-Valérien led them away to tables sparkling with white linen cloths and cut crystal and fine china. Somehow it was decided that Armand should sit next to Diane as a consolation for Tartuffe's being caught out by the comte and not getting her hand in marriage. Raucous laughter and the deafening noise of voices, babbling hilariously, swirled about them. As the supper progressed, chairs crashed backward to the floor in drunken, rowdy horseplay. Armand complained of a headache and forced down only a bite or two of roast beef. He looked pale and barely said a word to her. Madeleine spent most of the meal glaring at her and trying to catch Armand's eye. No need to feel jealous of me, Diane thought, not at all. There's not a trace of that intoxication left. Only a fleeting memory of her father's sword smashing down on her dressing table, and terrible guilt at having failed in her duty to the family, to her father. Odd, though, that such powerful yearning could be sealed away forever. Once, in reaching for his wine glass Armand's hand brushed her arm. And she felt nothing. How very odd.

Toward dawn Catherine made a nasty scene and insisted that they leave immediately. Before my father gets any drunker, she said. The room grew quiet for a moment, and the Saint-Valériens looked embarrassed as the comte, Madeleine, Sophie, and Diane followed Catherine to the carriage. There was hardly enough time to say goodbye, to thank their hosts, to hurry into their wraps for the return to Corcheval. Diane was appalled by Catherine's belligerence. How dare she! And poor papa, so cowed, humiliated. Really, she was insufferable, this sister of hers. Diane watched as Catherine's nodding head jerked upward again and settled back against the cushions. Ah, but poor, poor thing, she thought, staring at her sister's ravaged face. Is it any wonder?

The carriage slowed and swayed to one side as it turned into the tree-lined avenue. Straggling snatches of mist clung to the trees and bushes in the garden. Diane held Sophie's head with one hand and leaned forward and shook her father's knee. He opened his eyes and yawned and began to slap himself on the arms and thighs.

"Have I been asleep?" he asked, and looked sheepishly toward Catherine, whose head had slumped forward again.

Footmen appeared as if miraculously from the fog-wreathed chateau as the carriage pulled up to the entrance steps. Old Clovis carried a lighted torch above his head as he creaked down the stone steps, somewhat sideways, favoring his bad left hip.

Behind him, at the top of the steps, stood Philippe d'Ancy, somber in his fustian riding clothes, his head bare in the damp morning air. Diane took one look at his face and began to weep.

Diane breathed on the silver beaker and rubbed it vigorously with her handkerchief. She brought the beaker close to her face and smoothed her hair into place with her hand. The windows, mirrors, doorways, and beds in the room were draped in heavy black crepe. On the commode next to the door Clotilde had placed Diane's new black satin cap. Diane pushed her hair up under the stiff cap and raised the beaker to get a glimpse of herself.

The air smelled of clean, sweet straw. Diane took a deep breath. Not like the dank, moldy straw they packed around maman's coffin, she thought. The odor of mildew had lingered in the air as the footmen with their pastel gloves pushed and shoved the coffin onto the wagon as Uncle Philippe waited, his eyes never leaving the black lacquered coffin that held his sister.

Half-filled boxes and cartons of laces and ribbons were strewn about the room. Try as she might, she could not suppress her joy every time she looked at them, no matter how often she crossed herself and loathed herself for feeling such elation. She sat down on the bed, her head in her hands. It was not right to feel like this now that her mother was dead. But she could not help it. She wanted to cry; she wanted to pray for her sin of callousness, of indifference. But she could not. Not after her father had told her that he would be taking her back to Paris with him. As soon as he signed the papers with Roger Saint-Valérien. Paris! Paris! The balls, receptions, plays, concerts, the pageantry. This time she would be ready. Now she knew that she would have to marry, would have to accept the man that her father deemed necessary for the family fortunes. The idea still frightened her, but she was no longer a silly convent girl. This was the life ahead of her. And she must accept it without letting it destroy her as it had her mother. It had been good to come to the country, to get away from the sharp, smarting blow of being dropped by the King. Good to come to the country and miss the excitement of it all, miss it so much that it was a grinding ache that she woke up to every morning. Yes, this time she would be ready.

Book Four

17

Normally, Diane would have been in bed, fast asleep, hours before, but she sat at the piano playing as many of Couperin's gavottes as she had learned by heart, hoping to ease her melancholy with dance music only to find that each piece brought back a tangle of wistful memories of whirling through dance after dance in the King's arms.

Diane stopped playing and listened. Down below in the foyer she could hear old Clovis calling for Laurent's help. Her father, no doubt, coming home in his usual state after a long evening with the marquise de Sabran, his ever patient friend, who listened, tirelessly, it seemed, to his drunken ramblings about his ambitions, his schemes, his disappointments.

She lifted her hands to the keyboard again, then let them fall. Nothing seemed to go papa's way now, she thought, not since the King chose the beautiful shepherdess. Her father had lost his tiny, foul-smelling cubicle under the eaves at Versailles, he had been forced to give up his own apartment as well as her luxurious townhouse on the rue des Trois Pavillons and had established a residence for both of them on the rue des Fours. Though friends exclaimed over the fine taste and opulent furnishings, some of them hired, neither she nor her father was fooled. They knew that they had been diminished in the eyes of the fashionable world by moving to the rue des Fours. A somber mood reigned in the modest but elegant apartment.

Since coming out of deep mourning, she had attended a dozen or so dinner parties in the world she had known before her abject, confused departure from Paris. Although she had walked several evenings in the Cours-de-la-Reine with Madeleine and had greeted acquaintances with a nod or a handshake, she still felt removed from the life she had lived before she left for Corcheval. Around a crowded dinner table, as she listened to the familiar patter of gossip and flattery, the angling for advantage, the posturing, the preening, the boasting, she now felt content. Content with herself that at some point over the past year she had made peace with this world. She was relaxed, unafraid of the impression she might be making, not hungry for the words and attention that would make her feel beautiful and admired. The court now seemed to her a distant country indeed, one that she would visit in the future only as a foreigner, an outsider.

She sighed and resumed her playing. With any luck, her father would continue his tipsy way to his room and leave her to her solitude. She doubted that in her present mood, heavy with the loss of her mother and anxiety about the future, he would take much pleasure in her company. She spent most of her time alone, diligently working on her lessons or writing verse.

Behind her, the double doors burst open with a crash, and Diane cried out in alarm as a blur of dingy yellow fur flew past the piano, tangled itself in a rug, and leapt, clawing with all its might, into the heavy velvet draperies at the windows. It was the ugliest, dirtiest cat Diane had ever seen.

Panting, bellowing with laughter, the comte staggered toward her and swept her into his arms. "Shhh!" he said, putting his finger to his lips, "It's a surprise! A gift!"

"What? That dirty cat?"

"Not so dirty, my dear. A cat. A gift for Marianne!"

"Marianne hates cats."

"I know," the comte said, grinning blissfully.

"They terrify her," Diane said, trying not to laugh.

"I know," he said, rubbing his hands together with glee.

Diane laughed in pure delight. This was the father she loved best, the naughty little boy tickled pink with his silly tricks. High in the folds of the draperies, the cat clung to its perch and watched them with a baleful glare.

"But sit, sit, play me something to soothe my nerves." Her father spread his coattails and settled into a bergère next to the piano. "It's been a trying day. The King, I'll have you know, has purchased the title of Marquise de Pompadour for his new mistress. She'll have her own little stool, all the privileges of a duchesse. She's been officially presented to the King and Queen, escorted by the dowager Princesse de Conti. Can you imagine it? The Princesse agreed to the presentation on the condition that Louis settle her gambling debts."

Diane sensed his hilarious mood slipping away. The favorite's presentation at court spelled the end of his hopes, didn't it? Louis would not name Diane his titled mistress. Not now. Perhaps never. She felt as if someone had quickly stepped forward and closed the door to a bright, shining room, shutting her out forever.

"La Pompadour has even secured a sizable pension for Madame Lebon, the fortune-teller who predicted that she would one day be the mistress of Louis XV. It's just as the Queen says. It's the devil's work that this woman is up to. A sorcerer on the King's purse!"

"I'm sorry, papa," Diane said softly, her dark eyes moist with tears.

At that moment, the comte could not believe that a more beautiful woman could ever have walked the face of the earth. "Fie! Fie! *Mon trésor*," he reached forward and took both her hands in his. "What are those tears all about? Hein? Tell me you haven't noticed old Clovis staggering into my dressing room at noon every day with a tray piled high with gleaming white cards and invitations. And each one of them containing a handwritten postscript requesting the pleasure of Mademoiselle Diane de Fautrière's company as well. You're a celebrated beauty, my dear! They're all begging for the honor of entertaining you!"

And, he said to himself, even after the merely curious have satisfied themselves with a close look at the young woman who danced so exquisitely with the King, the aura of her fame and beauty will linger—long enough to secure her future *and* mine. He knew that he was drifting faster and faster downstream financially, and there were precious few lands left to mortgage or to sell. Nonetheless, there was no need to panic. Yes, lands were one thing—good, rich river bottom lands, and thick stands of timber spreading as far as the eye could see, and vast, rambling chateaux full of the treasures of the past—but the father of a famous beauty who had turned the head of a king could sleep a little more easily than the ordinary man in France in 1745.

With a loud thump the panic-stricken cat fell to the floor and streaked past them to the door.

"What in God's name was that?" asked the comte, stirring from his reverie.

Diane laughed gaily. "Your gift to Marianne. Remember?"

One day while I was attending Mass at the Jacobins' church, Rue St. Jacques, the Chevalier de V— entered a moment after me with an officer of the Swiss Guard whom I had never seen. They greeted me and sat down across from me . . . . The impression that we made upon each other was so overwhelming that we both swooned.

Marianne heaved an impatient sigh as Father Bertrand ambled from the side aisle and began to fuss around the altar table. Diane gave her a disapproving look, and Marianne shrugged and twisted her mouth into a pout. Recently, Marianne had begun to behave like a rude, unruly child at mass, and Diane had reluctantly complained to her father, who laughed and said that the little wench had plenty of spirit and had left it at that. Marianne spent more and more of her time gadding about the city doing the errands and making the purchases that the comte's steward used to be responsible for. Little by little, she had taken over the running of the household, and she dressed smartly for the part. And she had of late grown much bolder in expressing her displeasure with some of the requirements of her situation. Why must we be always running to mass? she would say. We don't live in a convent, for heaven's sake!

In particular, Marianne complained about the Eglise Saint-Jacques because it was damp and bone-chilling in the winter months, even when the coachman brought their foot braziers with them. But Diane was fond of the old church where few fashionable people brightened the gloomy interior with their gaudy, peacock clothes. Besides, the church reminded her of her mother, whom Diane had begun to idealize. Her mother, after all, had bravely defied fashion, the court and its frivolity, to give herself to good works and prayer. She was kind, gentle, pure; if only I can be like that, Diane thought, but how difficult that will be, now that she is no longer here to guide me.

It was All Saint's Eve and the little church with its peeling frescoes was still filling up with worshippers. The altar boys in their white starched surplices, each holding a large columnar candle, had taken their place next to Father Bertrand and in a few minutes mass would begin. Diane knelt and closed her eyes. Suddenly to her left she heard a sword clatter loudly against a chair, and looking up saw Jean-Christophe, now a commissioned officer courtesy of his aunt, stumble and awkwardly kick a chair forward as he went to sit directly across the aisle from her and Marianne. He uttered an oath as his sword caught in the rungs of his chair. Marianne laughed into her handkerchief and shot him a coquettish glance.

"He should look where he's going, the dolt!" Diane whispered angrily to Marianne. Diane bowed her head again, though she knew that Jean-Christophe was trying to catch her eye. She clasped her hands in prayer, but she was so annoyed with Marianne that she could not think of anything other than the scolding she intended to give her maid on the way home from church.

Diane could feel someone looking at her with eyes like busy, probing hands. Jean-Christophe, probably, and she tossed her head angrily, intent on ignoring him. She straightened and bowed her head in prayer.

Still, she could not calm her thoughts enough to begin to pray. And Father Bertrand, who conducted mass at a snail's pace even on his more vigorous days, kept fussing and delaying as his worshippers waited expectantly. Impatiently, she turned to the dimly lit fresco of the beheading of Saint Jacques, who had fallen to his knees before the bloody sword of King Herod. Dingy from the passage of time and the smoke from countless suppliant candles, the fresco depicted the saint's firmly muscled torso, his long, golden neck gushing dark streams of blood while his severed head gazed at the onlooker with beatific calm. Chastened, Diane made the sign of the cross and slipped into the quietude of prayer.

Soon enough, she again sensed someone looking her over with slow deliberation. She stared straight ahead at Father Bertrand, who had finally begun to say mass and had turned his back to the worshippers. Snippets of Latin phrases, barely audible, drifted in the air. Suddenly, she could stand it no longer. She turned her head to meet . . . not the warm, gentle gaze of Jean-Christophe but the luminous stare of a stranger. Their eyes met, and with lightning speed darted apart.

Dazed, she crossed herself, and stealthily looked again at the stranger across the aisle. He was sitting on the far side of Jean-Christophe, and she saw that he was also wearing a dress uniform, not like Jean-Christophe's, however. The dark-haired stranger wore the distinctive uniform of the Swiss Guards, whom Diane had sometimes seen in the parade of the guards on Sundays at Versailles when the King was in residence.

As if beckoned by her look, the stranger turned toward Diane. Her heart leapt into her throat. She wanted to look away but could not. At her side Marianne shifted impatiently from one knee to the other and sighed. *Dominus vobiscum.* Diane gripped the prie-dieu with both hands and tried to hear the words of Father Bertrand over the pounding of her heart. Was this what she and Madeleine had giggled about? A *coup de foudre?* A bolt of lightning? The sudden capsizing of her heart by a total stranger? It was absurd, really, as foolish as the romances that she and Marianne read. But, then, why did she feel overwhelmed, paralyzed by sensations of joy and excitement, thrilled to the very core of her being?

Afterwards, they stood together in the feeble autumn sun on the cobblestone square in front of Saint-Jacques. Simpering and toying with her new beaver muff, Marianne complimented Jean-Christophe for the second time on his handsome uniform and waited for her mistress to say something. Diane had managed to murmur a few words as Jean-Christophe introduced her to his friend. Beyond that, nothing. Despite her efforts, formulas of polite conversation died on her tongue. She felt as if she had indeed been struck dumb.

Jean-Christophe thought that Diane looked ill, pale and indisposed. "Are you sure you're all right?"

When Diane did not answer, Marianne happily spoke for her. "*Mais oui!* Mademoiselle is perfectly well. Merely chilled from those cold old stones. Such a dismal little church, Saint-Jacques!" She looked impertinently at her mistress, but Diane simply stared at Jean-Christophe, a bemused look on her face. The baron de Rothenburg . . . She had missed his Christian name, and at that moment it seemed unbearable not to know what it was.

"Diane, may we call on you this afternoon? After the dinner hour? The baron, as I said, has been pestering me to meet you for weeks."

Jean-Christophe's friend stood mutely at his side, his eyes shifting from Diane's face to his shiny boots and back again. The baron de Rothenburg. He did not move. He stood rigidly in place as if he were on guard in the public rooms of Versailles.

"This afternoon? I'm afraid that this afternoon Mademoiselle has promised . . . "

"This afternoon will be fine, Jean," Diane mumbled in a desperate rush.

The comte sat in a straightback chair, his face in the full sunshine of midday. Old Clovis, bending stiffly from the waist, held an oval mirror to one side, out of the glare of the sun, as Marianne lathered the comte's face. The comte no longer trusted Clovis for his daily shave. The old man's hands shook with palsy, and the razor had slipped rather dangerously a few weeks past. Another valet stood next to Clovis with a basin of warm water.

"*Bon sang!* You should have seen them both!" Marianne said loudly and the two valets exchanged a glance. Marianne had fallen into familiar habits with the master of the house, swearing coarsely like a scullery maid. Her vulgarity delighted the comte, exceedingly pleased with his plump and compliant housekeeper. Besides, rather than being simply a lady's maid, Marianne was proving to be indispensable in running his daily affairs. And in grooming him. A talented girl with very clever hands.

"They stood there staring at each other like lost lambs. Mind you, that young baron is handsome enough to strike any girl deaf and dumb. He's that *beautiful!* I've never seen his like! Not even the King! He's handsomer by far than the King ever was, I've no doubt." Marianne saw the comte stretch away from her razor to say something, and she was glad that he had too much lather around his mouth to risk it. He would be jesting and asking her whether or not he himself was handsomer than both the King and the baron, and she would have to lie and say, Present company excepted, or some such foolishness.

"The baron has the looks of an angel! Though why Mademoiselle should play such a fool with him, like the cat swallowed her tongue, when she has danced with the King himself night after night, and listened to him talking in her ear, and been given flowers and portraits, and I don't know what all. Along comes this young gentleman, and she loses her wits."

The comte stirred under the wide starched napkin tied around his neck. Marianne stepped back to survey her work. She dried the razor carefully and stropped it against a thick length of leather hanging from a ring next to the window.

The comte blotted the corners of his mouth with the napkin. "So you think that she is smitten with him? Is that what you're saying?" The two valets stared straight ahead.

Marianne threw up her hands in a theatrical gesture. "With Mademoiselle, who can say for sure what goes on in back of those big gray eyes? Who can predict what she is going to do with her heart? Any other girl would have fallen into a dead faint when the King looked at her and the next day would have been crying her heart out for love of him. They say the Pompadour woman, for all her scheming, is head over heels in love with the King. But not our Mademoiselle! The King whispers sweet nothings in her ear, she blossoms like a flower in the sunshine, and that's the long and the short of it."

The comte explored his cheeks with his hand and looked into the mirror. "I still don't see why you say Diane has lost her head over this fellow. She has her moods. They come and they go. She might have felt particularly quiet, I don't know, after mass. She's affected by those things."

"Well, you weren't there, were you?" Marianne said pertly. "The two of them looked at each other . . . why, you could *feel* it, it was so strong, passing between them. And the same when the chevalier came to call with the baron yesterday afternoon. You could *feel* it between the two of them."

"Hmmph!" the comte said.

"And all the while the chevalier is watching her and eating his heart out! It makes you . . . "

"The chevalier hasn't a *sou* to his name!" the comte said roughly. "He can pine after my daughter all he likes, but he'll get no further."

"He writes her the loveliest poems. Mademoiselle reads them to me. It's so tender. And how do you know that the baron is not just as poor as the chevalier, eh?"

"I don't," the comte said harshly, throwing off the napkin and rising to his feet. "But I shall find out, mark my words, I shall find out."

18

Each morning that Diane swung her feet out of bed and felt the shock of cold from the floor, she rejoiced. The icy winds of winter were setting in: there would be no more fighting in Flanders until spring. The baron would be on duty at Versailles, a short, vigorous gallop from Paris. To her young heart the ominous warmth of April seemed an eternity away. Ahead of her stretched hours and days and weeks with Paul de Rothenburg.

A steady, chill rain lashed Diane's carriage as it made its way slowly up the rue de Vaugirard, slipping on cobblestones slick with rain and debris from the morning market, toward the cheery lights of the marquise de Sabran's mansion. A sedate green canopy had been set up over the broad granite steps to protect arriving guests from the downpour.

"You're early. Again. And I wonder why," said Madeleine archly, as Diane handed her wraps to a footman.

"Am I overdoing it . . . as always? I think of this as my second home," Diane said, putting her arms around Madeleine's narrow waist and strolling toward the game room. "You and your aunt have made me feel like a part of the family. And Jean-Christophe, too, dear Jean."

"And you would be running over here for dinner every day even if our charming Swiss baron did not make this his second home, too?" Diane blushed, and Madeleine was annoyed that after more than a few years in Paris, Diane was still innocent enough to blush. On the other hand, Diane's infatuation with the baron had been a welcome, if unexpected, turn of events. There was little danger now that Diane would respond to Armand's lovesick glances.

That danger was past. Diane was hopelessly in love, as all the world, including Armand, could see. Armand had become less perfunctory in his caresses, but Madeleine could feel the desperate pride in his urgency. And the frustrated love for Diane that was still there, twisting his thoughts away, cooling his blood. Madeleine despised herself for wanting him so much anyway, even in his half state. But she did. And each day began and ended with schemes to get her lover the commission that would enable them to marry. For marry they would, if she succeeded. Armand would never let his feelings for Diane interfere with his passion for position and security, of that Madeleine was certain. He will stick with me whether he likes it or not, she thought bitterly, watching with envy Diane's radiant smile as she caught sight of the baron.

There were only a dozen or so guests around the tables in the game room. The baron had been seated on a canapé next to an elderly gentleman from the Franche Comté when Diane and Madeleine appeared in the doorway.

"Jean-Christophe wanted to play a game of quadrille before

dinner, but I begged off. Do you mind?" the baron asked Madeleine.

"Oh, no, why should I?" Madeleine searched for a witty retort and found none. The baron's gentle courtesy disarmed her tart tongue. "Have your walk around the garden, you two, and I shall learn something about the backward folk of the Franche Comté from your old friend there."

Diane and Paul walked toward the stone bench behind the tall boxwood hedge. It had become their favorite meeting place because they could talk as privately as they liked even though the garden was full of strollers before and after the dinner hour. Since their first meeting at Saint-Jacques when they had been so overwhelmed with emotion that they could not speak, the two young people never stopped talking. They heaped their deepest thoughts on each other, interrupting, finishing each other's sentences, laughing, crying, in their eagerness to bring their hearts and minds together. When they were apart, they wrote to each other long, passionate letters that Laurent posted to Versailles and that the baron's adjutant brought to the rue des Fours and gave (with an orange blossom from the King's hothouses) to Marianne as she prepared her mistress's breakfast tray. The baron had bought an exquisite blank book of shagreen which they exchanged, and each evening before she blew out her candle, Diane read the pages written by Paul before composing her response which she would pass on to him the next day. They wrote verses to each other, and Paul had set to music an ode by Ronsard celebrating passionate love.

"I half expected to see you during my toilette this morning," Diane said. "When you did not come, I rushed through my dressing so fast that Marianne lost her temper with me."

During the weeks when the baron did not have duty at Versailles, he stayed at the marquise de Sabran's townhouse and sometimes called on Diane during her toilette, usually with Jean-Christophe. They joined Diane's other admirers, sitting about the small room on straightback chairs. The chevalier de Montigny never failed to call in whenever he was in town, and the baron was astonished one morning to find the duc de Richelieu handing hairpins to Marianne as she dressed Diane's soft blond hair.

"I'm sorry. This morning I had to visit my family in Issy. My father sent for me." The baron's voice was soft and low, and, given his powerful military bearing, curiously seductive. His eyes were the same changing hue as Louis XV's, a piercing blue that could look as cold and as pure as ice. Even in the sunshine of the garden his skin looked cold, pale and austere, his features sharp and refined. He looks like an angel, a beautiful angel on the portals of Notre-Dame, Marianne said, in the carriage that day in October. Diane reached out and took his hand in hers.

"I should like to meet your father. And your mother."

"You will. Soon. My father had heard of you, and he wanted to talk about that."

"What do you mean? Heard of me?"

"Don't be alarmed! It's all right, truly it is. My father had heard that you were a great beauty, that the King thought you a great beauty . . . that's all."

"Does it . . . make a difference that the King liked me? With your father, does it matter?"

"At Issy, you know, my family is near enough to court to hear a great deal of gossip, and not near enough to be able to sort out the wheat from the chaff. They hear all sorts of things out there, and they don't always know what to make of it."

"But does it make a difference . . . with what they think of me . . . and of my father?"

"Oh, no, of course not. Your reputation remains perfectly unstained. My father is Swiss, and you know how we Swiss can be." He laughed and leaned down to kiss her brow. "The court is a shocking pigsty, morally speaking. Even after two years of unbroken service there I can scarcely credit what goes on." He paused. "In any event, I made it clear to my father that you had every opportunity to become the King's titled mistress but that you chose not to do so. As a result, my father thinks that you must surely have some Swiss blood in that ancient family of yours."

"I see . . . " said Diane. The moment passed when she should have corrected Paul, when she should have said, no, it was the King who did not choose me. She did not have the courage to say it. She sat quietly holding his hand, watching elegantly dressed men and women stroll along the parterres, which had lost the vivid colors of spring and summer. But, then, perhaps Paul knew the truth, perhaps he knew that the King had lost interest in Diane, perhaps Paul, despite his Calvinist rectitude had lied to his father—or rather colored the story in Diane's favor.

"You see? What do you see?" asked Paul, laughing.

"I . . . I forget . . . I must have been daydreaming a little. About the future, about our lives together. Papa grows fonder of you every day. You can't imagine how much that means to me. It is such a relief, to see him chat with you, laugh with you, and later praise you to the skies when we're alone together. He seems quite content, as if you were everything he has been expecting in my future husband. I feel that a great black cloud has rolled away into the distance. There is only sunshine up there in the skies now." She looked up toward the few puffy white clouds straggling across the pale blue November sky. "I don't have to worry anymore."

"You don't have to worry—and you don't have to exaggerate, my love. You make the comte sound like an ogre. And we all know that he is a charming man. I wish that I could be half as charming as he is. And so effortlessly."

Diane returned his smile. If they were at all lucky, the baron would never have to know her charming father's fits of black anger, his threats. If they were at all lucky, and she knew in her heart that they would be, she would forever inhabit the enchanted world of the heroines of her frivolous romances. Catherine and Madeleine, and her father, too, had made fun of her last summer, poring over her romances in the shade of the linden trees. But it was there that she learned to dream the right dream. And now her dream had come true.

"There they are . . . getting up on their own accord without having to be fetched by a footman. Such good children!" said the marquise de Sabran. The marquise and Diane's father stood on the landing in front of the broad entry way watching Diane and the baron in the garden beyond the low stone wall encircling the marquise's courtyard. "*Dieu!* what a beautiful pair! A pair of angels! No wonder Paris can talk of little else. Natier wants to paint them. Did you know that?"

"Natier? Can he tear himself away from his portraits of La Pompadour? And the King's purse strings." On some days everything and everyone reminded him of Madame de Pompadour's destruction of his plans. With every passing day she was becoming more and more of a force to be reckoned with at court. Ambassadors called on her at her toilette, and she had bested Richelieu in a struggle over the protocol privileges in her little theatre. The King had done as she commanded. Gossip circulated that he had looked up at Richelieu as he was helping the King remove his boots and had asked, How many times have you been sent to the Bastille, Monsieur? Richelieu needed no explanation of what the King meant. Richelieu quickly withdrew his objections to La Pompadour's wishes and soothed his vanity as best he could. When the comte had first heard of the marquise de Pompadour's humiliation of Richelieu, he had been inclined to gloat. Richelieu was no friend of his, and he knew it. Still, the real enemy was La Pompadour, all powerful Pompadour, who had the enamored King eating out of her hands. When he wasn't pouring France's gold into them.

"Watch your tongue, my dear! Or the cat will get it! The favorite has her spies everywhere. Perhaps in my own salons. Who knows who can be trusted?"

"Well, if I can't trust you and your friends and your reports on the baron, I shall be in a pickle. Not that my affairs bear looking into at the moment. But if the Rothenburg family's assets are not what you say they are, my affairs won't bear looking into at all. I shall not be able to tread water much longer."

"You worry too much, Michel. Your credit is still good. When your credit starts to fail, and when your tailor balks at turning out the latest pantaloons for you, then it's time to worry. Not before. Just look at Diane's fichu! It is so fine and transparent that it looks like gossamer! She'll start a fashion with those fichus of hers."

"She looks like her grandmaman in those old-fashioned things," the comte said peevishly. "The girl has a fine bosom and shouldn't hide it. I suspect that she's wearing a fichu to please her sanctimonious Swiss friend."

"What's got into you now? Are you calling the baron a prude? I thought you quite liked him."

As Diane and Paul came through the side gates and started up the steps, they waved and smiled happily.

"Judas Priest! You're right, Louise, he *is* beautiful!" the comte murmured, as if to himself, watching the young couple walk toward them. "I could lose my heart to him, too, if I don't watch myself." He took her arm, and grinned. "A young man that gorgeous can't be poor. God wouldn't allow it."

My father, more and more enchanted with the Baron, consented with pleasure to our marriage.

Negotiations for the Dauphin's marriage had been kept secret for months, but by early December of 1746, only a few months after Maria Theresa's death, the duc de Richelieu was on his way to Dresden to make an official proposal of marriage to Marie-Josèphe, the fifteen-year-old daughter of Augustus of Saxony. Richelieu, still peevish over Louis' choice of the chevalier de Montigny as the escort of the late Spanish infanta, departed for Dresden with his customary arrogant display. As Ambassador Extraordinary, Richelieu's enormous entourage included eighty-four pages, six running footmen, fifty ordinary footmen, and a dozen of his favorite *heyduques* in their exotic Hungarian dress. In Vienna and Dresden, much to the anxiety of a nearly bankrupt Augustus, Richelieu demanded the pomp and ceremony of betrothal entertainments that would satisfy his taste for opulent display. Richelieu reported to Versailles that Marie-Josèphe, though in no way a beauty, had every imaginable grace, and if put up to auction as a dancer at the Opéra, would create a scramble in the bidding. She speaks French very badly, he added.

On January 14, 1747, Marie-Josephe wept as she said farewell to her brothers and sisters before departing for her new life in France. Louis and the Dauphin rode out from Choisy to greet her, the Dauphin once again a sullen, reluctant bridegroom still mourning his beloved Maria-Theresa. At Versailles the young Saxon spent three hours getting into her wedding dress, which was so heavily encrusted with jewels that the skirt alone weighed close to sixty pounds. Richelieu almost tumbled forward on his knees when the King asked him to lift the train for the Dauphine. The wedding ceremony took place at midday, followed by a *grand couvert* and a ball in the riding ring of the Grande Ecurie. Chafing from chilblains after the long, wintry journey from Dresden, the Dauphine sat and watched as her new husband led out the ball with his sister, Madame Henriette.

Caught up in her own anxious betrothal plans, Diane listened absentmindedly to Madeleine's chatter about the Dauphin's wedding. Every now and again a memory of February of 1745 would leave her trembling with longing for the glittering world she had lost so suddenly. But the longing was confused and fleeting, and when it was over, she was left with the solace of her dreams of life with Paul.

The dreaded morning came when her feet on the rush flooring confirmed that the warmth of spring had arrived. The war in Flanders began again, bloodier and costlier than ever. Louis XV had over sixty Swiss guards in his household, and all of them were sent to the battlefields. They were hard, disciplined soldiers who could be counted on to make a difference in the fighting.

Reports from Versailles said that the roads between the battlefields and Paris were treacherous mud bogs, that horses had broken legs, thrown their riders, sometimes crushing them in their fall. Despite the drenching rains the baron made his way, with four changes of horses, to Paris for brief reunions with Diane. Sometimes he could stay only four hours before spurring his horse back through the downpour to his regiment.

During the long weeks and months without Paul, Diane fed upon his letters, which struggled through the vagaries of haphazard messengers to her door. Whenever Paul had even a few days' leave, he headed his horse toward Paris and the rue des Fours. They had become the talk of Paris society, the nobly handsome Swiss guard and the exquisite young woman whose celebrated beauty had once aroused the King's lust. Natier caused a stir by painting the young couple as Apollo and Diana. It was said that the King himself asked to see the painting before it was placed in the comte's sitting room.

Before the baron left for the battlefields, the comte had given his formal blessing to their marriage which would take place in Paris in November or December after the military campaigns ceased and the baron returned to his duties at Versailles. The comte and Diane had journeyed to Issy where the two fathers gave their word to the union, the contract to be worked out at a later date. The two families had a cordial dinner together and parted on the best of terms. The comte vowed to his daughter that, in his love for the baron, he was overcoming his prejudice against the priggish and provincial customs of the Swiss. As a matter of fact, Odile's reports on the properties the Rothenburgs enjoyed in their native country swept aside any restive prejudices the comte might still have. Besides, he enjoyed the *beau monde's* infatuation with his daughter and the Swiss guard. He always felt comfortable basking in the glow of admiration, even when he was not precisely in the center of it.

19

He had had a kind of lukewarm infatuation for Mademoiselle de . . . , a girl older than he who had thrown herself at him.

The sunny day had given way to rain and cold, buffeting winds. Diane looked out onto the bleak street below and shivered despite the cozy fire in her bedroom. She ran her hands nervously through her hair and sighed. At her desk she took out the packet of letters and began to read them again. She reread Sophie's letter first. Sophie wrote just as she spoke, in a breathless childlike sweep of words across the page, hilarious misspellings, no punctuation. Her penmanship, however, was exquisite. Diane made a mental note to compliment her when she next wrote to her. Sophie's letters were perfectly formed, clean, ornate, the penmanship prized by monks and nuns that only the best, most attentive pupils ever mastered.

She sat a few minutes staring at Catherine's letter, creamy ivory pages crumpled at the edges, ink-stained. Catherine was still in the convent, and Diane . . . Diane had been taken back into the glamorous whirl of high society. She had continued her expensive lessons. She found herself more popular than ever before. Then she met the handsomest man in Paris—who knows? in all of France— and they fell in love and soon would be married. It was a fairy tale. A romance. Catherine did not believe in fairy tales and romance.

Catherine's letter made no pretense of neatness or fine penmanship. Her irregular handwriting sprawled across the page, the "t's" and "l's" slanted forward until they were almost horizontal. Some of it was crudely printed in box letters. Ink spots peppered the pages, and Catherine had not even bothered to use sealing wax. She had simply turned over a burning candle and dripped wax into a dingy white blob with soot at the center onto the folded pages.

Diane smoothed the pages in her lap. She began to read the letter again and realized that she knew it almost by heart.

My dear Sister, I suppose that Sophie has told you, many times, how much she has grown since you last saw her, but should you remain in ignorance regarding your sister's height, I will tell you again that she has grown fourteen centimeters, according to the nail marks on one of the columns in the cloister. If the sisters ever find out who is scratching those nail marks on their precious column, Sophie may not be as tall as she was before you left. I don't believe you will find Sophie much changed, as I don't. She will always be a runt of a woman. I noticed the other day that she comes up to Uncle Philippe's watch pocket, but Sophie would say that Uncle Philippe is a tall man, and he is, but a watch pocket is not very high. My head is level with Uncle Philippe's shoulders. Still, if Sophie wants to think that her fourteen centimeters really make a difference, that's her privilege.

Despite the heaviness in her heart Diane looked up from the letter and smiled. Dear little Sophie. So lively and tender, letting down a floodgate of tears at maman's funeral mass. The bodice of Sophie's gown was soaked through, a dark black spot spreading over the black gown. Diane saw them pouring down, spilling onto her bodice. While Catherine twisted the black ribbon in her missal, and Diane sat stricken with grief, staring at the black lacquered coffin that seemed too large for her mother's slim body.

Diane took up Catherine's letter again.

Why Uncle Philippe took it into his head to come to see us, I don't know. Neuilly is out of anybody's way except for the bishop and the archbishop, and no one else in the family remembers that we are still here. Papa certainly wouldn't waste his time, would he? Of course, you would know more about that than I would. If papa hadn't heard that you were turning into something that men like him would be interested in, you'd still be here with us. Have you ever thought of that? I have, many times. He, maman, too, left us all here for three years, and now it is more than two years for Sophie and me. Not that I care about seeing his silly face and hearing his silly laugh.

I was glad to see Uncle Philippe, though, and to hear a little of what is going on at Corcheval and Joigny. Uncle Philippe didn't have much to tell. He is still making money on his lands and papa is still losing money. Same old news. If we stay behind these walls another ten years, the news will be the same, except that papa may have sold up everything by then. So I hope, dear Sister, that you are going to be the answer to papa's prayers at long last. I am counting on you because I can't count on anyone else to keep us from becoming as poor as church mice. Mother Superior said that papa plans to reduce our pensions to fifty crowns each. I don't believe the smelly old cat, though I wouldn't put anything past papa when it comes to money.

I asked Uncle Philippe about your engagement to the Swiss officer and either he did not know anything or he did not want to talk about it. Actually, Sophie and I probably know more than he does, but I didn't want to tell him that. A wife of a regiment commander came to stay at Neuilly while her husband was in the fields last spring, and she had a good bit to say about your fiancé. This baron de Rothenburg. Madame Périvier, the one whose husband was in the fields, is fonder of your fiancé than she is of her husband. That's what I thought, and so did Sophie. It seems that the baron de Rothenburg is the handsomest man that ever drew breath. Madame Périvier had never heard of you. But she had heard a great deal about another young woman the baron was pledged to marry. The banns were published in her church in the Savoie. Madame Périvier says that it is a "tragic tale" and that your poor baron was "duped" by this little schemer who was supposed to have buckets of gold louis in her dowry and then the buckets were as empty as the baron's own purse. Madame Périvier wept over the poor baron's plight. So did Sophie. I suppose we will all weep if the baron's purse turns out to be as empty as Madame Périvier says it is.

Diane folded the letter and slipped it into the side pocket of her petticoat. The thick letter made her pocket bulge uncomfortably. She removed it and placed it under a book. She stared into space and waited for the tight knot in her throat to ease. Before concluding her letter, Catherine had drawn up a list of books that she wanted sent to the convent, books that Diane knew would be seized by the nuns if they caught sight of the titles. Diane forced herself to think of these books, of going with Marianne to the little shop on the Place Saint-Sulpice and buying them, then sending them off by coach to the country.

She drew a deep breath. Words and phrases from Catherine's letter kept nipping and gnawing at her mind. The girl in the Savoie. She means nothing to me. She is nothing to me. Paul had said that, his dear, tender face, the face of an angel, streaming with tears. Believe me. He had not said that he had pledged to marry her.

There was a swift, loud knock on the door, and a draft of cold air as the door opened.

"La! Mademoiselle, what do you mean, sitting here in the dark? Still reading your letters, are you?" Marianne busily whipped the curtains over the windows and kneeled to replenish the logs. "Shall I bring in more candles?"

"Not yet, thank you, Marianne."

"You're missing him that much, Mademoiselle! You mustn't be doing that, he's only on duty for a fortnight, and he's back in your arms again, that angel of yours!"

"I'll sit for a little while longer," she said, "then I'll write to my sisters."

There was really nothing new and shocking in Catherine's letter about the baron and his "sweetheart" in the Savoie. Diane believed Paul, she had only to look at his lovely, pale face and believe. Someone like Catherine who read Voltaire and Diderot would never understand a man as idealistic as Paul. A Swiss. Catherine would laugh at Paul's idealism.

In the flickering light from the hearth, Diane could see the end of Catherine's untidy letter sticking out from under her book. Heavy-hearted, she looked at it as if Catherine, her scarred face twisted, grimacing, would rise from it and begin to mock her. The part about the money. That was what she must think about now. The girl from the Savoie, Paul had explained that, Diane understood how, in his youthful ignorance a forward girl, sensual and infatuated, could force him into her arms. The part about the money, though. Diane wanted to put her head in her arms and weep. It could not be! It could not be! The baron never talked about money, and she took his silence to mean that his fortune was so ample that he never had to think of it. What if it were true? To come so close to grasping her dream, and . . . then to have her father snatch it away! And he would. If he doubted the baron's fortune in the slightest, her father would take back his word and forbid her ever to see the baron again. What if her father never found out, or found out only too late? Too late to keep her from marrying the baron. Why should they care about a fortune? Paul would have his pension from the King. An assured pension. They could go to his native country, to the quaint little cities of Switzerland, and live there a clean, honorable life, far from the iniquities of the French court. It would be a good life. But, then, what would happen to Sophie? And Catherine? Where would money come from to provide for them? And papa, who was forever in debt, harassed by his furnishers?

20

Mademoiselle M—, a spinster at least fifty years old, became smitten with the Baron. She was ugly but rich. . . . She entertained the best society, and the simple, easygoing atmosphere in her house was very pleasant.

In the winter of 1748 the more socially fastidious grumbled that the popularity of Mademoiselle Malavelle's salon was a sign of the way money had corrupted their world's values. A newcomer to Paris society, this homely woman whose bulbous eyes, jutting chin, and pouchy neck made her look somewhat like an agitated, hungry pelican, was gay, witty, and companionable. A native of Languedoc, her unfashionable accent gave a piquant touch to her easy, familiar, earthy manner. Shortly after her entrance into Paris society, she had flung open her doors with profligate generosity. Hangers-on and social climbers and the greats at court elbowed each other around the luxurious rooms.

Approaching the venerable age of fifty, Mademoiselle Malavelle had never married. Under Louis XIV her father became the main supplier of horses and wagons for the royal army, and with one war following hard on the heels of another, Monsieur Malavelle acquired one of the largest fortunes in France. At the time of his death in 1732 he had married his youngest daughter to the marquis de Lorges, one of the finest names in the country. Some said that Mademoiselle Malavelle herself had missed her chance to take advantage of the family fortune by making a brilliant marriage. With a twinkle in her eyes, Mademoiselle Malavelle would correct anyone who, in view of her age, called her 'Madame.' "Not yet, *mon cher ami*," she would say coquettishly, "Not yet!"

Mademoiselle Malavelle claimed that she could not sleep well until she had feasted her eyes on Paris' favorite couple. Soon Diane and Paul were making the late night supper parties at Mademoiselle Malavelle's superb mansion a regular part of their day. After the summer and fall months of separation, Diane and Paul had again become the center of the social whirl. Apollo and Diana. The beautiful couple.

On this particular evening, since Paul would be coming straight to the supper party from Versailles, the comte proudly escorted his daughter. Already the vast reception rooms overflowed with guests. Every detail of the rooms bespoke Mademoiselle de Malavelle's staggering wealth. The ornamental moldings at the ceilings, doors, and wall panels were made of hand-carved wood, not plaster, and were finished in gold leaf. It amused Diane that while she herself dismissed Mademoiselle's display of her money as vulgar and *nouveau riche*, her father, like an excited child, relished every detail. "Just look at those champagne flutes!" he whispered as they made their way to the drawing room, "From Bohemia. I have it on the best authority! And the chandeliers!" Paintings by the latest favorites at court—bucolic idylls by Watteau, voluptuous women by Boucher, a still life by Chardin—crowded the steep walls.

As soon as Diane entered the drawing room, she could feel Mademoiselle Malavelle's eyes sweeping over her from head to foot.

"She admires you too much. Everyone does. You and Paul are the *coqueluches* of Paris salons," her father said, but the older woman's looks made Diane uncomfortable.

In the group clustered around Mademoiselle Malavelle, Diane saw Paul, leaning easily against her chair and laughing as she talked. Absorbed in the story Mademoiselle Malavelle was recounting, Paul did not see Diane and her father.

"I shall liberate Paul for you, *mon trésor*. I fear that politeness is another failing he has inherited from the Swiss," the comte said jovially, squeezing her elbow. Her father had been in wonderful spirits lately. He could talk of little other than Diane's wedding. One moment he wanted to organize the wedding party and set off for Corcheval, where the family chapel would provide the perfect setting for the marriage of the wonderful couple. The next moment he would be raging with impatience to sign the contracts and hurry through a simple ceremony in Paris and be done with the whole affair. He complained that the baron's father seemed to be dragging his feet of late. The main point, as the comte saw it, was to get the young couple married and established before the spring campaigns began again. Tonight he was cheerful and content. Next Wednesday afternoon they would gather at Issy to sign the nuptial contracts.

Paul joined Diane at a card table and began to teach her to play two-handed solitaire, much to the amusement of the other players.

"That's totally illogical, you know that, don't you?" asked the duc de Richelieu. Paul rested his hand on the table and stared at Richelieu. "Don't just look at me like that! I said, solitaire is solitaire. To play two-handed solitaire is not logical."

Madeleine, sitting next to Richelieu, leaned familiarly against his shoulder and made a great show of suppressing a giggle.

"This is a game, monsieur le duc," Paul said gravely.

"Ohhhh!" Richelieu said, rolling his eyes.

Diane noticed the exchange of amused glances around the table. "Let's walk about a bit, Paul," she said. "With so many people and the candles and oil lamps everywhere, it's stifling."

They strolled out onto the landing overlooking the foyer. A dozen or so latecomers down below were handing their wraps to Mademoiselle's handsomely outfitted footmen.

"I may not stay for supper tonight," Paul said, pulling a gold pocket watch from his waistcoat. "The roads to Versailles have been thick with carriages for the past few nights, and my horse is going to kill me with one of his tantrums. I'm afraid that he prefers open roads."

Diane stared at the watch. "No, don't close it yet. Is it new? I don't remember seeing it before."

"Beautiful, isn't it?"

"Yes. It's very beautiful. Is it new? It looks new."

"It is." Paul hurriedly closed the lid, hesitating a moment before putting the watch into his waistcoat.

Diane waited for him to say more. "Is it a present from your parents? Is it an engagement present?" Her father had talked of buying her a ruby and diamond necklace as soon as the nuptial contracts were signed. And Uncle Philippe would be giving her pearls.

The baron smiled sheepishly, and Diane felt her chest tighten with fear. "Yes. It's a present. But I don't know . . . maybe it is an engagement present. Maybe that's it."

"Don't you know? If someone gave you a present, you should know why. Paul?"

"Yes?"

"Who gave you the watch?"

"Oh," he said, plunging the watch into his waistcoat pocket, "Mademoiselle Malavelle gave it to me last night. And I'm so foolish about it that I keep pulling it out and checking the time. Like a little boy."

"Why on earth would Mademoiselle give you a watch? A gold watch? Why, it must have cost a fortune!"

"It must have," Paul said, brimming with enthusiasm. "It surely must have! You should feel it . . . it's as heavy as a stone." He worked the watch out of the narrow pocket and balanced it in the palm of his hand. "It must have cost thousands!"

"May I?" asked Diane, holding out her hand. She took the watch and brought it close to her nearsighted eyes. An intricate interweaving of two letters, one of them *P*—what was the other an *R?* a *C?* it looked very much like a *C*—covered the entire surface of the lid.

"Are those your initials?" she asked. "The *P*. And is that an *R?*"

"Yes. *P* and *R*. That's it." Suddenly he sounded nervous, and he strained to see Diane's face.

Diane pressed the thin catch, and the lid sprang open. On the underside of the lid, the pelican face of Mademoiselle Malavelle stared back at her, grinning coyly. There was no mistaking the face, despite the efforts of the artist to flatter his subject.

Diane closed the lid and held out the watch. "It's lovely. And, as you say, quite expensive."

"She's one of the most generous women, I've ever met. Bar none," he said, his face glowing.

For many nights thereafter Diane would remember that statement and be troubled by it.

"Generous, certainly. But did she say why she gave you such an expensive present?" Diane started walking toward the noise of the reception rooms.

"No. Of course, a woman as wealthy as Mademoiselle does not need reasons, does she? It's a whim. A charming whim."

"And you don't think this kind of present . . . a miniature of her . . . " Her spirits had sunk so low that she did not think she had enough energy to go on.

"*This* kind of present . . . ?" He sounded annoyed.

"I should say that this kind of present is . . . too intimate . . . a watch, a miniature. An unmarried woman to a young man. A much younger man," she said, an edge to her voice.

"Do you mean that it's improper? That I've done something improper in accepting the watch?" Paul hurried along beside her. He was clearly provoked. Diane had spoiled his pleasure in his new watch.

Mademoiselle fastened her eyes on them as they entered the room. Diane coolly returned her stare.

"Mademoiselle Malavelle. *Cécile Malavelle.* That's it, isn't it?"

But when she turned to Paul, he had already left her side.

After more than an hour of waiting in the drawing room Paul was summoned to his father's study at the end of the corridor. That morning he had received a message at his quarters in Versailles, a message in his father's usual imperious style calling for an urgent meeting to discuss "family" affairs. Paul had spent the rest of the morning chasing around the chateau for an officer to replace him on duty.

"You're late," the vicomte de Vaubois said, looking up from his papers.

"I've been waiting since four o'clock," Paul said gently, holding out his hand to his father.

"I expected you at three. You're late," the old man sniffed and blew his nose loudly as if to convey his vexation. He indicated a chair, and Paul sat down and waited. The comte looked far older than his fifty-six years. Chronic dyspepsia kept him thin and haggard, and he had lost most of his teeth to his voracious appetite for chocolates and creamy sweet pastries. He perched on the edge of his chair like a frail bird and looked at his son.

"The signing of contracts with the comte de Fautrière is to take place here at Issy next Wednesday," the old man said finally.

"Yes. I know that, father. Is that why you've sent for me? I was told that you had something urgent to discuss."

"We'll get to that . . . " the vicomte said, twisting one of his rings absentmindedly. His bony fingers glittered with ornate rings. He was vain about his fingernails and kept them long, though none too clean. "I've been hearing things lately."

"About Diane? I thought we had discussed that already. Several times. Diane's reputation is spotless. More than spotless."

"So you say. And, of course, I believe you, my son. Who more than you has an ear to the gossip at court? And I trust you not to bring dishonor on our family. I know that I can trust you for that."

"Thank you, father," Paul said, knowing that was what his father expected him to say.

"No, no. Rest assured that I am satisfied with your version of the—how shall I say?—ambiguous behavior of the King and Mademoiselle de Fautrière. I call it 'your' version, but others, Madame de Sabran, for example, have confirmed all that you say."

He leaned back in his chair and stretched his thin, spindly legs. "I've been hearing other things about the family that worry me." He paused and smoothed the front of his coat.

"What things?" Paul asked apprehensively. He knew his father's games only too well. The pauses, the absentminded gestures, the teasing silences. "What could possibly displease you in one of the oldest noble families of France?"

"No older than our titles!" the old man said sharply. "Vaubois and Rothenburg go back just as far, I've no doubt. We've only two left, to be sure, but that doesn't mean that we have to be ashamed of our lineage. Far from it." The vicomte sneezed and blew his nose again, and shook his shoulders vigorously like a flustered bird.

"Do you know a Roger de Saint-Valérien?" the vicomte asked, fixing Paul with his small, moist eyes.

"I've met Jules Saint-Valérien, his son. There is no *de*, as far as I know."

"Ah!" said the old man. "No *de?* That is curious." He stared for a moment at his nails. "It doesn't matter, I suppose. At any rate, I've had some business with this Roger de Saint-Valérien, this Monsieur Saint-Valérien, who, it appears, is a neighbor of the Fautrières in Charolais. A friend of the family, so he claims, and I am persuaded at the very least that he knows the comte well."

"And this man has reported matters that worry you?"

"Yes, indeed. That worry me a great deal."

"Can you tell me what they are, father?" Paul said, barely able to contain his exasperation.

"Actually, I was waiting . . . hoping . . . that you could tell me what they are, my dear Paul. After all, you spend most of your waking hours—when not on duty at the royal chateau—in the company of the comte de Fautrière and his no doubt admirable daughter. It seems to me a pity that a perfect stranger should be the one to tell me about the problems of the family soon to be united to us in marriage. A great pity, indeed, that my son should be so lacking in judgment, in perception, in . . . that he should see nothing and that a perfect stranger has to do my son's work!" The old man ended in a breathless rush.

"Problems! I haven't the faintest notion of what you are talking about, father!" said Paul, rising from his chair as if throwing himself out of a prison cell.

"Oh, I'm sure you haven't the faintest notion, my boy! Not the faintest! Has it never occurred to you that you might spend less time with your nose in your philosophy books, your poetry books, and more time looking over your nose at the world around you!"

Paul hesitated, then took his seat again, meek, dejected. He could never outlast his father. The old man knew how to wear him down, tear his patience to shreds.

"If you cared to do so, you would see that the comte de Fautrière is a miserable, vain fop who . . . "

"But I am not *marrying* the comte de Fautrière!"

"Of course not! Don't be childish! And don't interrupt. If you please." The vicomte waited a moment before continuing. "I saw Fautrière for the kind of man he is. All along. I did not need Roger whatever-his-name-is to tell me that his neighbor is a vainglorious fool who can count on more enemies at court than he can friends . . . "

"That's far from true! The comte de Fautrière has close ties with the princes of the blood, with the . . . "

"Oh, yes, oh, yes, oh, yes . . . I know what you are going to say . . . Such splendid examples of the court's piety, the marquise de Sabran, and that sort of thing. Relics from the old Regent's dustbin! And don't interrupt. I won't ask again!"

The vicomte clapped his thin hands. A footman peered around the door. "Some tea and sweets," he said, frowning and rubbing his stomach. "Ahhh! I must eat something to soothe these awful pains!" He covered his mouth with his handkerchief and burped convulsively.

"Shall I call for a glass of wine? Some water perhaps?"

"No! No!" his father said, shaking his handkerchief. "About this Fautrière . . . there's little to be said . . . except that the man is on the brink of ruin . . . teetering on the brink of ruin!" He mopped his forehead and took a deep breath. "Do you hear what I am saying, Paul? I have it on good authority, from a man to whom Fautrière has been selling his lands for years, that the comte is in debt to his ears, that his creditors are hounding the life out of him, that he can expect nothing more from the King, who will not forgive him his part in the plot against the old Cardinal."

"I knew the comte had . . . some debts. He has an expensive way of life. Like everyone at court. He is not unusual."

"Not unusual for a Frenchman, certainly. They are all careless wastrels at Versailles, and Fautrière is one of the worst of them."

His spirits sinking, Paul knew what his father was going to say next. He also knew that he would fight back.

"There is no doubt in my mind that when Fautrière submits his nuptial proposals, when he offers his daughter's hand in marriage, that hand will be empty. There will be no dowry!"

Paul said nothing.

"Fautrière has already hinted at this in our preliminary discussions."

"But . . . " Paul said softly, "You gave him your word! He gave you his word! You cannot change that! No matter how many debts the comte may have. You cannot take back your word, father!"

"We shall see . . . Certainly, you are right . . . in one sense. I did make a mistake. I should not have given my consent to a man whom I know only by 'reputation,' shall we say. But, then, I have given my word *mistakenly*. There is a difference. At least, *I* see a difference."

"Do you mean that after shaking hands with the comte and giving your consent to my marriage with his daughter . . . do you . . . will you now refuse your consent? Is this what you mean?"

"I say only that when the comte de Fautrière and his daughter arrive next Wednesday for the signing of the contracts, I shall put my name to no document that does not commit the comte to a dowry. And a sizable dowry at that."

"It's far too late for that, father. A man of honor cannot retract his word now. And even it you could, I won't have it! I won't have your mercenary interference! You've shamed me before, reneging on your word, like a commoner! Besides, with the King's pension I can afford to take a wife without a dowry. Assuming that Mademoiselle de Fautrière will not be provided with a dowry. Which, naturally, neither you nor I know for a certainty. I can afford to marry the most beautiful woman in the country, the gentlest, the most virtuous . . . "

"But not the poorest!" The old man laughed, a short, dry laugh like a sneeze. "You make me laugh, you young fool! Why should I expect you to know anything about other people! You don't even know yourself, you gibbering dreamer! Forever poring over your poetry books, muddling your head with . . . "

"Father, I must go!" Paul shot to his feet, his sheathed sword clapping against his boots. He could stand no more.

"You won't go far! Mark my words, my boy, you won't go far!" The old man slapped his thighs merrily. "You love luxury, you can't do without it! And you don't know it! Look at those soft gloves! Those boots! The finest leather that money can buy! And what about those . . . "

Paul bowed to his father and turned on his heels.

"Where is that man! Where are my sweets? I need my sweets!" cried the vicomte.

A servant brought my father a message from Mademoiselle M—, which he read aloud. She asked him to come to her house as soon as possible, because she had a matter of some consequence to discuss with him.

Mademoiselle Malavelle sat down and carefully spread the stiff folds of her skirt to each side of her chair. She was wearing an enormously wide pannier. The comte half rose from his chair and in doing so spilled port wine over his white stockings.

"Ahhhh! *merde! merde!*" he muttered. "Please . . . do excuse me, Mademoiselle, I didn't . . . "

Mademoiselle Malavelle laughed, the deep, hearty laugh of a portly, well-nourished man. "Have no fear, comte! I am not entirely ignorant of such naughty words."

She grinned, her brightly painted lips pulling back against pale pink gums and long yellow teeth. My God, she is an ugly woman, the comte thought, feeling suddenly warm in the stuffy little room. Everyone had departed for the night. Or had they? He thought he heard the voices of a quarreling couple in the distance, somewhere near the great rooms in the front of the house. It was late. He had no idea how late. For once he had gambled huge sums at *lansquenet*, and for once he had won. Such huge sums that the chevalier de Pradaillet had said that he would send his man around with the money tomorrow. Such a lot of money! Naturally he needed to celebrate with some of Mademoiselle's finest champagne. Then, why was he sitting in her tiny—God, it was the room of a midget, not a gangling spinster the size of Mademoiselle—boudoir drinking port wine? Which had just spilled down his leg onto his finest white stockings. What happened to his glass of champagne? And what time could it be? Should he ask Mademoiselle, or would that be impolite?

"I do hope I'm not keeping you, Mademoiselle?"

"Keeping me from what, *mon cher ami*?" There was a flirtatious lilt in her voice, and the comte thought that her eyes stared out at him like two wet, raw oysters. He felt sick to his stomach but was incapable of getting out of his chair.

"I wouldn't want to do that," he said, making an effort not to slur his words.

"You most definitely are not. An evening spent with a good friend cannot possibly be wasted —and you have become a good, good friend, haven't you, comte? As has your beautiful daughter. What would my *salon* be without her? Certainly not one of the most popular in the whole of Paris." She smoothed her skirts again. "I find these chairs quite ingenious."

"Oh, yes, quite. All the ladies say so . . . " The comte was listening carefully for clues. Perhaps he had asked to speak privately to Mademoiselle. Otherwise what was he doing perspiring in his fine silk shirt in this stifling room after spilling port over his stockings? Clovis would mutter under his breath, and Marianne would say that he smelled like a rotten old wooden wine vat and would put her foot in the small of his back and push him over onto the other side of the bed. "I wonder . . . " the comte began, and reached down to put his glass on the floor at his feet.

"Of course, you can, dear comte! Here I am boasting about my salon while I am being such a terrible hostess that I don't see that your glass is empty!" She rose briskly and started for the bell pull.

"No, no . . . " said the comte feebly, picking up his empty glass and shaking his head.

"Not port, no! You will be wanting champagne!" She pulled the cord and came back to her chair, carefully arranging her skirts as before.

I shall have just one glass, the comte thought, then one of the footman can see me to my carriage. But would the carriage be there . . . would Laurent be standing patiently in the cold night air waiting for his master? The comte could not remember whether he had sent away the carriage with Diane and the baron.

Mademoiselle sat down again, and immediately, or so it appeared to the comte, two footmen were pouring champagne into tall crystal flutes and he and Mademoiselle were toasting each other and laughing together like the best of friends. The comte felt reinvigorated, witty, debonair. He promised himself not to touch another drop of port. Ever. It seemed to him that he had never met a woman as genial, as hospitable—why, she anticipated his every wish . . . but, lord!, it was sultry in this little room!

"You know, comte, I love your daughter like a child of my own! Oh, la, I don't have a child of my own, but you know what I mean. Oh, la, you're getting me drunk, you are. But I know what I'm saying. I love that child."

"I know you do, dear friend . . . we all do. Louise de Sabran . . . who . . . well, she's a mother tigress with Diane. Loves her . . . my daughter . . . as much as I do. No, no . . . not as much, my daughter is my treasured pearl."

"I understand. *We* all understand. That's why we are so concerned." Mademoiselle Malavelle lowered her voice and twisted her glass between her long fingers.

The comte said nothing. He sat watching her glass twist back and forth. She wondered if he had heard.

"I can't bear to see Diane hurt, her reputation damaged, your family name."

"Diane? What's that you're saying?" The comte strained toward her, straightening his back and leaning forward. But his words were slurred, and an awful ringing started in his ears.

"I'm only saying what I . . . and I would guess others . . . have heard. And we don't want Diane to be hurt in any way . . . " She waited, her protruding eyes studying the emotions crowding into the comte's face.

The comte reached for his snuffbox, but his hands were too unsteady to risk taking a pinch. He jabbed at his pockets, found the opening and returned the snuffbox to its place. What had happened this evening? Had something taken place without his noticing?

"Has something happened? What is it?" he asked.

"No, please calm yourself, comte," she said gently. His face had gone from deep brownish red to stark white in a matter of minutes. "It's just that I . . . and I believe a number of *our* friends . . . have heard rumors about the baron de Rothenburg's past. We respect the baron, we all do. I admire him. And I am sure that there is some explanation, some justification."

"Justification for what? What is it?"

The loose pouch under Mademoiselle Malavelle's chin quivered ominously. She folded her hands in her lap.

"The baron, it appears, has a history of broken engagements. In other words, he has more than once pledged himself, betrothed himself."

"Do you have proofs? Where are they, these women?"

"Proofs? No. How would one prove such a thing without the parties to the act being present? But I have information—certain, verifiable information—that one rejected young woman—of a fine name, though not as fine certainly as Fautrière —intends to wait for the banns for the baron's marriage to Diane to be published and then she will charge him with a breach of contract. This young woman is . . ."

"Breach of contract! The baron? As fine a young man as I shall ever meet? A Swiss! A young Swiss!" The comte took heart from his own words. It was all too preposterous. The baron's physical beauty, good lord, he was so beautiful, Apollo would pale beside him, a young man that handsome would be bound to set any number of hearts throbbing, heads dreaming. Some young girl's fantasy, that's what it amounted to.

"That's exactly what I thought when I heard the rumors, my good friend. But then I said to myself, 'Cécile, I said, we French are always giving the Swiss too much credit for being the most virtuous people on the face of this earth. Maybe the Swiss can be tempted into error sometimes, too. Maybe the baron was tempted . . ."

"Do you know this girl? Have you spoken to her?"

"The next best thing to it," Mademoiselle shot back rapidly, and the comte failed to ask her what that might mean.

"I must speak with the baron immediately . . . and the vicomte de Vaubois. I'm sure . . . just as you say . . . there must be some explanation. The young baron is a superb *parti*. That can set a lot of foolish young heads dreaming . . . and scheming." As if inspired, he looked up at Mademoiselle Malavelle. "That's it! Perhaps this is no more than a scheme! The baron is simply the victim! Some little schemer is trying to get her hooks into him!" He felt better and better. His head was clearing.

Mademoiselle shook her head gloomily. The comte poured himself another glass of champagne.

"I think you'll find that the question is not that simple. Let us say that the young girl has right on her side. No, let us say that even if the young girl is merely a schemer, as you say . . . would you want your daughter's good name, her reputation, dragged into this mud? Diane is like a . . . "

"You're right, you're absolutely right. What fine judgment you have, . . . is it Cécile? Yes . . . Cécile . . . I can't, I simply can't allow Diane's name to get dragged into this mess . . . even if the baron is a victim of this little hussy."

The comte rose unsteadily to his feet. Mademoiselle rose and accompanied him to the door.

"What will you do now?" she asked, holding him firmly under the elbow. The comte smelled of sandalwood and leaned heavily against her as they walked.

"Oh, simply stall. Wait and investigate these rumors. I believe that we'll find them nothing more than rumors." The outer rooms were vast and cool with only a few candelabra burning to light their way through the shadows. "You know, Cécile, my good, kind Cécile, my little girl has lost her heart to the baron, and I want to see her happy with him."

"And she will, my dear comte . . . if he proves to be a man worthy of her trust! You mustn't let her make a false step now. You're her beloved papa, and you must look after her."

From the top of the stairs the comte could see a carriage waiting at the entrance. Mademoiselle's fine horses and a sleek barouche. No coat of arms, of course, but the very latest fashion in carriages.

"Ah, you are too good! I've kept you up and your household as well. I've been quite naughty, I'm afraid!" He embraced her warmly on both cheeks. Mademoiselle, gazing into his genial blue eyes, thought that only one man on earth was handsomer. Not the King of France. No. The baron de Rothenburg. He was handsomer. By far.

21

He concealed from me the conversation that he had had the day before with Mademoiselle M—.

Dark gray clouds streaked with black hung over the Jardin de Luxembourg as Diane and Paul made their final turn past the stone bench and halfway up the yew tree path to the marquise de Sabran's side gate. The streets beyond the garden had been abandoned for the fireside and cozy dinner tables.

The sullen wintry gusts of wind tugging at sodden brown leaves that clung to the gravel paths set Diane's nerves on edge. Wednesday had come and gone without the signing of the marriage contract. Her father, still in his dressing gown, unshaven, his eyes bleary with sleep, had hurried into her dressing room and had spoken confusedly of delays and unexpected complications, of misunderstandings that must be addressed with the vicomte de Vaubois before the young couple could proceed further with their plans. When Diane questioned her father about these complications, he had hinted that her honor, the Fautrière honor, was at stake.

They had been walking about for over an hour, and Diane's feet ached from the cold.

"Why didn't you come to Mademoiselle Malavelle's last evening? She asked everyone for news of you." The tip of Paul's nose had turned a bright pink. He could not keep the guilt out of his voice. Last night he had been relieved, glad when the clocks in Mademoiselle's game room had struck eleven, and still Diane had not appeared. He had relaxed then and had played several games of *comète* with Mademoiselle at his side, joking, paying him the wildest compliments! He blushed at the memory of them. She had brought him luck, all the while teasing him about his aversion to gambling. You should gamble more often, my dear baron, she had said. You should take a few risks. What do you know about risks, Mademoiselle, he had said, laughing, raking the pile of coins to his side of the table. He had gone home contented, though vaguely disturbed by his own contentment.

"Mademoiselle? I don't know. I was tired. My spirits have been low since Papa postponed the contracts."

"You mustn't despair!" he said gently, touching her arm. "*We* mustn't despair!" They continued their way toward the gate. "What did your father say? What reason did he give?" Paul had been astonished to learn of the comte's decision to postpone the signing of the contracts. His own father had wheezed and rubbed his stomach and finished off a whole dish of sugary comfits at the news. Then he had ordered Paul to get to the bottom of it.

"He didn't give a reason, I've told you. He just said that we must wait." She was ashamed to tell him that her father had invoked her honor and the honor of the Fautrière family. Absurd, it was absurd. Someone, but who? was poisoning his mind, turning him against Paul.

"How could you have been too downcast to spend an evening with me?"

"Rather, to spend an evening at Mademoiselle Malavelle's," Diane said, irritated. "I must confess that I don't feel terribly at ease with Mademoiselle any more. Not since she has begun to ogle you shamelessly in front of everyone there. Not since she has begun to make expensive presents to *my* fiancé."

Paul sighed. They were beginning to quarrel again. Over nothing. Or next to nothing. Trifles. Diane had become capricious, moody, dark dreary moods sweeping over her, taking him unawares. "Oh, come, come, my beautiful darling." He took her in his arms and lifted her face. The harsh wind had put a sparkle in her eyes and her cheeks glowed with health. She was an exquisite beauty. Beyond dispute the most beautiful woman he had ever seen. Or imagined. "Mademoiselle Malavelle does not ogle me! Or anyone else, for that matter. She's a good friend. A good friend to a young guardsman. You French may not understand friendship between a man and a woman, but in my . . . "

"And do friends spend thousands on a gold pocket watch, decorated with their initials in a love knot! A love knot! I know a love knot when I see one!" But she did not. She had described the interwoven initials to Marianne, who told her what it was. "And their portrait done in costly enamel!" Diane broke free and stood staring at the iron gate only a few feet away. "Well, she can spend a fortune on her portrait, the old crow! No amount of money will get rid of those ugly . . . "

"Diane!" Paul said quietly. "Don't you realize how unworthy this kind of talk is? One cannot . . . "

"Oh, spare me! Not another of your Swiss sermons," she groaned. Diane could not believe her own ears. She sounded like Catherine.

Paul caught the scorn in her voice, but he said nothing. He wanted to hurry away from the subject of Mademoiselle Malavelle. He knew that, as a man of honor, he never should have accepted the gold watch, not after she had carried on in such a preposterous way last month when they were alone together. But then the watch had been meant to apologize for that strange scene. She had said that she was sorry and had pleaded with him to take the watch as a token. He never should have fallen into the habit of spending an hour or two with her in the afternoons when he reached Paris too late for dinner with the marquise de Sabran. Yet how could he have known? How could he have suspected? And to find himself there, surrounded by warmth and luxury and the special treats that Mademoiselle would have made up for him, whatever the hour, coaxing him to enjoy, treating him like flesh-and-blood royalty. Nonetheless, he shouldn't have. Poor Mademoiselle had got quite carried away.

They stepped through the gate and started up the stairs. The sun suddenly burst through the lowering clouds, and Diane anxiously lifted her face to the sunshine.

On the landing at the top of the steps stood a young officer, his red uniform and gold braid glowing with color and fire.

"Armand? Isn't that Armand de Mézières standing there?" Diane asked.

At the sound of her voice Armand turned, and bounded down the steps, his arms opened wide.

"Armand!" she cried, rushing toward him.

The next morning, her callers having left, Diane was gathering up her sun mask for a walk in the Tuileries with Jean-Christophe, when Armand strode into her rooms, bringing with him memories of other mornings, before her father banished him from her company. Like two old friends they strolled along the paths of the Tuileries, deserted except for a few brave enough to face the chilly winds from the river. When Jean-Christophe failed to appear at their meeting place, Diane was not disappointed and did not stop to wonder at her faithful admirer's bad manners. Nor did she notice the look of satisfaction on Armand's face. Nor the way he clasped her arm tightly against him as they walked. She knew only that she was intoxicated with being alive in the chill, gray afternoon, feeling Armand strong and warm at her side, laughing down at her, stopping and turning her toward him, holding her closer, as he talked.

Afterwards, recalling their wintry walk in the Tuileries, she realized that she was happy with Armand in a way that she had never known with Paul. In a way that she could never be happy with Paul. There was excitement and danger in this happiness. It was a tainted happiness, fraught with the low desires she had come to fear in herself. With Paul there was serenity and security. She did not need her father to tell her that her feelings for Armand were treacherous. And disgusting.

She did not want to be like Madeleine, forever craving what only Armand could give her. No, no, Diane thought, with Paul there is peace, contentment, something, someone to strive for, trying always to get to that place of calm, free from the terrible longing for the pleasures that she did not understand, that swept her away into a kind of wild starving for more and more and more.

22

"My child," added my father, "there is worse still: The Baron has made to others the same promise he has made to you. And one in particular, a lady of quality, awaits only the posting of your banns to enter a caveat to the marriage . . . ."

The comte rose earlier than usual and spent the entire day, unshaven, still in this dressing gown and dimity mules, in Diane's rooms, bantering with her and Marianne. They played cards, scolding Marianne for her attempts to cheat, and Diane read aloud the letter she had received from Paul. It was a solemn letter describing their future together as a kind of noble journey of two kindred spirits. The comte found the style elegant, even learned, but asked to see the letter for himself, to look at the spelling.

The day passed quickly, and they separated only to dress for the marquise de Sabran's party celebrating the promotion of the comte de Lowendal to the rank of maréchal.

"I haven't yet satisfied myself in the matter of the baron's past conduct, *ma petite*," the comte said, as they alighted from the carriage. "But I suspect that Mademoiselle Malavelle has exaggerated the matter. She has your interests at heart, poor woman. In the meantime, I shall proceed with the formal engagement."

When Diane said nothing, he asked. "Does that please you?"

"Of course, it does. Oh, you know it does, papa!" she said. The comte, however, thought that she looked a little pale, that her enthusiasm was a trifle forced. They stepped into the huge foyer and reluctantly surrendered their heavy cloaks.

"Tourmelle will be here tonight. In all his glory. He was quite a hero at Berg-op-Zoom, and, besides, the marquise has taken him up. Should he bother you, however, let me know. I don't want the man annoying you."

It was the first time her father had ever spoken of Tourmelle in a disparaging way. "Believe me, papa, the man is a little crazy. He won't take 'no' for an answer. He behaves in the most preposterous way imaginable."

"He's a peasant, my dear. Peasants have never learned how to behave."

Paul swallowed hard and stared. "I'm sorry . . . I . . . I believe I missed what you said." He was stalling for time to comprehend that the grotesque creature sitting before him, her panniered skirts spread out proudly like a duchesse, had just proposed marriage to him.

"You heard what I said. You are at a loss for words. Am I right?" Mademoiselle Malavelle leaned forward and tapped his knee familiarly with her fan. In the candlelight of the corner where they sat, her face looked greasy, the pores as large as pock marks. She had streaked rouge across her broad cheekbones, and the white paint on her face made her teeth look even more yellow.

"I am . . . shall we say . . . surprised. Perhaps even shocked."

"Shocked? I fail to see what is so shocking about a marriage between the two of us. Am I that much of a horror to you?" Her voice became low, menacing.

Paul recoiled from the nasty thrust of her tone. He despised quarrels and misunderstandings. This surely was a terrible misunderstanding. "Oh, please, Mademoiselle. You misunderstand me. What I meant was, well, as you know, I am already engaged to be married. I have already given my word." Ah, now it will come, he thought, the nasty recriminations, the exquisite gifts. I shouldn't have taken a single one of them. He felt his throat tighten in panic.

"That was not my understanding from your father."

"My father! You've seen my father! You've . . . "

"Certainly. I wouldn't think of going about a matter of such consequence in a trifling manner. I've seen your father, and Madame your mother, as a matter of fact, and I've dined with your three charming sisters. Who will one day want to be married themselves, you know."

Mademoiselle Malavelle smiled coyly and waited for him to speak. In the distance Paul could hear the marquise's tall footman announcing, with a comical lisp, the names of arriving guests. They seemed very far away.

"My father must have confused you. The signing of contracts with Mademoiselle de Fautrière and her father is merely delayed. Postponed. My father is getting old. At times, he does not make himself clear."

"He made himself clear all right. Quite clear." She drew herself straight and gave him a haughty look that said that she was fast losing patience with him. "To be brief: your father considers his arrangements with the comte de Fautrière null and void. He maintains, and I believe him, that he entered into these arrangements under false pretenses. Quite simply, the comte held out certain expectations to your father. And it is now apparent that the comte has no intention of meeting these expectations."

Paul got to his feet. There was no reason to sit still any longer, politely enduring this preposterous situation, allowing his guilt over a few presents to muddle his judgment.

"What my father intends to do is one thing. What I intend to do is another. And I shall marry Mademoiselle de Fautrière. I don't need my father's consent for that." He held out his hand politely to help her rise.

"But, you do need *her* father's consent, my good man. Unless you propose to elope to Switzerland with her. And her father, the estimable comte, will never give his consent once he learns that the extensive properties and titles surrounding your name are . . . rumors, idle speculation. Or perhaps there is a politer way of saying what I mean." Her eyes bulged menacingly, showing wide strips of white. She ignored Paul's outstretched hand. Their talk would end when she decided. She was a stubborn woman emboldened by an increasing awareness of the power of her colossal fortune. She could begin and end interviews when she liked; she could marry the handsomest man in the kingdom—if she liked.

Paul, suddenly moved by her pathetic ugliness, said gently. "Come, let us be friends, Mademoiselle. I don't like to see you looking at me like that. So angry and disapproving." He lifted her hand, but she shook him away.

"I've never had much patience with fools," she said. "And at my age I don't intend to start now."

Watching Paul come into the concert room, weaving cautiously across the room, Diane thought that he looked dazed. He blinked his eyes against the bright light of the chandeliers and lustres. He was wearing his full dress uniform as befitted the occasion, and though it was already December, Paris was still celebrating the remarkable victory of the French forces at Berg-op-Zoom in the early fall. The comte de Lowendal, after feigning an attack on the enemy and retreating, had so thoroughly berated his men for their incompetence that spies within the camp had carried misleading intelligence to their leaders—intelligence which left the enemy forces vulnerable to a devastating surprise attack. The victory demonstrated brilliance and style, and the high society of Paris, having had few victories to cheer during the ragged progress of the war, determined to seize every opportunity to keep the festive mood alive. At least until harsher realities had to be reckoned with when the fighting began again in the spring.

"You're squinting something fierce," Madeleine said as she kissed Diane. "Almost as blind as a bat, you are. You really ought to wear glasses like my old governess in the attic in Poitou." Madeleine was smartly dressed in bright blue taffeta, and her hair, lightly powdered, was piled high on her head in the new style that was becoming popular with very young women.

"I was keeping an eye on Paul. He looks lost in this noisy crowd." As Diane spoke, Paul was engulfed by an excited group of guests, mostly brilliantly feathered and bejeweled women. "Look at them! They don't realize that Paul was not even in the battle!"

"Why should they care whether Paul was a hero or a poltroon? I can guess why they are flocking around him! Even the gods on Mount Olympus would stare!"

Paul did look stunning in his uniform, Diane had to admit. He stood tall and slim above his admirers, his dark hair woven into one long braid down his back. He was totally at ease, a center of calm and self-possession.

"I don't see Richelieu here tonight," Diane said.

"You won't. Our friend does not like to share the spotlight. Besides, Richelieu is already a maréchal."

"Why doesn't Richelieu like Paul? Why does he say demeaning things about him?"

"Does he? What things? What does Richelieu say?"

"Oh . . . I . . . He seems to think that Paul is not . . . good enough for me . . . " Diane said reluctantly. She had grown wary of Madeleine and her cold mockery. A few years ago, when they were both country girls from the convent finding their way through the maze of etiquette of court society, they had spent hours confiding in each other. Only Jean-Christophe was allowed into their secrets. And even he was excluded from their more intimate confidences. But after Madeleine fell in love with Armand, something happened. That love colored all of Madeleine's feelings. It made her mocking and hard and cruel.

"Well, I suppose I see what Richelieu means," Madeleine paused, looking at Paul, who had begun to disentangle himself from his circle of admirers. "After all, Paul is merely mortal, as it were. What I mean is, Richelieu was grooming you for the King of France, and here you are settling down with one of the King's household guards. Maybe that's what Richelieu means," she said, grinning coquettishly as Paul came up to them.

"You've made Paul blush," Diane said, as Paul asked Madeleine's permission to kiss her cheeks. It was one of Paul's habits that had begun to infuriate Diane, this bashful game of asking permission to give a kiss. So arch. So affected. When, as with Madeleine, that same permission had been granted a dozen times already. Paul looked at Diane with a guilty hangdog expression, and she felt ashamed of her impatience. Lately, in a polite, restrained sort of way, they bickered with each other. Diane deplored his dancing attendance on Mademoiselle Malavelle, and Paul began to make cutting remarks about the comte's frivolity, implying that Diane had been corrupted by it. The nuptial arrangements concluded, Diane was certain that everything would be perfect again. Just as it was in the beginning, before Mademoiselle Malavelle came to Paris.

"Voltaire is about to read his verses on the victory. If we can get through these people, we can grab seats close to the front," Paul said, giving his arm to each of them. The noise in the huge room had abated as groups dispersed for the reading.

"Oh, no! Again! That awful bore!" Madeleine groaned.

Near the double doors the crowd slowed, as swords in their slim, dainty sheaths got caught up in the ruffles and flounces of ballooning skirts, an opportunity for gallant compliments and teasing. There was a burst of full, throaty laughter, slightly drunken, a woman's provocative laugh as they waited to get through.

"Wait! Wait! Monsieur!" Odile laughed again, uncontrollably, squirming like a child being tickled. "Your sword will go right through to my petticoat!"

"I shall take great care, Madame, have no fear," the man said. His voice was gruff, his accent like the stable boys' at Corcheval. Diane recognized the voice immediately. It was Jean de Tourmelle on whose none too tidy uniform gleamed the Cross of Saint Louis. "My sword often misbehaves but never with a lady's petticoat," he said in a mock whisper, leaning toward Odile's ear. He drew back and turned his head, looking for recognition of his dash of wit. He did not see Diane, who ducked her head and tightened her grip on the baron's arm.

23

*D*espite the biting wind the day was sunny, and Diane did not hesitate a moment when the marquise de Sabran sent round her carriage to fetch her for a long, gossipy ride in the Bois de Boulogne.

"I do enjoy spoiling you a little," the marquise said, as her carriage made its way slowly through the fashionable byways of the Bois. "Besides, you must be a little lonely these days now that your baron's court duty has been extended to the end of the month. You poor dear." She patted Diane's hand.

"Oh, I suspect the time will fly by. Thanks to you, dear marquise. You fuss over me like a mother hen. Taking me out every sunny afternoon for a lovely drive. Buying me the most exquisite little gifts imaginable." In truth, when Paul's week *en service* stretched into over a month, Diane was surprised by her own indifference. The tenderness of their parting was grudging and tentative. She was convinced that Paul, irritated by the comte's haggling with his father, took out his ill humor on her. He found frequent occasions to chastise her shallow worldliness and seemed annoyed that his remarks did not bring forth the anxious tears to which he had grown accustomed. He had become desultory in his letter writing and no longer sent her romantic blossoms from the King's hothouses.

"Ah, speaking of little gifts . . . Dufour, you know the jeweler next to Madame Clarisse, he has such cunning little glove clasps. Gold with tiny diamond studs. Quite a novelty. Just perfect for your lovely young hands, my dear!"

"Heavens! There's no stopping you!" Diane laughed, fondly squeezing the marquise's hand. "But I really shouldn't linger this afternoon. I haven't seen papa for ages it seems. He has simply disappeared. I want to be at home for tea."

The marquise kept silent. It was hard to determine just how much Diane knew about her father's dissolute life, and she didn't want to alarm the young girl. Everyone at court was gossiping about the comte's latest folly. He was behaving like an adolescent with a young dancer at the Opéra, heaping expensive clothes and jewelry on her, borrowing money from Lévy, and drinking with the riffraff around the Palais Royal.

"I think your father is quite busy at court, you know," the marquise said after a moment. "Seeking a preferment of some sort. Look, isn't that the duc de Gevres' *berline*?" she asked, hurrying away from the subject of Diane's errant father. "How he manages to run his gambling den by night and gad about all day, I'll never know . . . Come, let's take another turn around the south side, and then we'll see what you have to say about Monsieur Dufour's glove clasps, shall we?"

Diane's hands trembled with exasperation as she struggled with the complicated pins of her bodice. Of late Marianne had fallen into one of her foul moods and was no help at all. She moped about the house all day, neglecting her toilette and drinking brandy at all hours. I really must speak to papa, Diane thought, as she hurriedly changed her earrings and checked her reflection in the mirror before rushing down the stairs to her waiting carriage.

Once at the marquise de Sabran's mansion, she sped up the deserted grand stairway. "Am I late?" Diane asked as the footman took her cloak. "Has the concert begun?"

The marquise winked knowingly. Though she congratulated herself on having spirited away the major attraction of Mademoiselle Malavelle's dinner table and salon, the marquise knew that it was a darkly handsome, newly commissioned officer who drew Diane to her drawing room, even on the coldest, most lugubrious evenings.

"You're in very good time. *He* isn't here yet." She was no fool. Diane's infatuation came as no surprise. She could forgive Diane anything, especially her taste for Armand's strapping good looks. Besides, the marquise did not share the popular enthusiasm for the baron de Rothenburg. She found him a bit of a prig. Let the child have some fun; it would do her good, she said to herself.

As Diane headed toward her favorite chair on a back row facing the door, she felt like a reckless child, disobeying her father, forgetting Paul and his severity. Even though most guests were meandering toward their seats, the duc de Gevres and a train of Diane's admirers rushed to bring her champagne, eager to compete with each other with their witty compliments, which she found more tedious than not.

They settled down as the concert began at last, and still there was no sign of Armand. It was a raw, wintry evening. Perhaps the roads were snowy, perhaps his horse had fallen, perhaps he had had an accident . . . She felt heavy with disappointment and anxiety. She closed her eyes and tried to concentrate on the music, and when she looked up, she saw Armand coming slowly toward her, his dark eyes fixed on her as if there were no one else in the room. Her heart raced as he came to stand behind her and rested his hands lightly on her bare shoulders, surrendering herself to the turbulent sweetness of his touch. His scent and his warmth made her light-headed.

Armand helped her to her feet as the concert came to an end.

"I was afraid you might not come," she said, reluctant to let go of his hand.

"The roads are terrible," he said. "But nothing would have kept me from seeing you tonight."

Smiling fondly, the marquise watched the young pair. The dear child, she thought, Diane is radiant, as happy as I have ever seen her. Thank Heaven, Madeleine has just taken up her new post in the Queen's service. I've no doubt she would not care for the spectacle of her husband-to-be unable to keep his hands off her best friend.

The marquise reached for a glass of champagne from the tray of a passing footman. "No more champagne for Mademoiselle de Fautrière," she said, nodding her head in Diane's direction. "See to it."

But as Diane settled into the narrow seat of a fiacre on that snowy night in February, she was far from sober.

"Where is my coachman?" she asked Armand. "And Laurent? Where is Laurent?" She was giggling like a schoolgirl. She did not really care. It was romantic to be climbing into a fiacre instead of pulling through the winding streets in her father's lumbering coach.

Armand had given half of the coins in his purse to Diane's coachman. The other half he had paid to the driver of the fiacre—to keep driving until Armand rapped against the window with his sword. Armand kissed her cold cheeks and pulled her into his arms. He opened his heavy cloak and spread it around her. Chilled from head to toe, she snuggled into the warmth of his embrace. The fiacre skidded and tilted to one side before crashing down noisily against the curbstone. They both laughed, and Armand once again pulled her against him and kissed her gently, opening her lips. His dark curls fell against her cheeks, like the caress of silk. She buried her hands in his hair, her lips reaching again for his.

With great tenderness Armand pulled her hips against him, his numb fingers struggling with the ribbons of her undergarments. His hands and mouth drifted over her body, releasing urgent spasms of pleasure so intense that he covered her mouth with his to soften her cries. Confusing, fierce sensations took hold of her body until she lay back in his arms, half stupefied, mesmerized by desire.

Gusts of icy wind whistled at the doors of the fiacre. They passed beneath a line of lanterns overhanging the street.

"Where am I?" Diane murmured, looking through the icy pane.

"In my arms. Where I have for so long yearned for you to be."

By the time Armand rapped on the window with his sword, the sky behind Notre-Dame was flushed with pink, and the weary driver turned his fiacre across the Pont Royal.

Diane crept forward and carefully opened her bedroom door. Not a sound. The entire apartment on the rue des Fours seemed to be under a spell, slumbering in the deep sleep of a winter afternoon. Icy sleet and snow pelted against the dark windowpane, and wind soughed and sighed in the elaborately glazed fireplace.

Diane sat down at her dressing table and hummed softly as she brushed her hair, smiling from time to time as she caught a glimpse of herself in the mirror, seeing herself in a completely new light. In the tormented hours after the long night in a hired cab, her only fear had been that she would never recapture the pleasures of those hours. It had been different from anything she could ever have imagined. So different that the entire world she had been familiar with dropped away, disappeared, melted away into a time long, long ago and very far away. Now there was much less mystery in the world she lived in. At Corcheval Madeleine, laughing scornfully, had said that the comte was making the beast with two backs with Marianne every afternoon, in the long, sultry hours of naps after dinner, and Diane had stared at her, dumbly, frightened by the image of a beast with two backs. In the house on the rue des Fours there were days when Diane never saw Marianne at all, and the upstairs chambermaid with a stony face did Marianne's work for her. Until Marianne would suddenly appear smelling of sandalwood and sometimes with brandy on her breath. Her father's perfume. Sandalwood. The beast with two backs . . . But there was nothing beastly about Armand, his gentle hands stroking her body, his voice full of desire, as soft and caressing as a fur rug warmed by the fire.

She wound her hair into a single golden coil and secured it with a large lacquered pin atop her head. Lightheaded with excitement, she laid down her brush and turned from her dressing table. Never would she have believed that she could be so clever. Or bold. Right under her father's very nose, and more important, right under Marianne's, she was giving herself up to her passion for Armand. Her mind had become devilishly cunning. Why shouldn't she stand up for her own happiness, no matter how brief? Quite simply, just after the dinner hour, the young lovers would meet in her bedroom. What better place, since her father had been away for weeks? And she could count on Marianne's laziness in the afternoons, especially these days when she seemed more interested in the comte's brandy bottle than in her duties.

The footed white Meissen clock on her desk made a tight, clicking sound, then after a short, meditative silence, struck five o'clock.

Already lamplighters were torching the lanterns along the dark, snowy streets. A noise. Someone walking in the hallway. She stood still and listened, holding her breath. Her heart racing, she moved swiftly to the door. Stealthily, she eased it open.

"Hello . . . ," Armand whispered. Quickly, Diane pulled him into the room and carefully closed the door.

"Did anyone see you?" Diane asked, laughing softly as he gathered her into his arms.

"No one. Laurent and the footmen were closing the shutters for the night."

Armand gently cupped her head with his broad hands and brought her lips to his, kissing her slowly, hungrily, like a parched traveler relieving his thirst at a cool mountain stream.

"Here," he said reaching up to Diane's hair, "Let me take that pin away . . . "

It seemed to Diane that he spoke very, very slowly, and in a voice so low that it was scarcely above a whisper. She could feel his warm breath against her face. He lifted a coil of her golden hair to his nostrils and inhaled deeply. "Lemon . . . you've been using lemon on your hair, haven't you? It smells delicious. Delicious."

Gently, he began to undo the buttons, pins, and satin ties of her bodice. He lifted away the bodice, slipping Diane's arms from the sleeves, and let the garment fall to the floor. His lips parted in a smile as he gazed at the homely laced corset that lifted her young, firm breasts. As if in a dream, she watched him slowly and deliberately unlacing the corset with the gentlest of motions, tugging to loosen buttons. When he had removed it, he ran his fingers slowly along the faint impressions left by her stays, and bent to kiss her breasts. Her knees began to tremble, and she leaned forward, clutching weakly at his cape, her warm breasts pressed into the cold buttons and braid of his uniform.

There was an impatient rat-tap-tap at the door. Breathless, Diane turned toward the door and waited, her heart thudding with fear.

"Mademoiselle?" Marianne shook the doorknob. "Your door is locked . . . Why is your door locked?" Her words were slurred, and she was obviously out of sorts. Alcohol never made Marianne happy.

Armand bent to nuzzle Diane's throat, his thick, glossy hair still full of the frosty evening air, and peppered her smooth, velvety shoulders with kisses.

"The wind, there was such a draft, rattling the door . . . I couldn't bear it."

Armand cradled her head in his arms and kissed her slowly and gently, as he shrugged off his heavy cape.

"What was that noise?" Marianne asked shrilly. "I heard something fall in there. What are you doing? It's early. Don't you want to play cards?"

"I . . . I'm not well, Marianne, really I'm not well," Diane said in a faint voice, her hunger for him unbearable. She kissed his eyes, his lips, his cheeks, still pink and chilled by the wintry night air.

"You sound peculiar. Open the door. I'll read to you." Marianne shook the doorknob again. "Mademoiselle?"

"I can't talk now. My throat is raw . . . "

Diane sounded so sincere that Armand looked at her with alarm.

"*Ah, pauchère! Petit poussinet!*" Marianne said. "You poor thing, I'll fetch you some parsnip tea. Just the thing."

Diane was instantly remorseful. She had never before lied to Marianne, whose patois terms of endearment touched her heart. "No, no," she said quickly. "Bed rest. That's all I need . . . just rest."

Marianne was silent, but Diane could hear her shifting her weight outside the door. "All right, then," she said finally. "It's just so lonely. I was thinking we could go together . . . to one of those smart cafés at the Palais Royal. Maybe we would see the comte there, or . . . Sleep well." Her voice trailed off pitifully.

They listened as her footsteps faded away down the long corridor.

"I feel very wicked," Diane said guiltily, her face flushed with desire.

"Then, what you need is some bed rest, *petit poussinet*," Armand said, lifting her into his arms.

Settled into the snug warmth of her feather bed, Diane soon found herself plunging into a place of pure sensation, losing herself in her passion for Armand, as the hearth fire purred and crackled, casting an orange red glow over their joy.

❦

Mademoiselle M— went to Issy to visit the Baron's father, a self-serving man. She spoke to him of her generous plans for his son, which would not be limited to him alone. . . . They parted, very content with one another.

"It's deuced cold in here? Don't you think? Or is it just me?" The comte rubbed his hands vigorously together, then held them over the fire. He looked worn and disheveled. Everything was coming down on him at once. He turned his backside to the fire and lifted his coat. "I can't get warm. I don't know what's got into me. I'm chilled through and through."

"Poor papa," Diane said gently without looking up from her tapestry work. She had never before attempted such a difficult piece, but Sophie's birthday was fast approaching, and she knew that her little sister would like nothing better than a new tapestry for her prie-dieu, a rickety affair, the cast off of one of the novices. Diane had chosen the Annunciation scene by an Italian artist because it was full of color and assorted animals, including a monkey smelling a flower.

"Aren't you going to ask me how my meeting with the vicomte went?" Yes. Everything was coming down on him at once, but if he could settle this marriage, if he could only get something promising in writing, he could shake off his creditors like a dog coming in out of the rain. What in God's name was happening? What kind of game were the wily Swiss playing now?

"I assumed . . . I hoped . . . that your meeting went well, papa." She smiled brightly at him, then went back to her work.

"They couldn't be going worse," he laughed wearily. "The old man . . . the vicomte . . . appears to have changed his mind."

"What! Changed his mind!"

"No, what I mean is, at first they rush forward, all eagerness to marry into one of the oldest families in France, and then, then . . . well, I don't know, I can't say for sure what is going on. But now the old man wants certain deeds of property to follow you into the marriage."

"What does that mean?"

"It means that the old man wants a dowry. And a sizable one at that. He keeps talking about other daughters to marry. Humph! As if *he* were the only one with other daughters to settle."

"Aren't there more properties, papa? More than Corcheval and Joigny?" Diane could not remember the names of the other estates scattered around Charolais. Catherine knew all of them, how many hectares there were on each estate, how many tenants, how many cows, the state of the roads and bridges and churches. "Weren't there more properties when maman . . . ?"

The comte waved his hands impatiently. "That's not the point! That's not the point! From the very beginning of our talks I have made it clear to the old man that you will have no dowry. From the very beginning. I've made no secret of it. And why should I? You have one of the noblest names in France. Many a rich bourgeois would go stark raving mad at the idea of marrying into our family. Being able to say that he has children with a mother whose name goes back to Charlemagne!"

"Papa! You wouldn't think of a bourgeois suitor, would you?"

"Of course not! Don't be absurd! I've rejected dozens of those already. I will never sink to a *mésalliance*! Never! The Fautrière name will never be linked with a hustling moneymaker who blows on his soup and wipes his nose on his sleeve. Never!"

"Then what are we to do?" The question sounded almost rhetorical, like a line repeated from a play that one has read too many times.

"I shall give the old man a little more time to come to his senses. And I will get to the bottom of this. Something is going on behind my back. Someone is pulling strings. I would bet my last snuffbox on it."

"But . . . who could that be?"

"Someone who wants to marry his daughter to the baron de Rothenburg. That would be my guess. Someone who is tempting the old vicomte with a big sack full of money!" His back to her, the comte held his hands over the fire again.

Diane grabbed at her tapestry hoop, which was slipping over her lap. Her stomach turned over. She folded her hands carefully in her lap. She must not panic. She took a deep breath. She had to marry Paul; she had to have a safe, secure life that would keep her in Paris and court society. Near Armand. Far from the sinister Tourmelle. Her need for Paul was as great—oh, it was greater! please God, it must be greater!—than her tormented longing for Armand. What happened with Armand during the long winter afternoons was separate . . . yet how could it be separate if she moved through the rest of the day in a trance, in a dream, waiting to be awakened to the fire of his caress? How could it be separate if she could think of nothing else, until she was back in his arms? So desperate for him that she did not care whether the servants knew, whether Marianne would find out, whether one day her father would burst in upon them as she . . .

"Paul! Marry someone else! It's not possible! He wouldn't, oh, papa, I know he wouldn't!"

The comte turned so quickly that he almost lost his balance. "Please, *ma petite!* don't shout! Don't get so excited!" He tilted his snuff box and shook it. He sniffed two pinches and licked his thumb to get out the small amount that was left. "I worry about you and your nerves. Your excitability. You're too high-strung, I've always said that. Like your mother." He crossed himself.

"I'm sorry. It's . . . You frightened me, papa. When you said that Paul . . . that someone might make an offer . . ." She looked down at her half-finished Mary, her arms folded meekly across her chest in complete surrender to God's message, and felt ashamed. She dared not look up. She was afraid of what her father would see if he looked into her eyes. He would see Armand. He would see her naked and panting in Armand's arms. He would see her sickness, her obsession with Armand, their honeyed afternoons when all the house was hushed, except inside the curtained bed, which rustled and whispered as they moaned and struggled in passionate embrace.

"Listen to me, Diane. No, now look at me. I want to ask you something quite serious. I worry about you, it's true. They've always accused me of making you my favorite of the children. Your mother said that . . . your uncle. I haven't made it a secret. It's true, you are my little one, and I want you to be happy. Truly happy. I know I can be harsh . . . but that's the way of a father." He paused and sighed.

"I know, papa. You mean well. I know that." She threaded her needle and began to fill in Gabriel's angel wings, a downy white, pure as fresh snowflakes on a window pane. Her father was about to say something dreadful, she was sure of it.

"And I . . . well, you understand that not every father cares whether his girls marry their sweethearts. You know that, don't you?"

"Of course, papa."

"So I'm not a monster hauling you out of the convent and throwing you into the arms of a stranger with a pile of money." He scratched his head, pushing his wig askew. The idea of not being a bad father seemed to have beguiled him into losing his train of thought. "Still . . . *mon trésor* . . . *if*, and remember that I am only saying *if*, I can't talk sense into this old fool . . . what I'm trying to say is . . . will it break your heart if our plans . . . if . . . "

He could not go on. Diane sat staring at him, her deep gray eyes swimming in tears. There was a succession of small, hollow sounds as her tears fell onto the tight canvas.

"Papa," she said, her voice hoarse, strained. "You don't understand. I . . . I have to marry Paul. I must marry him. You . . . please don't fail me, papa. Oh, please don't fail me!"

The comte dropped to his knees and put his arms around her to comfort her. She was wearing him out, this child of his. He ground his teeth in anger. That Swiss skinflint. Trying to worm his way out of a contract that would give his son the most beautiful woman in France. A woman who had turned the head of the King of France. Who had come within an inch of the royal bed, only to be tricked out of it by a scheming bourgeois hussy!

"I must go. I really must," he said listlessly, awkwardly rising to his feet. "I promised Mademoiselle Malavelle that I would call in tonight. She's a good friend to us. Right now, we need good friends like her. She may see some way to pull us out of this impasse with the vicomte."

"Oh, papa! If only she can . . . if only she can!"

The comte turned to close the door behind him and caught a last glimpse of Diane, her hands folded in her lap, staring into the fire. The refined beauty of her face glowed in the firelight, the smoothly arching brows, the perfect profile, the full curve of her lips. It had seemed so easy three years ago, he thought, so easy. As easy as bedding the chambermaid.

❦

While dressing, the comte emptied the small decanter of brandy that Clovis kept filled despite his old man's forgetfulness. Weary, cold—he could not stray from the fire in his dressing room more than a few feet without beginning to shiver—the comte nonetheless dressed with meticulous care. He painted his face carefully, rouging his cheeks with a new color that Marianne had found for him and sticking three beauty patches in the shape of stars at the side of each eye. Underneath his pale pink velvet coat and vest, he wore a woolen shift that Marianne had carelessly left behind in his bed the week before.

The drive across the river to Mademoiselle Malavelle's townhouse left him trembling with cold, though he had had Laurent put two more braziers into the carriage. It was still snowing. Mademoiselle would think him mad to turn up on such a night. He was so miserably cold that he did not care. He did not have enough energy to care.

Six or seven footmen were busy keeping the large half circle of steps swept clear of the falling snow. As the comte alighted stiffly from his carriage, a huge, bulky man mounting the steps turned to wait for him.

"A good evening to you, Monsieur de Tourmelle," the comte said, and for some reason, the sight of Tourmelle's broad, coarse face lifted his spirits. Tourmelle was an oaf of a man, beyond a doubt. He had no refinement, no manners. He chewed his food with his broad mouth open, he picked his teeth with his hand knife, he cleared his nose in the most extraordinary gesture. It made a person sick to watch him. But he did have his friends in high places. Very high places. The comte had learned to respect what Tourmelle had to say.

Before the two men could reach the foyer their shoulders were covered in thick, heavy snow.

Tourmelle's small dark eyes sparkled with pleasure as he gripped the comte's hand. "Three days, hein? And no end in sight. They say the road to Versailles is impassable now. Pity the poor buggers who are here tonight and think they will lose their pants if they aren't on hand tomorrow at the King's *levée*."

Only last year the comte would have been one of those poor buggers, as Tourmelle called them. That was before he lost his rooms in the chateau. Only one room really, with a shelf built into the wall where old Clovis slept. Even that little sop to his pride and his name was gone. The comte's knees ached as he mounted the stairs to the drawing room.

"I do pity them. I used to fly over those roads at all times of day and night, in all kinds of weather. It's a wonder I didn't kill myself many times over."

As they entered the drawing room, Tourmelle took the comte's arm. Tourmelle swung his large, peasant's head around the room. "And your daughter, comte? Your daughter . . . I don't see her anywhere at all."

"Actually . . . she's not here. She . . . " the comte was about to say that Diane had stayed at home because her fiancé the baron had guard duty and she did not want to spend the evening in society without his company. But, thinking better of it, he stopped and said simply, "She stayed at home. The snow . . . and the cold, you know."

The comte looked on astonished as Tourmelle's face collapsed with disappointment. The comte had never seen such a raw display of emotion. The great bear of a man seemed to slump by his side.

"Then I shouldn't have troubled myself tonight. I wouldn't come here at all if it weren't for the chance of seeing her, of just being able to look at her . . . " He looked utterly lost, dejected, standing there.

As a footman held back her chair, Mademoiselle Malavelle laid down her cards and strode rapidly toward them.

"I shouldn't come here for that one . . . that big Fish Eyes coming at us like a hungry shark. She's a hungry fish all right. And smelly. I don't trust Fish Eyes, I don't." He bowed toward the gawky spinster and turned away, toward the door. "You watch out for her, comte. She'll get you into some troubled waters. You don't want to end up smelling like a fish, too."

24

[M. de T—] was constantly in private conversation with my father, which worried me, for I suspected that I was most often the subject of their exchanges. I was not mistaken.

Over the years old Clovis had grown accustomed to half-carrying, half-dragging the comte, far gone with drink, from his carriage in the early hours before dawn. But that night when the comte returned from Mademoiselle Malavelle's, Clovis took one look at the comte and realized that neither he nor Laurent could get the comte to his bed by themselves. Laurent roused the portly cook to help them pull the comte out of the carriage and up the long flight of stairs to his rooms.

The comte was already delirious with a fever, which kept him semi-conscious for over a week. When the King learned of his illness, he sent one of his own surgeons to bleed him and to administer an emetic every morning at sunrise. Word was sent back to court that the comte de Fautrière suffered from a threatening case of pleurisy and that his recovery was most uncertain. Louis, who frightened easily at rumors of death, even the death of someone else, took the precaution of not sleeping with Madame de Pompadour for a week, lest God punish him for the miserable adulterer that he was, and, as at Metz, strike him down again in the midst of his joy.

While the comte lay pale and still, his laboring breath echoing through the upstairs hallways, Marianne fended off the swarm of creditors who had got wind of the comte's illness. Marianne was by turns charming, innocent, disarming, coquettish and haughty, shrill, abusive. The creditors to whom the comte owed serious debts proved to be the most accommodating. The butcher, however, cut off the household without another word, refusing the comte one more day of credit. To Diane's dismay, Marianne more or less closed down the kitchen and sent out for their meals from the cookshop on the corner, patronized mainly by servants in the quartier. The comte will never know the difference, Marianne said, in her practical way. With growing alarm, Diane watched the collapse of the rich chrysalis in which she lived. Armand had left the city on a mission with the duc de Richelieu, and Diane could not bear the thought of receiving a visit from the baron.

One day the comte lifted his bare leg, swollen and crisscrossed with slashes, and kicked the surgeon aside. Despite Diane's tears and old Clovis' mournful looks, the comte refused to be bled again. He cowered under the covers, and though he could barely speak, no one in the room dared defy his wishes.

Diane rarely left his side. The servants kept a huge fire blazing so that midsummer heat filled the room. The blowing drifts of snow had stopped, to be replaced by icy gales that frosted the window panes, and drafts underneath the doors fluttered the carpets on the floor. The cook made savory broths from ham shanks that Laurent fetched from the cookshop, and the comte gradually began to eat with the ravenous appetite of a hard-working peasant. One day, almost three weeks after he had collapsed in his carriage, he complained that he was bored, a wonderful sign, Diane said, that her father was returning to health.

She began to read aloud to him from *Pamela*, which she had first read at Corcheval the summer after she and her father had left court. Marianne and the comte listened, spellbound, to the story, hour after hour, until Diane's head ached from eyestrain over the poor print. Marianne and the comte agreed that the maidservant Pamela, faced with a French aristocrat, could never have preserved her virtue. Never. It was too farcical to imagine. Marianne sniffed knowingly, and the comte boasted that a Frenchman would have had his way with the modest, virtuous Pamela before the first chapter was over.

"Only an Englishman could have written such a preposterous tale!" the comte said. "Read on! Don't stop now, *ma fille,* we must see how our little maid escapes . . . "

A week later, by the time Diane reached the middle of the first book, Marianne and the comte were quarreling over the characters as if Pamela and Mr. B . . . had set up residence with them on the rue des Fours. Pamela had completely won over the heart of the comte, while Marianne claimed that she could not abide this whining ninny who used her so-called virtue to climb the social ladder. Soon Marianne began to call Pamela a shifty trollop, and Diane laughed so hard that she kept losing her place.

The comte and Marianne were arguing so rowdily one afternoon that no one heard Clovis announce Tourmelle as he strode into the comte's bedroom. Grinning hugely from ear to ear, his broken teeth glistening, Tourmelle went first to Diane and bowed over her hand. She could smell his clothes, a strong fleshy odor of horses and stables. He was finely dressed in sober brown velvet with grey silk stockings. Motioning to Marianne, Diane nodded in reply and quickly left the room.

After that afternoon Tourmelle called in every day, never at any fixed time, always as if by chance, as if passing by. This large, strapping man who towered over her, over everyone, frightened Diane. She could not leave the room fast enough, though her father scolded her bad manners and urged her to show Monsieur Tourmelle more courtesy. She could not. She ran from him as from a wild, charging animal bearing down on her.

Tourmelle remained closeted with the comte for hours. What they discussed remained their secret. Diane could not bring herself to mention the man's name, though she did put Marianne up to questioning the comte. The comte passed over these long visits in silence, turning aside Marianne's questions with a shrug of the shoulders. "I enjoy the man," he said once. And the comte's spirits did improve remarkably. He began to dress elegantly once again, even though he did not yet have enough strength to go abroad. Marianne shaved him every morning before noon and bathed him carefully in witch-hazel and sandalwood scent. His friends visited and mingled their complicated perfumes in the overheated room, but they were all dismissed with kisses and handshakes shortly after Tourmelle made his daily appearance. Before the month was out, the butcher's apprentice had brought round a handsome leg of lamb, compliments of the butcher, and soon the cook's larder was as well stocked as any other nobleman's establishment in Paris.

The marquis d'Ancy heard the news of his brother-in-law's near fatal illness as soon as he reached his home in Paris. Philippe had begun his journey back to Paris by riverboat, but further up, the Seine was icebound, and he had to use the coach bound for Paris at the end of the week. The roads were harrowing, icy and filled with drifting snow.

"You don't look like a man who has been snatched from the jaws of death," Philippe said jovially. "You look as if you're being cosseted like an old woman, Michel."

Diane stood next to her father's chair and fussed with the wide black bow that Marianne had tied around his hair. Philippe gazed at her young slim figure and wondered whether any woman could match Diane's beauty. She was breathtaking, a natural beauty. No paint or rouge could add to that glowing complexion. The Pompadour was a stick compared. And already showing tiny lines around the mouth, bloodless lips, showing the strain of keeping the King amused.

"And you look as if you had never seen your niece before, Philippe!"

Diane looked up and smiled.

"I was staring. Forgive me. I've been down in the country too long."

Philippe drew up a chair next to the fire as Diane gathered up her books and needlework.

"I promised Marianne that we would visit Madeleine today. We haven't seen anyone for months, it seems . . . because of papa's illness."

"Not even the baron de Rothenburg?" Philippe asked. A queer look passed over Diane's face. "Or have you found another admirer in your throng of suitors since I went away?"

"No, no," said the comte. "It's only that the baron has been called back with the comte de Lowendal to Flanders. The comte has taken the maréchal de Saxe's place until the spring."

After Diane left them alone, the comte appeared in no hurry to talk with his brother-in-law. Shifting about on his chaise-longue, he threw back the coverlet to show his bruised and swollen legs to Philippe.

"That's what our brilliant doctors know how to do! Pretty sight, hein?"

"So, when are we to celebrate my god-daughter's wedding, Michel? I want to do my part."

"There have been delays. The vicomte de Vaubois grows more demanding every day. At first, I thought that he was merely throwing the tantrums of an old man—he's close to seventy, you know. Now I'm not sure . . ."

"What does he want?"

"A dowry. A dowry big enough to insure an annuity for him and his family. Family being his wife and three daughters waiting to be married off." The comte gave a contemptuous snort. "An annuity! That's precisely what I went into this negotiation looking for! And now the old Swiss bastard is holding out his hand to me! Of all people!"

"Yes. You of all people. Still, he will have to be reasonable. The two young people love each other. I could never have imagined Diane so happy with the idea of getting married. He's perfect for her. Truly."

"Even perfect couples have to eat," the comte said morosely. He shifted his right leg and grimaced in pain.

"They will eat very well, you know that. The baron will have his pension from the King, whatever happens. They will not live grandly, but if they are happy together . . ."

"I won't have it!" the comte shot back so shrilly that Philippe drew back in his chair. The comte sat up and cautiously moved his legs over the side of the chair to the floor. "I won't have it! Settling for a pittance . . . a measly existence . . . for a girl who has been the sensation of Paris! Coveted by the King of France himself!" The comte's face and neck had turned a menacing red.

Philippe sat quietly, waiting for the storm to pass. It was his duty, to Aurélie, to Diane and the other two girls, not to let this fool's greed ruin the young girl's life. He owed it to Aurélie's memory not to let her child down now. His own boys were well established; their patrimony was safe from the spendthrift hands of Odile. Philippe had made sure of that.

"Who is this Mademoiselle Malavelle that Odile has taken up with?" asked Philippe. "Rich as Croesus I take it."

"Richer. You *have* been in the country a long time." The comte had grown calmer. He rose carefully to his feet and sat down again abruptly. "I still have no strength. My legs won't hold me up yet. This Mademoiselle Malavelle . . . she has been useful to me. She adores Diane. Everyone does. Anyway, Mademoiselle has tipped me off about the baron's unsavory reputation."

"Unsavory?"

"He's a young man with a history of getting himself into marriage negotiations, then withdrawing on suspiciously flimsy grounds. In other words, Mademoiselle Malavelle assures me that I am dealing with a fortune hunter."

Despite himself Philippe roared with laughter. Just the luck of this hopelessly incompetent fool to land in this predicament!

"Is she sure?" asked Philippe.

"I believe her. She had done some checking herself through relatives in the Savoie. That's one of the reasons this pleurisy knocked me over the head. It's a bad turn, there's no denying it. Especially with Diane set on having the man, whatever his fortune. But we can't all have what we want, can we?" The comte looked at Philippe coldly.

"What do you mean?"

"I mean that I have had dozens of offers for Diane's hand since we returned to Paris, the baron is only one among many, and I do have alternatives. I can pick and choose."

"And . . . have you someone in mind?"

"I wouldn't dream of a *mésalliance*, Philippe. I hope you don't imagine me capable of that," the comte appeared to be stalling.

"I will confess, however, that most of Diane's suitors have belonged to . . . well, the financial class. Out of the question, naturally," he said, darting a sheepish look at his brother-in-law. The comte paused. He lifted his legs to the chair and leaned back, exhausted with the effort.

"I'm looking favorably on a man from our part of the country . . . Jean de Tourmelle," he said in a low voice, turning his head away from Philippe.

"Jean de Tourmelle! You can't be serious! No, Michel, how could you for a moment!"

"Why shouldn't I be serious? A nobleman of great fortune! A military hero! Why shouldn't I be serious? Answer me that!"

"Calm yourself, man! You're as red as a beet! And shouting loud enough to bring down the house!"

"I'm a sick man, Philippe. And I'm very nearly down to my last *sou*. Why can't you see what it's like for a man in my situation? You've already married your sons into money enough for several generations, they're settled down on their estates, while here am I with my son and heir dead before his time only months after I purchased his promotion with loans I'm still paying five percent on. And with three daughters to be provided with husbands. One of them looking like a scarecrow, to boot. While her sister, the beauty of Paris, falls in love with a Swiss baron who has spent the last few years chasing a fortune with a wedding band. Now you want to tell me that I should turn up my nose to Jean de Tourmelle's offer? Just how can you presume to?"

"Michel . . . Michel . . . There's no need to shout." Philippe waited as the comte, with a petulant gesture, pulled a coverlet over his legs.

"I don't presume to tell you anything. I never have. Much as I would like to," Philippe laughed, and even to his own ears, his laugh sounded hollow. "I will speak my mind about Jean de Tourmelle, however. I owe my sister that much," Philippe said, anger creeping into his voice. "To put it baldly: Jean de Tourmelle is a brute. This is common knowledge. No self-respecting father would think of handing his daughter over to him . . . no! wait! let me speak my mind, and I'll have done. Jean de Tourmelle is not only a brute. He's a violent brute. I don't care how rich he has become or how many decorations he has earned from the King, the fact remains that he is a lout. A vicious boor who simply threw a Prussian woman over his shoulder after his men pillaged her village, then carried her off to Burgundy and locked her up in his chateau . . . "

"He has got rid of her. He swears it!"

"Got rid of her! After he set her shift on fire one night in a drunken rage! After he kicked her down the stairs and broke her arm in two places! And you want to give your delicate child to him! No amount . . . "

"You don't know him! He becomes as gentle as a lamb at the mere sight of Diane. He worships the ground she walks on . . . "

"Michel! Michel! How long would that last? Michel, listen to me! If you marry Diane to that coarse brute, you will kill her. It will break her spirit."

There was a short tap at the door, and Clovis entered the room, turning to bow deferentially to the marquis d'Ancy.

The comte lifted the calling card from the silver tray and nodded to Clovis.

"You've another visitor downstairs, Michel. And I must go." He extended his hand to the comte. "I will come again soon. For more talk. I beg you not to be rash. The girl is only seventeen. Believe me, there is no need . . . "

"You wouldn't know what need is!" the comte snapped, listening to the noisy racket of Mademoiselle Malavelle's sturdy boots as she approached his door.

She . . . told him that the Baron had just left her house and had confessed to her that he thought he had got me into trouble.

The comte could feel the icy chill of fear creeping up his legs, his spine, the nape of his neck. It had been over an hour since Mademoiselle Malavelle had left him. He had sent Clovis away with instructions that he must not be disturbed, not even for meals. His newly awakened appetite had simply disappeared. "Tell Mademoiselle that I am resting," he shouted into Clovis' cupped ear.

Resting, ha! the comte thought as Clovis clapped shut the door. Deaf as he was, the old servant had no idea that he jarred the room, making the tiny crystal baubles on the chandelier tinkle, as he pulled the door closed each time he left the comte's room.

Bon sang! Bon sang! the comte murmured to himself. What in God's name had he done to bring on these disasters! One right after the other! Thank God, he still had a few friends left! Without Mademoiselle Malavelle he might have drifted along, ignorant, unaware, letting his daughter blossom into a scandal right under his nose! After being the toast of the court, of Paris society. A stinking scandal ready to smell up every room she entered within a matter of months. Nine months . . . or less, probably! Or less! He could feel sweat on his upper lip. He searched for his snuffbox and could not find it. He kicked the coverlet off his legs, then groaned in pain.

She was a good woman, Mademoiselle Malavelle. Any other woman would have run around town spreading rumors in high glee. Poor woman, ugly as a goat with those eyes staring out of her head, but a heart of gold. At first he could not believe her, he could not bring himself to believe her! How could he? He lived with Diane, saw her every day—or almost—and during his illness, why, she had been a sweet, caring daughter. Not even the revolting business of the sickroom had kept her from his side. And the baron! The Swiss were celebrated for their gentle, chaste natures. People of discipline, character, restraint. The comte recalled the baron's fastidious complaints about the lewd couplings at court. He was above such base things, was he? Was he? Then how does it happen, monsieur le baron, that you have got my daughter, the most sought-after beauty in Paris, with child? The comte shuddered. He could not believe it. Diane was so innocent. A child. She is with child, Mademoiselle had said, she is with child by the baron. In these past three years in Paris together, or down in the country before her mother died, there was nothing to suggest that the girl could so deceive him. Surely Diane with her excitable nature could not conceal . . . would have given some sign. Though recently she had become more dreamy than usual, more shut up in her thoughts. Yes. Perhaps. Yet what would lead a man like Paul to confide such a secret to Mademoiselle? It was hard to believe. A stiff, proud . . . *priggish* . . . man like Paul, to mellow enough with a homely spinster to confess that he has to marry Diane. Abruptly, the comte sat bolt upright, crying out as pain shot through his legs and up his back. His heart raced. His mind flew back to the night he had left Diane to go to supper at Mademoiselle Malavelle's, the night he was carried home more dead than alive. He could see Diane's pale, anxious face, hear her distraught words. You don't understand, she had said. I . . . I have to marry Paul. I must marry him . . . Please don't fail me, papa. Oh, please don't fail me!

Ah, *mon trésor*, he thought bitterly, holding his aching head in his hands, you have failed *me*! You have failed *me*! Damn! Damn! Damn!

All the necessary legal arrangements completed, my marriage was celebrated two days later. The ceremony took place at midnight in the chapel of the chateau. . . . My head was spinning. I was no more than a mechanical doll . . . . Never was there a woman more unhappy than I.

As if from a great distance Diane could hear Marianne saying over and over again, "It can't be helped. It can't be helped. You have to walk to the chapel." Marianne was crying, too, tears washing over her plump cheeks. At the bottom of the back stairs, Diane leaned against the wall while Marianne grabbed a kitchen linen from a rack and wiped dry both their faces. At the end of the long corridor, in her father's library, Diane heard a clock strike the quarter hour, and she began to vomit, turgid spurts of pale yellow bile splashing to the floor, soiling her gown, her nose smarting as the bile oozed from her nose.

"Oh, dear Lord," Marianne said. "What am I to do with you? It can't be helped. You have to do it." She dabbed frantically at Diane's face and gown.

Diane closed her eyes and leaned against the wall as Marianne knelt to clean the bottom of her gown. She wore a pale gray velvet gown trimmed in white satin with a white silk petticoat. It was a new frock that Madame Clarisse had created for her to wear to her engagement party at the marquise de Sabran's.

They stepped from the chateau into the sharp air of the garden. The night was still, without a sound except for their harsh breathing. Faded moonlight illuminated the slate roof of the chapel at the end of the walk. No one was about. Diane wondered for a moment if there had been some mistake, some grotesque misunderstanding. Her legs were weak and shaky, the way they had felt as a child after a long illness. She lurched against Marianne, who grabbed her arm firmly and steered her forward down the path. The gigantic topiary animals that she loved almost as if they were domestic pets towered above her, indifferent, uncaring.

Marianne steadied Diane with one hand, and with the other, reached forward and pushed open one side of the wide double door. The blinding blaze of dozens of candles around the tiny space leapt into their faces. The chapel was deserted. Diane did not move. Marianne gently drew her into the chapel and took her hand and dipped it into the holy water font, shaped like an exquisite shell, at the door. Startled by the chill water, Diane mechanically crossed herself and, shaking her arm free from Marianne, walked directly to one of the two prie-dieux in front of the altar and dropped to her knees and bowed her head.

The familiarity of the place embraced her: the dozen prie-dieux with their sagging rush bottoms arranged neatly in two rows, the slender stained-glass windows behind the altar—Christ in his agony, his disciples looking perplexed and desolate—the two blood-red glass censers hanging on each side of the carved ivory altar. Over to one side, just in front of the communion rail with its bleached white lace, the bronze plaque where Louis-Etienne slept, never to awaken. While maman slept at Ancy, waiting for Uncle Philippe to join her.

A glimpse of a black skirt hurrying by, that would be old Father Durand. A cold wave of fear swept over her. So, it was real. It was going to happen. It was about to happen. She wanted to scream her terror. But who would listen now? There was a noise to her left. Uncle Philippe. Looking so fierce. As if he had just murdered someone and was proud of it. Suddenly, a clatter of high heels and the thud of hobnailed boots on the stone floors, a draft of the cold night air, and the warmth of someone next to her, plunging clumsily to his knees on the prie-dieu. Faraway in Flavigny, she heard the bells of the hilltop bell tower slowly, ponderously strike twelve midnight, and her stomach rose, the foul bile roiling at the back of her throat.

She raised her head, and Father Durand swiftly turned his back and began the nuptial mass. Numbly, she followed the liturgy that she knew so well.

Then, as if after a long, long sleep, someone was lifting her to her feet. Abbé Durand, his eyes downcast, raised his hand in benediction, "In the name of the Father, and the Son, and the Holy Ghost."

Behind her, she heard her father, drunk, giggling deliriously.

Book Five

25

Out of the kindness of my heart I took her into my home.

$\mathcal{P}$rotectively, Philippe took Diane's arm as they left the dining room for a walk in the garden. You must see my knot garden, she had said proudly, before he retired to his room last night. From his window this morning he had looked down in amazement at the formal garden stretching as far as the eye could see, greenery and bedding plants clipped and twisted into fantastic geometric patterns.

They stepped from the gloomy rooms of the chateau into the soft May sunlight of the garden, which spread out like a vast, multicolored piece of tapestry, so intricate down to the smallest clipped and trimmed shrub that it was like nothing Philippe had ever seen. It made him dizzy to think of the hordes of workmen toiling through the long summer months, planting, pruning, snipping. Such exquisite perfection lost in this wild secluded place. It was mad, really.

"Do you remember once, as a little girl, we came riding by Damfert and you stopped your horse and asked who lived here?"

"Did I? Whatever for?"

"You thought Damfert a terrifying place. So isolated and dark and ugly. You said you pitied any woman who would have to live in such a god-forsaken old chateau."

Diane de Tourmelle, looking past him into the distance, said only, "The garden looks quite refreshed this afternoon, after the rains last night."

Philippe wanted her to talk to him, to confide in him. He was, after all, her uncle, her godfather. Instead, for over ten years now, since her wedding in the chapel at Corcheval, Diane had retreated into silence. In the beginning of her marriage it looked as if she would be one of those women, like the good Queen Marie Lecszinka, whose fertility doomed her to chronic morning sickness and the constant cycle of pregnancy. Scarcely had Diane moved into her apartments in the chateau de Damfert, renovated with every conceivable luxury and comfort, before she gave birth to Jean-Baptiste. A scant year later a little girl, Adelaide, was born in the dead of winter, with only her husband and the servants to assist in the difficult, protracted labor and delivery. Then followed the miscarriages, one after the other, punctuating her life with pain and diminishing health. To Philippe's anxious eyes, Diane had taken on a look of wan frailty, a woman grown now and still beautiful despite her pallor, her thinness, and the spray of fine lines around her dark eyes.

She had been like a madwoman, those few days after her father brought her down to Corcheval. To get her away from the scandal mongers in Paris, he said. To force her into marriage with Jean de Tourmelle, that was the truth of it. There was no stopping Michel. Not after the smell of scandal followed Diane's name in and out of the salons of Paris. Michel had panicked. He had to cash in his chips before it was too late, before his beautiful daughter who had entranced a king entirely lost her value.

So, on the stroke of midnight, the traditional hour for marriages in Charolais, the high and mighty comte de Fautrière handed over this lovely child to Jean de Tourmelle. I shall never forget, until the day I die, thought Philippe, the open-mouthed terror on Diane's face that night. Handed over by her drunk and sniggering father to a peasant brute. Who stank like a barnyard, belched and picked his teeth with anything that happened to be handy. Never wore a wig, or only rarely, once or twice when the King might catch a glimpse of him. The King loved him, and called him his Burgundian demon. Tourmelle fought like a madman at Tournai, hacking and mutilating in an ecstasy of carnage. Women fled him like the plague. Even Odile. Ah, but money . . . Tourmelle made no demands. Not one. Michel for once must have had more money flooding into his pockets than he knew what to do with. Tourmelle's filthy money, of course, and that bourgeois goat . . . what was her name? How much did she pay Michel to go sour on the baron?"

"What was that spinster's name? Do you remember? The great tall woman with a pelican pouch for a chin?"

"Mademoiselle Malavelle . . . you must mean Mademoiselle Malavelle." Diane repeated the name carefully as if it were a foreign word from a foreign land where she had once lived.

"Yes. That's it. I haven't seen her for years. She's not the thing she used to be. Not that I am much of a judge about Paris society these days. Most of the court flocks to the gaming tables at Versailles on Sundays and Fridays. Or to the duc de Gesvres' place in Paris. It's a terrible habit, this gambling."

Diane laughed and squeezed her uncle's arm. "Ah, the duc de Gesvres. He tried to teach me tapestry work. Poor dear! I was hopeless. So clumsy with my fingers . . . he couldn't scold me enough! He should have had Catherine as a pupil. She would have made him proud."

"When will Catherine arrive?" he asked.

"Soon. In the next few weeks. She's left the convent to join Jean in Paris. She wants to see papa first, and papa is still in Paris. He won't be coming down to Corcheval this year."

"Catherine wants to hector him about the leases and timber at Joigny. A doomed cause, I'm afraid. Your father has lost all interest in his estates. Long ago."

A pet monkey chased by one of Tourmelle's hunting dogs streaked across the garden and skittered up a spruce which tilted and swayed dangerously close to the baying hound.

"A gift from Jean-Christophe!" laughed Diane. "He says that monkeys are still the rage in Paris!"

"Monkeys—of one kind or another—have *always* been the rage at court. Diane . . . " Philippe hesitated. "I wonder . . . I . . . do you think it best that Catherine come to live with you? I know that you cannot turn away your sister . . . but I wonder whether this is for the best. Catherine is a hard woman. You have your share of troubles already."

"Troubles? Oh, I have the usual share of troubles, I suppose.

Every woman does. Besides, where else is Catherine to go? Papa says that he cannot increase her pension."

"He could if he liked. Your husband has given him a very fine annuity. I am in a position to know." He wondered how much Diane knew of her father's underhanded financial arrangements. "Some of his creditors . . . your father has borrowed considerable sums against his annuity. That I do know. He could provision Catherine. He simply doesn't want to."

"Possibly." Diane did not want to hear the same old complaints about her father's wastrel habits that she had listened to for years. Without ever really understanding what her father's financial affairs had to do with her life. Until it was too late.

"Catherine's coming here is more than just a way of saving papa some money. Jean invited Catherine to live with us at Damfert. Do you know, they got on quite well at Sophie's wedding? Afterwards, Catherine started writing to him. Letters that go on for pages and pages. Jean puzzles over them for days. He thinks Catherine is the most sensible woman he has ever met."

"Ah, because she can talk yearlings and corn rot with him and his steward?"

"And how to build better piggeries! I'm not much good at that, am I?"

"What woman is? Or wants to be? At least, Catherine will be a little company for you. You must be lonely, my dear. Damfert might just as well be on the other side of the moon."

"Ah, but Damfert *is* on the other side of the moon, uncle!" Diane said gaily, her face lighting up mischievously. Briefly, for a moment, she looked young again, the slim, willowy blond whose beauty and grace had awakened a glow in the most jaded hearts of Paris society. "It is quieter, though, now that the children have gone. I hated to see them go. The tutors, the governesses, the pets . . . there was always a stir in the house. I . . . I wanted to keep them here a little longer. Especially Jean-Baptiste, who is so frail. The country air is good for him. But Jean says that I was making a sissy of the boy. And Adelaide. Then again, at her age I had already been in the convent four years. Come, I'll show you the ducks that Jean-Christophe sent up from Poitou."

That night, after Philippe pulled the curtains tightly around his bed and sank into the deep feather mattress that smelled of heather and rosemary, he lay awake wide-eyed, sleepless. He cursed himself for using too much snuff, drinking too much coffee, eating too much. Still, he knew that as soon as he turned his back on the fortress-like old chateau and headed to Ancy or to Paris, he would sleep like a baby again, no matter how much rich food he ate or how much wine he drank. There was something about Damfert that made his flesh crawl. There was something about the slight stoop in Diane's walk, the way she favored her left arm, her pallor, her gaunt frame that chilled him to the bone. He would stay another week.

Diane placed the thick letter next to her book on the table alongside her bed. The letter was carelessly tied with string and sealed with the Fautrière crest. Dear Uncle Philippe, he worries about me too much, she thought. I wish that I could look better for him, but I can't. She gripped the handle of her hair brush and waited for the pain to subside. She was bleeding profusely. Another miscarriage. Better that than a stillbirth. After the struggle, her body stiffening in an arc of pain, nothing. An armful of death. If she did not take care, the sheets would be bloody again tomorrow morning, and Françoise would mutter angrily under her breath as Diane finished her toilette and pretended not to hear. When Jean returned from Paris, she would make herself as beautiful as she knew how and she would ask him gently not to . . . she would beg him to leave her in her bed alone. Oh, she wanted to ask him, please never again, but she dared not. In the beginning, Jean had treated her so delicately, so tenderly, as if she were a fragile crystal glass that would break into a thousand glittering pieces if not handled just so. Such care, such gentleness, the great, burly bear of a man bursting into tears when his touch caused her pain. He kept himself as fresh and neat as a schoolboy, for her. So that she would smile at him and touch his face gently with her hand.

Unsteadily, she got to her feet, snuffed out the candles around the room, and carefully climbed into bed to read the letter that Laurent had brought in after supper. She sighed and picked up the letter. From her father, no doubt, complaining about his gout, about Marianne's laziness, about Madame de Pompadour's spite, etc. etc . . . and, with a flourish of signature and a postscript, a cross, cranky request for funds to be sent posthaste, etc. etc.

Diane untied the letter and recognized Catherine's loose scrawl slanting upward across the page.

Dear Sister,

Now it's my turn to be wining and dining in Paris while you are stuck off in a hole in the country. Every dog has its day. Right now I'm having mine. Jean—excuse me, I ought to say, Monsieur de Tourmelle . . . but I won't—Jean, as I say, won't let me sit still a minute unless I yell at him that my poor feet won't walk another step. We have bought every dress in every shop, every boot and fancy shoe, so many ribbons that I lose track of them, and you won't see any feathers or beads around Paris until another ship from the Antilles comes in. We've bought them all, and Jean won't be satisfied until he has found something else to give me. He says that you are going to be as jealous as a bourgeois wife when you see all the finery I bring home to Damfert and hear what fine times we have had, every night of the week. I laughed my head off when he said that. You are going to be jealous, though, when I tell you that I watched the Queen's dinner the other day, from the first course to dessert, and then the next day, I saw the King eating his dinner—and he ate an egg just the way you said he did— and before I leave, I am going to watch the Princesses, too. I have not seen the marquise de Pompadour anywhere around Versailles, though no one wants to talk about anything else. Your venerable father is one of them. You can't get him to change the subject no matter how hard you try. To hear him tell it, he would be the happiest man on the face of this earth if Madame de Pompadour had not come along and stolen the King away from his precious daughter. Your venerable father is losing his looks. If he would stay sober, he would not take as much snuff, or spill as much over his clothes and face. He is not the cleanest man I have ever seen, and all the perfumes in the world are not going to help if he doesn't bathe once in a while. By the way, I wouldn't be surprised if we don't have to call your former maid "stepmother" one of these days. I would laugh my head off at that. All the fuss and talk about mésalliance when you and Sophie had to be married off, and now look at him. He doesn't fool me. Marianne is smarter than he is, and soberer, most of the time anyway.

I will close now as there is no news. I am writing this while Jean is having his hair braided in two fat plaits because the gentlemen with two plaits get to dance all the minuets at the ball tonight. Jean says that he would write except that his spelling is worse than mine. Before I forget, I saw your friend Madeleine de Mézières big as life at the Queen's dinner. Your friend has got herself a place as one of the women of the Queen's chamber and makes a tidy sum of money selling once-lit candles from the Queen's suites. The furnisher of the Queen's playing cards also gives Madame de Mézières a cut on the profits. She is getting so rich in the Queen's service that I don't know why she walks around with such a long face. They say that she is barren and that her husband prays for more battles and more wars so that he can get away from her. All the women at court run after him as if he were another Richelieu, but he still looks like the same old Armand de Mézières to me. Jean says he is going to leave me behind if I don't seal this letter and clean my hands.

Before I close, Jean says that your boy is safe behind walls at the College Louis-le-Grand. Jean-Baptiste says that he likes school and hasn't got into any trouble yet. I say, just wait a little.

At the bottom of the letter Catherine had scrawled in wide, straggling letters, "Paris, the 24th of April 1758." As usual, she had forgotten to sign her name.

So . . . cynical Catherine was not immune to the brilliance and pleasures of Paris. Her high spirits fairly leapt off the page. And Jean, trailing about, buying her finery, he would love that. Spending his money, showing his power.

Staring blankly into space, Diane sat holding the letter, roused only when her bedside candle sputtered and guttered out. She welcomed the darkness and the old voices of her dreams—and nightmares—that were her constant companions. Some of these voices she had shut out forever, ten years ago when she married Jean de Tourmelle. Others lingered to soothe her pain, her loneliness. *Another Richelieu* . . . Yet Armand was unhappy, perhaps more lonely than she, shut away in the wild isolation of Damfert. No, it was not possible. Armand had Paris—the concerts, the music, the theatre, the gossipy broadsheets pasted over walls and doors, the excitement. The excitement! The crowds, the filthy streets, the bellman coming down the cobbled streets twice a day, summoning shopkeepers and householders to clear away the refuse round their doors and storefronts.

For months Diane had had no news of Armand. Only now and then Abbé Martin, on visits to the abbey at Cluny, picked up bits and pieces of court gossip. Only a little, but it was enough to feed her memories of Armand and being alive in his arms. Not dead and buried in the old stones and sultry green of Burgundy. Alive in his arms in her rooms in Paris and . . . at the little tavern at Bécage, tucked away in the forest. Arriving first, careful to keep her riding veil lowered, she took the key from the old innkeeper and mounted the short flight of the stairs to an immaculately clean room, bathed with the golden green light of the woods. After Armand pulled his horse under the window, he stood on his saddle and tapped softly on the shutters, then slipped effortlessly into the room through the window. He buried his head in her neck, covering her with kisses, warm, soft lips caressing, murmuring his love. . . . For hours that afternoon until she had to ride away, sweat foaming underneath her saddle as she whipped her horse through the forest, a shortcut to Damfert. Four summers ago. An afternoon of enchantment. Four years ago . . .

They had stopped writing to each other after Jean had caught her bending over a letter, crying hot, scalding tears. She had not heard him come into her room. After that evening, she dared not write again.

In the darkness Diane folded the letter tightly and placed it under her pillow. As soon as the light of dawn came, she would read it again, and Armand's face would come back to her, clear and bold and tender.

26

She became mistress of my house; the servants depended on her, not on me. They were forbidden to obey me.

*D*iane finished her toilette and got unsteadily to her feet. Good. Only the slightest bit of dizziness. After Uncle Philippe's departure the bleeding had worsened, leaving her weak and listless. When Jean came back to Damfert, one night—and it seemed more from habit than from real desire—he came to her room to say goodnight, and Diane had asked him, sweetly, holding his head and stroking his broad face, to be patient, to wait a little until she would be ready for him. He had grinned, a strange, lopsided grin, and had left her alone. No doubt he would go back to his old habits. Bedding the daughters of his tenants. Forcing the parents out of the cottage while he backed the girl against a wall and had his way with her.

After that night, the bleeding stopped, and the fevers began. Day followed day, week followed week, and still she languished, unable to leave her bed for more than an hour or two. Today, months later, she was actually going downstairs to have dinner. From the top of the stairs she could hear Tourmelle and Catherine gaily bantering.

Since Jean de Tourmelle and his pock-marked sister-in-law returned to Damfert, they had become inseparable. Diane marveled that they never seemed to run out of conversation; even from her room she could hear them arguing, laughing, joking, and gossiping from sunrise to sunset. Their rough laughter and loud disputes echoed throughout the solemn chateau.

"You shouldn't have waited. I'm so slow these days," Diane mumbled apologetically as she took her place at the dining table, feeling liberated from the loneliness of her bedroom.

Scowling, Catherine looked at her disapprovingly. "Not all of us sleep until nearly noon. Like some fine lady in Paris. With nothing to do." Diane did not answer. Jean had already begun to soak large pieces of bread in his soup. "Jean and I have been out in the fields since daybreak. Haven't we, Jean?"

"What? Hmmmm." He bent over his soup and did not look up at Diane.

He rarely paid any attention to his wife these days. He had not returned to Diane's bed. He never bothered to visit her even at the height of her fevers.

A place had been set on Diane's right. "Where is Abbé Martin?" she asked.

"He didn't stay for dinner," Catherine said.

"Why not?"

"Because he wasn't asked, that's why."

"What do you mean? He always has dinner with us," Diane said, her voice rising.

"He brought you some books. More of those trashy novels you two read. *L'Histoire de Madame de Luz!* Hmmph! *L'Histoire de Madame de Luz!*" she said again, as if she could scarcely believe it. "I put them in your dressing room. I didn't want the footmen seeing them lying around downstairs."

"The abbé always stays for dinner," Diane said again. She was furious that the kind and harmless young priest had been sent away like a common servant. "It's a very long ride from Flavigny . . . very tiring."

Her patchy eyebrow raised ironically, Catherine looked at Diane. "He ought to be used to it. He does it often enough. Besides, why should we sit around with a little Jesuit smelling up the table with his nasty *soutane*?" Eyeing Diane attentively, Catherine absentmindedly tore a piece of bread into small pieces, which she dropped alongside her plate. "Everyone knows why *soutanes* are made the way they are. The panel hanging down in front. And everyone knows what those filthy little Jesuits do with their hands in their pockets all the time. That's why their soutanes smell the way they do."

Dropping his spoon with a clatter, Jean de Tourmelle laughed loudly, a deep explosive laugh as if he had been hit hard in the stomach.

Catherine beamed at him. "Like yeast," she said. "Their nasty soutanes always smell like rising dough." Jean laughed again.

Diane stared at her sister. Catherine was talking like a harlot, like one of those painted women strolling in front of the Palais-Royal. That papa said were wicked and loose. And diseased. Catherine! Catherine talked as if she knew. But how could she? In the convent? Diane's throat and cheeks went hot as Catherine continued to stare at her mockingly.

Diane picked up her spoon and tried to eat. Jean noisily sucked at a bread crust. Jean seemed to have abandoned any attempt to imitate Diane's cultivated manners. He ate his soup like a peasant in a thatched cottage. During their schooldays at the convent Catherine had haughtily maintained an aloof superiority that she thought her due as a Fautrière. On occasion she had angrily scolded Sophie or Diane for becoming too familiar with an "inferior." Now Jean de Tourmelle's aristocratic title, purchased only two generations before him, obviously caused Catherine not the slightest qualm. Catherine seemed to revel in his coarse manners, his crude, often obscene, speech. Diane noticed that her sister had begun to speak with Jean's accent and to sprinkle her conversation with the local dialect of the peasants.

Catherine shook the crystal bell beside her plate, and footmen in white gloves came in to take their plates away.

"I haven't finished," Diane said.

"But we have," Catherine said, as Jean, looking up at her, smiled.

Diane folded her hands and drew back as a footman removed her plate. Since when had the bell been moved from beside her plate and placed next to Catherine's? She felt suddenly overwhelmed with weariness.

"We've had a letter from papa," Catherine said.

"He didn't write to me?" Diane asked.

"He wrote to me. Your husband. As etiquette requires," Jean said, and he sounded prissy and smug, Diane thought, as if his master had given him an assignment, and he had performed it well.

"Don't you want to know what he said?" Catherine asked.

"Yes. Of course. Though he usually writes something to me . . ." Diane said.

"He wants to come for a visit this summer. A few months, he says."

"That will be nice. I'm glad."

"He wants to bring Marianne. Remember Marianne, your maid during those *glorious* years in Paris? When you were the most sought after woman in . . ."

"Yes!" Diane hissed. "I remember very well!"

"Well, your papa wants to bring Marianne with him. It appears she needs fresh country air after all these years in Paris."

Diane clasped her hands tightly together and said nothing.

"We are saying 'no'," Catherine said levelly.

"'No' to what? To papa? Why, you . . ."

"'No' to Marianne. Of course. We don't want her here. What dear papa wants to do in Paris or at Corcheval is his affair. He cannot bring his trollop here." Catherine thrust her chin forward. Her deep-set eyes, to which her twisted, scarred brows gave a perpetually intense, puzzled look, glared at Diane defiantly.

The three footmen moved quietly around the large room, and it seemed to Diane that they, too, were watching her, that they, too, would like nothing better than to stamp their feet and shout their contempt for her. The enormous portraits tilting slightly forward on the walls around the room glowered at her watchfully, suspiciously, ready to cry alarm, their small, dark pig's eyes—like Tourmelle's—following her every move.

27

My father ... came to visit me during that time. I was so desperate that I told him of my ordeal. He had his own motives for dealing tactfully with my husband.

As Diane, in a freshly washed and polished carriage, sped along dusty roads toward Cluny, laborers with scarlet poppy blossoms tucked into their shirts looked up and waved their hats. In the summer of 1759 British raiding parties continued to bring shame and destruction to the coast of Normandy and Brittany while the King and court tried to make the best of the humiliating defeat of the French army under the comte de Clermont at Krefeld. But in the rolling gold and green hills of Burgundy, far from the sounds of the melee of war, wheat fields and vineyards basked peacefully under the summer sun.

Diane longed to see her father again. She had seen so little of him after Damfert became her home. The christenings of Jean-Baptiste and Adelaide, Sophie's wedding in the chapel at Corcheval. Happy times that soothed the pain of the last few days in Paris—parting with Armand, leaving forever the life of the court, running from the scandalous floodtide of gossip—and then her father drunk, raving drunk, abusive, hurling threats, thrusting her into the swarthy arms of Tourmelle, grinning—the smell of him! Time healed little by little every day the wounds that her father had inflicted and that she thought she would never forgive. Could never forgive. Papa is not bad, she thought, only spoiled, like Jean-Baptiste sometimes. She was determined never to whine, never to complain. Her marriage had brought an end to her father's financial burdens. For a number of years, at any rate. She had done what she was expected to do; that was the long and the short of it.

At the top of the hill as Diane caught sight of the spires of the cathedral at Cluny, her heart swelled with pleasure. She rarely left the grounds of Damfert, whatever the season, except for mass in Flavigny. As the carriage crossed the crowded main square, Diane saw the post coach in front of the auberge, and her spirits sank. The comte had always traveled in his own private coach, and there was no sign of one today. Her driver pulled up in front of the small timbered inn, and Laurent dropped down from the carriage and went to look for the comte.

On three sides of the square, peasants and itinerant vendors noisily hawked their wares. Chickens in wicker baskets squawked in alarm, pigs grunted, and children laughed and played around their mother's skirts. The air was filled with the smell of damp, rotting fruits and straw and horse manure. Dozens of rabbits, completely skinned except for their furry brown paws dangled from the butcher's stall, their thin carcasses, a shiny opalescent pink, twisting in the warm breeze.

Laurent came back to say that Monsieur le comte was refreshing himself and that Madame should be kind enough to join him. The inn would be thronged at this hour of the late morning, after the arrival of the coach from Paris.

Diane left the carriage and entered the cool, dim room. Directly opposite the door, in a high-backed wood chair, the comte sat drinking alone with a bottle of wine at a small table.

"*Mon dieu,* papa! You mustn't sit here alone like this."

Like a schoolboy caught misbehaving, the comte jumped to his feet and signaled for another chair. He looked resplendent in a dark chestnut waistcoat with coral pink vest and soft beige breeches.

"Papa! How handsome you look!" Diane said. The comte smiled and gently kissed the top of her head. After Diane's shortsighted eyes grew accustomed to the dim light in the smoke-filled room, she saw that he had aged. Yet in a kind and genial way. There was a general loosening around his face; his once sharply defined features had relaxed. White streaks lightened his dark brown hair, and snuff stains darkened the inner edge of his thin lips. His gray blue eyes were as piercing as ever, but bloodshot and the whites tinged with yellow.

"My child, you are staring at me with such a silly look on your pretty face." He spoke slowly, enunciating his words carefully.

"Ah, papa! I am so happy to see you! So happy! If only you knew. I've missed you . . . and Marianne."

He frowned. "Rather impertinent of your husband to turn Marianne away. Why was that, do you suppose?"

"I can't say, papa. I was told only that it . . . wouldn't be right, you know, to have you here with your . . . "

"Ah, my mistress. Is that it? *Très bien.* So, your husband is protecting the sanctity of his home. Admirable!" His voice rose as he trilled "admirable." "Then, your good husband has indeed refined his sensibilities. At Corcheval, the night you were wed, he had no compunction about cornering Marianne and ripping . . . *enfin!* He's *your* husband, my dear, family now, and one must respect the unity of the family." He sighed melodramatically.

Diane laughed. "Papa, you haven't changed at all! Thank goodness! We must go. It's getting late, and Catherine will be annoyed if we delay dinner."

"Catherine?" The comte belched loudly, and Diane could see that he was quite drunk. Light shone through the bottle on the table. Almost empty. "What the deuce does Catherine have to say about what goes on in her sister's house? Catherine, I am afraid, occupies that common but no less lamentable position of being . . . " he lurched to his feet and belched again. "A poor relation, an unmarried, unmarriageable spinster, in a rich household. You are the mistress of Damfert, my dear." He shook his finger in her face. "Don't ever forget that, my dear. If you do, Catherine will hound you out of house and home. You are the mistress of Damfert, my dear. Don't forget that."

"Yes, papa." She took his hand and led him, like a little child, through the crowded room.

Almost as soon as his head touched the cushioned banquette of the carriage, the comte fell asleep. At a crossing of the high road to Bécage, a flock of sheep slowed the driver to a stop, and the comte woke up.

"Bless my soul, I fell asleep," he said. His blue eyes twinkled. He looked young, refreshed.

"We don't have far now. Do you remember?"

"Not really. It's a gloomy country here. No one comes here. Oh, I'm sorry, my dear. But you understand my . . . "

"Of course. It *is* gloomy. And no one does come here, though at the moment I understand that not a few familiar faces from Versailles are in the country houses around us. Cooling off from their creditors until harvest time and revenues come in and leases are renewed."

"Versailles!" the comte said with disgust. "I don't care if I never go near the wretched place again. The place is entirely in the Pompadour's hands! Entirely! If you want to know who rules France!" He lowered his voice and leaned forward. "Though, my dear child, for a few weeks two years ago, after that madman Damiens tried to assassinate the King, for a while I thought that . . . that it was the moment to summon you back to Paris."

Diane was dismayed. "Back to Paris! What on earth for?"

"Well . . . ," he said, hunched forward, almost whispering, though there was no one to overhear what they were saying. "You know the King and his childish fears . . . Well, this Damiens merely pricked the King with a small knife. The slightest possible wound. You can imagine, a small penknife through a thick overcoat—it was bitter cold that night—does not do much harm. Never mind! The King takes to his bed, for nine days. Nine days! Do you hear? Night and day attendance of his doctors and surgeons naturally. And his confessor swishing in and out of the King's chamber as if His Majesty were about to . . . "

"I know. What I mean is, I have heard that this man tried to kill the King as he was coming down the steps to his carriage . . . "

"Yes, of course, your baron—did he tell you this?—was leading the way for the King."

"No, papa, no, I never hear from Paul. Naturally."

"Well, then, this fool—wearing his hat! Can you believe that? Wearing his hat in the presence of the King! Then expecting to escape unnoticed in the crowd! With his hat . . . "

"I know, papa, I know," Diane said, struggling with her impatience. "Jean and Catherine told me the entire story, in the minutest . . . "

The comte drew back against his banquette. "I merely wanted to say that during this silliness . . . the King confessing his sins and wailing for Extreme Unction and the Dauphin and the Queen and the Princesses fainting and throwing themselves around the King's bedchamber. Do you see?"

"I'm afraid not, papa." Diane sighed and gazed past her father's head, out the rear window at the swirl of pale gray dust. He was getting old, she could see that, old and confused. He rambled incoherently, as in the old days in Paris when he would drink too much, but now . . . now he completely lost his way.

"Well," he said frostily, "it's perfectly clear. Her high and mighty royal mistress came very close to losing her hold over the King. La Pompadour very nearly found herself thrown out on the streets like the duchesse de Chateauroux at Metz! It was a near thing! No one dared approach La Pompadour's apartments for eleven, twelve days. The King would not tolerate the mere mention of her name."

"Ah, but don't you see, papa, if the King repented his adultery with the marquise de Pompadour, it's hardly likely that he would be thinking of acquiring a new mistress." Catherine was right: the comte was indeed obsessed with the marquise.

The comte glared at her, his thin lips edged in brown drawn tightly together. "Not right away!" he growled. "Later! When all this foolishness with his little knife wound passed. Besides, the King has not bedded with the woman in years. She has some sort of female disorder, they say. She is . . . frigid," he said hesitantly, looking furtively at Diane.

"Yet she is the King's best friend. I understand that has not changed." That's what Paul had wanted, to be friends, to call each other "brother" and "sister," to love each other as friends, with the same chaste tenderness of their courtship. Paul had wanted that, after she had shut herself away at Damfert, waiting for the baby that fluttered in her stomach. Paul wrote to her every week, for a year. Over a year, to give her courage, to tell her not to despair.

"Is Paul still Captain of the Cent-Suisses, papa?"

"What? The baron de Rothenburg?" the comte asked brusquely. "Yes, he is. The assault on the King was not the baron's responsibility. He could have done nothing to prevent it. As you say, La Pompadour may not be the beauty she once was, but she is still clever enough to hold the King. In a vice! The woman is like a cat, always lands on her feet. Spending money on her chateaux and her china, hiring armies of . . ."

"Who is the woman the baron married?"

"What? A slight young thing. I forget the name. She won't appear at court, naturally. Her father's in finance. They all are these days," said the comte, dabbing snuff into this under lip. "He did well, the baron, to balk at marrying Mademoiselle Malavelle. She's gambling her fortune away. There's not much left, I hear, not much left over for the lackey who has been her lover since she left Paris." The comte brushed the front of his vest and straightened his jabot. The ugly old heifer, he thought, turning up her nose at my proposal. The comte de Fautrière, if you please! He could still see the look of amusement on her face, the smirk, the quivering pouch, spreading her skirts like an old flirt. I am honored, she said, but, no, I cannot think of it, dear comte. I cannot think of it . . . while my heart belongs to . . . Foolish old goat! Ha! Lucky for the baron that he couldn't go through with it, couldn't marry old money-bags. He'd have been in for a drubbing! She would have shouted it from the housetops, when she found out about the beautiful baron. She would have torn him to pieces!

"Does he have children, papa? Is he happy?" Diane persisted. She did not know why. She rarely thought of him, and if she did, he tumbled through her mind like some actor in a play she had never quite understood. She did not love Paul any more, perhaps she never had. She had loved the idea of Paul, his gentleness, his goodness. The serenity of Paul.

"Happy? Why should he be any happier or unhappier than anyone else? Than you, for instance, my dear. You have everything you shall ever want to be happy. Why all these questions about Paul? After all these years?" Forgetting his irritation, he leaned forward and smiled at her. "Believe me, *mon trésor*, Paul is not the man for you."

He hesitated a moment, then pursed his lips sagely. "Paul is not the man for . . . any woman."

"Where on earth do these confounded servants come from?" the comte asked. He had followed Diane into the gardens and waited patiently with a wicker basket as she cut calla lilies and dahlias for the reception rooms.

"Oh, from the villages around Damfert. Catherine has hired most of them."

"Scurrilous lot. I shout, I threaten, I cajole. They stand there like sticks, surly as you please, and then proceed to do exactly as they like. I shall go mad with frustration." In the mornings—or in the late morning hours before noon when the comte habitually rose—the servants mysteriously delayed in bringing the comte hot water for his bath. He had to call for soaps, for towels, for his morning coffee and hot bread, and none of the numerous servants could be released to serve as his valet. The comte had had no personal servant after old Clovis had been carried away with pneumonia and had made do with Marianne, who knew his habits and, in her own indolent way, cared for him. Even if Clovis had been alive, the comte could never have found enough money to pay for his coach fare to Damfert. He had drained his credit as far as it would go.

He set down the basket and mopped his brow. Clouds were gathering for another afternoon storm. "They're in league against me, that's what."

"Who, papa?" Diane turned to him, her voice full of alarm.

"Why, I don't know. The servants . . . your husband . . . your sister. All of them."

"Poor papa," Diane said, anxious to soothe his feelings, "It's only that Jean and Catherine are worried about the crops. Especially the vineyards. This awful rain, day after day, and now the vines are full of disease. It's not you, papa. They're just cross and rude because they're concerned about the harvests and the bad revenues if the pressings are bad."

"There, there, my dear," the comte said, picking up the basket again. "I understand."

While she pacified her father with facile excuses, in her heart, Diane was frightened. There *was* something sinister afoot at Damfert; she could feel it each time she was around Tourmelle and Catherine. Diane watched with suppressed fury as her husband and her sister hounded the comte into humiliated silence. Catherine sneered at her father's incompetence, baiting him with questions about his affairs that she very well knew he could not answer, while Jean contented himself with making the comte feel an intruder, a parasite forced to get his daily food at another man's table, Catherine criticized his expensive clothes, his vanity, his vices. . . .

What would become of her once her father had gone back to Paris? Or to Corcheval? Since Diane's illness, Catherine had taken control of the household, disciplining the servants, organizing their work, planning the menus. And, on the few occasions when they had a dinner party, selecting the guests. As well as the entertainment. Too late Diane tried to assert herself with the staff, beginning with Françoise, who had always been curt, insolent. Once Diane had complained to Jean, not directly criticizing her sister naturally, and he had stalked out of the room without replying. The look in his eyes told her not to bother to speak of the matter again.

Diane quickly grabbed a fan and a fresh handkerchief and hurried down the great stairway to the dining room. It was early August, and the weather had abruptly changed. A hot, searing breeze had chased away the dreary rains and had brought hope for the corn and wheat crops.

"The vineyards, do they look promising?" Diane asked, as Catherine and Jean took their seats.

Jean ignored her. He had not changed from the brown fustian trousers and heavy boots that he wore to the fields. In the evening they dined simply on a hearty soup, cheeses and fruit. Diane regretted that she had not decided to take supper in her rooms, like her father. But then the servants would have complained of the extra work.

"The vineyards promise to do nothing at all this year," Catherine said crossly. "What do you expect after that hail storm last week?"

Catherine twisted her head around like a great lady surveying a room with her lorgnette. "And where is our dear papa this evening? He's late for his supper."

"In his room," Diane said. "I'm afraid he's not feeling well."

Catherine and Jean exchanged glances. When the footmen filled their glasses, they smiled at each other and clinked glasses. Ignoring Diane, they began to talk of one of the tenants whose daughter had gone mad and abandoned her baby in the marshy reeds along the river.

Diane wished they would talk of the crops and the change in the weather. The whole land seemed drenched in misery. She crumpled her napkin and blotted the perspiration on her brow. She ate in silence, barely touching her food. The footmen moved quietly back and forth between the table and the sideboard and the kitchen. Looking up, she realized that Jean and Catherine had finished a second bottle of wine. They were becoming loud and playful. Diane looked across at them and smiled pleasantly, but they took no notice of her.

The meal was drawing to a close when, all at once, Catherine leaned toward Jean and whispered something in his ear. He laughed and glanced toward Diane. He laughed again, and across the table Catherine and Jean, their eyes gleaming with malice, silently watched Diane.

In the short passageway between the dining room and the kitchen Diane could hear tiny clinking sounds as the footmen arranged glasses along shelves in the pantry.

The dining room had grown still. No one moved. Diane rested both hands alongside her plate.

There was a loud, explosive noise as Catherine shifted her chair, scraping it along the floor, dragging it close to Jean. Reaching her hand toward Jean's lap, Catherine turned and fixed Diane with her crooked stare. Catherine smiled at her, her scarred lip twisted up at one corner. Diane could see her sister's outstretched arm, her hand disappearing under the table to Jean's lap. Jean, grinning from ear to ear, his fat lips wet and glistening, looked down and watched Catherine's hand. In the stillness of the room Diane could hear the sound of Catherine's hand, undoing, one after the other, the buttons of Jean's trousers. Diane sat, frozen in her chair, unable to move, unable to look away. After a moment, Jean looked up sheepishly and lifted the tablecloth to cover Catherine's hand. Catherine did not take her eyes off Diane's face. Jean took a deep breath, closed his eyes and threw his head back against his chair. His mouth half opened, he began to pant in short, guttural breaths. Catherine's mangy eyebrow lifted mockingly as she stared at Diane. Diane could see the starched white tablecloth covering Catherine's hand rise and fall. She stared in horror as Jean's breathing grew harsher.

Then, suddenly, with a wrenching effort, Diane, with both hands, pushed up from the table, scattering silver and overturning glasses. Her chair clattered backward onto the floor as she rushed toward the door, her hands cupped over her ears. As she pulled frantically at the door handle, she could hear the mounting crescendo of Jean's *ahhhhhh*, a sound like a whimpering puppy—a sound that she knew well. Catherine's low, voluptuous laughter, rich and loud, rang after her as she raced down the hallway toward the stairs.

Diane kept to her room, the shutters closed, sunlight throwing thin bars of yellow across the rush matting. Utterly disconcerted, the comte nudged open a shutter and looked down at the desolate garden, parching in the afternoon sun. Diane lay back in her chair, staring listlessly into space, rousing herself only to plead with him to take her with him back to Paris, away from Damfert. She would not say why. The comte had tried to read aloud to her and had to give it up. She would not talk of her life in the remote chateau, swathed on all sides, in every direction, with some of the finest vineyards in Burgundy. Since she had kissed him goodbye at Corcheval, her cheeks as hard and cold as ice, and had stepped into Jean de Tourmelle's carriage, she eluded any talk of her life at Damfert. The comte wanted to believe that his favorite daughter had simply faded away into the dull, boring quietude of aristocratic life in the provinces. Diane had produced a son and heir, little Jean-Baptiste, right away it seemed. Prematurely, as could be expected, given Diane's slim fragility. No one was in the least surprised. Particularly when another child followed within less than a year. A rather plain girl, Adelaide. When the comte last saw her, not long after she entered the Abbey de Fontevrault—at least the poor child had been placed in the most fashionable convent in France—the comte realized that Adelaide was doomed to look more and more like her father: broad peasant face, crooked strong teeth and a large nose, alas, slightly bulbous at the tip. Such a pity. With a mother whose face still turned heads and whose exquisite body, despite all those pregnancies, looked as virginal as the day she married.

Diane said, "Poor papa, it must be terribly boring for you here."

"Yes, quite frankly. I'm sorry to say, my dear. It is quiet. You don't see much society. I had thought you would. Given your reputation at court, I mean." It had been a mistake to come to Damfert, he could see that. But what else could he do? No peace day or night, creditors camping out on his doorsteps, filthy leeches that even Marianne's foul mouth could not drive away. I must get out of here, however, before the wine harvest, thought the comte. I must get out of here before Tourmelle can quote chapter and verse on why he cannot increase my allowance. With just a little more money, not much, a thin margin more, he would reform, things would go better. Back in Paris he and Marianne would economize, pay more attention to what went in and out of the kitchen, for instance. They were both careless. She more than he, certainly, but he should keep an eye out for chiseling as well. Mostly he must guard against his unhappy facility for buying without paying. Back in Paris! Away from this doleful life! Three months! It seemed an eternity. He looked at Diane, who sat quietly rubbing her long, thin hands together. What on earth can she be thinking of, driving herself mad! The comte had always dreaded Diane's "nerves," as he called them.

"What frightens you here, my darling?" he asked gently.

"Frightens me?" Diane gave a choked sound, a scoffing laugh. "Everything! Can't you see what they are doing to me?" Blue veins stood out along her thin neck.

"They? They?"

"My husband. And my sister. My sister hates me! She hates me, papa! Surely you must see that!"

"Catherine? Please, my dear, please. Shhhh . . . you must not excite yourself. You've always had that tendency, you know. To let yourself go, fly away with your nerves." Diane closed her eyes and rolled her head back and forth. "Catherine is a bossy woman. She likes to order everyone around. You know how she is." He had to mollify Diane; he had to calm her down. What else could he do? He could not take her back to Paris and risk putting a kink in his brutish son-in-law's tail. But there *was* something strange going on. He had felt it the moment he came through the doors. From what he could see, Diane might as well be invisible, as far as Tourmelle was concerned. He didn't even see her, he let her alone, which was a good sign. It may not always have been so, however. Diane did not look well, though after he had arrived, at the beginning of the summer, she had put on a little weight, she had seemed cheerful. Still, there were little things that worried him. The way she forgot herself, and . . . carried her left arm when she walked. And when she sat down, her left hand would lie, useless, in her lap.

"It's more than that!" Diane exclaimed. She got to her feet like an invalid and walked to the window and threw open the tall shutters. The setting sun had churned up deep orange clouds over the treetops on the hill. "Catherine torments me. Day and night she dreams up ways of tormenting me. Setting the servants against me! You've seen it! Don't pretend you haven't. You see how the servants have treated you since you came to Damfert. That's Catherine's doing! And my husband lets her do it! My husband has let her take over my house!"

"And is that such a bad thing? She's a hearty woman, Catherine, strong as an ox. You're fragile, my dear, you're . . . "

"I won't have any more excuses!" said Diane sharply, whirling around to face her father. He moved quickly away and sat down on a tuffet next to Diane's empty chair. "I'm tired of making excuses for them!" She could feel the blood throbbing in her neck and in her temples. She reached out to a commode to steady herself. Her father slumped forward, his head in his hands. "There are no excuses for what they are doing . . . for what they are doing to me."

Diane was silent. The comte looked up and waited for her to speak.

"Catherine is my husband's mistress," she said. "They do horrible things together . . . in my presence . . . they don't . . . "

The comte began to giggle. "Diane, dear Diane, you are raving!" His shoulders shook with laughter. Catherine grew uglier with every passing year. Catching sight of her in Paris, watching her coming toward him on the promenade, before she saw him . . . he had waited, taken her in, her livid face, painted a bluish white with great gashes of red on her mouth and scarred cheeks. Revolting. She was a repulsive creature, as she swayed coquettishly along on Tourmelle's arm. In a dress that dipped low over her taut, full breasts, swelling up . . . milky white and lovely smooth shoulders, bare in the late afternoon sun. The comte saw Catherine and Jean again, as clear as a picture, the two of them, strolling along oblivious, laughing, joking, leaning into each other like . . . Like . . . Oh, my God. The comte cleared his throat and looked down at his feet.

"Oh, papa," she pleaded, "You must let me come away with you. You must! Please. Please. I can't live in this cursed place another day!"

The comte rose and took her into his arms. "There, there, *ma petite*. We will think of something. Trust your poor old father. Trust me, my dear."

28

The torments that I endured at home reduced me to a kind of stupor that prevented me from thinking clearly. A hundred times I left home, taking a few clothes and escaping across the fields.

From the commotion in the hall Diane knew that her father's trunks and boxes were being taken downstairs to be loaded into the carriage. She rolled over and buried her face in her pillow. He had not come to her room to say goodbye. Toward midnight, when the old chateau was quiet, she had crept to his room and pleaded with him once more to take her with him to Paris in the morning. Nervously, his ear cocked toward the door, the comte promised to send for her. When? she had asked, more to embarrass him than to get an answer, for she knew that her father would never have the courage to send for her. He was too afraid of Jean, too afraid of losing the handfuls of gold that his son-in-law threw in his direction. Scornfully, like a man throwing scraps to a dog.

Diane folded the plump pillow and placed it under her head. Curiously, she felt stronger, lying there in the dimness, listening to the footmen swear as they bumped the comte's belongings down the stairs. Her father would never help her. He would roll away to Paris and would forget her very existence. A few charming letters on her saint's day, perhaps an inquiry about the children. Little more. He would retreat into his life of pleasure and intrigue, more obstinately fascinated with the marquise de Pompadour than the King himself. If her father would not help her, she must help herself. She clenched her fist and pounded the bed, once, twice. And Uncle Philippe. He would not desert her. Once he knew what Jean had done to her. How he had beaten her. For no reason. Only because he was drunk, and he had said that she put on airs with their neighbors. And he would not tolerate her grand lady pretensions. At first she was terrified, the first time; he kept hitting her over and over again, with his fist. Her eyes swollen closed for days, the servants sniggering behind her back. No wonder they despised her. The other times . . . the other times she did not cower, she did not plead, she would wait and let him strike her. If he was very drunk, he would soon lose interest. He had better things to do, he said. She was not worth his time. Since Catherine . . . there had been no more beatings. Not for a long time, not for over a year.

In the days that followed the comte's departure from Damfert, Diane overflowed with cheerfulness, determined not to let her sister and her husband know how frightened she was of being left alone with them. She never mentioned her father; the comte was forgotten. Whereas before, whatever her feelings, Diane had dutifully written to him and fretted over his health, his finances, she could not think of anything more to say to him. She busied herself in the garden, doing the work herself if the under-gardeners had been taken away for duties in the vineyard. In the evenings she went to bed tired but invigorated. Her pale complexion, lightly touched by the sun, looked radiant, and she was gradually regaining the use of her left arm.

She wrote Jean-Baptiste and Adelaide long letters full of motherly advice and encouragement. Her affectionate correspondence with Sophie took on a new urgency. The charming, bumbling letters of Sophie, her little sister Sophie, were kept in a large leather portfolio on Diane's bedside table where they could be reread each night before she went to sleep. For her little sister was becoming with every passing day the lodestar of Diane's hopes and dreams.

Diane reached for the portfolio of Sophie's letters, and she immediately felt calm. She, too, feared her "nerves," as her father called them, the furies that shook her from head to foot, that sent her moods swinging high and low, so that she could not fight back.

Against Catherine or Jean or anyone else. Now she had to fight back, she had to escape. She knew herself well enough to understand that her fragile nerves would not be able to withstand the torments of Damfert much longer.

She picked out Sophie's last letter and laughed softly. Such spelling! Worse than Jean-Baptiste's! She thought of her son toiling over his long piece of foolscap, the pink tip of his tongue sticking out at the corner of his lips—broad, beautiful lips like his father's—straining to join his letters neatly, to please his tutor, to make his mother smile and run her hand through his glossy thick curls—deep mahogany, like Armand's. She let herself drift for a moment into memories of Armand's warm, scented curls tumbling down to his dark brows, over his drooping lid with thick black lashes.

Sophie started her letters with a great leap forward and only after a sentence or two remembered to add a hasty "dearest sister" or "Very Dear Diane," in towering capital letters as if this were indeed Diane's official title.

Mainly what I have on my mind is you, Very Dear Diane, and my happy, happy news! First, let me say that Charles sends you his most affectionate greetings, a warm, brotherly kiss on both cheeks—and one more kiss, for good measure!—to our sister Catherine, too, and let us not forget, Monsieur de Tourmelle—for I was about to do just that, forget Monsieur de Tourmelle, I mean! My happy, happy news! You will have guessed already what it is, you are so clever and always have been. My hand is shaking so that I can scarcely write it! Yes! It's true! I am still carrying the baby, and I know that this time will be the lucky time for me and Charles. Diane, dear Diane, it has to be! My heart will break if I lose this one. God would not do that to me again. I have not forgotten my guardian angel and all the saints that I prayed to at Neuilly. I am praying my heart out now, dear sister, please pray with me! Oh, listen to Sophie! I need you here to tell me what a silly goose I am being, worrying all the time and down on my knees praying too much. Very Dear Diane, please write to me. Your letters bring me such comfort, they always have. At Neuilly I used to put on a clean apron every time one of your letters came from Paris with all the news of court and the King and Queen and

the Princesses. Write to me and tell me that I am in your prayers. I pray for you too, dear sister, I don't know why, but lately, in your letters, you sound very lonely and sad. Think of your little Sophie, sunning herself in her garden, and getting as fat as a fat toad. Oh, Diane, I am so happy! But now I am tired. Please write to
Your loving Sophie

Diane replaced the letter in the portfolio and, taking the bedside candle, sat down at her desk and started another page to add to her letter to Sophie. Diane's hands were cold as ice and stiff. Nerves, she thought, and a great wave of inertia swept over her. What is the use? What can Sophie do? Her little sister with big hazel eyes, clinging to the skirts of Diane or Catherine. Tagging along, making a nuisance of herself, but always ready to smile, to hug, to kiss. And now a grown woman. Baby sister expecting a baby of her own.

Diane dipped her pen in the porcelain inkwell, an exquisite piece of Dresden that the marquise de Sabran had given her for her sixteenth birthday, and forced herself to write, fighting against the dark wave of despair. Sophie was a marquise, too, the marquise de Rostaing. Sophie had married the dashing, young Charles de Rostaing, not as wealthy as the comte would have liked, but a fine title of the sworded nobility, an old name. While visiting Neuilly-les-Dames with a friend who had come to call on his fiancée, Charles had fallen passionately in love with Sophie. His friend's fiancée claimed to have a handsome singing voice, and, jokingly, to put her to the test, the young men had sent for Sophie to come and play accompaniment on the pianoforte. Charles had taken one look at the pretty, baby-faced young woman and had lost his heart. His mother, the dowager marquise, had been appalled. The comte de Fautrière was a well-known wastrel who would not be able to put two gold louis together to dower his daughter. Charles persisted. You will love her as I do, maman, he said. And she did. Sophie melted the heart of the despotic old dowager. The old marquise could not wait to carry the dear little thing away from her pokey convent to the family seat in Champagne, where she could cluck over Sophie and pamper her like an old mother hen a young chick.

The night of Sophie's wedding at Corcheval Diane had helped her dress while Catherine sat at a mirror and painted her face again. The comte had ordered the dress from Madame Clarisse, Diane's dressmaker in the little shop at the Palais-Royal. Sophie blushed scarlet when she saw the dress, alarmed by its extravagance. It was made of the finest silver brocade and the bodice embroidered with glistening seed pearls, an exact copy of the first Dauphine's dress when she married in 1745. Little Sophie, such a child! If only she could have seen the toilettes at the grand receptions in Paris and Versailles! The men as sumptuously dressed as the women. Ah, such a time it was, such a time. Diane sighed, and slumped forward.

A man's broad hand slapped noisily against her door, and, startled from her reverie, Diane splashed ink across the page. "Good night, dear wife, good night, good night, goo . . . " Tourmelle crooned mockingly as he staggered along the hallway. Someone crashed heavily against a closed door, and she heard her sister laugh and mutter drunkenly.

Diane stared at the whorl of ink, slowly spreading across the page. She watched fascinated as her hands began to tremble. For a moment, she held her quill aloft, poised over her letter to Sophie, before dropping it, like a dirty, useless object. Why bother? she said aloud to the darkness. Sophie was far away, in Champagne, with her own family, her own worries. Tourmelle and Catherine were all powerful. Damfert was indeed a fortress chateau from which she would never escape. She would never see Armand again. He would weave in and out of her wretched loneliness only as a snatch of gossip, a word, a smile, an anecdote from faraway Paris and Versailles. Uncle Philippe said that Armand had set up an actress as his mistress and that Odile claimed that he picked up prostitutes at the Palais Royal and brought them home just to enrage Madeleine. Madeleine . . . How she would laugh, Diane thought, to see me now. Close to thirty and already a thick streak of silver in my hair. Diane shook out her hair and encircled the graying streak with her fingers. She contemplated the shining bulk with grim satisfaction. It would do Madeleine's heart good to see that she is not the only unhappy woman on the face of this earth. She thought of that summer long ago at Corcheval when Madeleine watched Armand like a hawk desperate for prey. And I was so blind that I did not see the love in his eyes.

With her strong hand she grasped her damp hair and twisted it into a tight coil and wrapped it around her head like a halo. Bending her head to search for her hand mirror, her hairpins loosened and the heavy coil collapsed into jagged loops along her neck. Suddenly despair overwhelmed her. She held her mirror in front of her thin face and watched fat, luminous tears racing like schoolboys down her face into the brackets around her quivering mouth. Like a tired old woman, she rose from her chair and, with dragging steps, moved toward the curtained bed.

More and more isolated, Diane fought against her fraying nerves as the dismal months of harvest limped along. Too late, dry, scorching heat lay across the vineyards where the vinedressers shook their heads over the wretched sight of rotted vines and grapes. Tourmelle retreated into a surly rage and drank himself into a stupor every night with Catherine. They still laughed together, but it was a strange laughter, full of menace, without joy. Nonetheless, they were inseparable. They were at each other's side from the early morning hours when they groggily pulled on their boots and drank steaming bowls of coffee with thick, lumpy cream, until the late hours of darkness as they drank together next to the fire, sharing a clay pipe, cursing the weather, grumbling, laughing, or irritated by lust, coupling in a chair, against a wall or a table, quickly, viciously, like animals with a tormenting itch.

Tourmelle and Catherine made a great show of being busy thrashing out the new tenant leases and overseeing the harvests, or what remained after the disastrous rains. They contented themselves with treating Diane as if she did not exist. They took no trouble to conceal their intimacy from either the servants or Diane. They boldly indulged in lewd caresses, their hands roaming insistently over each other as they sat at table and drank wine. Half tipsy, Catherine would climb upon Jean's lap and rub herself against him as Jean squeezed her breasts, pulling them out of her gown's shallow bodice and fondling them. The footmen would gawk and whisper, while Diane stared straight ahead, stolidly chewing, until she finished her meal. Then she would fold her napkin carefully, like a well-trained schoolgirl, and leave the room.

During the long days of the dry harvest season when there was very little to harvest because the crops had rotted under the punishing rains of spring and mid-summer, Diane returned to her dream of freedom, of breaking free from Damfert. Every day she grew stronger in her resolve, she would do it, she would flee her hellish life and never return. Her whole life had been a story of impotence, of being passed along from one life that she had not chosen to the next, from one bondage to the next. She prayed not to let go of the thin threads of hope to which she still clung. She willed herself not to give in to despair.

She began to experiment with the idea of simply running away, of disappearing into the woods. She would go to Abbé Martin for help. Little by little, on the pretext of going to mass, she would take along a few necessary items, would leave them in the keeping of the abbé, who would accompany her to Cluny, where she would take a coach to Sophie's chateau. First, she would test her stamina for the journey on foot.

One day she rose before dawn and dressed sensibly, putting on sturdy boots, and quietly left the sleeping chateau. Before midday she had walked to a hamlet with a small church, the ruins of a medieval chateau, a few thatched cottages, and a cooper's shop. In the afternoon she set out again, across bare fields, exhilarated by her freedom, but even more by confidence in her own strength.

With only a short stop along the way for her meal of bread, a little cheese, and an apple, she felt not at all weary. Toward sunset, nearing Flavigny, the skies began to rumble and flash. The end of the dry spell, thought Diane, the storm would be fierce. She hurried along, panting now and feeling a sharp stitch in her side, she managed to push aside the church door just as the skies emptied and sent sheets of water roaring around the tiny church. As the skies darkened and the drumming rains continued, she realized that it would be impossible to set out again for Damfert. Who, after all, would miss her there? Certainly not her sister and Tourmelle. She spread out her cloak and lay down on a bench. The old church groaned and creaked under the storm. She slept fitfully during the night, waking cold and cramped while it was still dark.

Stepping into the dim foyer at Damfert, Diane stopped short and listened, overcome by the feeling that something was amiss. A footman came forward to light the wall lustres around the circular foyer. He paid no attention to Diane as she gripped the thick red velvet rope along the wall and began to toil up the steps. She was bone weary and could not wait to step into a soaking hot bath and go to bed.

Nearing the top of the staircase, she heard footsteps rushing toward the stairs.

Their faces in shadows, their backs to the light, Catherine and Tourmelle stood waiting for her, as a little breathless, she stepped onto the landing.

"Good evening, sister," Diane murmured, lowering her head and turning down the hallway toward her room.

A fist clamped around her arm and jerked her backward. Tourmelle, his face black with anger, pushed her against the wall.

"And your husband, madame? Aren't you going to greet me this evening?"

"Of course," Diane said weakly. She thought that her legs would give out under her and that if he released his grip on her arm, she would slide to the floor. "I was just going to my room."

Catherine stood to one side, her blotchy eyebrow twisted with amusement.

"Ah! Ah! To *your* room? Is that it? Whatever for?" Tourmelle trilled, mocking her. "Whatever for? Except to rest up after wearing your little priest's prick down to a . . . "

Diane could hear her own screams echoing down the long hallway. Dark yellow flashes of light exploded in front of her eyes. From her nose, a trickle, then a spurt, of warm blood ran down over her lips. As if she were no more than a rag doll, Tourmelle, with one hand, jerked her back and forth, knocking her head against the stone wall. Thud. Thud. Thud. Like a flimsy rag doll.

Laurent sat on a bench near the fire in the scullery and rubbed the huge round silver tray with a soft rag. His hands were black, and Julie, the scullery maid, had draped one of her aprons around his neck so that he would not soil his uniform.

"That's enough now. You've finished it. Here, give it to me." Julie took the tray from Laurent's hands and gave him a milk pitcher. "Here, take this, my beauty. You'll be needing another rag for the polish."

Laurent looked up at her as she took away one rag and put another in his hands. "Thank you, Julie," he said, smiling with all his might. He watched as she arranged pitchers and sauce boats along the bench next to him. "Go along, now," she said. "You mustn't just watch me, you know."

Briskly, Julie rumpled his long blond curls and gave him a friendly pat. "He does a fine job, if only you show him the way."

She picked up a basket of potatoes next to the cellar door and carried them to the table and began to peel them. A plain girl with an affectionate nature, Julie felt sorry for the tall, handsome footman and his mistress. While the other servants made fun of Laurent and played tricks on him, Julie looked out for him and found special treats for him in the kitchen when he seemed downcast.

Several of Tourmelle's servants had found reasons to quit Damfert after Catherine's arrival. Though they were used to the ravages of disease, smallpox in particular, and the deformities of nature, still there was something in Catherine's scarred face and manner that made them quake. The country folk hated her, peasants and gentry alike, Julie knew that. Practicing her witchcraft, they would say, striking fear in the hearts of innocent folk! When Tourmelle's peasants revolted and refused to give him his two days of *corvée de bras* at haymaking time, whom did he send to do his dirty work for him but his witch of a sister-in-law, and more than just a sister-in-law if the tales of the goings-on of those two demons be true? She got the peasants back to work, his Mademoiselle de Fautrière. She's the one that scared the wits out of them with her evil eye. And when the grapes rotted on the vine and mold turned the stalks black, why shouldn't they blame her and her fiendish face? Even the wild poppies in the vineyards turned black and rotted.

On the other side of the room, at the window, the cook stood at the sink and chopped chunks of cabbage into a blackened pot. An older woman who had been caught stealing provisions and had been sent away by the monks at Cluny, Simone had caught Catherine's eye at market one day and had been engaged on the spot.

As the house servants called for their wages and slipped away, Tourmelle gave Catherine free rein in finding and training new servants who would please her. Of all of them, Simone was the most fiercely devoted to Monsieur de Tourmelle's sister-in-law.

"Hmmph!" said the cook. "How many jobs does he have now that Mistress High-and-Mighty is wasting away upstairs?"

"Shhh . . . !" Julie turned to see if Laurent were listening. Laurent, his head bent, dipped his rag in cook's mixture and rubbed the milk pitcher. "You never know how much he understands. You never know. He's a lot smarter than we think, is what I say."

"He's a lot smarter than his mistress upstairs, is what I say. Mistress High-and-Mighty hasn't eaten a morsel of food out of my kitchen for ten days now. I've counted them. Let her go, says I to Mademoiselle. Don't you worry about the likes of her, says I." The cook was a broad woman who swayed from side to side as she talked, her wooden sabots screeching against the gritty flagstones.

"May be that Madame is sickly," Julie said to the cook's back. It scared Julie to think of what went on at night in the dark old chateau, which had room upon room that not a soul had ever seen in the broad daylight, that lay shrouded in linens from one year to the next. Julie had worked at the chateau since she was nine years old when her grandpa brought her to Monsieur de Tourmelle and left her there and never came back.

"And why shouldn't she be, is what I say. Let her sit up there and starve herself to death. It'll but serve her right." Simone shoved her knife into a fat cabbage head and split it in half. She rocked from side to side and shook her head.

Crossing over to Laurent, Julie took away the pitcher and put a tall pricket into his hand. Laurent looked at her meekly and reached for the polishing rag.

"You see? That's right. You've got the hang of it now, haven't you, my pet?"

Julie glanced at Laurent. He sat bent over the pricket. He appeared lost in his own thoughts.

What could the poor fellow be thinking of, sitting there listening to cook making fun of his mistress, and his mistress shut away upstairs. A fine lady who has been to court and is used to fine things. It's no way to treat a fine lady. It's worse than what Monsieur did to the Saxon woman who spoke so queer that no one could understand. The Saxon woman, that was whipping and beating and hitting, women know what that is. But turning a fine lady like Madame into a shadow. That's worse. Though Françoise says that she never saw any woman come through a beating the way the Saxon woman did. Time after time. She lost half an ear one time. Françoise saw it herself. Found the piece of ear on the floor. It looked like a piece of dark, dried up mushroom, she said. So pretty Madame was, when she came to Damfert, and after the baby boy, lying up there on her chaise-longue in her laces and perfumes, while all the fine visitors came to call. Monsieur said that was the way ladies in Paris did, after they had their babies. He was ever so proud of her then, Monsieur, fussing over her and running the household ragged to look after her properly and tearing down all the timber on the south side and building a pond and a fountain and all that for the garden, such as no one had ever seen before. Like the King's very own. That was before Monsieur fell back to being the way he was with the Saxon woman and the girls from the village that came into the house before it was cleaned up for Madame. And Madame's own sister, she made Monsieur worse than ever, egging him on in his meanness. No shame at all about what the household says or about the nasty tongues wagging over the dinner tables every day. Spreading the tales of her own sister trying to kill herself with pieces of broken glass, cutting her arms and bleeding over everything. So much blood that salt and vinegar in the sun won't bleach it out. Now starving herself . . .

"It's no way to treat a fine lady," Julie said. Laurent raised his head and smiled at her.

"Phew! Open those windows!" Holding a handkerchief to her nose, Catherine kicked aside a chair and pulled at the tall shutters. "*Jésu!* What a stench! Get them open, damn you!"

One panel of a shutter clattered back against the wall, and Françoise strained to turn the handle on the window.

"Like as not, it's frozen shut," wheezed Françoise, pulling at the window.

Next to the ashen pink embers of a brazier, Diane sat watching them in open-mouthed bewilderment.

Françoise stumbled back as one of the tall windows came open in her hands. A gust of ice-cold air swept through the room.

"Get Laurent up here with hot water. Buckets of it. Where is her slipper bath?" Catherine threw open the door of an armoire, which creaked and sagged on its hinges. "Her slipper bath, I said. Where is it?"

Sucking on the remains of a rotting front tooth, Françoise waddled toward Diane's dressing room and rolled the slipper bath out of a dim corner. Catherine hurried about the room opening drawers and chests, heaping shifts and ribbons and hoops out onto the floor.

"Don't just stand there sucking your teeth. Get down to the scullery. I want that girl up here giving me a hand with her clothes. I'm going to need all morning, from the looks of it to get her cleaned up and ready to leave."

As Françoise hurried from the room, leaving the door wide open behind her, Diane slowly turned her head to watch her go. Catherine pulled one gown after another out of the armoire. Diane stared at her but did not move. Her hands were folded in her lap; her small bare feet, rough and grimy, rested on an embroidered stool.

Catherine snatched a black taffeta gown with velvet trim from the back of the armoire. It was the gown Diane had worn to the ball at the Opéra on a wintry night in February 1745 when she and the King had dressed as Spaniards in honor of Maria-Theresa, the Dauphin's bride.

Catherine shook out the folds of the gown and held it against her body. She was as round and voluptuously curved as Diane was rail thin. "Here. This will have to do. It's going to hang on you like a stick but there's no help for it." She tossed the gown over a chair.

She came over to Diane and gripped her arm and pulled her to her feet.

"Come on. Get up. We've got to get you cleaned up and dressed. You've got to look pretty for papa. One last time."

29

The comte had always said, when the subject of death arose, that he wanted to be buried in his own private chapel at Corcheval. He had never been able to understand his wife's aversion to the chapel, which he had designed for her pleasure. He himself confessed that he was quite vain about it and could not think of a more hospitable resting place.

Not that the comte ever devoted much thought to death or his final resting place. Least of all on that fateful night after a Twelfth Night party at Saint-Cloud when he began to cane his lackey. It had been a large party and the comte had indulged himself without restraint when the hot, succulent dishes were placed before him. Lately he had put on a great deal of weight, despite the irregularity of his meals at the rue des Fours, and his clothes pinched uncomfortably. He had lost his youthful, lean body, which had filled him with such pride for years. Marianne grumbled that the ironmaster in Ancy cut a better figure than the comte.

Twelfth Night, the *fête des rois*, at Saint-Cloud was hardly the time for discipline, however. And when the comte found the gold ring in his piece of cake and was crowned with a laurel ring of gold leaves made by the flirtatious duchesse d'Orléans herself, the comte felt it his duty to carry the party to a fever pitch of gaiety. He drank, he danced, he cavorted in a darkened wardrobe with a young lady-in-waiting to the duchesse, and after the young lady complained of his disappointing performance in the wardrobe, the comte returned to the table and drank some more.

The sun had already made a half-hearted effort to warm a gray, gloomy Paris morning when the comte's hackney cab pulled into the half circle drive of the rue des Fours. He had fallen asleep as soon as the driver pulled away from the chateau at Saint-Cloud, and when he awoke, groggy, with a fierce headache, he flew into a temper because there were no footmen to assist him from the cab, no one to fling open the doors and help him up the stairs to his room. The house looked empty, as if it were still closed for the night. He had to stand on his own doorsteps and turn the bell to awaken a footman.

Clearly the staff had expected Monsieur le comte to stay the night and much of the following day with his hosts at Saint-Cloud. Instead, the comte de Fautrière had been one of those less consequential guests with a ticket entitling them to attend the party but not to stay on after it ended. The comte's status in the court circle had declined over the years since his beautiful daughter departed under a cloud of scandal. Moreover, it was well-known that the comte had not had a titled mistress in years and that he made do with his daughter's former lady's maid.

By the time the comte had climbed the stairs to his bedroom door, his face and neck had turned an ominous brick red. A thin white line rimmed his lips. The veins in his throat bulged as he shrieked at a footmen to bring up a bottle of brandy. In his bedroom, the hearth was cold, and the curtains were pulled over the shuttered windows.

The lackey sent up to build the comte's fire was a lad of ten, who had joined the household only a month before. As he darted past his master toward the hearth, the comte fell upon him with his cane and would have done the unfortunate boy terrible injury, had the comte not been seized by an apoplectic fit. When Marianne, awakened by the commotion, pulled him off the boy, the dead comte was still clutching his cane with both hands. It was a very sturdy ebony stick with a carved ivory handle. Soon after her father brought her up to Paris, Diane had discovered it in a little shop near the Pont Neuf and had given it to him for his saint's day in 1744 when the comte marked his fortieth year.

The marquis d'Ancy was the first to learn of the sudden death of his brother-in-law. Even before Marianne had absorbed the finality of what had happened, she dispatched a footman to the marquis' residence for help in sorting out what to do next. Accustomed as he was to the comte's daily catastrophes, Philippe paid little attention to the footman's noisy arrival downstairs. Without undue haste he completed his work with his secretary before admitting his brother-in-law's man.

With great effort he roused himself and began the necessary arrangements for the comte's burial by his family at Corcheval. He was relieved when Sophie and Charles arrived to collect Jean-Baptiste, a large, watchful boy of twelve, from the College de Louis-le-Grand before proceeding to Corcheval. Little Adelaide had pneumonia and was judged too feverish to leave her sick bed for such a long trip in the harsh January weather.

Naturally the comte's final journey forced Philippe to dig deeply into his purse once again. In death as in life the comte traveled expensively.

"You won't be opening up that ground in Charolais in January! No, Monsieur!" the fellow had said, though Philippe suspected that he was looking for an excuse to gouge more money. So Philippe agreed to have the body sent down to Corcheval in a casket filled with fifty gallons of Antilles rum. It seemed a fitting way to lay his brother-in-law to rest.

"That ought to keep him until spring, if need be," the mortician said, patting the casket after he had sealed it shut.

Nothing astonished Philippe more than Odile's devastating grief. He would never have imagined her capable of such emotion. He was certain that Odile and the comte had not been lovers for years. Whenever he saw them together in society, they behaved like wary competitors, jostling with each other for a vantage point. They did not seem to be friends at all. Nonetheless, Odile was so distraught by her loss that Philippe consented with relief when Marianne insisted on accompanying his wife to the funeral service at Corcheval. They departed, the lady's maid and the marquise, sitting opposite each other in stony silence, tears streaking down their painted cheeks. Odile had been so grief-stricken that she bought no new gowns for the occasion.

Confused and frightened, Diane sat very still in the chair where Sophie had placed her. A flurry of fat, damp snowflakes had ceased, and the fields outside Corcheval lay stiff with cold. There were crowds of people everywhere, streaming in and out of the great rooms of the chateau, lingering in groups along the reflecting pool, shaking hands, embracing, their faces solemn, sad. They looked as if something terrible or unlikely had happened. Diane, however, felt much better. She lifted her hand and inhaled its fragrance. Clean and perfumed! Before getting dressed and starting on the journey, she had had a wonderful, long bath with soap and suds and sponges. And now she smelled clean again.

Odile, with Marianne at her side, came near, crying, keening in sorrow, holding on to each other. "You see, everyone loved him! Look at this crowd. The dead of winter, yet they've all come to pay their respects. We all loved him, didn't we?"

Diane shrank back in her chair. Why did every one talk so fast? And loud? Sophie squeezed her hand, and Diane felt safe again, even though she knew that Catherine sat on the other side of Sophie.

People kept streaming past, milling around, crossing themselves as they went by the magnificent coffin covered in a blanket of deep burgundy velvet with a crest worked in silver thread. A lion rampant, keys, a palm tree . . . silver and burgundy, papa's colors. The Fautrière crest. The palm tree for one of their crusader ancestors. Sophie said that papa was in the beautiful coffin, but no one had seen him there, and, how could he be? Papa died long ago after a summer of terrible rains that rotted the vineyards in Burgundy.

"I've lost the baby. I've lost my father, and now, I've lost my sister. My dearest sister who was always good to me when I was a little girl. She never forgot about me when everyone else did. She and Clotilde took care of me. I can't bear any more, Charles. No more."

In truth, Charles was as defeated as his wife. Away from his strong-willed, hearty mother, he was frightened. Hope was stronger than despair whenever his mother was at his side. There had been too many deaths. And the babies never came to term. And now his sister-in-law, a broken woman, withdrawn, mute, terrified of her own shadow. She hovered about like an old woman, repeatedly lifting her hands to smell them. Her old-fashioned black dress hung in loose folds from her sharp, thin shoulders. Staring disconsolately at his feet, which he scuffed nervously back and forth against each other, Jean-Baptiste had sat next to his mother during the funeral mass. From time to time he would look at her shyly. When she first saw him as he alighted from Sophie's carriage, Diane had cried out in delight. Then she had lapsed into absent-minded silence, as if she had made a mistake, as if she had mistaken Jean-Baptiste for someone else.

Charles gripped Sophie's hand tightly as they made their way to the library. "Courage, my love," he said, "Diane is not lost yet."

Sophie and Charles had waited for friends and the priest to leave before asking Catherine to speak privately with them in the library. They had made up their minds to take Diane back with them to Champagne.

The wide double doors of the library were open, and, as they stepped into the room, they both gasped and drew back. Catherine had changed from her black mourning clothes to a vivid blue silk gown with only a token black crepe armband to indicate bereavement. She had painted her face stark white with large round circles of burgundy red on her scarred cheeks and scarlet on her twisted lips. She sat at the comte's desk, surrounded by his papers and portfolios. Smiling, she leaned back in her chair—the comte's chair—and enjoyed their consternation.

"That's all he deserves," she said scornfully, glancing down at the armband. "You cannot imagine how that nasty little man has fouled up our patrimony. Fortunately, you and papa's favorite have me to set things right."

Before the funeral arrangements for her father were completed, Catherine had set to work securing power of attorney over her father's affairs from his administrative notary. She turned and with a grand gesture indicated chairs for them to be seated.

"No, thank you, Catherine," Sophie said, appalled by her sister's behavior. "We'll stand. We'll only take a moment of your time. As you're quite busy, it seems." She looked at the documents on the desk. "Charles and I would like very much to take Diane back to Champagne with us. To live with us. And since Monsieur de Tourmelle has not seen fit to attend his father-in-law's funeral, we are asking you to carry that message to him."

Tourmelle had not accompanied the sisters to Corcheval for the funeral, because Catherine had done her work only too well. In poisoning his mind against Diane, Catherine insinuated that the comte had deliberately duped Tourmelle into marrying Diane off his hands. He adored his stout, good-looking son, and for all her power over him, Catherine could not persuade him that Jean-Baptiste was not his son. Nonetheless, Tourmelle harbored a gnawing resentment that somehow the comte had foisted damaged goods upon him.

It was easy enough for him to forget that for years he would have moved heaven and earth to marry Diane and that he had for a few years been happier with her than at any time in his life.

Catherine stared at Sophie as if she had never heard anything so preposterous in her entire life. "Diane's place is at Damfert! With her husband. With me, her sister. Somebody has to keep her disordered imagination in check!"

"But, Catherine, don't you see? Surely you must," Sophie said.

"Diane is unwell. She is not herself," Charles said. It simply had not occurred to Sophie or Charles, that Catherine would have any objection to their inviting Diane for an extended stay in Champagne. Catherine was, after all, an unmarried spinster living as a dependent in her older sister's household. In the absence of Tourmelle, they wanted her to spare them the long drive to Damfert to inform him of their invitation. And now Catherine reacted as though she were in effect her sister's guardian.

"She has not been herself since papa filled her head full of nonsense," Catherine sneered. "That's all that's wrong with her. She has had to come down off her pedestal. It drives her crazy not having flocks of men telling her how beautiful she is. That's all that's the matter with her."

"Then we shall have to return to Damfert with Diane and speak with Monsieur de Tourmelle ourselves, Charles," Sophie said dryly, cutting her sister short.

The next day, after most of the trunks had been loaded onto the tops of carriages, Catherine sought out Sophie and Charles in the orangery. Sophie turned, and before Catherine could speak, said, "My maid is helping Diane. She will be driving back to Damfert with us."

"I've thought it over," Catherine said. She seemed nervous and even a little diffident. "Diane might enjoy the change of air, after all." She glanced at the dilapidated room with dead and dried plants in cracked pots. "I've got weeks and months of work to do here, untangling the mess of the liens and debts on the property. Diane is bound to be a nuisance. She'll be just another burden when there is so much to do."

Sophie smiled pleasantly and said nothing, content to have avoided a tiring journey to Damfert, relieved to have brought Diane under her wing.

Diane, Catherine had concluded after a good night's sleep, would indeed get in her way at Corcheval. She could not count on Diane merely to mope around or try to starve herself to death. Besides, it would be wonderful to return to Damfert without her. Then there would be nothing to interfere with Catherine's happiness with Tourmelle. They were a team. A fine matched pair. She was determined not to lose him. For months Tourmelle had not seen Diane or expressed any interest in seeing her. He had turned her over to Catherine. She's your sister, he said. Deal with her as you see fit. And Catherine turned her over to the servants, who mistreated her and neglected her and tormented her. Which served her right, as far as Catherine was concerned. She had *earned* Tourmelle's affection. But she had not liked the way Tourmelle stared at Diane when she came out of the house and got into the carriage. Oh, my God! he said. She is so thin! Catherine could hear the sob in his voice. He was about to weep over Mistress High-and-Mighty! She is still such a pretty thing, Tourmelle said dreamily, as they drove away. So, Catherine would return to Damfert, and Diane would not. Because Tourmelle and Catherine were a team.

Book Six

30

I had a married sister in Champagne who, concerned about my misfortunes, urged me to spend some time at her home.

Sophie smiled as Diane successfully reached, and held, a high note with her clear voice, as young as a girl of sixteen. She was singing "Le Perfide Renaud" from *Armide*, while Sophie played accompaniment, and her mother-in-law turned the pages of the score. Soon, Charles would be returning from settling a dispute in one of the parishes on the estate, and then nurse would bring down the baby and all of them would settle onto blankets under the water oaks while Diane-Françoise tottered about, drooling onto her apron, a toothless grin spread across her impish little face.

With tenderness and gratitude Sophie looked up at her sister. What miracle had dispelled the tension and sadness from their lives? The dead babies, the miscarriages, Charles' weak lungs? What miracle except Diane? It had to be Diane, who had come to live with them, chasing away the disappointments, the heartaches, the woeful dark-of-night dread of the future. Even the dowager marquise had not been immune to the gloom that had begun to settle over their lives.

Three years ago no one would ever have suspected that Diane could be brought back from the shadows of Damfert. At the comte's funeral she had sat like an *abrutie*, a brutish lump only intermittently aware of what was happening around her. After her initial shock on seeing Diane's condition, Charles' mother had treated Diane's nervous breakdown like any other job. She rolled up her sleeves and got down to work. Her affectionate nature overflowed like her embonpoint. She never kissed when she could embrace and kiss, too; she never shook hands when she could kiss. She quickly saw that above all else Diane needed affection. And Madame de Rostaing was a patient woman.

At Ussé Sophie's servants had been afraid of the thin, mute woman who emerged from the family carriage. Madame's sister from Burgundy, they whispered. Without Laurent to help, Sophie did not know how they would have managed. In unfamiliar surroundings, good, slow-witted Laurent was almost as frightened, as disoriented, as his mistress. But he had doggedly stayed at her side, soothing her spirits, fetching her bath water, bringing her flowers from the garden. When they arrived at Ussé, Laurent had two ancient suits of livery, both of them faded and frayed at the collars, the silver braid on his sleeve unraveled into dangling loops. Stubbornly, Laurent refused to give up his uniform, and Charles, relenting, had the comte's livery copied into fresh versions.

That was the first time Diane really laughed at Ussé: when Laurent came to serve her breakfast in his handsome new livery. They could be heard crowing like two children with new toys.

Sophie and Charles and old Madame de Rostaing kept close watch on Diane's firsts: the first time she smiled at one of Charles' jokes, the first time she let her maid dress her hair with diamond pins, the first time she had a new dress made, the first time she played the piano and sang.

The household put aside its worries with Sophie's efforts to produce a child and concentrated on Diane. At Damfert Diane had spent months isolated in her rooms. At Ussé she was rarely left alone. They were a sociable group, the old mother-in-law, Sophie, and Charles. They had grown used to spending their days quietly together, looking up from their needle work or their books for a bit of conversation, singing together around the piano in the afternoons, playing a few hands of piquet after supper, then walking in the park before going to bed for the night. Slowly, they drew Diane into the calm rhythms of their country life. In time their friends in the neighboring manor houses and chateaux came to call and went away charmed by the marquise's striking sister, so much quieter, however, than the little marquise, who was quite a chatterer.

The day Diane stepped clearly into the light of day, however, was the day Sophie announced that she was pregnant once again. While Madame de Rostaing and Charles lowered their eyes fearfully and spent more time than usual on their knees in the chapel of the chateau, Diane radiated optimism. Like all women her age, Diane had suffered her share of miscarriages, and she had learned a thing or two. Now Diane became the caretaker. Here you are again, Sophie would say, nursing me along, just like those years in the convent.

It turned out to be a happy time for all of them. Sophie even developed a taste for Diane's foul-smelling brew of arrowroot tea, though the day after she gave birth to Diane-Françoise, she declared that she never wanted to taste another drop of the stuff. Until the next pregnancy. Sophie named the baby Diane-Françoise after her sister and her beloved mother-in-law. They called her Fanette.

Three weeks after her niece's birth, Diane celebrated her thirty-third birthday with fine champagne bottled on the Rostaing estate. After Sophie had gone to bed, Charles and Diane and Madame de Rostaing sat around playing cards and singing until almost dawn when Sophie came down and scolded them. They locked arms affectionately and staggered up the stairs to bed.

"Oh, Charles, you missed Diane's song from *Armide*!" Sophie said as Charles walked through the French windows into the music room.

"Not altogether. I listened crossing the park, and it couldn't have been lovelier, Diane. Brava." A footman lifted a tray expectantly to Charles.

"Ah," he said, taking an envelope. "This must be from Tourmelle, Diane." A thick veil of tension fell over the little group in the music room.

Charles noticed that his mother stiffened. The "irregular" situation, as she preferred to call it, of Catherine de Fautrière and Diane's husband distressed the kind-hearted old woman. To her mind, it was incest, pure and simple. To be sure, the King himself had gone from one de Nesle sister to another, three all told, and during one period taking two of the sisters as his mistresses. It was no less a sin for all that, even if the King himself was the sinner. Madame de Rostaing dreaded the days, they were rare, once every three or four months, but she dreaded them nonetheless, when a letter from Tourmelle arrived with a remittance for Diane.

"What is it? What does it say?" Diane asked, her voice anxious. One day a letter would arrive demanding that she return to Damfert. She was certain of it. They had not finished with her yet.

Charles took the letter and sat down next to the window to read. Catherine had never once written a word to her two sisters. There were no New Year's cards or letters, nothing on their saint's day, though Sophie and now Diane sent her greetings throughout the year. As far as Catherine was concerned, her two sisters had ceased to exist. Charles learned through Philippe d'Ancy that Catherine had fought like a wildcat against the pack of creditors descending on the comte's estate after his death. Catherine had set out to win, to turn the extended properties into productive moneymakers. The times conspired against her. And the comte's hopeless prodigality doomed her efforts before they began. Catherine learned that the loan her father had taken at five percent to purchase Louis-Etienne's commission encumbered her every step. She set up a costly tile-kiln at Joigny, which hobbled along for a year before failing altogether. She sold off timberlands, and timber rights, all to no avail. The very agents who had been so clever at cheating her father outwitted her as well. The chateau and title of Corcheval were sold to a tax farmer three years after the comte's death.

"The usual. Nothing more," Charles said, running quickly through Tourmelle's letter. There was the note for the same amount of money that Tourmelle had decided upon shortly after Diane had gone to live with Sophie and Charles. It was a decent, though not an extravagant sum of money, given Tourmelle's fortune. With the note Tourmelle included a short, old-fashioned letter, using the formulas and turns of phrase Charles' late father would have found to his taste. In the letter, before closing, Tourmelle admonished Charles to keep his corrupt and sinful sister-in-law (Tourmelle never referred to Diane as his wife) from shaming Tourmelle's good name any further.

Charles looked up at Diane. She and Sophie, forgetting about the letter, were teasing each other, Diane insisting that it was

Sophie's turn to sing. In the fading light of sunset they looked as young and as carefree as two maidens let loose from the convent for an evening. Diane's face was soft and trusting. She appeared unmarked by Damfert and Tourmelle and Catherine.

My sister's charming mother-in-law, being forewarned of my troubles, tried to find ways to make me forget them.

"Have they left you here all alone, maman?" Diane crossed the yellowing lawn to Madame de Rostaing. The remains of the afternoon *goûter* had been cleared away. The old lady sat reading in the shade of the water oak.

"Sophie went up with nurse to bathe the baby and settle her down for the evening. And Charles was lured to the stables. A mare is foaling, and he is convinced that she can't do it without him."

"I've brought you a shawl. The wind is coming up. The day's are getting shorter."

"And the sun doesn't warm these old bones the way it used to do. Sit. Sit, my dear. Keep me company. I like reading under a tree, don't you?" Diane settled the shawl around Madame de Rostaing's plump shoulders. "Not that I mind being alone, but it's always better having company."

"I don't like Sophie climbing those steps so much. That's twice today." Diane frowned.

"It's all right. She's the very picture of health. The doctors say as much themselves, and you know they see the worst in everything, with their leeches and cups and knives. Foolish bunch! You mustn't worry like that. Look at Charles and me. The last time, when little Fanette was in the making, we couldn't smile to save our souls, we were that scared. You got us over that, and now just look at you!"

Diane gazed anxiously across the lawn as she picked up her workbasket. Her back rounded, she looked strained as she hunched down over her embroidery hoop. Her daughter Adelaide's health was a constant worry. Once, after Tourmelle took Adelaide away to Damfert for the summer months, the little girl's fainting spells kept her confined to the convent infirmary for a full year. A pale, broad-faced child, Adelaide was plagued with nervous tics that made going into society a nightmare for her. During Adelaide's visits to Ussé, Diane tried to bring her out of her shyness by having her read aloud, correcting her diction, asking her questions on each passage. Adelaide, pleading headache and fatigue, would beg off, preferring to spend her days at Ussé walking slowly around the paths of the park, head meekly bowed, hands clasped behind her back.

Jean-Baptiste, healthy and robust, came to visit during every school holiday. His voice had changed, and he grew so tall that he towered over his diminutive aunt. He was shy and respectful around his mother. Though they talked little, they spent hours together during his visits, and when the carriage called to take him back to school, Diane would place her tear-soaked face against his cheeks when they said goodbye.

A gust of wind swept through the ancient water oak releasing a shower of shriveled copper leaves. A few clung to Diane's soft woolen skirt. She did not move to shake them off.

"I like it when you call me 'maman'," the old woman said, breaking the silence. Her heart ached for this lovely young woman, reduced to being just another dependent female in her sister's house.

Diane looked up and slowly smiled. "Do you? I suppose I never thought about it. I must have picked it up from Sophie and Charles." Diane rested her embroidery in her lap. Madame de Rostaing had folded her hands expectantly. She wants to chat, Diane thought. "Strange, though. It occurs to me that Sophie always called our mother '*ma mère.*' Never 'maman.' Isn't that odd? I had forgotten that. It's been so long ago, ages since maman died at Corcheval."

Diane swept her eyes around the spacious park where they spent most of their waking hours, taking comfort in its tranquil beauty.

"Sophie loves you," Diane said after a moment. "And she's not afraid of you, the way she was of maman. Our mother, I mean."

"Afraid of her? Sophie afraid of her own mother?"

"Oh, not really, I suppose. It's just that Sophie never spent much time close to maman. Sophie was away at school, and maman was just a beautiful lady who came by from time to time to visit. To see that her aprons were not torn, and that her nails were clean."

"I know, I know. The kind of mother I've always been to Cécile. The kind of mother we noblewomen were brought up to be. And are still taught to be! Though Cécile would never be afraid of me!" They both laughed at the idea of haughty Cécile cowering before her kindly old mother. "Ashamed of me, yes. With my old-fashioned clothes and my country ways. I don't come up to the mark of Cécile and her fine friends at court. I know that as well as she does."

"Ah! Don't talk like that, maman," Diane said, reaching across and tugging affectionately at the lace of Madame de Rostaing's sleeve. "We all love you here at Ussé. Sophie has never stopped singing your praises since Charles brought you to the convent to meet her."

"That little vixen! I'll remember it until the day I die! Cross as I was, driving all that long way over the muddiest roads in the kingdom! She stole my heart away!" The old woman shook her head. "She stole my heart away!"

Diane looked at her fondly. "What would Cécile say if she could hear you talk like that?"

"Cécile?"

"Yes, Cécile. Don't you think she would be jealous?"

"Jealous? Why should she be?"

"Why, I don't know, jealous of your love for my sister. Perhaps, of preferring Sophie to her. Tell the truth now. If Sophie and Cécile were drowning and you could save only one—only one, mind you!—which one would you rescue? Hmmm? Which one?" There was a mischievous glint in Diane's eyes.

Madame de Rostaing tossed her head irritably. It was clear that the question had touched her to the quick. "That sounds like the kind of games you young people play at court. You wits. You intellectuals! It's foolishness, that's what it is."

"All right, then. Tell me, which one would you save?" Diane asked solemnly.

Madame de Rostaing straightened her cap and pulled her shawl tightly across her broad bosom. She gazed at the gnarled roots of the oak, silver gray in the afternoon sun.

"I would rescue my daughter, of course. I would save Cécile from the waters." She paused and took a deep breath. "Then I would drown myself with my daughter-in-law," she said quietly, lifting her head and looking steadily into Diane's eyes.

They were still sitting quietly looking at each other when Charles' old hunting dog loped under the shade of the tree and thrust his wet muzzle into Diane's lap.

"It's Charles," the marquise cried happily, squinting into the sunlight. "I hadn't expected to see him before supper time."

Charles walked toward them, his head bowed and his hands behind his back, his long, glossy curls shining in the late afternoon sun. Laurent, his noble head held high, his face calm and impassive, followed Charles at a short distance.

Watching her brother-in-law crossing the lawn, Diane knew immediately that something was wrong, and her thoughts flew to Sophie.

"What is it, Charles? Is Sophie all right?" Her embroidery work fell to the ground as she stood up.

Under the shade of the huge tree Charles' face looked bloodless; pale brown freckles were sprinkled over the bridge of his thin nose.

Charles went to Diane and took her in his arms. He patted her back gently. "No, no," he said softly. "It's not Sophie. It's not Sophie."

31

I was left alone with my son, my daughter having died in tragic circumstances.

In the park, under the water oak, the servants were beginning to set up tables and chairs for the afternoon *goûter,* as gardeners raked the gravel paths circling the fountain. Diane could hear the house steward calling for Laurent to fetch his mistress. Under the massive old tree her niece was trying to climb onto the back of one of Charles' hunting dogs. Fanette kept sliding off, while the old dog lay patiently submissive. Watching the flaxen-haired toddler at play, Diane smiled, her eyes filling with tears. Poor, melancholy Adelaide, even as a child she had not known such simple pleasures. What had given Adelaide pleasure? Diane had not the slightest idea, and it pained her to think of how little she really knew her own daughter.

Diane opened her jewelry casket and put away the gold pendant earrings she had inherited from her mother and wondered whether she should take the casket with her to Paris since she would be in deep mourning and would wear no jewelry. Her mourning dress, the same one she had worn for her mother, though still a perfect fit, was old and completely out of fashion, but she did not care. The black bombazine dress with black crepe trim was heavy, weighing her down physically and emotionally like her grief. She had only one black silk hood and one pair of black shammy leather shoes and gloves. She reminded herself not to forget to take a black crepe fan.

On her desk lay a full-page, eloquent letter of condolence from the King. She picked it up to read again. It touched my heart, he said, when you named your sweet child Adelaide after my own beloved darling. He spoke of the death of his ten-year old grandson, the duc de Bourgogne, and how bravely he had endured his cruel sufferings. A good man he must be, thought Diane, unable to stop her tears, to write such a letter to soothe a mother's heart. They say the King is like a mother to his children, overly fond.

At the door she turned and surveyed the sun-filled room, where her trunk looked like a dark, ominous intruder, and was overcome with fear. Fear of leaving Ussé and the soothing monotony of the days there, the slow, ponderous change of seasons, the quiet domestic habits, the affection of family. Fear of seeing again her tormentors, though she doubted very much that Tourmelle and her sister would bother to attend little Adelaide's funeral at her convent in Paris. Fear of Paris itself, its memories, pleasures, and temptations. Now that the door had sprung open, she was afraid to venture forth, to take the high road to Paris, the forbidden city of her desires.

But go to Paris she must. Though Charles offered to accompany her, he was easily persuaded by Diane and Madame de Rostaing to remain with Sophie, who looked desolate each time anyone mentioned his going. The next morning in the early hours as milky patches of mist clung to the dank stubble in the fields, Diane climbed into the carriage alone. Laurent, immaculately groomed, his pale, blond hair plaited into a thick braid, sat alongside the driver. Diane's traveling trunk, its hinges rusty from disuse, was strapped over the rear springs of the carriage.

The trunk contained only a few sober black gowns, outmoded, unfashionable, to see her through the few days that she would remain in Paris after Adelaide's funeral mass. A week, perhaps two, to visit with her son, to rest from the journey and the shock of losing her daughter to an epidemic of gangrenous throat infections that had swept through the convent and taken away eighteen girls.

In the streets scrawny-necked children hawked dirty songs about the King, thrusting the stiff sheets of paper into the open windows of the carriage, despite Diane's black veils and the black ribbons on Uncle Philippe's carriage. The words, mocking and obscene. They said that La Pompadour coughed and kept to her bed, her beauty vanished, her lips shriveled and yellow. They said that she had become the King's procuress, slipping young girls in and out of the pavilion of the Parc aux Cerfs, young girls who would do anything the King wanted.

To Diane everything seemed different in the Paris that she had left so many years ago when she had been driven in the middle of the night to Corcheval. Changes everywhere. The Opéra had burned down in late spring. Mansions had been built all the way to the tollgates at Vincennes. She stared in amazement as her uncle's carriage jerked and twisted through the streets. New squares with huge fountains. The vast Place Louis XV, gigantic, stretching over what used to be scrubby land from the Tuileries gardens to the Champs Elysées. The King celebrated the end of the hateful Seven Years' war, Pompadour's war, her enemies said, by opening the Place with balls and fireworks. In the middle of the great space, on a pedestal, a bronze statue, enormous, resplendent: Louis XV on his favorite mare. Around the base of the statue the sculptor Pigalle had cast an allegorical figure at each corner: Force, Prudence, Justice, and Peace. The King's four mistresses, that's what they are, scoffed the broadsheets: Mailly, Vintimille, Chateauroux, and Pompadour. Mock the King? Belittle His Majesty? What had come over the people? Louis the Beloved. What had become of him?

At the door of her uncle's suite of rooms in his mansion on the rue de Varenne a footman sat in a straightback chair and nodded drowsily. Startled by the rustle of Diane's skirts, he sprang to his feet and showed her to her uncle's bedside.

Except for the whir and ticking of numerous clocks placed about the huge room all was quiet and still. The marquis slept, his gaunt head turned to one side, his purplish lips parted as he breathed noisily through his mouth.

Carefully, Diane tugged her uncle's nightcap over his ears and covered his outflung arm, her heart overflowing with love for this kind, gentle man. A footman lifted a chair and placed it next to the bed.

Diane sat down and pulled her cape tightly around her shoulders. It was cold in the room. Yet sweat covered her uncle's lip and dampened wisps of hair on his forehead. Diane gazed at the emaciated man in the bed and thought that he looked sicker than the week before when she had last seen him. Tall, barrel-chested Uncle Philippe. What had become of him? Where had he gone? More changes, and this one cut to the quick.

He had said that it was nothing, that it was only an attack of the "purples," as he called them. He would get up soon. From his estates his stewards sent up roebuck and jam and snails and mustard and all the little delicacies that improved the marquis' appetite and put him back on his feet. He would soon be up and around town, at the King's *levée* and morning mass, at the theatre. He had laughed and winked at her, and she tried to smile back. After bleedings for a fortnight, provided there were no infections from the cuts, Uncle Philippe insisted that he would be back in his carriage, hustling about here and there, going about his business as usual.

The room was growing dark. A footman entered with a twist of burning rag and began to light candles. Soon the candlelight made the fading daylight look like darkness.

Philippe d'Ancy stirred and turned his head toward the light. "Is that you, Diane?" He managed to raise himself on one elbow before falling back again. The marquis' valet hurried forward to prop him up against his pillows. "Have you been waiting long?"

"I'm the one, uncle. I've kept you waiting. I was late, and you fell asleep." He looked so very ill, his eyes watery and unfocused.

"You aren't too warm, are you, my dear? It seems to me hot in here for this time of year." With a feeble lift of his hand Philippe motioned for a drink of water. "You look very pretty. I won't say 'handsome.' That wouldn't be enough. You look lovely, my dear." Tired, he leaned back, sharp pains shooting through his thin arms where the surgeon had cut him last. In the candlelight, her features softened, Diane did look beautiful. And young, though her eyes had faded.

"The air of Champagne has done you a world of good," he said.

Diane laughed, her spirits lifting.

"When will you be going back?" he asked.

"Soon. I wouldn't want to miss Sophie's confinement. And afterwards we'll have a great party with Charles' best champagne."

But even as she spoke, the joy drained away and left her heavy-hearted. In the deepest recesses of her heart she knew that she had for years longed for nothing more than to go to Paris and to find Armand again. She could not help it: with every corner turned she had thought to see him, strolling along with friends or alone, his dark head lowered, preoccupied, sad. How many times in the past few days she had thought she caught a glimpse of him just disappearing into a street, a shop, a doorway. It was driving her mad, this longing for the sight of him. Only this morning she had strolled through the Tuileries gardens, her eyes darting here and there like a hungry animal in search of food. And the gorgeously dressed men followed her with their eyes as she walked, ogling her despite her antiquated black gown, watching her sway along the paths, Laurent at her side. That much about Paris had not changed.

She could not truly say, to her uncle or to herself, why she wanted so desperately to stay in Paris. Forever. It was not just Armand, the addictive dream that one day she would turn a corner, and he would be there, coming toward her, ready to love her as if she were seventeen years old again. It was not just Armand. Yet the ache for him had not gone away. It was the vivid world of the court and its scandals. The magic presence of the King. It was not just Armand.

"I want to spend a little more time with Jean-Baptiste. I want to be near him just for a while. It will make me feel less lonely when I return to Ussé," she said with a wistful smile that broke Philippe's heart.

"Of course, you do, my dear. Why, Jean-Baptiste is a man grown, his father has just bought him a commission in the gray regiments. He's as happy as a clam, Jean-Baptiste! Swaggering about in his scarlet waistcoat trimmed in gold!" Philippe was fond of the boy. Up to a point. A terrible braggart, he was, this Jean-Baptiste. And as vain, he thought, as Michel de Fautrière ever was. More vain. He was damned handsome, no one could gainsay that. A peacock, just like his grandfather. Throwing away thousands on fancy uniforms and swords, chasing actresses like a wolfhound off his leash.

"Of course, I understand, *ma petite*," Philippe said. His rush of energy on waking had disappeared. He felt exhausted. He closed his eyes and thought of the trip to Burgundy. The roads would be a trial until they got further south, but what did it matter? To get out of the clammy darkness of Paris and into his own bed at Ancy. He could not bear the thought of dying without seeing again the drafty old chateau of his childhood. He and Aurélie loved the homely old place. Dear Aurélie, her sick lungs caving in on her, snuffing out her life. Insisting, almost hysterically as she lay dying, that she did not want to lie beneath the stones of that strange little chapel, tormented by the mere idea of having her dead body laid to rest in the chapel built by the man who had betrayed so much of her young faith and innocence. So little happiness in that life. Like her daughter, so little happiness . . .

Marianne's maid, splendidly dressed in hunter green serge with a sparkling white apron trimmed in fine lace, stood aside as her mistress poured out tea. Clearly puzzled, Diane surveyed in silent admiration the exquisite taste of Marianne's apartment—the Boucault chairs of carved walnut, a "D"-shaped commode with a pink marble top and brass mounts. How was it possible? A lady's maid?

"It *is* pretty, isn't it?" Marianne said, enjoying Diane's astonishment. She had been delighted when Diane's note finally found its way to her. And why not? They had had such good times together. Mostly. Her silly old father, randy as an old goat in bed. Stingy and bad-tempered in the mornings, though. Always broke. Lord, Lord, he could make them all laugh!

"Do you remember that daft novel by the Englishman about the serving maid who was so virtuous she made her fortune with her . . . ?" Marianne stopped herself and hooted with laughter. Fresh from the country, Mademoiselle de Fautrière—or rather Madame de Tourmelle—might not be used to the kind of talk that went on in Paris.

"*Pamela*? You mean the novel we read when papa was so ill?" Diane asked.

The young maid looked up in surprise as the two women broke into peals of laughter, rocking back and forth, steadying their teacups.

"Oh, Marianne!" Diane said, "It is so good to see you after all these years. I've missed you. Can you believe me when I say that?"

"Of course, I can. For I've missed you . . . and the comte." Her lively face clouded over. "I cared for him, you know. More than anyone before . . . or since." As soon as she said it, Marianne wondered whether it was true. Perhaps not, but she had been awfully fond of the comte, all the same.

"I know, Marianne. We both loved papa. Despite his faults. But you haven't answered my question. When did you move to this side of the river?"

"Not many months ago," Marianne said. "Shortly after I left the service of Mademoiselle Sergent. Yvette Sergent, the actress."

"Yes. I know." Diane fought down the tremor in her voice. She carefully set down her cup. Yvette Sergent had been Armand's mistress. Was perhaps still his mistress.

"Then you must know that she was your friend Armand's mistress for six years," Marianne said boldly. No point in pussyfooting around. Besides, if the truth be told, she was certain that Diane had sought her out to learn what she could about Armand. I'm being nasty and unfair, Marianne thought. Diane looked pathetic in her dowdy black weeds and countrified coiffure, though her eyes, when she smiled, were just as fine as ever and her complexion like a creamy peach still.

"Yes . . . " Diane said hesitantly. "I heard that, too."

"Until he left her. Or she left him. That would be more exact. A man like Mézières cannot afford to take an actress for a mistress. He doesn't have the means. A noblewoman, yes, he can afford that. Aristocrats take their lovers like so many flowers to add to their bouquet. To set on one of their commodes for their fine friends to admire. The Mademoiselles Sergents of this world," Marianne said with authority, "have to make their fortune while they can. They won't be beautiful forever. Mademoiselle Sergent had to look to the future. So farewell to Colonel de Mézières." Marianne made a wide, sweeping gesture with her hand.

"A colonel? I had forgotten that Armand is in uniform." Diane lowered her eyes. Marianne was too clever. She would read Diane's secrets in her eyes.

"It suits him," Marianne said rather tersely. "It suits any man, particularly a man as well set up as Mézières. Handsome! He makes many a woman swoon when he walks into a room." She could sense Diane's discomfort and was ashamed of herself for enjoying it a little. "He was good to me, the colonel. After your father died, I had nowhere to go. Madame Odile went queer over religion all of a sudden. She lost her looks, she lost her figure, she lost the comte, and—*voilà*, she finds the Lord Jesus Christ! Hrrmph!" Marianne knew that she was on safe ground there. Diane had always detested Odile.

"I'm glad he was able to help you," Diane said listlessly. Suddenly it all seemed hopeless, staying on in Paris, trying to recapture those giddy days, sleepless nights. It was too late. Armand must have had many mistresses by now. He would have the most beautiful mistresses in Paris, she was sure of that. Why should he still care for her? After all these years? Diane looked at her hands. They were pale and thin with thick veins, bluish gray, threading their way toward her wrists. An old woman's hands, she thought. Thirty-four years old. No proper woman could dance at a ball after she was twenty-five. I would have to sit and watch.

"Do you go to balls, Marianne?" Diane asked.

Marianne looked at her in surprise. "Balls?"

"Yes. I mean, do you dance?"

"Sometimes. It depends. My friend . . . My friends and I like small supper parties. And the gaming tables. There are more of those now than when you were here. The King himself gambles like a madman, you know. He never used to, in the old days when only the duc de Gesvres was allowed tables."

"But, you could dance if you wanted to, couldn't you? Now that . . . you're older?"

Marianne laughed. The velvet patch next to her lips slipped upward into the swell of her apple cheeks. "Ah, that's it, is it? I wondered what you were getting to. Of course, I dance when I've a mind to. At masked balls you do whatever you like. Your friend, Madeleine—you haven't asked about her—led out a quadrille at the Hotel de Ville as if she were the Queen herself. The brazen hussy. Some mornings she must wake up and think she *is* the Queen. Even if she were the Queen, Armand de Mézières would turn up his nose at her. He despises that woman. And I don't blame him. She's hateful. Hard. A heart of stone."

"Then she must have changed. Madeleine was always good to me. And she loved Armand with all her heart."

"Good to you!" Marianne's voice rose. "Oh, yes, indeed! She loved you like a sister, didn't she? She and Mademoiselle Malavelle." Marianne sank back in her chair. "Madeleine loved you so much that she ran to your father and told him that you were pregnant so that he would marry you off to Tourmelle before . . . before you lost your value completely. And not even Tourmelle would be fool enough to take you off your father's hands. First, Mademoiselle Malavelle, then Madeleine. Your father couldn't run the risk of not believing them."

Diane sat stunned. She said nothing.

"That's how good Madeleine was to you, my dear. She was afraid of you. She stopped at nothing to get what she wanted. She wanted you out of Paris before Armand did something foolish and romantic. Like eloping with you and making her the laughingstock of the court," Marianne said, yawning and stretching her arms. She had relaxed in Diane's company. It *was* like old times. The comte never did stand on ceremony and neither did Diane, after they got to know each other.

A lump hardened in Diane's throat. She wanted to cry out against her own stupidity. Never once in all these years had she suspected Madeleine behind her father's frenzy that night as they left Paris. Never once. Such a simpleton, she was. Not knowing herself that she was expecting a child, Armand's child. Knowing only that her young body was changing in mysterious ways. And somehow her father must have guessed that something was going wrong that frightened him and made him ashamed of her.

"I only thought that papa had guessed . . . that something was wrong with me," Diane said at a last, her face flushed. She was ashamed to have Marianne talk about her secret as if everyone had known. After her marriage, when her slim body had swelled, and Tourmelle, happy, his face shining with joy, had watched the doctor examine her, she knew immediately what the strange malaise meant. It meant that she would give birth to Armand's child. She thought that had been her secret all these years.

"Well, Monsieur de Tourmelle never guessed. That was what mattered to your father." Marianne yawned again.

"How did Madeleine know?" How could she know, Diane wanted to ask, when I did not know myself that I was with child.

"Madeleine makes it her business to know what concerns her. That handsome fiancé of hers was driving her crazy. He was the last one. When she got over him, she got over all men. She's the one who drives *them* out of their minds these days."

"Madeleine? A success at court?" Diane stared. Madeleine? It was not possible.

"If you call having men make fools of themselves, doing cruel things to please her, yes, she makes more conquests than any woman in Paris. Wait a little. You'll start hearing the stories. I'm surprised you haven't already. She pulled off her worst trick three months ago. She teased one of her flirts until he panted after her like a spaniel. But before she would let him get close enough to lick her boots, she made him vow that he would go back to his last mistress and get her pregnant. Then and only then would he have his way with Madeleine de Mézières. The great oaf did as he was told! And crowed all over town about how he got into Madame de Mézières' bed. His poor little mistress has been down in the country ever since. She may never show her face in court again."

What an extraordinary story! Her girlhood friend, Madeleine, turning men into her slaves, her playthings. Diane felt sick to her stomach.

"Not that Madeleine is any beauty. The Queen has fifty-two women in her entourage, each one uglier than the next, and Madeleine happens to be the only one with any appeal whatsoever. Her face was never anything to brag about, you know that, but she's as shapely as ever. Barren. No little ones dragging her down. That's a help. Still, she always had a figure to make a man's head turn her way."

Marianne glanced up nervously as the clock on the mantelpiece struck five. Suddenly, she seemed restless.

Diane felt embarrassed, as if her former servant were dismissing her for being such dull company. She stood up and held out her hand to Marianne, who half reclined in her deep chair.

"I must go, Marianne. I'm afraid that I have some serious thinking to do. I must make a decision."

Marianne lazily rose to her feet. She smiled and took Diane's arm, discreetly steering her toward the door. "Look here, go back to the country to your sister's if that pleases you. If it doesn't, stay here in Paris, and we'll have a marvelous time. I'll see to that. I promise you that." She squeezed Diane's waist familiarly. "With a few new gowns and a stylish coiffure, you'll be as sought after as you were years ago." Diane looked at her with an ironic smile. "Well, maybe not the way it was when you were a girl of fifteen and had the King himself making a fuss over you. But you'll see. You'll have a different kind of fun now. We'll go to the theatre, to Saint Cloud, to the masked balls at the Palais Royal."

The smartly dressed maid helped Diane with her cape as a footman stood holding the door open.

"Do you ever see the colonel? Colonel de Mézières, I mean?" Diane asked softly, bending her head as she fussed with the clasp of her cape.

"Armand? Oh, yes, usually. When he's in town, I see him about. And my . . . friend knows him quite well. Quite well. He has lent Mézières a good deal of money, I believe."

"Then, you would know where I might see him? Or send a letter to him? Or . . ."

"I could find out. Armand is still in Bordeaux. He's attached to Richelieu's entourage. The old lecher has been named governor of Bordeaux and lords around like the King himself. You could write Armand there. I'll find a courier for you."

Marianne yawned and gently urged Diane toward the door. It was silly of Diane, really, trying to fan the embers of a love affair that was dead and gone. Move up and move on, that was the thing. "I must get my beauty sleep," she said. "Otherwise, I may frighten my friend away this evening. And we wouldn't want that, would we?"

32

In Diane's small apartment fires had been lit in every room, and a brazier of hot coals placed in the foyer. In the candlelight Diane looked like a pretty schoolgirl as she bent over the desk in her bedroom. The mild winter of 1763 had turned glacial, overnight it seemed. Snow fell every day for a week, and ragged men, their faces smudged black, hawked lumps of coal and charcoal on street corners.

Dear Family, she wrote, and then leaned on her elbows, staring into the candle flames. What would they be doing at Ussé this evening? Not much. Reading or playing piquet. Sophie would be great with child now. Diane dipped her pen and began to write again. *I've worried myself sick about Sophie and the baby, and still you don't write to me. Is it the weather? The storms? I haven't been out at all for the past few days.* Her daily visits with Marianne truly did not count. It was not at all like going about in society. She took tea with Marianne, ordered gowns and hats and gloves and shoes . . . really her own clothes were little more than rags and someday she would be out of mourning entirely. *The weather is frightful beyond belief. But how is my little family? How I long for news of all of you, of little Fanette, my adorable little godchild! Busy as I have been with getting settled in my little place, I have not stopped thinking of you one moment. Uncle Philippe has been a dear. He has given me some very fine pieces of furniture, loaned them to me, really. Sophie, you would love my little apartment! It's not a fancy address—14 rue de Grenelle— but Marianne, my lady's maid, do you remember? Who came to Paris with Papa and me? She was at papa's funeral in Corcheval. Marianne has helped me make it very smart and comfortable. Marianne's residence is quite luxurious. I believe she has come into money of her own, for she lives on quite a grand scale. I won't say that I am envious, for how could I be, but I never step into her sitting room without catching my breath!* Marianne was changed. And yet she was not. She still laughed and winked and joked at everything. She still lolled about eating sweets and drinking brandy, even in the afternoons. The little maid in green serge no longer made any pretense of bringing in the gleaming tea tray at four. Instead, she brought in sweet cakes and brandy. At first, Diane had not been able to tolerate much of the strong drink. It burned her throat and made her choke and cough. Then, after a while, she began to dip her cake in her drink and suck it like her morning croissant. Lately, Diane quaffed her glass just like Marianne. Without cakes. Sometimes she had two or three if they talked and laughed long enough, or if one of Marianne's furnishers called in with his goods. *Marc*, Marianne called it, a liqueur from Burgundy that was her friend's favorite. This friend of Marianne's . . . It was a man, Diane knew that. My friend this, and my friend that. No more. Marianne told her nothing about him. He must be an admirer, perhaps a lover. Leaving Marianne one evening, Diane had glimpsed a portly man, short, swaddled in furs, alighting from a carriage. Not a nobleman. Not someone from court. There was no coat of arms on the shiny sides of his carriage.

Diane rang the bell for her maid, who soon poked her head into the room.

"Bring me some brandy and a glass, Claudine," she said. Despite the toasty warmth in the little room, a glass of a spirits would be just the thing on such a blustery night.

"Brandy, mademoiselle?"

"And a glass, please."

"But we've no brandy, mademoiselle. No brandy at all. Not even a bottle of wine."

"Then remind Laurent to buy a bottle tomorrow. Perhaps two. We may have guests."

Uncle Philippe found the perfect little maid for me, a child really, for Claudine is not more than ten if that, and so frail that I mustn't ask her to do too much. My good Laurent is as devoted as ever. He was knocked down by a wagon in the streets a month ago, and his left leg troubles him. He limps along, poor dear, without a complaint. Maman and Charles, you must take good care of Sophie now that I can't be at her side. You must not forget her herbal teas. Massage her ankles at least once a day, preferably in the mornings to get rid of the bad blood that settles in the feet as we sleep. Ah! I should be there right now making sure that our Sophie is taking care of herself. I won't delay here much longer. I would never forgive myself if I were not at Ussé when our baby is born.

Diane dipped her pen. How many months? She counted on her fingers. Four more months . . . April . . . spring . . . She would leave for Ussé then. Surely Armand would return soon. It had been two weeks since Marianne gave her letter to her friend's courier. Over two weeks. Would he simply ignore her? As if he had never loved her? *I am counting the days until I can rejoin my family in dear old Ussé. Though I mustn't forget my own duty to Jean-Baptiste. A cruel fate it is to be a mother! Dear little Adelaide, swept away by such a terrible disease. The King wrote me a note of sympathy, did I tell you? Yes, I must have. My only daughter perishing only a few months after she became a canoness. The child's dearest wish, to wear the white veil of the canoness. Had she lived, Adelaide would have had to leave the convent walls that she loved so well. Tourmelle would never have allowed her to take vows. Never! He and that black-hearted sister of mine would have married her off to any scoundrel looking for a proper "connection." As if the Tourmelle name went back to the Crusades!*

Charles, it pains me to talk of the blackguard who has ruined my life, but I must ask you to send to me as soon as you possibly can, any orders of payment from Tourmelle. I have borrowed, more than I ought probably, from Uncle Philippe. And I must confess that Marianne has helped me with my expenses as well. Tourmelle's notes will put me in the right. I count on you for this, dear brother. I tremble lest Tourmelle and my sister discover that I am in Paris near my son. Neither troubled themselves to attend the pitiful ceremony of Adelaide's final journey. Should we be surprised, mired as they are in their den of iniquity at Damfert? Mother Superior told me that Tourmelle sent a purse for the celebration of masses for Adelaide's soul, though I know for a certainty that the reprobate is a free-thinker like my sister. They no doubt sent a fat sum to mock the dear sisters and their faith. I must not think of the evil pair now. I trust you all to help me keep from them my present circumstances.

I must close now. Uncle Philippe remains much the same, though he insists that he will see the apple trees at Ancy come into bloom before he departs this world. May God grant him this wish!

I embrace you all, my loving sister, brother, and maman.

Diane sprinkled sand over the letter and tapped it around the sheet before tipping the sand back into the china box and replacing the lid. A windowpane rattled in the wind. A dreadful evening. She stared guiltily at her letter. Half-truths. Rather half-lies. How easily they came to her, it was dismaying. And for what? Armand? Her letters to him might as well have been sealed in a bottle tossed into the sea.

She rang for Claudine. After a few moments the maid appeared, rubbing her red, chapped hands together.

"Are you sure there is no brandy or wine in the house? Not even a drop or two in one of cook's bottles for the kitchen? Ask Laurent. He will know. Laurent has a wonderful way of finding things to make me happy."

Christmas holidays came and went quietly. Harsh, cold air clung to the city. Sitting at her window, looking down into the icy, cobblestone streets, Diane was bored but not tempted to brave the cold for a drive past the Luxembourg gardens or the Palais Royal at the promenade hour. She waited patiently, dreaming before her mirror of seeing Armand again, of melting into his strong arms. She would have to be patient. She could not ruin everything by putting aside her mourning too soon and going back into society.

She must wait. Even Marianne cautioned her against being foolish. You've nothing to gain, she said, and everything to lose. Your friends like the marquise de Sabran will welcome you back with open arms when the time comes. But not before. And that husband of yours might get a whiff of gossip and set on you with a *lettre de cachet*. Diane would be patient.

In the mornings she kept to herself, reading the latest scandal sheets and novels, writing a little poetry, but mostly writing long letters to the family at Ussé. Sophie was in wonderful spirits, although her letters were filled with anxiety about Diane, alone and bereaved in the big city. In the afternoon, Diane went to dine with Marianne, if she happened to be alone, and afterwards stayed on to gossip and drink brandy and let Marianne brush and curl her hair into clever, fantastic swirls. In the darkening shadows of the afternoon, Diane felt like a young girl again.

Once, Marianne's stout friend whom Diane had one day glimpsed stepping down from his carriage appeared, unannounced, unexpected, for dinner. Marianne introduced him as Monsieur Fabian, though she called him Emile, and invited Diane to do the same. Almost as short as Marianne, round and dark-haired, Monsieur Fabian ate each plate ravenously, his large, moist brown eyes fixed on Diane. They took coffee and ices in Marianne's boudoir, and Monsieur Fabian held Diane's hand and clucked sympathetically as she told him the sorrowful story of her marriage. Flushed with wine and brandy, Diane talked on into the late afternoon as Monsieur Fabian squeezed her hand, murmuring *pauvre petite, pauvre petite* with a wheezing sigh, while Marianne dozed on her chaise-longue.

At the end of April, though frail and hobbled by disease, the marquis d'Ancy packed up for the country, anxious to escape the raw winter weather that clung to the city like a death's shroud. He was in hearty spirits and determined to get back to his beloved fields in Ancy.

"Promise me that you'll go back to Ussé, my dear. This city is no place for you now."

"I know, uncle. I'll be packing to leave soon. You've been so kind, so generous, as always. And I must repay you. Somehow. The loans, I mean."

"Nonsense. You'll do no such thing. Paltry sums. Not worth mentioning. I can still afford to indulge my favorite niece a little."

He smiled and gathered her in his arms for a farewell embrace. She worried him, this favorite niece. At night, when the pain in his legs awakened him, deep misgivings about her troubled him and kept him tossing and turning until the light of dawn. Diane was up to something. That was his only way of putting it to himself. Her situation was equivocal. Why should she be so obstinate? By all accounts, Sophie and her little family had done wonders for Diane at Ussé. Rescued her. Healed her shattered nerves. Made her whole again. Sophie loved her, and Diane loved her sister. She was happy there. She said so many times with tears in her eyes. Last week Diane had ignored him when he asked whether she planned to return to Champagne for her sister's confinement. That was your plan, wasn't it? he had asked again. Diane had begun to fuss with his hairbrushes, asking where he had them made and whether the silversmith might be able to create a set for her.

What could Paris offer her now? An older woman, close to thirty-five. Beautiful, of course, but fading. She was spending too much time with that maid of hers. Whatever for? Madame de Sabran had seen Diane out and about in the shops and had hinted that she was spending money by the handful at the most expensive furnishers. Refurbishing her tired old wardrobe, she said. As if she planned to settle in Paris indefinitely. She's up to something, he thought gloomily.

A jubilant letter arrived from Sophie: a boy! She had given birth to a healthy son and heir. *Oh, Diane,* she wrote, *I never thought that I could have a healthy baby without you by my side with your dreadful arrowroot brew. Little Charles-Louis-Philippe took us all by surprise, waking his maman up at three in the morning and insisting on being born that very day, the 24th of April 1764! Oh, happy, happy day! I long for you to see him. We all long to see you, dearest, dearest sister.*

All afternoon, Diane sat reading the letter. With so much love and contentment waiting for her at Ussé, why did she spend her days in drab, lonely rooms, her only society the shopkeepers who took her orders and her former maid? She had let her daydream of Armand take possession of her life. Nothing else seemed to matter now until she could discover whether the dream was worth dreaming all those years.

Days and weeks inched by, and still Armand did not return from Bordeaux. Diane's letters, for she had written more than a dozen by the end of April, remained unanswered. Marianne, her patience short, grew shrill and abusive when Diane begged her to find out why Armand lingered in Bordeaux.

33

The card was delivered by a chimney-sweep whom my footman followed to the door.

Outside Diane's heavily draped rooms, the late morning sun washed through the narrow streets. Inside the small room, candles burned as if it were the dead of night. Embers glowed on the hearth. The thick red taffeta draperies tightly closed, the red canopied bed, the dark chairs cast a soft red hue over Diane as she sat in a peignoir, a book of poems opened in her lap. She was not reading. She was staring into space, waiting for a knock at the door.

The day before, in the late morning, calling by the marquise de Sabran's townhouse, hoping for an invitation—to tea, to a late supper, anything—Diane had glimpsed the duc de Richelieu's large, gilt-edge calling card. She recognized it immediately, for she knew it well. In the old days, when Richelieu was shepherding her toward the King and the *petits appartements* at Versailles, the duc called every day—morning, noon, or night, it didn't matter.

The marquise is *en service* this week, her lady's maid said, but Diane was already heading toward the door. She had got a piece of information more precious than an invitation to the marquise's salon: the duc de Richelieu had returned to Paris. And with him, most certainly, Armand de Mézières.

Instead of sending Laurent with a message, Diane gave a few *sous* to an urchin, a chimney-sweep, strolling through the streets calling out for jobs. She could not even be sure that the boy had understood the address or the directions she gave him. Armand might recognize Laurent, might send him away, might not take the message. A young chimney-sweep, she loved the romance of it.

All through the afternoon she had trembled with expectation. He is coming! He must come! She had waited too long, throughout the fall, the dreadful winter and the raw, reluctant spring. She had waited too long for the man who had made dreaming the most essential part of her life.

She had bathed, painted her face, and put on one of the costly new gowns that she had chosen for the summer season, a green taffeta creation with gold *passementerie* covering the bodice. After her bath she scented her body with oil of *muguet*, dipping her fingers in the fragrance and running her hands over her thighs, under her full breasts and over her neck and shoulders. She made up her face carefully, smiling into a mirror and making wide circles of rouge on her cheeks. She frowned at the deep lines that framed her mouth and felt a moment of panic. She would keep the draperies closed, the candles lit. Candlelight, soft rose candlelight. She would look as beautiful as ever.

When all was ready, she sat down with a book of poems and rang for Laurent and a bottle of brandy and two glasses. Dear Laurent, devoted Laurent—his startled, round-eyed stare told her that she had succeeded, that she was indeed as beautiful as ever. In her elation she drank several glasses of brandy to calm herself. She closed her eyes to drowse a little, so that her eyes would be bright and refreshed when Armand came through the door.

At some time during the long night Diane realized that he was not coming. For over an hour she sat motionless, fighting with the idea that he would not come. At last, wearily, she rose to her feet and undressed. She scrubbed off the paint from her face, loosened her hair and brushed it. She threw her new gown over a chair and put on an old cream-colored silk peignoir, so worn that it was as soft as butter. She tied it loosely around her waist and sat down again.

For a moment she thought she must have slept, that she must be dreaming. She thought that she heard a slight tapping, scratching noise at the door. A scratching at the door . . . someone from the other country. She stared at the door. She saw the knob turn, and the door part slightly.

Then, Armand stepped cautiously into the room. He hesitated a moment, his eyes searching for her in the dimness of the room.

"Diane?"

At the sound of his voice, Diane sprang from the chair and ran to him. It was no dream at all. She had not gone mad again. Armand was here, and she was in his arms. It was not a dream.

Armand stood still, clasping her to him. His strong, square hands kneaded her back. "Diane, Diane," he whispered. He buried his face in her long, thick mane of hair, and she realized that he was crying.

"Oh, don't! don't!" she said, taking his face in her hands. He kissed her hungrily, raking his mouth harshly against her lips, all tenderness gone. He swayed and staggered forward a little, but still he kissed her, his hands moving down over her hips, crushing her against him.

"Oh," he said, lurching clumsily, "we shall fall down. Here . . . " He lifted her as if she weighed nothing at all and carried her to the bed, and with his knee, parted the bed curtains.

Diane's eyes never left his face as she shrugged off her peignoir and reached up to pull his head down to her.

Later, Armand lay on his side and looked at her. "Extraordinary. You don't look a day older. Honestly. I can't believe it. You look even lovelier than that afternoon in Bécage. Do you remember?" He leaned over and kissed her. Great waves of tenderness welled up in him.

"You know I remember. You know that you are all I have to remember. My happiness with you. Why didn't you answer my letters?"

"I . . . don't know. I just don't know." He knew that he had had a mistress then who had been driving him wild with her caprices, playing him off against the old duc. Running hot and cold. Diane's hectic letters came to him, without fail, at the wrong moments. It was easier to ignore them. He could not face the pain he read there. What a fool he had been. What a stupid fool.

"There were so many of them."
"Were there?"
"You know there were."

I will not attempt to repeat all that we said during our meetings. People truly in love, especially those who find themselves in a similar situation, will easily guess what we said to each other.

The misery of the years they had spent apart was sealed over with the intense pleasure of their reunion. For weeks the two lovers were content to spend most of their time in Diane's dingy little rooms. But with the fine weather, Diane boldly set aside her mourning and appeared on Armand's arm in all the smart meeting-places around Paris.

They often took afternoon coffee at the Café Procope, opposite the new Comédie-Française where actors and actresses, musicians and writers sat at tables and preened and gossiped all day. A table was reserved for Voltaire, who made a noisy entrance with his entourage at five o'clock every day and stayed on until the curtains rose. Diane thought that he looked like a cross old gnome with his thickly powdered wig towering over his small, wrinkled head.

They preferred the spacious terrace of the Café du Foy, a smart new establishment at the northernmost end of the Palais Royal, where fashionable courtiers came to dine or to sip rose-scented drinks as they watched the parade of women of questionable morals.

"Ah! Should I be jealous?" asked Diane, mischievously, nodding her head toward a flamboyantly dressed "horizontal," who brushed by their table, brazenly giving her petticoat a quick hitch as she ogled Armand.

"No, I wouldn't bother if I were you." He laughed and bent to kiss her golden hair, warmed by the afternoon sun. Finding Diane again filled the deepest recesses of his emotional yearning. Since her marriage he had lost all serious interest in women. He had drifted along from the arms of one mistress to another, until promiscuous coupling itself became a habit. Singers and dancers at the Opéra mostly. Or a torrid week or two with the odd comtesse or marquise from court. His conquests were facile, and—he hated to remember them now—sometimes savagely carnal.

"But I would have been jealous of Yvette Serjent," she said solemnly. "You spent four years with her. I can't bear to think of it."

"Yvette was touching, very naïve in certain respects," he said slowly. "I grew used to her, comfortable even. Then, she sent me packing. She did not intend to waste her youth and beauty on the likes of me. And why should she? After all, she was a mistress. Not the woman of my life. Not the love of my life."

Armand glanced around at the fashionable women sitting on the terrace. He could not imagine a woman more exquisitely cultivated, engaging, and entertaining than Diane, such refinement joined with a sweet and tender nature.

Though Diane talked of what might have been if they had been able to marry, Armand never did. He listened to her tearful sighs and stroked her hair and said nothing. Marriage had nothing to do with what they felt for each other. Armand had never regretted his marriage to Madeleine. It was necessary. His way into the clergy was blocked. Only a military life was open to him. Without Madeleine and her aunt's help he would have had to leave for the colonies in the New World. A god-forsaken life in a god-forsaken country. No, he had never regretted his marriage. It was a damned pity that the comte had panicked and married his daughter off to a petty provincial aristocrat. Buried in the country, far from Paris, that was no life for a cultured woman like Diane.

Only when Diane spoke of the children they might have had, did Armand feel his heart dip and sink like a dead weight. Well before Diane fled Paris with her father in the middle of the night, Armand knew that she was carrying his child. Caressing her one day his hands had lingered there, over the hard swelling, and he had known. In her innocence she had no idea that she was with child, and he was afraid of frightening her. She had taken away with her his son. His son, who called himself Jean-Baptiste de Tourmelle.

"I would like to go with you one day to the Petite Ecurie, when Jean-Baptiste returns to court, to see your son." Then, he added hesitantly, "Our son."

Diane looked up quickly. She leaned forward and caressed his hand. "Really, would you? *Our* son . . . Of course, why not? Except that he's no longer a page at the Petite Ecurie. His . . . Tourmelle has purchased a commission in the King's regiment for him." She reached for her glass, her hand trembling slightly. "But . . . you can't imagine, he is the very image of you. Years ago, it broke my heart to pack him off to school. It was like losing you all over again." She set her glass down and clasped her hands in her lap. Her eyes filled with apprehension.

If Jean-Baptiste ever saw her with Armand, he would know the truth immediately. How could he not? Father and son resemblance could not be more pronounced—the face, the dark, curly hair, the eyes, the manly build. And if Jean-Baptiste heard any gossip about her, about her going around with Armand, it would take only a hint in a letter, and her paradise with Armand would be over. Her life would be over.

"I expect he'll be returning to court soon," Diane said with a weak smile.

But Armand had caught the glint of fear that leapt into her eyes and knew at once what it meant. He reached for her shawl and carefully spread it over her shoulders, his hands full of love.

"Come," he said, taking her hand. "At this hour they'll be unloading oysters at the Grand Véfour. Are you tempted?"

As the months melted away, Diane spun a thicker and thicker cocoon around her happiness with Armand. She was happy, thoroughly happy.

Men had never found her more alluring, not even when her smooth, creamy complexion was still untouched by time. She drew men to her like frantic bees to a honeycomb. They crowded round her, brought her drinks, carried her fan, her shawl, left little presents on the commode of her modest sitting room. Armand, at her side, was delighted, though he jealously guarded their passionate afternoons in the tiny room in the rue de Grenelle, where their joy in each other unfolded effortlessly, endlessly.

Until this balmy afternoon when word came to Armand that he must soon return to Bordeaux with the duc.

"You mustn't be sad. The duc hates Bordeaux in the summer months. He can't stand the humidity, and the oysters and mussels go off in the heat. I'll be back before summer begins. For a certainty." With a gentle caress under her chin, he lifted Diane's face.

"Of course," she said, trying to smile.

Armand reached for her hand and brought it to his lips. The desolation in her eyes broke his heart.

Diane sat next to the window in the sunshine and combed out her hair, letting it spread out along her shoulders. Then, with a few deft movements, she swept her hair into place, wispy curls clinging to the nape of her neck. She wore no paint at all.

"You look lovely," he said.

"I shall look like an old hag once you walk out that door." she said, her eyes filling with tears. "You are my beauty cream."

And it must be true, he thought, she needs no paint to take my breath away.

"Shall we stay in tonight? Laurent can fetch us some supper from the cookshop on the rue du Bac. Would you like that?" he asked. Tonight of all nights he did not want to go into society. He did not want to share her with the usual flock of admirers in the marquise's salon or with the fancy crowds around the gambling tables.

"Perfect!" she said, bringing her hands together in a childlike gesture that went straight to his heart.

The next morning, in the weak light of dawn as he hurried into his clothes so that he would not miss the duc de Richelieu's *levée*, he gazed at Diane, naked, still half-asleep in the disheveled bed. She had a young girl's body, her legs long and smoothly muscled. Her clothes were scattered here and there over chairs and tables. He smiled to himself, remembering their lovemaking. The innocent little simpleton from the convent, what had become of her? How many times he had mocked her for Odile's amusement. When, despite himself, he had fallen in love with her, it was Diane's innocence, her virginal cleanliness that had captured his heart. Her beauty, yes, her wondrous face and supple body. But it was the distance of pure innocence in her eyes that made him long to hold her close forever.

34

As soon as she read the letter, Diane tied on a hat and sent Laurent to find a fiacre. Although Marianne lived only a short way from the rue de Grenelle, Diane's driver was soon delayed by a maelstrom of carriages and coaches at the Pont-Royal and could not budge. A gay crowd of courtiers was taking a boating party down to Bellevue to see the glass works.

Diane averted her face so that she would not be recognized. Hunched over with anxiety, she pulled the letter from her skirt pocket and read it again.

Our very dear Diane, please forgive the haste of this letter. I have no time for the usual polite phrases or for the kind words that are in all our hearts when we think of you. I must tell you that I have received a most frightening letter from your sister Catherine, the sum of which is that Tourmelle has learned that you are residing in Paris. He accuses you of licentious behavior, which has besmirched his good name at Court. He has ordered a lettre de cachet for your immediate arrest, and he threatens to bring action against me and your sister for deceiving him as to your whereabouts. You must, dear sister, return in all haste to us here before you are apprehended and put away, God knows where. Sophie and Maman are utterly distraught. Send a messenger by return post, I beg of you.

Laurent had jumped down from the rear of the cab and was trying to make way through the crowd. He looked back over his shoulder at Diane, staring wild-eyed at the pushing and shoving crowd of vendors setting up their stalls on the quays. She bowed her head to the piece of paper again.

Diane could feel her heart thudding hollowly in her chest. At the convent no one ever spoke of *lettres de cachet* except in whispers. It was a phrase whispered behind cupped hands, from bed to bed in the dark dormitory, while sister in her chair at the door nodded over her breviary and candle. At services, darting fingers would surreptitiously point out the daughters . . . and wives . . . and sisters who had been whisked away from their families, seized by the magistrates, and placed behind convent walls. Sometimes they didn't leave. Sometimes they died there. Laure Pellegrin. They said her husband took her dowry, everything, even her jewels, then got his friend the minister to give him a *lettre de cachet*. His wife had been intimate with one of the footman, he claimed; so they took her away, shut her up in Neuilly. Diane had glimpsed her once, laboring up the narrow, twisting stairway to the drying room under the rafters. Laure Pellegrin had pulled to one side and covered her face as Diane stepped past her.

Racing up the stairs to Marianne's sitting room, Diane took no heed of the footmen carrying crates and boxes down to the courtyard. She found Marianne shouting angrily at her maid.

"Stupid slut!" she said, wheeling around. "She claims she can't find my ruby earrings! Liar!" she yelled at the maid's back as she scuttled toward the door.

Sweat poured down Marianne's unwashed face. Under her arms dark, damp circles stained her nightshift. Diane was too terror stricken to wonder why Marianne should be standing barefoot in her drawing room at this late hour in her nightshift. "Filthy rats! Deserting a sinking ship. They have a nose for that!" Marianne said, falling into a chair. "Sit down! You look as if you have seen a ghost!"

"Marianne . . . I'm in trouble. You've got to help me." She could not bring herself to sit down.

"What do you mean? Are you . . . " she narrowed her eyes as she looked at Diane's waist. "Are you with child? Sit down. You look as if you have hounds at your heels."

Diane made a wide, dismissive gesture and sat down.

"Well? What is it?" asked Marianne impatiently.

Diane pulled out the letter and opened it. "I've had a letter from my brother-in-law . . . Sophie's husband. Catherine has . . . Tourmelle knows I'm here. In Paris. He's obtained a *lettre de cachet*. For my arrest."

Marianne sat up sharply. "*Bon sang!*" she said. "*Bon Sang!*" She stared at Diane solemnly. "A *lettre de cachet!*"

Tears flooded Diane's eyes. "Yes. For my arrest . . ."

Marianne stood up. "Well, I always thought you were foolish not to work out your situation better than you did. While your uncle the marquis was here and could make everything look legitimate. That's what I would have done." She began to pace back and forth. "Look at what these parasites have done," she said, kicking at a wooden chest.

"But, what can I do now? Run away? Go back to Ussé?" Back to Ussé, the very idea chilled her heart. To give up the joy of having only to reach out her hand and find Armand there. To touch his cheek in the lonely hours before dawn, to watch him fall asleep in her arms.

"I have very little money," Diane said. "I've been living on credit since . . . for a while. I can't remember."

"And where is Armand?"

"On a mission with Richelieu in Bordeaux. What must I do?"

Marianne sat down again. "I think it's better to stay here where you have highly placed friends. Your husband has been in the country a long time, away from court. The King hasn't seen him in years. The marquise de Sabran, have you seen her yet?"

Diane shook her head. "I came first to you. I . . . the marquise has been out recently. I haven't . . . " The marquise found Diane's situation in Paris "irregular," that's what Armand had said. Lately, when Diane called and sent in her card, Madame de Sabran never found it convenient to receive her.

Diane's face turned red in splotches over her neck and forehead. "Everyone talks here. About nothing. They make up scandals to amuse themselves." Diane felt ill.

Marianne studied her coldly. "You haven't been discreet," she said finally. "You go to extremes. Your father always said so. You let yourself get carried away. You and Armand."

"Help me, Marianne, for the love of God, help me!" she begged.

"Well," she said harshly, "can you leave Paris, leave Armand, and go back to your sister's? Your brother-in-law might . . . "

"I would rather die," Diane said. "Without Armand I have no life anyway."

"Don't be absurd! Of course, you have a life without Armand! You talk like a fool."

"I have to make a decision! I have to do something! Right away!" Diane said shrilly. Her stomach was in a tight knot. Every minute wasted would cost her dearly, she was sure of it. She might be arrested as soon as she returned to her rooms. Thrown into a convent again! Or worse, prison.

"All right! All right!" Impatiently, Marianne smoothed her shift over her knees. "You must go plead your case with the minister who issues the *lettres de cachet* for the King. That would be Berryer. I suppose Tourmelle has declared that your conduct is not that of, let us say, a proper wife, that you are dragging his good name through the mud, and so forth and so on. Am I right?"

"Yes."

"Go to Berryer. I've met him once or twice. I have no idea whether he will listen to you or not. But, I have heard this." Marianne was warming to her task. "They say that he has a weakness for pretty ladies. Especially ladies with a fine name like yours. Remind him of who your father was. The comte did have plenty of friends, after all. Tell him your sad story."

"But what can this man do if Tourmelle has already obtained the letter?"

"Berryer has jurisdiction over Paris. If he does not use the King's seal on a letter, nothing can happen to you. Berryer has the final word. You'll want to wear your most flattering gown. Keep his mind on you, not on your husband and his good name."

For the first time since opening the awful letter from Charles, Diane felt some hope. A feeble beacon of light.

She reached for her hat and got up.

Marianne followed her to the door. "Do your best," she said, taking Diane's arm as she turned to leave. "Be nice to him," she said, looking at Diane as if they were sharing a secret.

"Of course," Diane said.

"Be very nice to him, Diane. It may help."

"Oh, I shall be quite humble and polite, never fear," Diane said, impatiently shaking off Marianne's hand. As soon as the door closed behind her, she hiked up her skirts and ran down the steps to Laurent and the waiting fiacre.

I told him all my troubles ... He then took my hand and while sitting close to me, he said, "Don't worry. Never will there be a lettre de cachet against you. ... He is not a man," he said, looking me in the eyes, "because no real man could ever treat you harshly. He is a beast."

The minister's offices were located in a broad street behind the two identical buildings that Gabriel had designed for the new Place Louis XV. The cobblestone street was paved in a fan design that made Diane dizzy as she hurried along, head down, to Berryer's office.

She arrived just after the dinner hour, in the early afternoon, the hour when she and Armand would take their siesta, then make love, and afterwards dress for a walk in the Tuileries gardens.

In halting words, trying not to be overheard by others in the crowded antechamber, Diane explained her visit to an aide, who listened impassively for a moment before taking her card in to the minister. Diane searched the aide's face when he came back into the antechamber, looking for some clue that would inspire hope. Finding none, she sat down in a chair and numbly waited to be called.

The crowd of petitioners dwindled, and still Diane sat in the cold waiting room, her back rigid, her chest tight with anxiety.

It was early May, and darkness still fell early. A footman lit a few candles for the aide, whose pen scratched back and forth over a pile of papers.

Diane felt weak with hunger. She had had nothing to eat since supper the night before, and being alone without Armand, she had taken only a little soup with bread. The scratching of the man's quill made her flesh crawl. The room had been empty for almost an hour. She wondered if she should ask whether the minister could see her now. She cleared her throat, but the man did not look up from his papers.

"Ahhh, *chère madame!*" An unctuous voice boomed into the deserted room.

Startled, Diane jumped to her feet.

Coming toward her with outstretched hands, she saw a short, dark man with thick, bushy eyebrows. He wore no wig, and his long hair, falling loosely over his shoulders, was as black as pitch.

"*Chère madame,*" he said again, taking both her hands in his. "Can you forgive me for keeping you waiting in this wretched antechamber?" He nodded at the aide, who sat, mouth agape, watching them. The aide folded his papers and began to clear his desk.

Berryer led Diane into his office, a handsome room which looked very much like an elegant salon with its tulipwood desk and showy commodes rimmed in bronze doré. The richness of the furnishings reassured her.

Berryer motioned for Diane to sit down on a low sofa, and he drew up a chair facing her.

"Ah," he said, "you sit down with such grace, Madame. There is nothing quite like the pleasure of watching a beautiful woman. The way she carries herself, the way she sits down . . . "

The minister spoke with the lilting cadences of the south of France. He smiled at her and clasped his hands expectantly.

Diane did not know where to begin. Her glance settled on two large paintings that dominated the room. In one, numerous naked women frolicked about with fat, merry cherubs, and in the other, a beautiful blond woman, all round masses of breast, buttocks, and thighs, sprawled against a mossy green bank next to a bubbling stream. A cherub, hovering over her, tweaked one of her nipples, as if it were a delectable comfit that he would pluck and that would melt sweetly away in his rosy-lipped mouth. Pulling her gaze away, Diane was about to speak when Berryer said, "I knew your father. The comte de Fautrière . . . " He winked at her. "The rascal!"

Diane, who had prepared a sad face to begin her plea, was caught off guard. She hesitated a moment, then gave him a tentative smile. "Oh, yes . . . papa . . . "

Berryer tipped his head to one side. "And you, his beautiful daughter, are you a bit of a rascal, too? Hein?"

Startled, her eyes blank with terror, Diane burst into tears. Huge drops of tears flooded down her cheeks.

"Oh, *mon dieu! mon dieu! mon dieu!* What have I done?" Berryer sank to one knee in front of her and began to dab at her face with a big square handkerchief, stiff with lace. "Oh, my dear woman. Please do stop! Please don't go on like this."

Diane's shoulders trembled and shook. Deep sobs shook her, and still the tears came. Berryer took her awkwardly into his arms and patted her back, murmuring soothing words. Gradually, her sobs subsided into long, ragged hiccups.

"Here. You must have some brandy," he said, steadying his hand on his knee and pushing himself to his feet. He brought her a glass and held it to her lips and watched with satisfaction as she drank it down as if it were water.

"Thank you, monsieur. You are ever so kind," Diane said, her voice low and husky from the brandy and from crying. His thoughtfulness touched her. Suddenly emboldened, she was sure that he would be sympathetic to her situation.

Berryer poured himself a glass of brandy and another for Diane. He sat down facing her again. "Now, *chère madame,* tell me why you are so distressed. Tears should never dampen the face of a beautiful woman like you," he murmured, wondering whether he should not sit beside her on the sofa. No, he could have a better look at her from his chair. Such a face! And such refinement. Every gesture, every look. A lady . . . though with the tempting body of a Venus. He liked older women. He was not ancient and decrepit like

Richelieu, needing a whorish girl in order to perform like a man. Berryer studied the curve of Diane's breasts in her low cut gown and stretched his legs with contentment.

Diane sipped her brandy and began her story. Since Berryer had known her father, she talked of him and his position at court until old Cardinal de Fleury persuaded the King to banish the comte to Corcheval. She told of how, when she was almost fourteen, her father had taken her from the convent and brought her to Paris for lessons and . . . And then how the King had taken a fancy to her patter and her dancing.

In the candlelit room Diane had no idea of what time it was getting to be. The shutters outside the windows were closed. From time to time Berryer filled her glass. It was pleasant and warm in the office with its the rich furnishings, the soft candle glow, and the minister's kind attentions. Berryer seemed in no hurry for her to leave. At some point, when Berryer came to sit beside her, she was somewhat startled, then reassured by his large, sympathetic presence. And when she talked of her marriage and began to cry again, gently this time, no heaving sobs, he drew her head against his plump chest and caressed her face and hair.

Much later, as Diane started to repeat parts of her story, Berryer interrupted to soothe her fears.

"My dear lady, I promise that no harm will come to you. Ever." Diane could feel his warm breath on her ear as he bent his head down to hers. "If you'll be nice to me . . . " he murmured.

"No harm? Do you mean no *lettre de cachet?*" she asked. "Of course, I will be nice to you, monsieur. Of course . . . " She stumbled over the words, her tongue thick. Her heart pounded with joy. He had promised!

She tried to sit up straighter, to turn to look at him, to thank him with all her heart. Unsteadily, she sat up and smoothed her hair. To her astonishment, Berryer pulled her into his arms and quickly began to fumble with the hooks of her bodice.

He gazed at her with amusement. "Ah, have you forgotten? You said that you would be nice to me? Don't you remember?"

The next morning Diane woke with a dry throat and a dull hammering in her head. The first thing she saw was Charles' letter, crumpled up into a ball. Berryer had done that. He had read the letter and crushed it into a ball and tucked it into her pocket. And then he had taken her into his arms and kissed her again—a long, wet kiss that made her cringe. I am so grateful, Diane had said, remembering his promise. Ah, no, *chère madame,* it is I who am grateful, he said.

Diane found Marianne drinking a cup of tea and staring out the window of her empty sitting room. The parquet floor echoed hollowly under Diane's heels as she crossed the room.

"Marianne! What's happened? Where is all your furniture? Your beautiful furnishings?"

"I'm moving. I'm looking for a better place," Marianne said sardonically and turned back to the window.

"Marianne," she said, hoping to raise her spirits, for Marianne did not sound at all happy about finding a better place to live. "My dear friend, I must thank you for your advice. I have Berryer's . . . "

"You, what? You saw him and it's done! He will protect you!" Marianne's face lit up. Diane had plenty of starch. Like her father, just when you wanted to strangle him, he did something unexpected, something gay and wonderful. "We must celebrate!" She looked around at the empty room. Sitting around hanging her head would accomplish nothing. Diane's good luck might be contagious. "At the Café Procope! We're fine ladies, aren't we? We'll celebrate at the Procope. My credit is still good there. What about yours?"

At the Café Procope Monsieur Edouard had to arrange a larger table to accommodate the flock of revelers crowding around the two women's table. It mattered little to Monsieur Edouard that they took up his best table for the entire afternoon. They were a drinking crowd, and the men with the two finely dressed women were flush with money.

While Marianne animated the group with her salty comments and her hearty laughter, Diane sat demurely in her shadow, smiling sweetly, sipping her brandy and basking in the unabashed admiration of the men who joined them. Most of them were Marianne's acquaintances, friends or associates of Emile Fabian. They were not aristocrats. They were involved with money: financiers or tax-farmers. They displayed their wealth in their jewelry and the rich fabrics of their clothes.

Diane found them charming, a trifle vulgar and rough, but charming nonetheless. Her relief in escaping from Tourmelle's clutches created a great swell of affection for these good-hearted men, their eyes so adoring, their purses so vast and open.

When she and Marianne escaped for a moment for a breath of fresh air and the conveniences in the courtyard, Marianne confided that her "friend" had abandoned her for another woman, a cheap slut of an actress who had made most of her money with Madame Surville, the richest madame in Paris. Gone the sumptuous apartment, the high life of the gaming tables. Marianne was more angry than sad. She was glad to see the last of Emile Fabian, but his money, ah, that was another story.

In her half tipsy state, Diane stared at her former maid with awe. Marianne had not inherited money after all. She had been a "kept" woman. Diane knew that her father had slept with Marianne from time to time. She was not blind to her father's comings and goings in the house. But that was different. Marianne was a part of the staff, paid to be Diane's lady's maid. And when Diane had married and moved to the country, well, Marianne had simply stayed on with . . . other duties. Diane had given it little thought. Naively, Diane had assumed that Monsieur Fabian gave Marianne expensive presents the way all admirers do. The King once sent Diane a portrait of himself, framed in expensive shagreen. But she and the King were never lovers. Presents were only a pretty way of paying compliments to a woman you admired.

Diane regarded Marianne in a new light. What she herself had done with Berryer, how was that so different? Diane had turned a corner, and she knew it. She had taken a plunge into a world that she never dreamed she would ever inhabit.

That night, Diane was shaken from sleep by a nightmare in which she was trapped in a small skiff that had lost its tiller. She crouched down in the tiny craft, entirely at the mercy of the pounding waves. One moment she was rushing toward the shore, closer, closer, ever closer, her heart racing with joy . . . only to be swept back again, away from the shore, out to sea. On the shore, still and impervious as a statue, stood Armand, watching her plight with cold indifference.

35

Some festivities were organized at Saint-Cloud to entertain the Duc de Chartres, a thirteen-year-old child who fell into such depression that one feared for his health . . . . I went there regularly with my circle of friends. I danced, seeing that all of the women in my situation did so.

Lonely, her financial situation increasingly desperate, Diane gradually succumbed to Marianne's pleas to join her and her friends. At the very least, Diane could count on a good meal, which would mean enough savings to keep Laurent eating well for a week. Soon, the two women found themselves at the center of a group of fun-loving party-goers. By late afternoon each day they were swept along in revelries that frequently did not end until after dawn.

As days grew longer and warmer, Marianne's friends often went to Saint-Cloud, where the duc d'Orléans staged one extravagant gala after another at the chateau to cheer his chronically depressed son, the duc de Chartres. Jugglers and puppeteers spread over the parks and grounds in sumptuous tents. There were fireworks and balls each night. There were shooting contests, fanfares on the river, tumbling acrobats in tents, and small orchestras playing in the groves of the park.

It was the first time that Diane had joined her new friends in their excursions to Saint-Cloud. As soon as she alighted from the carriage, she saw across the park a party of finely dressed courtiers standing alongside a pleasure barge on the lake getting ready to step on board. Wasn't that the marquise de Sabran in the yellow gown?

"I'll be right back," Diane shouted gaily over her shoulder. She hurried toward the marquise, who turned to watch as she came near.

"The lovely Diana," cooed the duc de Gesvres, bowing theatrically.

Two of the courtiers and a woman Diane had never seen before turned their backs and stepped on board the barge.

"Diane? What on earth? How did you get here?" the marquise asked rather haughtily, her voice high and cold.

"With my friends," Diane replied quietly.

"Your friends?" The marquise peered at the little group standing around two ostentatiously expensive carriages. "Why . . . isn't that, I do believe it is . . . isn't that your lady's maid? The one your father . . . ?"

"Yes. Marianne. Her name is Marianne. She's been very kind." Diane felt like a misbehaving schoolgirl called to account by Mother Superior. "I shall see you later, then, Madame," she said, turning away.

"Later? At the ball? Do you have an invitation?"

"No," Diane mumbled.

"Then I shan't see you," the marquise said with unbearable finality. "However, you'll notice that the duc has had his workers set up seats on the terrace for bourgeois . . . and respectable folk. You may watch."

The duc de Gesvres smiled weakly at Diane before following the marquise onto the barge.

Diane stood quite still watching the marquise as she fussed with her skirts before settling into her chair. She had felt the marquise's rebuke like a physical blow, and now she was furious. What gave the marquise the right to treat her like a scullery maid?

But, as the night wore on, Diane found herself having such fun that she forgot the marquise and the humiliation of not having an invitation, of having to remain separated from the duc and his numerous aristocratic guests.

Months passed, and she grew used to the moist-eyed admiration of Frédéric Lacombe, a rich tax-farmer who was captivated by her refined manners and her delicate ways of eating and drinking. He followed her about like a lovesick boy. On fine sunny days he began to take her out for drives in the Bois de Boulogne in his immense carriage, lacquered a dark green, on each side of which were panels painted by Boucher depicting a sleeping shepherdess being awakened by a handsome rustic of rosy delicacy and charm. Afterwards, he would insist on buying her a few trifles at her favorite shops: a dozen pairs of gloves, stockings, silk shawls for evening, ivory fans, silk parasols.

One night, returning from a spirited evening at Saint-Cloud, Diane allowed Lacombe to kiss her on the drive back to Paris. And to fondle her a little—though she was quick to put an end to his more venturesome caresses.

I was quite shaken at the sight of such a treasure, which was enormous for someone who had but eighteen francs and had to wash her own laundry.

Diane was dozing when Laurent came to her with Fredéric Lacombe's calling card. She looked at it with dull incomprehension. Laurent said that the gentleman was waiting below in his carriage.

Her hands began to tremble. Fredéric Lacombe! She scribbled a note and sent Laurent down below to the carriage. Then she flew about the room getting dressed. She was in too great a hurry to paint her face. Besides, her hands were too shaky. She put on a simply cut gown that showed off her waist and breasts, and she pulled her hair away from her face so that her large gray eyes looked even larger.

When she took Lacombe's hand, he gazed at her with reverential awe. Diane thought that she saw him brush away a tear as he helped her into the carriage.

They lingered over dinner, for Diane spoke of her dreadful circumstances. She tearfully confided that she had no maid, only a faithful footman whose wits were slow but who was tall and large and ate enough for two men. Finally, she confessed that she had no money and feared that her son would not provide for her on his return to court.

Lacombe listened patiently and declared that he loved her even more after hearing her touching story. He had missed her desperately when she failed to appear at the Café Procope. He had sought her out, and she had made him the happiest man in the world by dining with him. They drank champagne and smiled at each other through their tears.

When Lacombe left her rooms shortly before dawn, Diane stared in disbelief at the purse of coins that he had placed next to her brush on the dressing table. Packed to bursting, a bulging chamois purse, supple and furry to the touch, and inside, gold louis. Quickly, she took up the purse, loosened the string and tumbled the coins out onto the rumpled bed. She gasped. A fortune! A fortune!

36

Though Lacombe had rescued her from loneliness and chased the wolf from her door, Diane prayed each day for Armand's return and anxiously rehearsed how she would elude Lacombe's attentions. Lacombe interpreted her nervousness as the delicacy of a true aristocrat and congratulated himself on having found a mistress of such breeding.

One August day as the heat wave persisted and the splendid Bouchardon fountain in the rue de Grenelle opposite Diane's windows slowed to a trickle, baskets and bouquets of flowers poured into Diane's rooms.

From ten in the morning until well past noon they continued to arrive, and when the tiny rooms could take no more, Armand appeared, exclaiming, with a mischievous look, over Diane's fragrant bower.

After a tumultuous afternoon in bed, Armand lay watching Diane scribble a few notes for Laurent. "Errands," she said nervously. "There is absolutely nothing in the house. We live like monks. A crust of bread here. A piece of cheese there." She laughed and tossed her thick mane of hair away from her face.

It was beautiful hair, still silvery blond, though he had noticed more gray streaks around her face. Something was changed. He lay watching her profile, his eyes narrowed. She bent over her desk. She looked older, that was it. But he had been gone only a few months . . . Her clean, sharp jaw line had grown slack. A tiny pouch of flesh underneath her chin spoiled its girlish curve. She had gained weight. He felt guilty looking at her like this, coldly. Without love. Her flesh looked flabby, puffy. A little like Odile . . . Great God, no, not like Odile.

Diane turned to him and smiled. "I'll call Laurent."

She padded across the room in her bare feet and waited for Laurent to appear and then slipped him the notes through the half-opened door. She whispered a few words to Laurent and closed the door.

"Whispers? What was that all about?" Armand asked, stretching lazily.

"Nothing." She returned to the desk and carefully put everything in place.

She is nervous because she was not expecting me, Armand thought. She is tense and high-strung. Even when we were making love. Usually Diane lost herself in lovemaking. This time there was a distance. We have been separated too long.

"Come back to bed," he said.

※

They took up their life together again. Their enchanted life, as Diane called it, refusing to recognize that, now, there were subtle changes. On Armand's arm, she returned to the exclusive salons of Paris with literary wits, intellectuals, and fashionable courtiers milling through beautiful rooms. She and Armand played lansquenet, listened to arias from the new opera by Beaumarchais, and applauded politely as their host read his own composition, an ode to the dear little monkey which the aged marquise de Préville always carried around in her muff.

They received a few invitations to intimate suppers, but not many. A definite chill spread over the room when Armand and Diane appeared. Diane no longer enjoyed the same success of the previous year. Men looked her over, then moved on. Armand felt the difference. Diane tried not to. Almost always they noticed a sudden surge of talk as they left a room. Armand sometimes went to the marquise de Sabran's receptions alone. Diane was not invited, and the marquise no longer wanted to speak of her.

Increasingly, Armand had to accept invitations excluding her. Diane urged him to go alone, and, inevitably, he drank too much, gambled too much, burdened by a loneliness that chilled his soul.

Diane used her time away from Armand to placate Lacombe. Meek, worshipful Lacombe had become a tormenting beast, suspicious and insulting. When not flying into a jealous rage, he pouted. He was hurt, offended by her coolness.

Diane ground her teeth with impatience and kept quiet. Inwardly, she raged against herself for falling into a life with the likes of Lacombe. Vulgar, uncultivated men of commerce. She bitterly resented the time she was forced to spend with him. All the more so because she realized how tenuous her connection with the world of the aristocracy had become. Without Armand, what invitations could she expect? Few, if any. While her father was alive, she had made no close friends among her class in Paris except for Madeleine and her aunt. Diane had taken for granted her father's privileged connections. The comte selected and arranged her invitations, or she had gone about with Madeleine and her friends or with the marquise. Jean-Christophe had disappeared into his estate in Poitou. It was said that he drank and lived little better than the peasants on his land. Madeleine was out of the question. She could not renew her ties with her, even if Madeleine would allow it. Madeleine had already betrayed her once. What would she not do now that Diane was back in Paris and passionately involved with Armand? The marquise, ah . . . if she was not Diane's enemy, she was definitely not her friend. Without Armand she would be cut off from her world forever. A flutter of fear rippled over her.

When Laurent refused him entrance one afternoon, shaking his large head ruefully from side to side, his cornflower blue eyes unclouded, empty, Armand knew what was going on upstairs in Diane's rooms. He had seen the expensive carriage and liveried lackeys. He had only the vaguest idea of Diane's financial affairs, and he had no intention of inquiring, but he gathered from certain remarks that her situation had become precarious after his departure for Bordeaux. On his return, however, he could not help noticing signs of ample provisions . . . to say the least. Her jewelry, for one thing. So much of it new. He could not help noticing that she welcomed his absences from time to time. She drank more. Her conversation in society was hectic, nervous, strident. She had stopped reading. And she never mentioned her poetry. She was losing her beauty.

For whatever reason, she seemed desperate.

Armand decided to wait. He thanked Laurent, then strolled up the street to a café, where he bought a few pamphlets from a street urchin and sat drinking until he thought it reasonable to return to Diane's.

Outwardly, Diane appeared calm when Armand called on her.

"Almost six and you're still in your peignoir?" he asked.

Diane yawned prettily. "I've had a lazy afternoon. I fell asleep over Sophie's letter . . ."

Her eyes were bloodshot, and her hair looked freshly brushed.

"Then, you forgot? You forgot that we were to call on the duc de Soubise. Don't you remember? He invited us to look at the pavilion he has had built at the foot of his garden. The murals have caused a lot of talk. They're gamy, it seems. The duc thought you might appreciate them."

Diane blushed scarlet and sprang to her feet.

Armand regretted his cruel remark. But it was true. The duc had looked at him with a curious leer and had said that the murals were Madame de Tourmelle's "sort of thing." Armand had not given the duc's remark a second thought. Until now. Armand clenched his fist. He felt cold and mean. He looked at Diane as if she were a stranger.

"Well," he said, "shall we go?"

She stared at him, her eyes wide with fear. "No," she said weakly. "It's too late."

They looked at each other in silence. Finally, Armand said, in a harsh voice. "Yes, my dear Madame de Tourmelle, it *is* too late." He looked at her a moment longer. The woman he had loved with all his heart was as filthy as Madeleine and Odile.

Armand turned and left the room.

37

In December of 1765 Jean-Baptiste de Tourmelle had been plunged in the ceremonial splendor of Versailles for several months. It was there on a bleak, windy Sunday afternoon that he awaited his mother.

Tall, squarely built and not quite eighteen years old, Jean-Baptiste de Tourmelle could already survey his brief young life with satisfaction. During his schooldays in *pension* at the Collège Louis-le-Grand, he had discovered a gift for making useful friends. After finishing his studies, he had had many occasions to practice this gift. His father having purchased a commission for him in the King's grays, Jean-Baptiste had the good fortune to be sent to Lorraine, where he ingratiated himself with the family of the devilishly clever comte de Stainville. Stainville, with the marquise de Pompadour as his patron, became Louis XV's prime minister, receiving from the King the title of duc de Choiseul. When the lodestar of Versailles became too strong to resist, the powerful duc de Choiseul himself found a place there for the promising young Tourmelle.

For a moment Jean-Baptiste did not recognize the tall, slim woman whom his valet admitted to his sitting room.

"*Ma mère,*" Jean-Baptiste said, his voice high and reedy. "Sit down! No, over here. You're as pale as a ghost."

"It's the stairs, my dear. Give me a moment to catch my breath." Diane lifted her veil. She was panting and beads of sweat stood out on her forehead and upper lip.

"I know . . . the stairs. They take some getting used to," Jean-Baptiste said, strutting a little as he crossed to a chair facing his mother. "Isn't it wonderful, *ma mère,* to see me in rooms at Versailles?"

"Your grandfather had rooms here for years," Diane said sharply.

She was exhausted. For weeks a suffocating cold had kept her in bed, shaking with chills and fever, with only Laurent to care if she lived or died. Long before she fell ill, Lacombe had already shrugged her off.

Jean-Baptiste swallowed his annoyance and put on a contrite face. Why shouldn't he be proud? Not every one his age had such eminent people for friends.

"I'm working with the prime minister—the duc de Choiseul. And the comte de Saint-Florentin. Refitting our naval yards, our ships. It's an enormous undertaking. The Pompadour's war left our navy in a shambles."

Diane sat looking at him coldly, as if she were inspecting him.

Jean-Baptiste softened his voice. "Your letters . . . they are wonderful, *ma mère.* You have truly a poetic touch. I'm not a letter writer myself."

"You could have sent some sort of reply. You don't have to write me a sonnet, you know."

Her mouth creased into bitter lines. Her hair was carelessly twisted into a chignon. Only her large, luminous eye imparted a hint of beauty to her face.

Jean-Baptiste squirmed uncomfortably. He should have answered her letters, he should have sent her money—or arranged to have some loaned to her. It was a damned nuisance, really. Having his mother in Paris, on her own, no close kin . . . and the curious ménage at Damfert, she couldn't very well go back there.

"You're looking well, *ma mère*. Despite this dreary weather."

"What? Looking well? When I've had to crawl from my sick bed to come to see you?" Diane's eyes glinted fiercely.

"I'm sorry. Truly I am. What I mean to say is, you shouldn't be here at all. Sick and alone. You should go back to Ussé. To Aunt Sophie and Uncle Charles, who will take care of you and love you . . . as you deserve, *ma mère* . . . as you deserve. The air of Paris is pestilent. In the winter particularly. Look at our unfortunate Dauphin. He has taken to his bed. His lungs, you know, the damp winter weather crucifies him. The King is utterly distraught, for fear that he will not survive the winter."

"The Dauphin survived the smallpox in '52, you wouldn't remember that, but I do. I suspect he can live through a few foggy mornings."

Diane knew that she sounded querulous but could not stop herself. Little by little, her heart was hardening against her son. She had humbled herself to a lowly beggar before her own son. Suddenly, she saw herself again on that wretched night, weaving toward the chapel, her stomach heaving in fear of the brute who would become her husband. And now, her son standing before her—rich, glossy in velvets and gold braid, every finger clogged with rings of precious stones, the buckles on his shoes worth a fortune.

"Which reminds me," Jean-Baptiste said, shaking the lace of his sleeves (like papa, Diane thought, and tears stung her eyes). "The King is having a mass said for the Dauphin's recovery, and I mustn't be late." He smiled brightly at his mother.

A condescending smile, Diane thought. The kind of smile you give to a dog that you know you're going to kick out of your way in the next few minutes.

"Naturally," she said, "you mustn't be late."

They both stood up. Jean-Baptiste held out his arms to embrace his mother.

"Before we go," Diane said, her face stony with anger. "I need money. I must have money, or I shall be turned out on the streets like a . . . "

"Please, please, *ma mère!*" said Jean-Baptiste, frowning and holding his fingertips to his temples as if her words had rattled his brain. He sighed and left the room. She could hear him scraping furniture across the floor.

When he returned, he carried a small chest of carved birch.

"Here, take all of it."

Diane seized the chest. Its weight reassured her.

"The chest is handsome. Shall I keep it?"

"If you like. It was a gift from Aunt Catherine."

"Ah, well, then, since it has sentimental value, I shall see that it is returned."

They had reached the door. Jean-Baptiste stood aside to let his mother pass.

"*Ma mère,*" he said, touching her arm. He thrust out his chin a little, and his voice affected the whimpering, drawling high notes of a court dandy. "*Ma mère*, I'm afraid I have to warn you that this will be the last. Money, I mean. I have a position now, and I have to . . . well, ah, there are enormous expenses involved."

"Naturally."

They walked along in silence to the landing. Diane had lowered her veil. To have come to this—to slink through the corridors of the chateau which she knew as well as her own home, where she had danced with the King in the hall of mirrors. To sidle along, stiff with the fear of being recognized. To have taken a rackety common coach, a *pot de chambre,* filled with the stinking hoi polloi of Paris going to see the King and the royal family dine. When she had stood in front of the King's table holding in her arms an exotic bouquet of flowers! Handed to her by the King himself. Holding the flowers in her arms while the King's bleached blue eyes stared and stared at her . . .

"Will the King declare a mistress before the year is out?"

"I should think that His Majesty's chief concern now is the health of the Dauphin," Jean-Baptiste said, pursing his mouth primly. "I shall have to leave you here. You know the way, I'm sure. I must fly away to the duc de Choiseul's apartments first."

In truth, Jean-Baptiste, an ardently ambitious courtier, dizzy with the triumph of having rooms in the King's palace, if only now and then on a temporary basis, had no desire to be seen strolling through the halls of Versailles with a slightly dingy veiled woman on his arm whom someone might recognize as his mother.

Before she had finished counting all the coins in the chest, Diane realized that she would not have enough money to last through the winter months. Since Lacombe had dismissed her—that was the way she thought of it now—she had learned a great deal about money. Mainly, how to get along without it as much as possible. Still the rent had to be paid, she and Laurent had to eat. The thought of returning to Ussé made her skin crawl with shame and guilt. She was no longer fit for the sweet serenity of Ussé. She had been corrupted, and when she stopped to think about the infernal downward spiral of her life, she was appalled. She could not trail the foul odor of her life into the fragrant halls of Ussé.

As soon as she had counted the money, Diane separated into a pile the price of a coach fare to Ancy for Laurent. Whatever he did, however much he wept, she must send him away from Paris. She would put him on a post coach and send him in his bedraggled livery to Uncle Philippe's estate, to the shelter of the Charolais where he had grown to manhood. She was determined that he would not see her living like an animal. He had seen too much already.

Epilogue

Night had begun to fall earlier as autumn ended, and the first snows of winter cloaked the statues and the sundial in the middle of the small courtyard of the modest convent. A lantern cast a feeble round of light in the corner next to the table where a little old woman sat hunched over a cup of ale, her withered face turned toward the light.

"Bless you, child," Marianne said, trying with all her might to still the trembling of her hands as she clutched the cup. "And was Madame de Tourmelle buried properly with her eyes turned toward the heavens and her head toward the chapel? Like a proper Christian?" She began to cry again.

"Oh, yes, Madame, don't you fret about that," said Sister Ursule.

The little old woman had asked those questions at least a dozen times. They had gone together to stand over the freshly mounded grave in the moldy cemetery behind the chapel, useless ground, filled with shadows where the sun never reached. Mother Superior had not wanted to admit her at all. She said that she was filthy, her clothes in rags, and her hair crawling with vermin. In the refectory she drank three bowls of ale and ate stale black bread that even the porter would not touch.

"Oh, the sorrow of it all," Sister Ursule sighed, and she began to cry, too. "Four years in the convent, and I her only friend really. The others scoffed at her, or avoided her, a sinful woman paying for her sins. Shut away from the world by her own son's *lettre de cachet*. An aging beauty who drinks too much, full of herself, they'd say, though Mother Superior and Sister Justine have been known to stagger away from the refectory, giggling, their rosaries catching on the backs of chairs. I've seen them myself. Many a time. Madame de Tourmelle was not the only one to take a nip on the sly."

"We were like sisters, the two of us," Marianne said, her rheumy eyes fixed on the old pewter cup. She took a slow sip of ale. I should have looked after her, she thought. I was older. More experienced. She never did get over being an innocent country girl. I should have warned her that men want good return on their money, no matter how glamorous and beautiful a woman may be. I should have warned her that Armand, sooner or later, was going to find out. And he did. And that was the end of the only bit of happiness she ever had in her entire life.

"I wonder if I could trouble you for another cup of ale?" she asked in a genteel manner she was sure Diane would approve. "And then I must be on my way. You've been more than kind, my child."

"You mustn't think of leaving on a night like this," Sister Ursule said, placing the warm cup in Marianne's dingy hands. "I wish you wouldn't go."

She watched as Marianne greedily emptied the cup. "Tell me, Madame," she said almost in a whisper. "Were Madame de Tourmelle's stories true? That she was the most celebrated beauty at the court of Louis XV, charming the King out of his senses so that all other women ceased to exist after he took one look at her? The handsomest king who ever lived, losing his heart to a young girl of fifteen?" Sister Ursule could feel her heart beating a little faster.

"Of course, they were true. The King couldn't resist her. She was a beautiful creature. Divine. The whole court knew that she would be the next titled mistress of the King. It was magic."

"Magic . . . " Sister Ursule sighed, her dark eyes bright with wonder. "I knew it was true! The others laughed and called Madame de Tourmelle's stories tiresome, but I never did. Never. I wanted to hear them over and over again. I know them all by heart."

Marianne rose stiffly from the table. "If I don't keep moving these old bones, they'll seize up on me." She tried to laugh, but it was only a tired, wheezing sound.

At the refectory door Sister Ursule pulled a small shagreen frame from her skirt pocket. "She gave me this," she said. "Look."

Marianne knew it only too well: it was Diane's portrait of the King, her treasured gift from the King himself.

"Tonight, after chapel and evening prayers," Sister Ursule said, "I will place it on my night table, next to the candle. To ease my loneliness, now that Madame de Tourmelle is no more."

Acknowledgements

My sincere thanks to my ever faithful readers, Darryl Boner and Kirsten Bruno, for their enthusiasm and suggestions, to Martha Hoffman for her astute editorial guidance, and, above all, I am deeply indebted to my friend and former colleague, Nicole Vaget, who introduced me to the haunting story of the comtesse de L—.

Printed by Libri Plureos GmbH in Hamburg, Germany